DESERT STAR

LISETTE BRODEY

SABERLEE BOOKS

Published by

Saberlee Books

Los Angeles, CA
United States of America

saberleebooks@yahoo.com
lisettebrodey.com
facebook.com/BrodeyAuthor
twitter.com/lisettebrodey

Copy Editor: Laura Daly / laurajdaly@earthlink.net
Cover Design: Lisa McCallum
Typesetting / Graphic Design: Lisa McCallum
Cover photos: iStockphoto; Star: Lisa McCallum
Back cover photo: Lisette Brodey
Book is set in Minion Pro 12pt. type

ISBN: 978-0-9909606-1-4 (paperback)
ISBN: 978-0-9909606-0-7 (e-book)

1. Young Adult Paranormal—Fiction

Printed in the United States of America

This book is dedicated to my mother, Dr. Jean L. Brodey

I miss you, Mom.

"Miracles are not contrary to nature, but only contrary to what we know about nature."

—*St. Augustine*

ACKNOWLEDGMENTS

To Laura Daly, for your expert editing.

To Lisa McCallum, for designing this cover and for helping me with absolutely every aspect of this book.

Thanks to the following people who provided valuable information in my research: Heather Barnett, Rich Burlingham, Joy Katzen-Guthrie, Vicki James, Christine Toy-Johnson, Cynthia and Mike Pecoraro, and Michael Putini.

To the following people for your ongoing support and kindness with the writing, publication, and promotion of my work: Talatha Allen, Shykia Bell, Kenneth Brodey, Mark Cote, Dody Cox, PattiAnn Cutter, Henry A. Leighton, Jr., Dionne Lister, Stuart Ross McCallum, Charles Roth, Jaidis Shaw, Laura Schultz, Sheri A. Wilkinson, and Leigh Ann Wilson.

There are so many more people who have supported me in so many ways. I wish it were possible for me to thank each and every one of you. I hope you all know who you are. And last, but not least, thank you to my fellow authors for your support, advice, inspiration, and friendship. You all mean so much to me.

DESERT STAR

Chapter 1

Larsen Davis generally looked down when he walked through the hallways of Mystekal High, so if someone were to smile at him, he'd hardly notice. But he always knew precisely where he was, and his keen peripheral vision always told him when he was approaching his two least favorite senior classmates, Jax Reinhardt and Antonio Reyes.

Six foot four and muscular, Jax could be physically intimidating without saying a word. And often, just because he could, Jax liked to puff up his chest and get in someone's way. On most days, Larsen was his favorite target.

Larsen stopped short of walking into Jax, who had stepped into his path to block him from moving. "Hey, gay boy, I know it's only October, but I couldn't help but wonder. Got a date for the prom? Picked out what dress you're gonna wear yet?"

Jax turned to his friend. "Whatcha think, Tonio? Pink sound like a good homo color for our boy here?"

"Yeah, or maybe purple. As long as he has matching shoes and purse."

The two teens exploded in laughter, while Larsen took a step to his right to get around Jax. But Jax took a step to his left.

"C'mon, homo boy, what's the matter? Don't you want to stay here and chat with us?" Jax flashed an evil smile. "We gotta know, is it true about you black dudes? Do you guys all have logs in your pants? Or is yours a wittle bitty stick?"

Larsen looked up at his tormentor. "Shut up. Just let me pass, Jax."

"Nah, maybe not."

Approaching the trio, River Dalworth, who only days earlier had noticed Jax bullying his classmate, was fed up. "Dude, why don't you man up and leave the guy alone?"

Antonio laughed. "Rio, sup with you? If anyone should be manning up, it's this little homo boy."

Undaunted, River stepped closer to the bullies and stood boldly, distracting them just long enough so that Larsen could get away.

Jax shrugged. "Proud of yourself? Letting the little queer escape? Well, there's always next time."

River looked Jax in the eyes. "One of these days your shit is going to land you in prison. And then, as you're so interested in the phallic measurements of your brethren, you'll find out firsthand, via your anal sphincter muscle, everything you're wanting to know."

"What the fuck are you talking about, Dictionary Dick? Who talks like you?"

"I talk like me. I don't talk like anyone else. I didn't get my dictionary out of a gumball machine."

Gina Dennison stood across the hallway by her locker, admiring River. She had been crushing on him for two years, but he had always been oblivious to it. But now that they were both seniors, and River was displaying a sense of self she hadn't seen before, he was all that much more attractive to her. He used words nobody else knew, he was smart, and he didn't follow anybody's ways but his own.

Jax glared at River. "I don't know what to make of you, but sticking up for homo boy like that, I'm just thinking you're two peas in a pod."

"Yeah, you think? Bet you don't even know what a pod is."

Jax looked at Antonio for help, but he had no idea how to respond to River either.

River chuckled. "Really, Jax. You shouldn't be using big-assed words like 'pod' if you don't know what they mean."

Gina smiled and vowed to herself that she wasn't going to wait any longer to get to know the mighty River.

📖📖📖

River was just leaving school for the day when Gina caught up to him. "Hi there, River."

"Oh, hi, Gina."

"I was just wondering …"

"What? If I'm as good-looking close up as I am from a distance?"

Gina giggled. "Well, maybe."

Just as River was about to respond, Larsen appeared at his side. "Sorry to interrupt. I was wondering if I could speak to you for a minute. Before you head home."

Gina looked disappointed. "Guess I'll talk to you another time, River."

"Sure thing." River turned to Larsen as Gina walked away. "Let's go outside and hang a left. I think they spray for bullies there."

"Ha! I think they do. Thanks, Riv." As soon as they walked around to the side of the school, Larsen leaned against the wall and exhaled. "Man, it's been a bad day."

"I'm really sorry about Jax and Antonio."

"They cornered me right after Ms. Carrow's class."

"Sucks, dude. Sorry I wasn't there."

"Listen, River. I wanted to thank you for standing up for me. People rarely do. I wasn't so sure Jax wasn't going to punch you out."

"I wasn't worried."

"I really appreciate what you did. I just don't want you to get caught up in my nightmare."

River shook his head. "No. It's everyone's nightmare when nobody stops bullies."

"I sure wish more people felt like you did. Wish they had your courage. I should be able to stop them without any help."

"Reinhardt's a big guy. Antonio is a body builder. We all need a little help now and then. Just try to go home and chillax."

Larsen looked down and kicked the dirt. "Home. That's a joke. I'm gonna tell you something, Riv, because I know I can trust you."

"You can. What's up?"

"Let's just say that being at school is better than being at home most of the time. And considering I've got two jerks bullying me, that doesn't say much, does it?"

River looked dumbfounded. "School is better than home? What's going on?"

"I've got a mother who's the biggest bully of them all."

"Your mom bullies you for being gay?"

"That's about right."

"How about your dad?"

Larsen's eyes began to water. "My father died when I was eleven. My mom says that the lack of a good male role model is what made me gay. She's clueless. You know, Riv, when I was ten, my dad took me to the mountains one day. We were just sitting there, looking at the view, and he told me, 'Son, when you grow up, there are gonna be some people who will bust your balls for being different. But take it from your old man, it's okay to be whoever you are.'"

"So your father knew you were gay?"

Larsen wiped away a lone tear. "Yeah, he knew before I did.

And I think he knew he was sick. That's why he told me. I'm sure of it."

"Oh, damn, dude. I'm sorry. What did he die from?"

Looking right, then left, Larsen paused before answering. "Some kind of lymphoma. My mother won't talk about it."

"Sorry, Lars. I really am. So, what's up with her?"

Larsen looked in the distance and saw Jax and Antonio jump into a black Mustang where the driveway to the school met the main highway. "Let's go, Riv. You don't need to stand here and watch me hold the building up."

River laughed as he and Larsen started walking away from the school, toward the large expanse of desert where several students were still milling about, waiting for rides, or just talking. "I'll tell you, if you can hold the building up, you can take care of those two clowns."

Larsen frowned. "Yeah, maybe. Anyway, my mom, well, she's embarrassed to have a gay son. Tells me all the time that it's hard enough being black, so what the hell did I have to go and be gay for. I keep telling her that I had as much choice in being gay as I did being black. But she's not buying that. She told me she's gonna squeeze the gay right out of me one day."

"Yeah, right. C'mon, come over to my house. Hang with me for a while. I live about a mile down the road, off to the right."

"I live about a mile and a half in the other direction. Oh, man, Riv. What if someone sees us walking to your house together?"

"Then it means their eyeballs are in good operating condition. C'mon."

Surprised but pleased, Larsen walked alongside River.

"You're a pretty good guy."

River was embarrassed. "I'm okay. Tell me about your mom."

"She works as a waitress in Palm Desert. She goes in before I get home from school and gets off work around ten-thirty."

"She's not around to cook dinner for you?"

Larsen sighed. "No. I eat mostly frozen dinners. Sometimes on the weekend she cooks up a pot of something and leaves it for me to heat up. Or I cook a little something myself. But that's not the worst part, Riv. My mom picks up men all the time. And she doesn't know them that long before she brings them home. She says she's doing it for me. Wants me to meet 'real men.' They stick around for a couple of weeks and dump her."

"Wow, dude. That's some lame shit."

Larsen picked up a small rock and threw it as far as he could. "She told me the last guy dumped her because he couldn't sleep in the house with a homosexual in the next room. What kind of idiot thinks that gay people are attracted to just anyone of the same sex? Or that we're all sexual perverts? Makes me mad. Anyway, Mom told me I'm ruining her life."

River bit his bottom lip while Larsen's words replayed in his head. "Sounds to me like it's the other way around … sorry, I shouldn't have said that."

"S'okay, Riv. I'm down with the truth. Your parents gonna have any problems if you bring me home. I don't want to—"

"No. No way. My family isn't like that. We've got our own history, you know. Nobody in my house is going to judge you. This is probably TMI, but my mom split on us years ago and went to live in LA with some loser producer. It's a long story, but she came home, stuff happened, and then she and my dad fell in love again and got remarried. When she first left, we thought she was gone for good. So you never know. We've even got a dog now. Maybe things will get better for you."

"Don't think so, Riv. My mom hates me more every day."

📖📖📖

Arielle's burgundy RAV4 pulled up to the house just as River and Larsen were approaching. River, often a loner despite his easy charm, rarely brought friends home. Pleased to see him doing so, Arielle was smiling as she got out of her vehicle, followed by an enthusiastic border collie mix.

"Hey, Riv. You brought a friend home."

River bowed dramatically, and then made a sweeping hand gesture toward Larsen. "Greetings, royal mother. This is Larsen Davis." River turned to Larsen, grinning. "This is my mom. But you don't have to bow. That's only something she makes us do. Oh, and this canine rascal is Muggins."

Larsen laughed as he put his hand out. "Hi, Mrs. Dalworth. Hey, Muggins. Nice to meet you."

Muggins wagged his tail and after a quick round of roughhousing with River, jumped up to meet the stranger.

"And very nice to meet you, Larsen. I see you've already mastered the art of not taking my royal offspring seriously. Excuse me for looking like I've been crawling through a dusty building, but that's exactly what I've been doing. Let's go inside and get out of the sun."

Larsen was beaming. As River held the screen door open, Arielle and Muggins walked through, as Larsen followed behind them. Arielle led Larsen into the living room and stopped by the couch. "Have a seat. Can I get you boys something to eat or drink?"

"You don't have to wait on us, Mom. Lars and I can raid the fridge in a few." As soon as River sat down, Larsen did so as well.

"Okay, if you're sure." Arielle sat in the armchair opposite the couch, and Muggins jumped up into her lap.

Larsen smiled warmly at Arielle. "I'd love to hear why you were crawling through a dusty building."

"Well, as you know, our humble town of Mystekal is undergoing a complete redevelopment."

"Yeah, I just moved here with my mom in the summer, but I heard that the guy who used to be principal was a murdering creep who owned the town."

"That's right. Ernest Carrow. He met his untimely demise right in the hallway of our alma mater! Mom and my sister, Jessie, and I saw the whole thing." River paused. "A ghost choked the fuck out of him."

"Really? I heard about that, but my mom said it was probably a stroke or something. That's what the papers said."

"Nuh-uh. The ghost of the guy he whacked a long time ago killed him—strangled him until his eyeballs bulged out of his head and popped wide open. The right eyeball went rolling down the hallway and was carried away by a giant cockroach. *La cucaracha, la cucaracha ...*"

"Riv ... that last part didn't—"

"Carrow left all his money to the school nurse, Anna Nimble, but turns out she hated his homicidal guts all along. She was only pretending to like him. Who knows what he might have done to her if he knew how she really felt. After he died, she gave most of the loot to his daughter, Eve, our English teacher. Now she and Jinxsy Patterson, who turns out to be Ms. Carrows daughter, which really blew everybody away, especially Jinxsy, are Mystekal's head honchos. The Jinxster is my sister's BFF."

"Wow! That's unreal!" Attempting to process all of the information that River had just given him, Larsen turned to Arielle. "You were going to tell me why you were crawling through a dusty building. Maybe that'll be less taxing on my brain."

Arielle laughed. "Ah, yes! Well, I'm in charge of the renovation and expansion of the Desert Theater. I'm working out of a trailer behind the building. We're not only going to restore the theater to its former glory, but we are also going to add onto it. The abandoned paint store next door to it is going to be made into classrooms for a new performing arts school. I'm still working it all out now. But it's going to be fabulous!"

Larsen looked excited, then sad. "Sounds great. What a dream that would be …"

"Are you interested in the theater, Larsen?"

"Yeah. I've wanted to be an actor my entire life. I'd really like to do musical comedy except I can't really carry a tune with a handle on it."

River turned to Larsen. "Mom's an actress. She's been in some movies and shit, but we don't talk about that too much these days because that was a bad time for our family."

Arielle's stare bored a hole through River's forehead. "Riv, since we don't talk much about that time, let's not talk about it *right now*, as well. What do you think? Good idea?"

"Ha ha, Mom. You crack me up."

Arielle resumed talking to Larsen. "I hope you will follow your dream, Larsen. If you want to act, you should go for it. Why do you look so sad?"

"I guess you should know that River was nice enough to bring me to your home today because at school these … uh … these dick …"

Arielle finished the word for him. "Dickheads?"

Embarrassed and surprised, Larsen continued. "Well, yeah, those guys at school were bullying me again. For being gay. Thing is, Ms. Dalworth, like I told Riv, my mom hates that I'm gay and thinks she can 'straighten me out.' She thinks theater is a 'gay profession' and said she will never support me doing gay work with other gay people."

Arielle banged her head three times against the back of the armchair. "Oh, Larsen. I'm so sorry. Would it help if I spoke to her?"

"Oh, shit no! I mean, no, thank you. She would probably think the only reason River was nice to me is because he must be gay, too, and then she'd think you were messed up for being okay with it."

"Well, my son isn't gay, but if he were, I would be fine with it. And just for the record, I'm fine with him having gay friends. In this home, we care about associating with good people. That's numero uno."

River blew a large puff of air through his lips. "Yeah, dude. You should have seen the douchebag movie producer my mom used to live with in LA. Creepy Phil Hodges. In fact …"

"Riv, let's save any walks down Memory Lane for those special times when there is absolutely no other possible choice for conversation. Like when we're all dead. How about that?"

Larsen and River both cracked up.

"Damn, Riv, no wonder you're an okay guy. You've got the coolest mom."

"You're making me blush, Larsen. Listen, you guys help yourself to food and drink."

River turned to Larsen. "Otherwise known as sustenance and libation."

Larsen's face screwed up in confusion.

Arielle smiled. "My son, the language lover. You've probably noticed he's a bit bizarre, but, well, we love him. Mars wouldn't take him back, you know. His dad and I searched the desert for the spaceship he landed in, but it apparently went home without him. No forwarding address. Now, if you'll excuse me, Larsen, I need to shower and get this plaster dust off me. You're welcome in our home any time. Muggins, stay here and entertain the boys."

Larsen was choked up. "Thanks, Ms. D. I mean—"

"You can call me 'Mrs. D' Larsen. Or Arielle. Either one is fine. See you later."

River noticed Larsen's eyes welling with tears. "Hey, Lars, you okay, dude?"

"Yeah, I'm fine, Riv."

"What's up with those lacrimal gland secretions?"

"Say what?"

"The tears."

Slightly embarrassed, Larsen wiped his wet face with his forearm. "Nothing wrong. It's just that this is the nicest I've been treated in a really long time. Oh, and one more thing: I think your mom is right. You might really be from Mars after all."

Chapter 2

"Where the *hell* have you been?"

Closing the front door of the apartment, Larsen looked stunned to see his mother, Raylene Davis, sitting in an upholstered living room chair with a wooden tea table in front of her, sorting dollar bills and change from the day's tips.

Larsen walked over to her. "I was at my friend River's house. He invited me over after school, and then his mom asked me to stay for dinner. His parents and his sister are really nice people. His dad just drove me home. How come you're so early, Mom?"

Raylene slapped her hand on the small table, causing the pile of quarters she had just stacked to fall, most of them onto the floor.

"Now look what the hell you made me do. I'm asking the questions. How come you're home so late?"

"I just told you, Mom."

"You should have called."

"Why? You're never here at this hour." Larsen knelt down and began picking up the quarters from the carpet and putting them back on the table.

"Well, just so happens that I went in four hours early today to help out a co-worker. She had a doctor's appointment. Pregnant. I worked early, and she worked late. Okay, Mr. Nosy?"

Larsen placed the last of the quarters on the table and stood up to face Raylene. "If you were worried, how come you didn't call my cell?"

Waiting for an explanation, he heard the flush of a toilet. He looked down at the floor in disgust. His mother had brought home a new man. Another stranger.

Larsen was disgusted. "Oh."

Raylene sat up straight in her chair. "Don't you be 'ohing' me like that. Larsen, meet Reggie Lee White."

Larsen turned to see a large, black, brawny man coming from the only hallway in the small two-bedroom apartment. The man eyed Larsen as if he were the intruder in his home.

Larsen wasn't about to let the strange man take control so easily. "What the—"

Raylene grabbed the wad of bills from the table and stuffed them into her bra. "I hope you weren't planning on disrespecting our guest. Especially when I've asked him to help you."

"Help me do what?"

Reggie walked behind Raylene and faced Larsen. "Evenin', son. Your mama's told me all about you." Reggie leaned in and began to massage Raylene shoulders. "This feel good, baby?"

Raylene purred. "You know it does."

Refocusing on Larsen, Reggie altered his stance and stood tall. "See son, I drive trucks. All over the country. It's a good living. Your mama said you needed some help planning for your future. Well, I can help you get started. Tell you everything you need to do to be a trucker. By the time you graduate, you'll have a career waiting. A good one. Make an honest living."

Larsen rolled his eyes. "Seriously?"

"I don't play, young man. Not when it comes to earning the almighty dollar."

No. You just play when it comes to hopping into bed with my mom. You probably haven't even known her for twenty-four hours.

Raylene impatiently waited for Larsen's response. "Answer the man. Thank him for his generous offer. Go on."

Defiantly, Larsen looked into the eyes of the stranger. "Thank you for your generous offer. But I have no interest in being a truck driver."

Reggie looked at Raylene, then again at Larsen. "It's a job for a real man. You have a problem with being a real man?"

Larsen challenged Reggie with his eyes. "No, not at all. I am a real man."

Raylene leaned back in her chair and threw up her hands to the sky. "Oh, Lord, there he goes again. Telling those damn lies on himself."

Larsen was quick to protest. "I am a real man, Mom."

Shaking her head, and waving him off with her arms, Raylene disagreed. "Real men don't stick their johnsons into other men."

"Yeah, they do. But for the record, I haven't had sex yet."

"And that's exactly why I want you to drive a truck."

"So I can be a gay truck driver?"

Emphatically, Raylene slammed her hand on the table as the quarters fell to the floor again. "I give up!"

Larsen sighed. He was so tired of the same argument, but tonight his mother was having it for the sake of the stranger she had brought home. "Mom, I could go the rest of my life and never have sex. And I'd still be gay. I could drive a fleet of trucks, and I'd still be gay. It's who I am."

Reggie shrugged, as if to say to Raylene, *I tried, he's your problem,* then took a seat on the old black leather couch.

Larsen started to head for his bedroom, but his mother stopped him. "Go sit on the couch. I'm not done with you."

Respecting his mother's wishes, Larsen took a seat on the couch, as far away as he could from Reggie. "What else, Mom?"

"Who's the new friend you have? Another gay boy?"

"No. He's not gay. And even if he were, that doesn't mean I'd like him that way. I mean, you don't like every straight man you see, do you?"

Reggie looked as interested in her answer as Larsen.

"No. Of course not. But that's different. I am very selective about the type of man I like."

"And you think that gay people aren't selective, right? We just want to do it with anyone of the same sex, right? Well, I'm here to tell you that's bogus."

"Who's the boy?"

"River Dalworth."

"White boy?"

"Yeah. So?"

"You like white boys?"

"He's my friend. He's a cool guy. He stood up for me today."

"Stood up for you? What does that mean?"

Larsen had opened a door he didn't want to walk through. "Never mind."

Reggie turned sharply to Larsen. "Respect your mother. She asked you a question."

"Some guys were bullying me at school. Two against one. River stood up for me."

Raylene reached down to the floor to pick up the change that had fallen. "Well, I'm glad to hear there are boys at your school with some common sense."

Relieved, Larsen smiled. "Yeah, Mom. There are. Riv's a chill guy. You'd like him."

"Not him, stupid. The ones who don't like gay boys. Maybe they're the ones to squeeze the gay out of you."

It took every ounce of strength for Larsen not to cry in front of his mother and the stranger. He jumped up from the couch, ran into his bedroom, closed the door, and was unable to stop the tears that flowed down his face.

It had been three days since Gina had mustered up the courage to talk to River, and by Friday, she was determined to try again before the weekend came and went.

In Mystekal High's cafeteria, Gina had worked out a plan. With her brown-bagged lunch ready to go, she waited one minute after she saw River take a seat, then walked over and sat down in the empty chair across the table from him.

"Hey, River."

River finished chewing the large bite he had taken out of his sandwich. "Hey, Gina."

Nervously, Gina spoke the lines that she had rehearsed. "I wanted to talk to you on Tuesday after school, but then Larsen came along and—"

"Yeah, the dude went through a lot that day."

Gina smiled, trying not to look overly flirtatious, but send her message all the same. "I thought it was really cool the way you stood up for Larsen. I know that a lot of people don't like the way that Jax and Tonio act, but you're really the only one to do something about it."

"I couldn't not do something about it. Especially when that kind of stupidity is in my face. Lars doesn't deserve it. He's a good guy."

Gina could feel her heart pounding. "I really admire you, River. I've wanted to get to know you since we were sophomores, but I didn't think you'd want to know me."

Oblivious to the fact that a girl was melting in his presence, River continued to eat his sandwich. "Why's that, Gina?"

"Well, because of my sister, Taylor. She was always a real bitch, well, a bully to your sister and Jinxsy. Sort of the way Jax and Tonio are to Larsen. I figured you might think I was just like her.

Only I'm not. My sister's kind of screwed up because my mom wasn't really there for Tay when she was younger. My mom messed with a lot of drugs, and even after she got clean, Tay never forgave her, and they've just never gotten along so hot. Tay moved to LA the day after she graduated. She told my family that if we ever want to see her again, we'll have to come to LA because she's never coming back to this dusty hellhole."

"I remember your sister. And, no, she wasn't very nice to Jess or the Jinxster. But they handled her all right. What's she doing in LA?"

"Working at some vintage clothing store on Melrose Avenue. Living with some much older guy who's high on weed all the time. Getting high too. Partying. Going nowhere but thinking she's on the fast track to being a wardrobe person in the movies because celebs come into the store once in a while."

"Will that help her? Meeting actors?"

"Probably not, especially if she's high all the time. My dad told her she needs to get her you-know-what together and find an apprenticeship or something—you know, get her foot in the door and learn the business. Just because you're in the same neighborhood as a dream doesn't mean it's going to find you. You have to go after it, you know?"

River put down his sandwich and took real notice of Gina for the first time. Her long, blond, curly hair framed her face nicely, and she had bright blue eyes with a smile to match. "I like what you just said, about being in the same neighborhood as a dream. That's kind of cool."

Gina blushed. "How about you, River? Do you have a dream? What are you going to do after we graduate in June?"

"I draw shit. Well, mostly people. I'm an artist."

Laughing, Gina tried not to make her infatuation any more obvious. "Right, I've seen some of your work. You're not good, you're freakin' amazing. Have you been drawing all your life?"

"Yup. So, how about you? What do you want to do?"

Just as Gina was about to respond, she gasped as she glanced over at the kids waiting in line for a hot lunch. River turned to see what she was looking at with such horror.

As Larsen was telling the cafeteria supervisor, Kathryn Winterstrom, what he wanted to eat, Jax and Antonio were positioning themselves on either side of him, squeezing against him until he fell to the floor, his salad tumbling on top of him. Jax and Antonio, mission accomplished, laughed as they left the line and hurried out of the cafeteria.

Looking up, angrily brushing salad out of his face, Larsen saw that River was ready to jump to his defense. He tried to wave him off. Not picking up the signal, River rose to help his friend.

Gina, very aware of what Larsen was trying to convey, spoke quickly. "River, wait!"

"What, Gina? I've got to help my friend."

"No, Riv. This time you'll help him more by doing nothing. The damage is already done. He can get up on his own. If you rush to his side, people will start saying even more—"

"Even more what?"

Angry that she let it slip, Gina struggled to mask her own words. "People will start saying even more cruel stuff to Larsen. That's all."

Now fully tuned into her station, River wasn't buying it. "Nope. That's not what you were going to say at all. Kids have been spewing crap about me and Lars, wondering if I'm gay because I'm friends with the guy. Am I right?"

Gina looked downcast. "Yeah."

"Gina, it's okay. Just because you told me that, it's not like I blame you. And it's not like I'm surprised, either. Think I don't know that the addled brain misfires? Well, I do. People can talk all the bullshit they want, and it won't change who or what I am. You were right to stop me. Lars knows how to get up all by himself. Bullshit just makes *my* brain misfire sometimes. And for the record, I do like girls."

Distraught by what she had just witnessed, Kathryn called a coworker to take over her duties and raced from behind the counter to help Larsen.

Handing him a moist towel to wash off the salad, Kathryn looked as if she wanted to cry. "I'm so sorry, son. If I had been on this side of the counter when those boys did that, it wouldn't have been a pretty sight."

Embarrassed, Larsen didn't want to make a big deal of it. "It's okay, Mrs. Um …"

"Winterstrom. Kathryn Winterstrom. And you are …?"

"Larsen Davis, ma'am."

"It's my pleasure to meet you, Larsen Davis. Let me get you some lunch. On the house."

"That's okay, Mrs. Winterstrom. Jerks like that kind of make a guy lose his appetite."

"No, no. You must have something. I certainly understand if you don't want to sit here in the cafeteria. But how about if I make you a nice sandwich to slip into your backpack? If you get hungry later, between classes, you'll have something to eat. It would make me feel a lot better."

Larsen smiled. "Sure."

"I'll tend to that right away. And you listen to me. If you ever have any problems, and you don't want to involve the other kids, you come find me. I couldn't be more serious."

"I really appreciate it. You know, it really sucks having those guys bully me, but I try to find the good in things, and, well, because of them I have met some of the nicest people in this school."

"It's called looking for the silver lining, and it is a wonderful philosophy to have about life. I wish …"

Kathryn stopped speaking in midsentence, and her eyes filled with tears. Larsen knew there had to be a very good reason. But that would be for another day.

"Let me go make your sandwich. Give me five minutes and meet me over there. At the end of the counter. How does that sound?"

"Great. Thank you."

Gina, seeing that Larsen was on his way over to River, decided to leave the two friends to talk. Pumped about how well her conversation had gone with River, she was already dreaming about the next time.

📖📖📖

"I hope everyone's written the essay I assigned on Monday. Vanesa, will you please collect everyone's work and bring it to me?"

Vanesa Chavez rose from her chair. "Sure, Ms. Carrow."

Jax let out a sigh to inform everyone, especially Eve Carrow, that he was bored. "What were we supposed to write about?"

Eve, who was known for her usually cheerful demeanor, tried to hide her annoyance. "*Lord of the Flies.* You were to share your thoughts on why we make the choices that we do. Why do some choose civility and others savagery? Is that ringing any bells? I know it's been four very long days since I assigned the essay."

Jax twisted his face. "You being sarcastic, Ms. Carrow?"

"I'll leave that to you to figure out, Mr. Reinhardt. And I'm not going to repeat the entirety of the assignment. If you did it, then you know exactly what I asked for. If you didn't do it, you'll get a big, fat F."

Jax looked over at Larsen and whispered. "F as in faggot?"

Larsen looked straight ahead, refusing to acknowledge the ugly words.

Barely keeping her composure, Eve took the papers from Vanesa, then turned to address Jax. "Was there something you said to Larsen that the entire class should hear?"

River shot a warning glance at Jax, who opted out of Eve's offer. "Nope. I'm good."

Gina smiled as she made note of River's quiet threat to protect his friend.

Eve leafed through the essay papers. "Well, looks like you've done the work after all, Mr. Reinhardt. Let's see what you had to say."

All eyes were upon Eve as she scanned Jax's essay. The shaking of her head and the biting of her lip didn't bode well. "What the heck is this nonsense?"

Antonio laughed. "What did you write, Jax?"

"Just that it's hard to be civil when degenerates and homos walk among us."

Jerome Lincoln turned sharply to Jax. "I'd agree with that, Reinhardt, because I'm finding it really difficult to be civil to a degenerate scum like you. So maybe you've got a point."

"You black dudes just stick together. You got a thing for Davis?"

"No. Just got a thing for decency. Now, why don't you shut your mouth. You have no right to spew that kind of nasty shit."

Jax nodded defensively. "First Amendment says differently."

Eve, taking a deep breath, took control of the conversation. "Aren't we all lucky to live in a country where our right to free speech is protected? That right is something that many of us take for granted because we've never known otherwise. But in this world, people are killed for saying a lot less than you just said, Jax. And while I respect our constitution, you're going to respect the rules of my classroom. This is a bully-free zone. This entire school is a bully-free zone." Eve looked over at Larsen, who hung his head. "At least it should be."

Jax sat up straight, ready for a confrontation. "Really, Ms. Carrow? That's funny coming from the daughter of the biggest bully of them all." Jax turned to Vanesa. "Principal Carrow hated your sister, Sophia, didn't he? Wasn't he going to behead her or something for chewing gum? Didn't like Mexicans, either. When we were in the tenth grade, he told Tonio that the whole lot of them ought to be sterilized until they die off."

River noticed that Antonio looked shaken as he recalled the former principal's vile words.

Jax turned to his best friend. "Go on, Tonio. Tell Ms. Carrow what else her old man did."

Antonio, now looking sick to his stomach, waved Jax off.

Vanesa turned to Jax. "I hate the way Mr. Carrow treated my sister and everyone else. But that's not Ms. Carrow's fault. She suffered more than anyone. So get off her case."

Jax laughed. "Ass kisser. Pucker up. Lips on butt. Mwwwah!"

Eve glared at Jax. "My father was a horrible man. I will never know what made him so evil; I only know that he was the cruelest human being I have ever known. And, ironically, you've unintentionally made a very good point about the subject of our essay. It is well known that William Golding wrote *Lord of the Flies* because he was deeply affected by the brutality and violence he saw in the Second World War, when he served in the Royal Navy. He participated in the invasion of Normandy, and for those of you who pay attention in history class, you'll understand the profound effect that an experience of that magnitude would have on any human being with feelings.

"But Golding didn't brutalize people because he witnessed it. He recreated the horrors that haunted him only by writing about them. I wish my father had simply written about the demons that plagued him. But he didn't. Instead, he chose to live a hate-filled life, torturing people with his words, and killing them, too."

Gina looked alarmed as she saw Eve's eyes well up. "You okay, Ms. Carrow?"

"I will be. Thank you, Gina. It's no secret anymore that my father killed my boyfriend in high school. I will live with that for the rest of my life. And now that my father is gone, I will never know what turned him into an evil monster."

River looked uneasy. "Maybe his ghost will come back and tell you."

"I don't think so, River. My father is burning in hell. His eternal home. They don't give out day passes for homecomings."

Larsen looked thoughtfully at his teacher. "Do you believe there is a hell, Ms. Carrow?"

"Honestly, Larsen, I have no idea. But on most days, when I think about my father, I'd like to think there is. How about you? Do you think there's a hell?"

"I don't know, either. Some days I'm pretty sure there's a hell on earth, though."

Everyone, including Antonio, turned to look at Jax, but he'd long gone quiet.

📖📖📖

Gina's timing was perfect. River was just opening his locker when she walked by. "Hey, Riv."

River looked up. "Oh, hi, Gina. How's it going?"

"I'm so glad it's Friday. I live for weekends." She grunted and let her backpack fall to the floor. "I swear this thing gets heavier every day."

River grinned. "Must be those rocks I keep slipping in there."

Gina laughed. "Things got a little heated in Ms. Carrow's class today, huh? I feel so bad for her, having to live forever with the horrible things her dad did."

River corrected her. "He was her father, not her dad. He was never a dad to her, you know? Any dick can be a father."

Gina looked embarrassed. "Yeah. You're right. The wrong word just slipped out."

River laughed. "Don't look so upset. No biggie. I'm not going to send you to vocabulary jail."

"But that might be fun. Would you lock me up and throw away the key?"

Larsen, who had just approached, saw Gina flirting with River and tried to keep his distance so as not to interrupt.

"There are no keys in vocabulary jail. You just have to say the right words to get out."

Gina smiled coyly, trying not to let her infatuation show. "Like what, Riv?"

"Oh, I don't know. Maybe something like, 'Let me out of this hellhole! I'm sick of eating alphabet soup!' "

Gina giggled as she picked up her backpack and put it over her shoulder. "You're so funny. And different. Good different. So, what are you doing this weekend?"

"Just stuff."

"You know, since they reopened the movie theater, there are at least three movies there all the time. There's one I'm really dying to see."

River, taking some books out of his backpack and putting others in, nodded. "Yeah, this town has come a long way in two years since Ms. Carrow and the Jinxster took ownership. New housing development, motel, shopping center, and a facelift for this old-assed school. We've got thirty percent more kids now. Oh, and my mom's the project manager for the Desert Theater renovation and expansion. She's going to run the place when it's finished."

"Mystekal's getting another movie theater?"

"No, this isn't a movie theater. It's the kind of theater that has a stage for flesh-and-blood actors to flub or forget their lines on. That kind of theater."

"Sounds fabulous. I'd love to see what she's doing with it!"

Noticing Larsen, River shut his locker door and rested his backpack on the floor. "Hey, dude. How are you doing? My mom called earlier and wanted to know if you'd have dinner with us again tonight."

Larsen brightened while Gina simultaneously looked jealous.

"Yeah, I'd love to, Riv. That's really nice of your mother to ask."

"Well, don't get too much of a swelled head. It was really Muggins who wants to see you again."

"That is the coolest dog, Riv. I'd love to have one, but you know that's impossible. At least for now."

River looked over at Gina. "Have a really good weekend, okay? I'll see you on Monday."

"Sure, River. See you Monday."

As Gina hurried off, Larsen turned to River. "I know you're a really smart guy, so please tell me that you're not as dumb as you appear to be right now."

"What are you talking about?"

"Man, that girl has got it bad for you. She's so hot for you, she's burning up. Whew, I can still feel the heat!"

River looked embarrassed and picked up his backpack. "Get out of here."

The two boys walked down the hall toward the front door and outside into the afternoon sun.

"Man, Riv, she tried like crazy to ask you to the movies with her. And when you didn't bite, she told you she'd love to see the theater your mom's working on. And you're just like 'Duh, whatever.' And then go on about everything that's new in Mystekal. I'm not so sure you didn't do that on purpose. Anyway, that's your business. All I know is that she's a really cute girl who digs you. You should ask her out."

"I don't know, Lars …"

Larsen rolled his eyes. "You're the only guy I know who's fearless when it comes to facing the school's biggest bullies and scared to death of a pretty girl."

Chapter 3

Larsen was stunned to see his science teacher, Henry Sledge, walk into the Dalworths' house, at precisely six-thirty, with a woman.

Noticing his surprise, River burst out laughing. "Ha ha ha! You should see your face, dude. I guess I forget to tell you that Mr. Sledge is now Uncle Henry. He married Aunt Stella."

Stella gave River a big hug. "You thought you'd never get rid of me, boy, but aside from missing your faces every day, I'm finally a happy woman."

"Hi, Aunt Stella!"

"Jessie, my beautiful niece. How are the classes going?"

"Fine. Still trying to figure out what I want to do with my life."

"How about something in the science field?"

"I don't think so, Mr. ... I mean, Uncle Henry. I'm not wired for math or science. I'm really enjoying photography a lot. I took the class just to fill my schedule, but it's opening up a whole new world for me. I'm loving it."

"Any samples of your work for Henry and me to see?"

Jessie sat down as Henry and Stella took their seats. "Well, actually, I have a few photos of numbnuts and Muggins I took last weekend. They're covered in awesome sauce ... if I do say so myself."

Larsen looked at River. "Numbnuts? Is that you?"

"My sister is delusional. I didn't see you take any photos,

Jess."

"You were too busy playing with Muggs in the side yard. I captured you candidly. Actually, Aunt Stella, I'm thinking about becoming a photojournalist. But I want to be one of those photographers who capture the seedier side of life, the gritty underbelly of the world that few people understand but many fear. The world is filled with bizarre specimens of the human species. That's why Riv makes the perfect subject."

Larsen laughed. "C'mon, Riv. Your sister's funny. Laugh."

"No worries, Larsen. Riv doesn't like tasting his own medicine. He spits it out like a little boy." Jessie still enjoyed teasing her brother. "Got a girl on your mind, maybe?"

The corners of Larsen's mouth turned upward, and River shot him a look to keep quiet.

Swiftly picking up on the exchange, Jessie smiled. "OMG. Is there a lover girl, Riv?"

"No, there is not!"

Stella laughed. "I'm betting there is. So, Riv, where are your parents? And the dog, for that matter?"

"They went out to pick up stuff for dinner. Mom and Dad are like swooning lovebirds since they got back together. Can't even go to the supermarket without each other. 'Love you, baby.' 'Love you more, baby.' Kiss. Kiss. Kiss. Ha ha."

Jessie rolled her eyes. "Dad's still working two jobs, and Mom's spending every day at the Desert Theater, so they don't really get that much time together, especially since Dad has to work some weekends. And Muggs went with them because he loves Mom more than anyone. He's her son. The normal one with four legs and a tail."

Everyone laughed, and River noticed Larsen trying to mask the sadness that washed over his face. He knew exactly what his friend was thinking; he wanted to have a family just like River's.

"Hey, Mrs. D. Can I help you with the dishes?"

Arielle took her hands out of the soapy sink and turned to Larsen. "You're a sweetheart, Larsen. But, no, please go join the others in the living room. I'm actually having fun being domestic. I didn't think I had it in me."

"All right, but I wanted to thank you for inviting me over again. I feel like a different person when I'm here. Well, maybe not a different person, but a much happier one."

Arielle dried her hands on a dish towel. "Come here, Larsen. Let me give you a hug."

As he felt the warmth of Arielle's embrace, Larsen tried desperately not to get too emotional. "Thank you. I didn't think there was anyone left to care about me."

"Oh, honey, I'm so sorry that your dad is gone and the situation with your mother is so bad. I wasn't always the best mother to my children. It's something I profoundly regret, but if it weren't for all that I've gone through, I wouldn't be who I am today. Maybe your mom needs some time to come around. Even though she's your mother, she's got a lot of growing up to do. Just like I did. Just like many of us do."

"But you would have never been happy that your kids were being bullied at school because you agreed with the bullies."

Arielle made a sad face. "Riv told me. No, I wouldn't have done that. But I did say a lot of pretty stupid things. I used to think Jessie's life would be better if she dolled herself up with makeup and wore designer clothes. It gives me chills to think about how shallow and out of touch I had become."

"You're a really good person, Mrs. D. I know you must be thinking some pretty bad things about my mother that you wouldn't admit to me. And I'm down with that. Because they're true."

"I can't speak for your mom, Larsen, so I won't. But you're always welcome here, and you can always talk to me." Arielle paused. "Oh, excuse me, I've got a call coming in."

She grabbed her cell out of her pocket, and Larsen nodded politely and went into the living room to join the rest.

Leaning against the sink, Arielle smiled as she saw the call was coming from her best friend, Lisa Finlay. "Hey, girl. What's cookin'?"

"Oh, all kinds of things. I've got pots on every burner. I miss you being here in LA, but I've never heard you happier than you sound now. Phil really sucked the life out of you."

"He did way more than that, Lis. I don't know if he has a woman in his pathetic life now, but if he does, I pity her. Is he still in LA?"

"Uh, yeah. He is. I guess I should tell you. He's taken an office just down the hall from mine."

"Are you effing serious? An office for what? What's he doing now?"

"My assistant, Petra, is a bit hot to trot for Phil's assistant. From what I've been able to suss out from her, your scar-faced ex is producing something for another cable network. Thankfully, not the same one I work with. The house in Bel Air is history, and he's downgraded to a two-bedroom condo in Hollywood. Word has it from other sources that he's been seen around town with some blonde nobody knows. Probably picked her up in a bar on the Strip. He's drinking a lot. That's about all I've heard through the grapevine."

"Hmm. Well, thanks. That's about all I can stomach to hear right now, anyway. So, how are things with you?"

"Doing great. Ross is in preproduction for the new film, and I'm doing something kind of fun here that I'd like you to be involved with."

"Really? You know that I'd love to help, and saying no will probably kill me, but my life is here now, and—"

"Nothing like that, sweetie. I'm your bestie, remember. I'm the last person who would ever want to lure you back to LA. Hear me out. One of the documentaries I'm working on is about building restoration, the preservation of local and national landmarks, and on and on. We'll be filming all over the country. I'm not sure exactly how we're going to structure it, but I want to include your theater in it. And I don't want to wait any longer, because if I do, I won't be able to get footage of the renovation in progress. Soooooooooo, I'd like to come down to Mystekal, with Josh, my favorite cameraman, shoot the work in progress, and interview you about everything you're doing. How does that sound?"

"Like perfection, Lis. Not only will I love being part of your documentary, but it will be great publicity for the theater. We're still in the process of carefully getting rid of the old, so it would be perfect timing to shoot before we put in the new. And I took photos and footage of the place before any work was done, so that should be helpful as well."

"You're prophetic and a genius! So, you're going to be the director once the building is finished, yes?"

"You'd better believe it. The whole thing has been a dream. I've never felt more fulfilled. I want this theater to put Mystekal on the map!"

"Phantasmagorical. I've got to run, Ari, but I will be in touch, and we'll arrange a time to do this. I believe in you. I know you can do anything you set your mind to accomplish. Oh, and one last thing: don't glam yourself up for the cameras so much that nobody will believe you're working in an abandoned theater."

Arielle laughed. "You know me too well. That's scary. But I've evolved since those days. Trust me."

📖📖📖

"That sounds wonderful, baby!" Mick Dalworth got up and put his arms around his wife. "I'm so proud of you and everything you're doing. Things are really falling into place."

Mick gave Arielle a big kiss, and River nudged Larsen. "Lovebirds. Just like I said."

"Mom, that's amazing! I'm so happy for you. Look, even Muggins is wagging his tail. He's proud of you, too."

"Thanks, Jess. I'm eager to share with Eve and Jinxsy. Will Jinxsy be around this weekend?"

"No, she's going to Big Bear with some friends from college. She'll be around next weekend. But I can tell her about it."

"I'd appreciate that, honey."

"Congrats, Mrs. D. You're going to be a documentary star!"

"Thank you, Larsen. But I'm really hoping this opportunity will do more for the theater than for me personally."

Stella rose and hugged her sister-in-law. "I never thought I'd like you this much, Arielle. But you have turned into one damn fine woman."

River laughed, then turned to Larsen. "Aunt Stella used to hate Mom."

Mick gave his son the mock evil eye. "Zip it, Riv."

"Ha ha. You used to say that to me all the time."

Mick smiled. "I sure did. And if your filter continues to malfunction, you're going to be hearing it a lot more."

"Okay, Dad. I'll get my filter fixed."

Mick laughed. "That's gonna be a pretty expensive repair job. I'm wondering if a repair is even possible. Well, nothing a good roll of duct tape can't fix."

"Ha ha. You're funny, Dad."

Larsen's laughing face turned sad. "I've had a great time here tonight with all of you. But if you don't mind, Mr. D, I'm going to have to take you up on that ride home again. I need to be there before my mom gets home."

Larsen popped in a DVD of *West Side Story,* sat on the couch, then began to watch the movie he'd seen many times before. He was worried about Raylene and silence only made it worse. He grabbed the remote and turned up the volume to try to drown out his bad thoughts, but it didn't help. It was already after one-thirty, and his mother wasn't home yet nor had she called or texted. Unlike the first night he had dinner with the Dalworths, this time he had texted Raylene to tell her where he'd be, but she never responded. When he tried calling, he was only able to leave a message on her voicemail. Now he was really starting to fear the worst.

For a moment, all of the problems he had with his mother vanished and were replaced by frightening scenarios of what might have happened to her. Two minutes into the most frightening "what if" of all, he heard loud voices outside the front door, followed by the sound of a key struggling to turn a lock. Just as he was going to get up and open the door, Raylene and Reggie came staggering into the living room, reeking of whiskey and barely able to keep from falling.

Reggie, not even noticing Larsen or the television, was grinning like a Cheshire cat and chasing Raylene. "Here kitty, kitty, kitty! C'mon, you're going to give me some of that—"

Larsen stood up. "Whoa! That's my mother you're talking to!"

Reeling back in surprise, Reggie wasn't about to let Larsen stop him. "Well, look who's here. You go to your room, boy. Your mama's got some poontang to deliver to Reggie Lee."

"No, I don't think so."

"Gay boys don't even know what poontang is."

Larsen felt his heart racing. "This one does!"

Raylene stumbled as she tried to keep her balance, then fell lopsided into the armchair, narrowly missing a collision with the dining room table. "You don't tell me or my man, um, my man, Reggie, um, what to do in the house that I pay for. And what the hellllllllll would you know about what men and women do together, anyway?"

"Don't bring my sexuality into this, Mom."

Raylene pointed to the television. "And what the fuck is that you're watching?"

"*West Side Story*, Mom. You know what it is. It's a musical. Takes place in the 1950s in New York. Remember?"

"I don't remember shiiiiiiiit. There you go again, watching those gay stories all the time."

"It's not a gay story. It's about two rival gangs, the Jets and the Sharks. What's gay about that?"

Reggie, disgusted that Larsen had interrupted his game of cat and mouse with Raylene, picked her off the armchair, sat down, and put her on his lap. Raylene giggled for a moment, then her face grew ugly as she turned back to her son.

"Well, um … I think what you've said just proves my p-p-point."

Larsen, working overtime to control his anger, quietly addressed his mother. "What point would that be?"

"Well, you've got two gangs. Now you and me both know there's a whole lot of testosterone in these boys. But what are they doing? They're dancing in the streets like faggots. Real men don't swish from side to side like that. Look at that one in the tight red shirt sticking his booty out. Like a goddamn mating call to see if the other one's in heat."

Reggie howled with laughter. "Y'ain't lyin', Raye."

Snarling at Larsen, Raylene continued to rant. "Look at those boys, all snappin' their fingers together."

"Oh, boy, Raye! Now the homeys are swishing their hips."

"They sure as fuck are. Now look at them. Making kissy sounds at each other. You gonna tell me that's what heterosexual boys do?"

"Mom, please. Just stop!"

"Aw, hell, look at them now, piroufuckinetting through the streets of New York. Twirling like ballet dancers through the alley. Now you listen to me, Larsen. These boys in this damn movie have all taken years of ballet. You go to any ballet school in the country, and what you're gonna find is a class full of almost all gays. And don't you be trying to tell me no different."

Larsen put his head down. "Okay, so some of the dancers probably were gay men. Does it matter? It's not a gay story. It's a tragic love story. Tony and Maria's story was inspired by *Romeo and Juliet*. You know, by William Shakespeare. And so what if it were a gay story? The dancing is beautiful to watch. Someday I'm gonna dance like that."

"You will never take a dance lesson while you're under my roof, boy. What you've got is a trash pile of wasted asssspirations."

"I love musical theater. More than anything."

"Well, if God thought you should do this nonsense for a living, he'd have given you a voice for singing. Even the church choir didn't want you."

"Just like you don't want me."

Raylene pretended not to hear. "So, you went to that white boy's house again."

"Yes, I went to River's house again. His family likes me."

"They know you're gay?"

"Yeah, they know. I already told you that. And they don't care. They just like *me*. Is that too difficult for you to comprehend?

That someone could just like me for who I am? That the whole world doesn't care about my sexual orientation?"

"Hush up, boy. Turn off your fag DVD and go to your room. Leave Reggie and me alone."

"Come on, Mom. Can't you two at least go into the bedroom?"

Reggie, who still had Raylene on his lap, reached around and grabbed her breasts with both hands. "Maybe the boy wants to stay here and watch. Maybe that'll be what cures him."

Larsen grabbed the remote and turned off the TV. "I can't believe what I'm seeing and hearing. You should be ashamed, Mom."

"I *am* ashamed, boy! I am ashamed of *you*!"

Unable to control himself, Larsen screamed back. "There's no way in hell you could be as ashamed and as disgusted with me as I am with you. That's impossible! You make me sick!"

"Don't you be talking to your mutherr like that!" Reggie fiddled under Raylene's shirt. "Damn, woman, you got you one stubborn brassiere here. Unleash these hooters. I ain't got all gotdam night."

Larsen shivered with revulsion, hurried into his small room, and slammed the door shut. He was almost sure this was child abuse, but if he called the authorities, they might not believe him. And God only knows where he might end up. At least in Mystekal he had friends now. That was more than he'd had in a very long time.

Burying his head into his pillow and sobbing, he cried until he fell into a merciful sleep.

Chapter 4

Searching through his backpack, River finally remembered that he had shoved the latest class handouts from Eve Carrow into the front, zippered pocket. Reaching his hand in to retrieve it, he pulled out a piece of pink-lined notebook paper, folded in fourths. It was likely something Jax had slipped in there, just to torment him for being Larsen's friend.

Hey, Riv,

I really enjoyed talking to you today at lunch. It's pretty lame that it took me two years to get up my nerve, but better late than never.

I think you're hot and very cool. LOL! Wait! That makes no sense, but you get the idea. What I'm really trying to say is that I like you. You make me laugh. I'm thinking maybe you like me okay, too, but I get the idea that you might be shy when it comes to asking a girl out.

Okay ... so I'm going to be a bit rad and try to slip this note into your backpack at the end of the day. I hope you'll find it SOON. Trust me, I've never asked a guy out before, but I was wondering if you'd like to go to the movies with me over the weekend. Or maybe next weekend if you're busy or want to think about it for a while. I hope to hear from you soon. My number is 760-244 ...

River reread Gina's note three times to make sure he wasn't hallucinating. She was a cute girl, and right from the beginning, he felt comfortable with her. He was seventeen and had never asked a girl out before. He was way overdue, and Gina had made it easy for him.

All he needed to do was to call her and then come up with some excuse to leave the house so that no one in his family would know.

📖📖📖

When Larsen woke up the next morning, the first thing he did was check the living room. It was a squalid mess. Dirty plates and glasses lay overturned on the coffee table and floor. Ants were feasting on the crumbs from an empty package of crackers. His mother's clothes were strewn everywhere, and she lay naked on the braided rug, snoring heavily. He had no idea when Reggie had left, and he didn't care.

He just knew he had to get out of the house. Brushing his teeth was a chore because his hand trembled as it gripped the brush. Larsen was not used to seeing his own mother naked, especially after having had sex with a near stranger, and he did not want to be around when she woke up. He hopped into the shower, got dressed, and quietly left the house, with no idea where he was going. It was too creepy to leave a note anywhere if it meant having to see her naked again. Even for a second.

When he got outside, he remembered hearing Gina tell River that there were three films playing at the new-and-improved local movie theater. A dark theater would be the perfect place to lose himself and his troubles.

📖📖📖

Larsen had three choices: a psychological thriller, a Hollywood superhero movie, and a film about an older couple struggling through a midlife crisis.

He chose the third one, simply because it began an hour before the other two, and he wanted to go inside and sit down, even if he had to wait forty minutes for the film to start.

He was the first person there. Larsen sat in the middle of the theater. He put his head back, closed his eyes, and tried to destress. He felt thankful he was anywhere but home. He had thought about calling River, but the last thing he wanted to do was to lose his welcome at the Dalworths' home so soon after it had been extended.

After sitting alone for a while, he heard a voice speaking to him. "Excuse me, son. Are you all right?"

Larsen opened his eyes to see a kind-looking African American woman, in her late forties, sitting next to him.

"I-I'm okay."

"You don't look okay. I'm surprised to see a young man like you coming to a movie about older folks with marital problems. I've been sitting a couple of rows behind you, off to the right, and I couldn't help but notice that you seem very upset." She stopped talking to smooth out the lap of her dress. "You know, this is really none of my business. I think I should go back to my original seat. Very sorry to have disturbed you."

"No, wait. It's really nice of you to care about me. Not a lot of people ... I mean, I'll be okay ..."

"My name is Martha Joy. If there's anything a stranger can do to help, I'd like to try."

"That's nice of you, ma'am. But there's nothing you can do. Just a bad scene at home, you know?"

"Please, call me Martha Joy. Or just plain old Martha. But I do prefer Martha Joy."

"My name is Larsen. And you're a very pretty lady. I wouldn't call you plain at all. Or old."

Martha Joy managed a laugh. "Well, you're very kind. I guess

I'm not too shabby. Just not feeling very pretty today, that's all."

"Well, you are."

"Sure I can't lend an ear? Trouble with your parents?"

"My dad died when I was eleven, and my mom hates me for being gay. She treats me like the scum of the earth. That's why I'm here, just to get out of the house. When she leaves for work, I'll go back home."

"Your mom works on a Saturday?"

"Yeah, this is her best day, actually. She's a waitress, and the crowds are bigger on weekends."

"I see. Well, no shame in being gay, Larsen. I know you don't feel 'specially good right now, but there are a lot of gay men and women who struggle with their sexuality. Some can't accept what they're feeling, and others are so afraid of being scorned by family, friends, and the world at large that they stay in the closet. I think it's wonderful that you are secure with who you are. That doesn't make the hard times any better today, but having pride in yourself will serve you well in the future. Just try to remember that. And take it one day at a time. I've only known you two minutes, and I can already see what a fine man you are."

Larsen smiled. "Thanks. I really needed to hear that. I'll remember those words, Martha Joy. Promise. I'm not sure what will happen in my life after I graduate from high school."

"You're welcome, sweet child. Do you have a career in mind?"

"I want to be in musical theater. I can act and dance, but I still need lessons. I can't sing, though. All the lessons in the world won't help me there, so I'll probably just pursue acting. My mother thinks theater is for gays, and she doesn't want any part of it. She said I'll never take dance lessons while I'm living under her roof, even if I could pay for them myself."

"Listen to me, son. Everything about you tells me that you're going to be a star. Your mama has her problems, God bless her, but you can't let them become yours. If you do, you'll never be all that you can be. You will be haunted by your past and stuck in a place where you can't move on. Please hear me, Larsen."

"I-I do. I hear you, Martha Joy. Thank you. I mean it. I feel hopeful just talking to you."

"That makes my heart smile."

"How about you?"

"What about me?"

"You're just as sad as I am. I can see it in your eyes. And you said you're not feeling very pretty today. Why not?"

"Ah, it makes no never mind."

"It does to me. I care. Not that it matters. But I do."

Martha Joy glanced around the still-empty theater as if to make sure no one was within earshot. "I think my husband is cheating on me. We've been married for twenty-eight years. Guess he doesn't find me attractive anymore."

"Are you sure? Did you catch him?"

"No. But I just know."

Larsen pressed. "How do you 'just know' something like that?"

"Well, he's a truck driver. He used to work more, but the laws were changed to reduce the number of hours that a trucker can legally drive. You know, to keep the roads safe and all. But my husband doesn't think I understand all that, and sometimes he tells me he's working more hours than he actually is. Fool doesn't think I notice a difference in his paycheck, either. Twice this week he said he was on the road, but I was in Palm Desert on Tuesday night, visiting our daughter, Ellie, who lives there, and I passed his truck outside this restaurant. I figured maybe he was there with his buddies and would come home later. But he never did.

"Last night, he was home like always, and then around nine

gets a call. Says he has to go help a buddy whose rig is stranded. Kind of gave me a bunch of double talk, but I tried not to pay it too much mind. 'Round three-thirty in the a.m., he comes home, crawls back into bed, smelling like a bottle of Jack Daniels mixed with a heavy dousing of cheap perfume. I pretended to be asleep. He fell out and snored like a freight train. Three hours later, his alarm goes off, and he's back on the road."

Larsen had no words. He just stared at her.

Martha Joy looked embarrassed. "I'm sorry, Larsen. So sorry. I had no right to burden you with my business. None whatsoever. Martha Joy White needs to mind her Ps and Qs."

"White. That's your last name?"

"That's me. You sound surprised."

"Um … no. Not at all. Just wanted to make sure I heard correctly. Because, uh, maybe because someday, when I'm happy and successful, I'll remember the pretty lady in the movie theater who spoke the kind words to me. And I'll want to know who to thank." Larsen exhaled, then took a deep breath. "You didn't burden me at all. We just shared our problems, right?"

"Yes, indeed we did. That's very sweet of you to say. My heart is smiling again, but now it's time for me to return to my seat. Your words are wise, Larsen. I do believe the good Lord brought us here for this short time to share our troubles and divide our pain. I'd like to think so, anyway. It was very nice meeting you. And just remember, life isn't happy now, but it's going to be glorious. I just feel it. Good-bye."

Before Larsen could say anything, Martha Joy was gone. He wanted to call after her, but he could tell she was uncomfortable sharing her problems, and under the circumstances, it was best to let her go.

Larsen wondered. If Martha Joy was right, and if God had wanted them to meet, just to help one another, did God also want

Larsen to know that his mother's new sex partner happened to have a wife?

When the movie was over, at one-thirty, Larsen looked around the theater one more time for Martha Joy, but once again, he figured it was for the best that she was already gone.

As he stepped outside the theater, wondering how to kill another hour before he could safely go home, he heard a female voice call his name from a distance. Expecting to see Martha Joy after all, he was surprised to see River and Gina together.

Waving enthusiastically, Gina rushed over to him. River, who had never been seen with a date before, looked a bit embarrassed. Larsen hadn't known River very long, but he easily recognized his friend's awkwardness, and it amused him.

"Hi, you two. Well, isn't this a surprise!"

Gina, who was glowing just being with River, spoke first. "Hey, Larsen. What are you doing here? Are you going to see a movie, too?"

"Already saw one. *Uncertain December.*"

River screwed up his face. "Dude, isn't that about old people having a midlife crisis?"

Gina laughed. "Well, if they're having a midlife crisis, then they're not that old."

"True. But still, how come you went to a movie in the morning, Lars, and how come you saw that one?"

Larsen's face fell. "Just needed a breather. It was the first show of the day, so my decision was kind of made for me."

"Some bad shit happened at home, didn't it?"

"Yeah. I'm not going to lie. But I'll deal. You guys enjoy your movie, okay?"

Gina gently took hold of his arm. "Hey, not so fast. You really look like you could use your friends right now."

"You're da bomb, Gina. But I'm stepping out of the way here, okay? And you better get in line and get your tickets."

River disagreed. "Our movie doesn't start for a half hour, and if we miss it, there's one after that. Your shit is going down right now. Let's go over to the Kalifornia Kafe and have a drink or something. On me. There's an empty table right on the sidewalk. We can talk and watch the weirdos walk by, too."

Gina giggled and looked at River, her eyes sparkling. "What do you think, Larsen?"

"I think that if I'm sitting next to my weirdo friend, River, I'll be too distracted to see any street weirdos. A guy can only take in so much weirdoism, you know? You two rock, but I'm not into being a third wheel."

The more Larsen protested, the more certain River was that his friend was in trouble. "Come on, Lars. You're not getting out of this one. Let's grab that last table before someone else does."

📖📖📖

Gina and River listened in shock as Larsen recalled last night's events, then described what he had seen in the living room upon waking.

Horrified, River's face displayed the extreme emotion he usually kept under wraps. "Man, that blows. I used to think I had it bad during the years my mom was gone, but this is so much worse."

"And you know what, Riv? There are a whole lot of people who have it way worse than me, and I bet they'd be happy to trade places. Sick as that sounds."

Gina agreed. "You're right. Someone's always got it worse, but that doesn't make our stuff hurt less, just to know there are people out there who are really suffering. Well, I guess it does in one way, but not in another way. Like I told Riv, my mom is a drug addict. She's been clean for years, but I always wonder if she'll slip back into it. She started using when she was younger than we are. Was high off and on for years. My older sister, Taylor, got the brunt of it. So that's why she's so angry and messed up. Sorry for rambling. You never even knew her. Enough about my family. I only mentioned them to let you know that I haven't lived a storybook life, either. But this is some bad stuff you're going through. Bad enough dealing with Jax and Antonio at school, and bad enough having your mom hate on you for being gay, but everything else, wow, I mean, that just totally sucks."

Larsen took a sip of his lemonade. "Thanks for listening, guys. I know I can trust you."

River, who had been quietly absorbing the impact of Larsen's story, nodded. "No, just listening isn't enough."

"River's right."

"There's nothing either one of you can do for me. Just being able to talk about it makes me feel so much less alone. But I'm stuck with my mom until I graduate, and who knows if I'll have any kind of money to get out then. I know one thing, though. I'm gonna give it everything I've got."

"Dude, you can't go home to this every night. It's just not right. You need to hang out with me more often. My family loves you."

"Yeah, but they're your family. And as much as I appreciate the invitations to hang out and have dinner, I've got to be a man and handle my own problems. I do, Riv."

"Having support doesn't mean you're not dealing with things. Excuse me. I've gotta hit the head. I'll be right back."

As soon as River had gone inside the restaurant, Larsen turned to Gina. "I need to say this quickly. I know how much you like this wacko guy, and I also know that I always seem to mess up your time together. Being the needy friend is one role this actor doesn't want to play. You know? I'm glad to see you guys together today. I was hoping it would work out."

Gina was intrigued. "What do you mean, you were hoping it would work out?"

"I see the way you look at him. And I saw you slip a pink piece of paper into his backpack by the lockers yesterday. In fact, I made sure to keep talking until you got the pocket zipped up."

"You saw me? Should I be totally embarrassed? Yes, I should."

"Hmm. Let me think. No, I think you should be commended. It worked, right? You're here with Shy Guy, right?"

Gina blushed. "Well, yeah. We are. I guess he wouldn't have called if he didn't like me, too."

"And that's why I'm not messing it up. Trust me, I would feel worse if I knew I'd ruined your first date. I'm going to split before Riv gets back. Take care, Gina."

"Larsen, wait …"

River got back to the table just in time to see Larsen quickly walking down the street. "How come he didn't say good-bye? He should have stayed and hung with us. I need to call him."

Gina put a gentle hand on River's arm. "No, you don't. Remember the other day in the cafeteria when I told you not to help him up?"

"Yeah."

"Well, it's the same thing here, River. We listened to Larsen talk, and it really helped him. And we offered more, but he didn't want it. The guy really wants friends, but he doesn't want to be a burden. Or a third wheel. And even if we don't feel that he is either of those things, it's important that *he* doesn't feel that way, you know?"

"Damn, Gina. You're almost as smart as I am."

Gina's face brightened as her laughter filled the air. Her hand, still on River's arm, squeezed him a little bit tighter. River smiled as he looked into her eyes. "I'm kind of diggin' you, girl. I might even hold your hand in the movies."

Chapter 5

For Larsen, after the hell of the prior weekend, five days passed without incident. Raylene, embarrassed that Larsen had witnessed even a hint of her sexual activity with Reggie, and relieved in believing that he had slept through the unsightly aftermath in the living room, kept to herself. The awkward silence didn't make Larsen happy, but the absence of abuse made life at least bearable.

Even at school, things were better. But on Friday afternoon, as soon as English class had finished, Jax was on the warpath.

Cornering Larsen in the hallway, just as the class was emptying, Jax unleashed his ugliness. "Hey, gay boy. I hope you didn't think I'd forgotten about you."

Larsen looked the bully in the eyes. "I never gave it any thought. Maybe that's because I don't give you any thought."

"Liar. Today in gym class, I saw you checking out my package."

"You're delusional, Reinhardt. You're not my type."

"Aw, come on. Any man with a dick between his legs is your type."

"You think?"

While the rest of the class hurried to their lockers, River and Gina stood and watched. River, though it went against his nature, had learned to let Larsen fight his own battles, whenever possible. But he wasn't going anywhere until he knew his friend was okay.

River kept one eye on Jax and the other on Antonio, who stood quietly against the wall not saying a word.

"Yeah, I think so, homo."

Larsen kept strong. "You know, guys who hate on gays usually do so because they've got a little gay thing going on themselves. Maybe you need to check yourself in the mirror. You might even fall in love."

Jax's face reddened, and he bit his lower lip with rage. "You calling me a faggot, faggot? Tonio, come help me teach this cocksucker a lesson."

Antonio looked uneasy.

Jax snarled at his best friend. "What the fuck, homey? You gonna just stand there while this queer insults me?"

"Actually, man, I've got to get going. Bianca is waiting for me. Word out!"

Embarrassed and angry that Antonio had refused him publicly, Jax was even more upset that his best friend appeared to have lost his taste for bullying altogether. Looking down the hallway at Antonio as he hurried around a corner, Jax mumbled "pussy" under his breath, then turned back to Larsen as his rage intensified.

Without another word, Jax grabbed Larsen by his shirt, and swinging him around in a three-hundred-and-sixty-degree circle, was just about to bash Larsen's head into the wall, when River got between them. The force of Jax's weight pushed River into the wall, but Larsen's head landed safely in River's chest, though the impact was painful for both. The principal, Hal Dreighton, who had been alerted to the incident, came tearing down the hallway, followed by Sherman Brown, the custodian.

"You boys okay?"

Larsen nodded. "Yes, thank you, Principal Dreighton." He turned to River. "And thank you, man. You practically had your head split wide open for me. You okay? Did you hit your head?"

"Nah. Almost. But no, I'm fine." Seething, River glared at Jax, but seeing that Gina was standing there looking like she was going to cry, he rushed to comfort her.

With Sherman Brown beside him, Principal Dreighton grabbed Jax's arm and forcibly led him down the hall to his office, as Jax, humiliated, protested loudly every step of the way.

River, still seething, watched them go. "Reinhardt's getting suspended. And if he tries this lame shit again and gets caught, he's getting expelled."

Gina attempted to smile. "I'm just so glad that neither of you were hurt. I was really scared. And I'm so glad that Principal Dreighton witnessed it. Maybe this craziness will come to an end."

"It'll be okay, Gin. Stay here with Lars, okay? I'll be back in a few."

River rushed around the corner and ducked into an empty classroom, then pulled his cell phone out of his pocket to make a call.

"Hey, Riv. What's up, honey?"

"Hi, Mom. Listen, remember when I told you everything had been okay for Lars since last Friday night's freak show with his mom and her boyfriend?"

"Of course. Was there another incident?"

"Not at home, but just now at school. I don't want to get into it, but I wanted to ask you if I can bring Lars home for dinner. "

"Absolutely, honey. In fact, I was just going to text you and ask you to do so. Not only would I like to see him, but there's something kind of cool I'd like to talk to him about."

"Yeah, really? What?"

"Be patient. You'll find out when he does."

"Okay, thanks, Mom."

"Riv?"

"Yeah?"

"One more thing."

"What's that?"

"Maybe you'd like to bring Gina home for dinner, too. I think we'd all like to meet your new girlfriend."

Stunned that his mother or anyone in the family had a clue, River stood there with his mouth open.

"Hey, Riv, rhyme to the wise, close your mouth before you attract flies."

"Mom, how do you—"

"I know you, son. I don't have to see you. I know you. Now, are you going to ask Gina for dinner?"

"Uh, yeah. I guess."

Arielle laughed. "Looking forward to it. We can't wait to meet lover girl."

📖📖📖

River, Gina, and Larsen were relaxing in the living room when Muggins came bounding in and leaped on River's lap. River groaned. "Hey, boy. How are you doing? Good day at work? You'd better get down. Dad's not gonna be happy if he finds your fur all over his chair."

Muggins licked River's face, then jumped down and went over to greet the visitors seated on the couch.

Larsen stood, put his arms out, and gave the dog, who was standing on his hind legs, a hug. "Did you miss me, Muggins?"

The dog licked Larsen's face, nuzzled his head against him, then went over to greet Gina.

"Hey, cutie, who are you?"

Muggins, without waiting for an invitation, jumped up on Gina's lap and began wildly kissing her.

"Ha ha. That's my mom's chauffeur. Also my brother. Muggins."

Gina, giggling as Muggins eagerly showed his affection, kissed the dog back. "Hey, Riv, don't get jealous now."

Arielle, carrying a heavy briefcase, walked into the room. She put the briefcase in a corner and turned to greet her guests.

"You must be Gina Dennison."

Gina smiled as she stood up. "It's so nice to meet you, Mrs. Dalworth. My mom says you and Mr. Dalworth were in school with her and Dad."

River looked surprised. "How come I didn't know that?"

Gina smiled. "Don't know, Riv. Guess you don't know everything."

Arielle laughed. "He wishes he did, but, no, he doesn't. How are Nate and Denise? Please, sit down again."

Gina resumed her seat. "Um, well, they're good. Um …"

"I know about your mom's battle with drugs, Gina. You can speak freely with me. It's okay. Is she doing all right?"

"Yeah, she's been clean for years. I didn't know if you knew and—"

"Well, I do. And it's fine. I've fought my own battles, honey, lots of them, so don't ever worry about me judging your mom, okay?"

"Thanks. I'm so relieved."

"Well, then I am, too. And I'm very happy to meet you. My son has excellent taste."

Arielle looked over at River, whose face was now crimson-red, then turned to Larsen. "Hello, my friend."

Larsen stood and gave Arielle a big hug. "Glad to see you, Mrs. D. Thanks for having me over again."

"You're welcome, honey. Riv told me about last Friday night. I wish you would have come by the next day. You shouldn't have to suffer that kind of pain. And certainly not without friends by your side."

"I appreciate that, Mrs. D. I just didn't want to be a burden."

"Nothing could be further from the truth." Arielle looked at the seat Larsen had just vacated. "Please, as you were, Lars. Before everyone else gets here, I have some business to discuss with you. I hope you'll be as excited as I am."

Larsen took his seat on the couch, but he could barely sit still. "Tell me, Mrs. D. I'm going nuts trying to guess what it could be. Ever since Riv said you had something to talk to me about, my brain has been in overdrive."

Arielle smiled and sat in her favorite chair. Muggins, who had just finished kissing Gina, hopped onto his mother's lap. "Sheesh! I swear this dog weighs more every day ... all good things are worth going a little nutso for, don't you think?"

His eyes smiling, Larsen leaned back on the couch and stretched his arms lazily in mock relaxation. "Okay, then, if you don't mind me going cuckoo before your very eyes, just keep torturing me. But I warn you, I can go around the bend pretty quickly."

Arielle laughed as she scratched the dog's neck. "Gee, a girl can't have any fun. You win. I'll spill. Well, if you'll recall, last Friday night when you were here, you know that my friend Lisa called from LA to ask me to be a part of this documentary she's producing on the restoration of vintage landmarks ... down you go, Muggs."

Muggins reluctantly got down, sitting by Arielle's feet, and looking up at her with sad-sack eyes.

Larsen leaned forward. "I think Muggs is trying to make you feel guilty for making him sit on the floor ... sure I remember. Sounds incredible."

"It is. Well, I've spent so much of this week preparing for the interview that I realized my life would be infinitely better with an assistant helping me a few hours every day. Larsen, I'd love it if you'd come to work for me at the Desert Theater. You can work as many days as you can handle. As long as the job doesn't interfere with your schoolwork, I'm flexible. I really need you. Twelve dollars an hour."

Larsen looked incredulous. "Are you kidding me? That's like the best thing that anyone's ever asked me. What would you need me to do?"

"A little bit of everything. Pick up supplies and samples around town. Sweep up after the workers have gone home. Maybe some email correspondence, Internet research, take Muggins for a walk when he looks hopelessly pathetic as you see him now."

Larsen laughed. "And you're going to pay me twelve bucks an hour?"

"Absolutely. But I'm not done. After the theater is renovated, I'm producing and directing an area-wide talent show to open it. So I need to get the word out that we're looking for theatrical talent of all ages from the neighboring towns to participate. The grand-prize winner will receive a thousand dollars and a starring role in a future production, but we'll have other winners, too. I want to involve as many people as we can and make this theater something special. I'm planning to promote this like crazy. So … not only do I want you to help me organize the event, but I hope you'll participate in it, too."

"I'd love to, Mrs. D. I'd love to do a monologue, maybe. I really am a good actor."

"I don't doubt it. And I'm bringing in industry professionals from LA to judge, so you can't count on me to play favorites. But I'll be rooting for you."

Larsen fell back against the couch. "Really? I'm blown away, Mrs. D."

"Wow, Mom. That's so cool. Lars will be the best assistant ever."

"Thanks, Riv. You know I'll give it everything I have."

"You might even get discovered, dude." River lowered his voice. "And you can save some money and have a real job to put on your resume. Things are looking up."

Larsen was overjoyed. He thought about the words that Martha Joy White had spoken to him the previous Saturday. Her uplifting faith in him had found a place in his heart. He hoped she'd hear about the talent show and come see him. His mind was racing as he considered all of the positive things that could come from Arielle's offer.

Gina reached over and gave Larsen a hug. "I'm so happy for you."

"Thanks, Gina. Thank you all. And thank you, too, Muggins."

Muggins wagged his tail and nuzzled up against Larsen's leg.

"You know what? I think today is going to turn out to be one of the best days of my life."

📖📖📖

As Larsen sat on the couch reading *The Scarlet Letter*, the next assignment in English class, he found it difficult to keep his mind from wandering. Not only was he thinking about the possibilities that his new job might bring him, he was hoping that the embarrassment of the previous Friday night would put his mother in the right place to receive his good news.

It was eleven-thirty, and she wasn't home yet. Mick had dropped Larsen off at ten o'clock, and the nervous wait for his mother seemed endless.

At twelve-fifteen, Larsen gulped as he heard her key turn in the door.

Nervously, he clenched his fists and noticed how sweaty his palms felt. "Um … hi, Mom."

Raylene looked at him suspiciously as she walked into the apartment and closed the door behind her. "You waiting up for me like you did last Friday night?"

"Sort of. I thought you'd be home around eleven. I was getting a little worried. Plus, uh, I have some news."

Raylene put her purse down and flung herself on her favorite armchair. "It's Friday night. Can't a woman unwind after a long day of work?"

Larsen swallowed the lump in his throat. "Sure, Mom. It's just that you never text or call anymore, so when you don't come home at the regular time, I worry."

"I'm the mother. You're the son. You report your whereabouts. I don't report mine."

Larsen sighed. "It's not like that, Mom. I just want to know that you're okay."

"I'm as fine as a woman can be who has to be on her damn feet all day serving people to keep a roof over our heads. What the hell would you know? You don't work."

"I'm in high school, Mom. Remember? It's a big building with classrooms where teenagers go to get an education."

"No need for sass."

"Sorry. But speaking of work, that's what I wanted to tell you. I got a job. Part time. A few hours a day."

Raylene smiled. "Well, well. Miracle of miracles. My son has got himself a job. Haven't had a Davis man working since Nathaniel got ill when you were only nine years old. I've been busting my ass ever since. It's about time you contribute. Guess at your age you'll just be making minimum wage, right? Well, that's okay. A job is a job. A respectable start."

Larsen didn't know if it was wrong not to correct his mother when she just assumed he'd be earning minimum wage. But he didn't know how much she'd expect him to contribute, and he had to make sure he was able to save for his future. He hated lying, but necessity and survival demanded it. Maybe, if things went well, and they started getting along better, he would tell her that he got a raise. But for now, even though he was lying by omission, he had to do it.

"I'm really glad you're happy, Mom. I was hoping you would be."

"What's the job? Flipping burgers at Mickey D's? Pumping gas? Supermarket bag boy?"

Larsen took a deep breath. "I'll be working with River's mother, Mrs. Dalworth. She's the project manager for a building restoration in town, and I'm going to be her assistant. You know, run errands, sweep up, do stuff on the Internet."

Raylene nodded. "I see. Well, that doesn't sound so bad. Actually might be better than the jobs I just mentioned. Maybe you'll learn some good skills."

Filled with relief, Larsen got up and went over to give his mother a hug. He couldn't even remember the last time he had done so, but it felt good, despite the very weak hug he got in return.

"It means everything to me to have your support, Mom."

Raylene looked up at him. "Can't be unhappy about your working. As long as it doesn't mess with your studies, I'm okay with it."

"It won't interfere, Mom." Larsen walked back to the couch and sat down. "I like to study. You know that. And Mrs. D said the same thing."

"So, what kind of building will you be working in? That old church on Main Street?"

Larsen could feel his heart racing. "Um, no, Mom. The Desert Theater."

Raylene didn't say a word. She just sat there in the chair, her eyes moving from side to side, as if she were trying to process what Larsen had just said. As he watched her, his heart raced even faster as he waited for her to answer. Finally, she looked him square in the eye, and he looked back, forcing a smile as he did so.

Without warning, Raylene turned up the volume full blast, giving her vocal cords a workout. "Oh, hellllllllllllllll no! Don't even get me started, boy. You finally give me something to feel proud about, and you're planning to work in a gotdam theater."

"What's wrong with that, Mom? When I was a little boy, I remember going to see a show with you and Daddy in Palm Springs. Don't you remember? We went a few times. That's when I first knew I loved the theater."

"Biggest mistake of my damn life. That's when I first knew—"

"What? That I was gay?"

"That's right, Larsen. That my only son was going to grow up to be a damn homosexual."

"Well, if you knew that before I did, then you should know that I didn't have a choice. You should know that it's who I am and who I was meant to be. Honestly, Mom, you can't possibly think that taking me to the theater made me gay, do you? Because that's ridiculous."

Raylene stood up. "I don't know what the hell I think, Larsen. I just don't like my son being a damn gay! And you ain't working in that theater. I'd rather see you flippin' burgers. You hear me, boy?"

"Mom, I'm going to work for Mrs. D. This is the best thing that's ever happened to me. And I'm gonna do it."

"The hell you are!"

To Larsen's surprise and disgust, the front door suddenly banged open, and Reggie came storming in. Noticing the look on Larsen's face, he tried unsuccessfully to appear intimidating and stand tall. But he was unable to stop himself from wobbling and had to rest the palm of his empty hand on the wall. "Don't look so shocked to see me, boy. I got me a key now."

"What?" Larsen turned angrily to his mother. "You gave this guy a key? No way! No way, Mom!"

"Reggie's the new man in my life, Larsen. You think I don't

deserve that? You think that my life is meant to be nothing more than waiting on rich folks?"

"But ... but you haven't even known each other two weeks."

Raylene eyed the bag containing a bottle that Reggie was holding in his free hand. "Open that damn bottle and pour me a drink 'fore I lose my damn mind." She looked angrily at Larsen. "We met a month ago, Mr. Know-It-All, and we've gotten real well acquainted. So don't you be sticking your nose into my personal business where it don't belong."

Reggie took his hand off the wall and tried again, with no luck, to steady himself. "That's right, boy. Listen to your mother!"

Larsen ignored him and continued to address his mother as he watched Reggie walk crookedly over to the coffee table and pour two drinks into the empty glasses sitting there. "It *is* my business if this stranger is staying in the same house with me. You better believe that's my business."

"You watch your mouth, boy. Don't you be giving me any back talk!"

"Mom, you don't understand. Not only is he a stranger, he's got a—"

"He's not a stranger to me, Larsen. And before long he won't be to you, either." Raylene reached down to grab one of the drinks that Reggie had just poured and took a healthy swig. "My man stays; the job goes. End of conversation!"

There was no way Larsen was going to let his mother ruin his life. No matter what he had to do or say, he was going to win this battle. "There's something really important you should know, Mom. About Reggie."

Raylene stood up and walked up to Larsen, who stood immediately as he saw her approach. Standing only inches from his face, she lowered her voice in a quiet rage. "And what the hellllllllll might that be?"

Larsen looked at Reggie, who had just downed his first drink and was pouring another, and then at his mother. "He's got a wife, Mom. He's a married man."

Raylene turned sharply to look at Reggie. "You got a wife, Reg?"

"I sure as hell don't, Raye. You ought to know that. I took you by my place last week. You think I would do that if I had a wife? Stop your lyin', boy. That's a filthy gotdam lie."

Looking as if she wanted to strangle him, Raylene grabbed Larsen by the shoulders and shook him. "Why would you say such a thing? Isn't being homosexual sin enough? You need to be a liar, too?"

"I'm not lying, Mom. I met her. Last Saturday."

Reggie downed his second drink and threw his glass, watching it shatter as it hit the wall and fell onto the floor. "Filthy liar, boy!"

Larsen and Raylene both reacted in surprise as the breaking glass interrupted them. Larsen backed away from his mother and walked to the end of the couch. "I'm not lying. She was a real pretty lady. She had her hair up on her head, and there was this white flower in her hair. I met her at the movie theater. I went there in the late morning because I got up and saw you …"

Raylene gasped, realizing that Larsen had seen her lying naked on the living room floor.

Fearlessly, Larsen pressed on. "I had to get away. I got to the Mystekal Sands about forty-five minutes before the movie started. The theater was empty, but I didn't care. I just needed to be alone. Then this lady came over to me. She said she was very sorry to bother me, but she was worried that I might not be okay. We talked, and she told me her name was Martha Joy."

Reggie's eyes opened wide. "What the hell!"

"I didn't figure exactly who she was until she said her whole name, Martha Joy White. She told me that her husband was a trucker and that he cheated on her, and that he didn't get home until three-thirty last Saturday morning. She said he reeked of Jack Daniels and cheap perfume. That's *exactly* what she said. I'm not lying, Mom. I swear to God. I swear on Dad's memory."

Raylene turned to Reggie. "You lyin' son of a bitch!"

"I'm not lying, Raylene." Reggie sat down on the nearest dining room chair he could find. "I had a wife. Her name was Martha Jonette. Only she hated her middle name because it was her grandmother's name. Jonette Washington was one evil woman. Martha was full of joy. So she renamed herself Martha Joy, but not legally. She just called herself that. Only me and some close friends knew. How the hell did you find out, boy? You snooping in my business?"

Larsen looked stunned. "I'm telling you for the last time. She told me!"

"And I'm telling you, boy—and you, too, Raye—Martha Joy White is dead. She died five years ago last week on what would have been our twenty-eighth wedding anniversary. You don't believe me, boot up the gotdam computer and put her name in the Giggle whatchamacallit. You'll find her obituary sure as I'm standing here. I'm gonna say it one more time:

Martha Joy White is dead. God rest her soul."

Chapter 6

"Dude, I'm so glad you came over today. Would have hated for you to spend all Sunday wandering around town just to keep some distance from your mom. But I wish you'd called yesterday."

Larsen, sitting on the large beanbag chair in River's bedroom, looked glumly at his friend. "Well, today and Monday are her days off. I didn't want to stay cooped up in my room. Especially with my mom not talking to me. What a joke. It sucks when she *is* talking to me, and it's awkward as hell when she's not. Just a bad scene all around."

"She's not speaking to you?"

"Nope. But she's real good at shooting daggers in my direction."

"Why is she angry with you? You just told her how you met that Martha lady."

"Well, for starters, on Friday night, after her brand-new boyfriend got over the shock of me describing his dead wife and knowing her name, he and my mom held court, yours truly being the defendant, only in my case, I didn't get to mount a defense. The verdict came in, and the jury of two drunks decided that I had gone sleuthing on the web and found out a whole lot about Mr. Reggie Lee White and then used it to purposely break them up.

"If that wasn't enough to keep her angry with me, she's way pissed that I accepted that job with your mom at the theater. This morning she told me to tell your mom, 'Thanks, but no thanks. Find another gay to work for you.'"

River was furious. "No way, Lars. You need to work with my mom. I don't know how, but you'll find a way around this."

"Trust me, I will. This is the best opportunity I've ever been offered in my whole messed-up life. But when your parents come home later, I do want to tell your mom everything that happened. Is that okay?"

"Yeah, sure. She'll want to know. But she won't let you turn down the job, either. She and my dad went hiking at San Jacinto Mountain for the day. You ever been there? There's a kickass view of the Coachella Valley. Anyway, Sunday's usually Mom and Dad's only day together; the lovebirds like to go on day trips so they can coo at each other without making Jess or me nauseated."

"You're a trip, Riv. And you're one to talk. You've got a girlfriend now. A really nice one, too."

"Yeah, she's pretty cool."

"Are you sure you wouldn't rather be with her today?"

River lay back against the headboard of his bed. "Yeah, I'm sure. I really like Gina, but I don't want either one of us to get into a routine. I spend a lot of time drawing, you know. I need that escape time."

"I wish I had a fantasy world to escape into … if I did, I might never come back. That's quite a gift to be able to draw the way you do."

"Too many freaks out there in the world, Lars. Someone's got to draw them. Record those mugs for the history books. You know?"

Larsen laughed, but he was alarmed to see River's expression change so quickly. "Hey, what's up? You're going all serious on me."

River paused before responding. "I'm just thinking about what you said about your mom and that Reggie White guy accusing you of snooping on the Internet. Do you think he really believes you were checking him out, or do you think it's just an excuse?"

"I think he's totally convinced. And yesterday he took my mom to his apartment and let her search through the whole place to prove that there's nobody living there but him. So, yeah, they both believe I went snooping just to mess their stuff up. Only they're wrong."

"Do you think the lady you met was a ghost?"

"Wow, never been asked *that* before … Well, It was kind of dark in the theater, but she looked and sounded real to me. I never met a ghost before, so I don't know."

"Well, I have. And they can look just as real as you and me. Sometimes."

"Reggie said that even if I actually met a woman, which he knows I didn't, then she was probably Martha Joy's older sister going around town trying to make trouble."

"That doesn't really make sense. How would her sister even know to say all of that to you? And why would she have been in the same theater? That's actually more far-fetched than seeing a ghost, which for this town, isn't far-fetched at all. You hear me, Lars?"

"Yeah, I do. But my head is just spinning from all of this."

River sat up. "Okay. Hear me out. So, if good old Sir Reginald Lee of White thinks that you found some damning shit on the Net, then I'm banking on the very real possibility that there's something to find. Grab your board, Lars. You and I are going surfing!"

After jumping off his bed and booting up the computer, River went into the dining room, grabbed a chair, and brought it into his room. "Here. Take a seat next to me."

Wasting no time, River typed "Martha Joy White," but there were no matching results. "Look, Lars, nothing. If the lady's nickname for herself isn't on the Net, how did you find it there? What did you say her real middle name was?"

"Jonette."

River typed "Martha Joanette White" but there were still no results.

"Try taking the *A* out of 'Joanette', Riv."

River typed "Martha Jonette White," and immediately, the search engine results offered several hits. Choosing the first link, River double-clicked.

"That's her, Riv! That's the lady I spoke to. Look, she's even got the white flower in her hair in the photo."

River didn't respond. He just stared at the computer screen.

"Say something! Don't you believe me, either?"

Reaching to his left, River grabbed his sketchbook, opened it up, and handed it to Larsen.

"No way! This is Martha Joy! Did you see her somewhere? You drew her? Crying? Was she crying? Where? Tell me, Riv. You're killing me here!"

"When Gina and I went into the movie theater, Gina went to the ladies' room, and I waited in line to get popcorn for us. This lady was standing against a wall, crying. I've always had this weird thing about people crying. I don't know. I just notice them. It was weird because nobody else even seemed to see her. Or care. If I wasn't in line, I might have asked if she was okay. In fact, I was going to talk to her after I got our food, but then she was gone. Like I said, Lars, I can see ghosts. But I don't always know they are ghosts. Not at first."

"And you managed to remember her face and draw it so realistically?"

"Dude, not to be the poster boy for immodesty or anything, but I've got some gifts. I can see dead people, and I can draw. From memory. I'm sure I've got some gifts with girls, but I haven't discovered them all yet. Ha ha."

Larsen cracked up. "You're a piece of work, Riv. But I'm freaked. Go back online. What does her obituary say?"

River scanned the obituary. "Just says she died unexpectedly on October 19. About five years ago. She is survived by her son, Devon Reginald White, Los Angeles; her daughter, Ellie White-Sharpe, of Palm Desert; her husband, Reginald Lee White, and her grandchildren, Amelia White, Trevor White, and Bethany Sharpe. After raising her children, she worked at a hospital in Rancho Mirage. She loved gardening, singing in the church choir, theater, and movies. Her friends fondly remember her love for the Mystekal Sands Theater ... get this, Lars, it says she and Reggie went to the movie theater on their first date and almost every week thereafter until their son was born. That makes sense."

"Seriously? Nothing's making much sense to me."

"Listen, dude, ghosts hang around places where they were really miserable or really happy. Sometimes those places can be one and the same."

"Okay, so if she's been dead for five years, why did she tell me that stuff about Reggie cheating on her last week? You know, when he was with my mom?"

"Because she wanted you to know who she was and pass it on to your mom, I guess. She wanted you to know her husband has always been a cheater, and your mom should beware. I'm just guessing here. Stop me any time before I plunge into vapid elucidation."

"Say what?"

River laughed. "Nothing, dude. Just cuddling up to some vocabulary. So, what are you thinking?"

"Well it's not that I think you're wrong, Riv, but there's got to be more. Do me a favor; type in 'Reginald Lee White Mystekal,' okay?"

Within seconds, not only did Reggie's picture pop up in one of the hits, but it was a police mug shot. "Way to go, Lars. We is cooking with gas, my friend. Freakin' A!"

Larsen was trembling. "What? Tell me. I can't read sideways.

You're blocking my view."

"Give me a sec to read this … Okay, here's the scoop. Martha and Reggie were married for twenty-something years. He was a trucker for a produce company. One night, he told her he was on the road, in Texas, so she went to visit their married daughter, Ellie, in Palm Desert. Only on the way to Ellie's house, Martha saw the dude's truck at a restaurant, one with a bar that's a real popular hangout for truckers. She called her daughter and told her that she was going inside to see what was going on. She parked her car, went inside, and saw Reggie kissing on some woman at the bar."

"Is that what it says in the paper? That he was kissing on some woman?"

"No, dude. I'm paraphrasing. Using my own words."

"Oh, sorry. Go on."

"Anyway, when he saw his wife eyeballing him, he threw down his money on the bar and went racing outta there. Got in his truck, drunk as hell, and tried to drive away. Meanwhile, Martha was so hysterical she tried running after the truck. He was smashed and wasn't even looking where he was going, and she was killed by *his* truck, instantly. Whoa! That's horrible!"

Larsen was choked up. "I-I can't believe that."

"The dude lost his trucker's license for life and was sentenced to three years in prison. So, if he served his full term, he would have just been out for two years. Whatever he does for a living, he's not a trucker anymore." River leaned back in his chair to absorb the shocking information he had just relayed. "You going to tell your mom?"

"And risk her going off on me again? And him, too? No. Not now, anyway. This is some seriously messed-up stuff." Larsen took a few moments to catch his breath and think about all that had happened. "You know what Martha Joy told me? She said I shouldn't let my mother's problems become mine. She said if I did, they would haunt me forever, and I wouldn't be able to move on … Wow … guess something like that happened to her. She was right, Riv. I'm not going to let my mother's sickness get in the way of my happiness. I don't know how I'll get around her objection, but I know one thing: I'm taking that job with your mom."

📖📖📖

Larsen walked aimlessly up and down the supermarket aisles trying to figure out what he could buy before going home. When Arielle had called River to say that she and Mick would be home around eight, two hours later than planned, Larsen decided to leave the Dalworths' home. Just having been a guest for dinner on Friday, he hated the idea of being there when Mick and Arielle got home from a long, tiring day. No matter how much River insisted he stay, Larsen was adamant that it was time to go.

He planned to tell his mother he had eaten dinner at the Dalworths'. He didn't want her cooking for him when she wasn't even speaking to him.

"Larsen?"

Surprised to hear his name, Larsen turned around. "Mrs. Winterstrom. From the cafeteria, right?"

"That's me. And, please, call me Kathryn."

"I couldn't …"

"Really, it's fine. And I'm very impressed you remembered my last name. I don't think it's a very difficult name, but I often have to repeat it several times before a person learns it."

Larsen smiled. "When someone shows me a kindness, I make it a point to remember his or her name. It's only right."

"You're a very polite young man. What are you doing on a Sunday evening walking down the snacks aisle? If I'm not overstepping my bounds by asking."

"Uh, just looking for something to eat."

"Don't you have food at home, Larsen?"

Hesitating, Larsen looked down at his shoes, then raised his head to answer Kathryn. "Yes, I do. But I don't really have the best home life. It's just me and my mom, and she …"

"She what, Larsen?"

"Um … she just doesn't like me too much, that's all."

Kathryn shook her head. "It breaks my heart to hear that. You know, Larsen, I had a long week preparing lunches at the school. And tomorrow starts a brand-new week. I don't feel like cooking tonight. I'm in the mood to get a nice hot dish at the deli and sit in the food court and eat my meal. I hate to eat alone, though, and I do that most every night. Would you let me treat you to dinner? The company would sure mean a lot to me."

Looking into her kind, eager eyes, Larsen could not refuse her offer. "Thank you, Mrs. Win … Kathryn. That's very kind of you."

Twenty minutes later, Larsen and Kathryn were comfortably seated at a booth in the food court. Having told Kathryn the condensed story of his home life, he felt very much at ease with her.

Kathryn daintily wiped her mouth. "Thank you for telling me your story. And I'm very sorry that your mother doesn't want you to take the theater job with Arielle Dalworth. I hope she'll have a change of heart. If it's okay, I would like to tell you something about me, and maybe you'll understand why I feel such a connection to you."

"Sure! Please, I'd love to know more about you."

"Well, I've been alone for many years. I used to have a wonderful son, Peter, and a handsome husband who both made me very happy. My son was a bright, shining star in my life, Larsen. And like you, he was gay, and like you, he had theatrical aspirations. He had the most beautiful baritone voice I've ever heard. It was so distinct, so rich. A music critic from Palm Springs once referred to Peter's voice as having 'lusciously dark tones.' It was nearly impossible to hear Peter sing and not feel uplifted and joyous."

Finishing the last bite of his dinner, Larsen laid his fork on the plate. "Just from what you've said so far, it doesn't sound like you had any problems with him being gay."

"My biggest worry about Peter being homosexual … that was the accepted word back in 1968 … was that he would go through much of what you're going through. Only back in those days, there was a lot more open prejudice than there is now. That said, there's still way too much today. Our society has not come nearly as far as I had hoped."

"Yeah. For sure."

Kathryn sighed. "Peter often worried that he had disappointed me. I told him I would rather have a happy homosexual son than an unhappy heterosexual one. And I meant that. I just wanted to see him graduate, follow his dream, and live a fulfilled life."

"Wow. I can't imagine my mother ever feeling like that. I hate to ask, and you don't have to tell me, but what happened to Peter?"

Kathryn took a sip of water to fortify herself. "Well, when Peter was fifteen, he met a young man who was also gay, and they fell very much in love. I worried for him. This was 1971. Peter's boyfriend's father was not supportive or tolerant in any way." Kathryn paused to drink some more water. "That's putting it mildly. Believe it or not, Larsen, this man was far angrier than your mother. He threatened our family on numerous occasions, telling us to keep our 'damn queer' away from his son."

Larsen looked angry. "He wasn't accepting that his son was gay, right? He was one of those people who think being around someone else's gay child is the only thing making their child gay."

"You've hit the nail on the head. That's exactly right."

"Nicholas, my husband, tried to warn Peter and his friend to, at the very least, keep their relationship secret. For a short while, they did, but due to circumstances, it was rather impossible." Kathryn lowered her voice. "I haven't told anyone this story in a very long time. It still feels like a fresh wound."

"You don't have to say any more; it's okay."

Kathryn spoke with emotion in her voice that took Larsen by surprise. "I absolutely do. I would never tell you this much and stop here, but for now, I will leave out the details. Instead, I will tell you that the other boy's father followed through with his threats. He staged an accident to kill not only my son, but also his own flesh and blood."

"Say what?"

Kathryn managed to maintain her composure. "Larsen, Peter died at the hands of this monster. His own son survived, and he went on to brutalize him until he died."

Larsen reached out and grabbed her hand. "I'm so sorry. That's just awful."

"I miss Peter every day of my life. I miss his smile. I miss his passion for music and his beautiful voice when he sang my favorite songs. I miss his hugs, his laughter. Oh, he had a terrific sense of humor. Very dry. I would have given anything to see my son grow up and live the life he deserved."

Larsen hung his head. Kathryn's pain encompassed him. He related to every nuance of her tragic story and felt her sorrow as if it were his own. "What happened to your—"

"To my husband?"

"Yes. If you don't mind telling me."

"Nicholas could not handle his grief. He wanted to grieve with me, to comfort me, but he couldn't. He blamed himself. He was so angry."

"Oh, no, I hope he didn't—"

"No. After two years, he just left me. We divorced, and he moved away. I have no idea if he's dead or alive. I've never tried to find out. Being abandoned was more than I could take. I had to rebuild my life as best I could. Dwelling on my ex-husband just pulled me back into my pain."

"So how did you get through it?"

"It was very hard. It still is, though the pain has dulled over the years. I had a very wonderful neighbor, one of the kindest people I've ever known. She was my best friend. Her empathy and warmth saw me through many hard days. She saved my life. And so did my work. I found a job as a housekeeper for a terrific family. I stayed with them until their children were grown. Then I came to work at the high school."

"Didn't the guy who killed Peter ever get caught?"

Kathryn took another sip of water. "No, Larsen. He didn't. And I should explain that it wasn't until many years later that I learned that Peter's death wasn't an accident. My husband was long gone, and there was nothing I could do. My heart couldn't handle it, either."

"Thank you so much for telling me."

Kathryn's face brightened. "No, thank you for listening. I rarely tell the story, and it is almost never that my listener understands as you do. I have spent my life working around children, and it brings me as much happiness as I will ever know."

"So, I want you to come to me any time you need me. I'm going to give you my phone number and email address, too. You are welcome to contact me any way that is good for you. I want to be there for you if you'll let me. And I want you to stay safe above all else. Please, Larsen. Stay safe."

Chapter 7

The split second Larsen opened the front door, he regretted coming home.

Drunk and disheveled, his mother sat slumped on the couch with a glass of Jack Daniels in her hand, and Reggie, with his shirt off and his fly unzipped, sat next to her, eating corn chips and salsa, watching a recap of the San Diego Chargers' game.

Raylene curled her upper lip as she looked at Larsen. "Well, if the little gay liar hasn't come home. Hungry, boy? Hope not, because I'm not getting off this couch to cook you squat."

"I had dinner with a friend."

"Didn't know you had but one friend."

"Well, Mom, there's a whole lot about me you don't know."

Reggie chewed the large handful of chips he had just shoved into this mouth, then swallowed them uncomfortably. "Damn, Raye. Looks like he's got himself a boyfriend."

"Oh, helllllllllllllllllllll no!"

"I don't have a boyfriend. Not that it's any of your business if I did."

"Everything you do is my business. I hope you told that Dalworth lady where to stick her job offer."

Reggie let loose with a large belch, then picked up his drink and took a huge gulp.

Larsen was disgusted but ignored the interruption. "She and

her husband had plans this weekend. I haven't seen her since Friday night."

Raylene grabbed the bottle and refilled Reggie's glass as she spoke. "Well, I don't give a rat's ass about some strangers' weekend plans. You just make sure you turn that job down, boy. You're not going to embarrass me any more than you already have by working in a damn theater."

Larsen was stoic. "Who have I embarrassed you in front of, Mom? Name one person."

"For starters, Reggie here. Didn't even have the decency to let him teach you how to drive a truck. You could have learned something."

Larsen snorted with disgust. "Really? I embarrassed you because I didn't let a guy who lost his trucker's license teach me how to drive a truck?"

Livid, Reggie stood up, trying unsuccessfully not to wobble. "How the hell do you know I lost my trucker's license? Like I told you, Raylene, this boy is a lying snoop. Seems pretty clear to me why he made up that story about my poor deceased wife, God rest her soul. Only the likes of pond scum would stoop so low like that just to deprive his poor overworked mama of some male comp'ny."

Raylene looked up at Reggie. "You lost your license?"

Reggie fell back onto the couch. "Ancient history, Raye. Nuffer now."

Revolted, Larsen couldn't stop himself from speaking. "What does that mean, 'nuffer now'?"

"He said 'Enough for now,' boy! Seventeen years old, and you're losing your hearing already." Grabbing a chip and shoving it into her mouth, Raylene chewed as she spoke. "Well, isss one story you damn well isss gonna tell *me,* Reginald Lee White."

Larsen looked into his mother's eyes. "You thought he was a truck driver all this time. And you call me a liar?"

Washing the chip down with Jack, Raylene narrowed her eyes as she looked at Larsen. "Reggie never told me he was a truck driver. Told me he used to be one."

"That's right, boy. I work on a date farm outside of Thermal. Not that it's any of your damn business. Still know how to drive a truck. Could've hooked you up with any number of good buddies I have."

Raylene cackled with inappropriate laughter as she taunted her son. "Ha! Cat's got the liar's tongue. Liar, liar, pants on fire!"

Walking toward his room, Larsen turned to Reggie. "Better than having my pants unzipped."

Embarrassed and boiling mad, Reggie stood, zipped up his fly, and called to Larsen. "You ain't going any damn where, boy."

"Dat's right, Larsssssen. You don't be speaking to my man that way. Now you get back here and stand up to him like a man. Not that you'd know anything about that."

Larsen took a calming breath. He did not want to be involved in the escalating madness and knew he had to stay cool and maintain what little control was left. "I *am* a man. I am a proud gay man."

So drunk that in her anger she knocked over what was left of her drink, Raylene stood, shouting at Larsen. "You are a mistake! You should never have been born! I never want to see another homosexual as long as I live!"

He wanted to scream back at his mother. He wanted to shout a thousand things that had been festering in his mind and in his soul for years. He wanted to turn the coffee table upside down and throw the four dining room chairs, one by one, against the wall, until the room looked exactly like the tornado whirling in his head. His mind felt like the homes of the hoarders his mother watched on reality TV: junk, piled high, everywhere. Nowhere to walk. So many things that everything, even the most valuable of treasures, became worthless junk. He could not navigate his way out. As his mother continued to scream at him, voices, in his head, screamed back at her, while Larsen stood there, seemingly still and almost utterly unaffected.

Raylene continued to scream at him, her anger intensifying with each ugly word. "Answer me, you lowlife, pathetic excuse for a son!"

With great difficultly, Reggie walked toward Larsen. "Answer your mutherr, boy. Show some gotdam respect, you spineless SHIT!"

"Is everything all right in there?"

Larsen exhaled as they all turned toward the front door. Immediately, Reggie hurried back to the couch and sat down.

The strange man's voice grew loud. "HELLO, IS EVERYTHING ALL RIGHT IN THERE?"

Larsen ran to open the front door to find a concerned neighbor, who looked sorrowfully into his eyes. "You okay, son?"

"Thank you. Thank you for coming."

"It's all right, son. The police are on their way. My wife and I heard everything."

Without looking back, Larsen nodded in gratitude, then, running for his life, he took off into the dark desert night.

📖📖📖

River had tried for hours to reach Larsen on Sunday night, but every call went to voicemail.

Walking to school on Monday morning, River's stomach flipped and flopped as he thought about his friend. As he approached Mystekal High, earlier than usual, he was surprised to see what appeared to be someone or something on the ground against the side wall of the building. Running quickly toward it, River was stunned by what he saw.

"Lars! Are you okay? What happened, man?"

Dazed and half awake, Larsen, wearing the same clothes he

had worn the day before, sitting on the ground with his back against the wall of the school, looked up. "No, not okay. Not ever gonna be okay again."

"Sure you will, dude. I know it's bad. I know it's worse than any shit that's ever happened in my life, but don't give up. That's not like you."

Larsen looked down at the ground. "Whatever."

"How long have you been here? Lars ... come on."

River noticed as a look of shame washed over Larsen's face. "Dude, you been here all night?"

The look on Larsen's face was the only confirmation River needed. "Oh, man, I know some heavy shit must have gone down. What I don't get is why you didn't call me and come stay at my house."

"No, Riv. I'm not going to impose on your family like that. Besides, all you need is a sleepover with me to really get people talking."

"Eff that bullshit. What do you think matters more to me, where my friend sleeps at night or what drivel spews forth from the pieholes of the ignoramni."

"I never met anyone who talks like you do."

"You've already told me that before. C'mon, don't change the subject on me."

As more students headed for school, those who noticed the boys on the side of the school craned their necks or whispered their speculations to the person closest. But when Kathryn saw Larsen sitting on the ground as River stood over him, she ran toward them as quickly as she could.

"Larsen! Are you all right? Who did this to you? I'll have them arrested! Was it Jax Reinhardt and his friend Antonio?"

Ashamed to make eye contact, Larsen looked down. "No."

"He's been here all night long, Mrs. Winterstrom."

As Kathryn realized Larsen was wearing the same clothing as he had worn the night before and looked as though he hadn't slept in days, she gasped and put her hand to her mouth.

River tapped Larsen on his shoulder. "Dude, can you get up?"

Larsen looked vacantly out into the desert. "I don't know. Does it matter?"

Kathryn fought to hold the tears inside. "Please, Larsen, River and I will each give you a hand. You need to get up, okay?"

Without waiting for a response, Kathryn and River each extended a hand, and Larsen stood, immediately leaning back against the wall, as if he weren't sure he could keep his balance.

"Oh my. Did something awful happen at home?"

Larsen nodded.

"Come on, we're going to Principal Dreighton's office." Kathryn spoke with fierce determination. "This nightmare you're living is officially over, and I'm just the person to end it."

📖📖📖

River had no idea what had happened to Larsen. Kathryn Winterstrom had taken him directly to the principal's office, and he hadn't heard a word since. At lunchtime, River went to the cafeteria to find Kathryn to see if he could get some news, but she wasn't at her usual place behind the food station. Just as he was wondering what was going on, Principal Dreighton's secretary walked into the cafeteria to find River and ask him to follow her.

In Hal Dreighton's office, River was relieved to see Larsen looking much better. He had showered and was wearing a brown Mystekal High T-shirt. And he looked happier than River had ever seen him.

"Hey, Riv!"

"Well, hey there yourself, dude. You had me worried. You

were, like, zombie of the desert this morning. My whole family has been worried. My mom's been texting me all day."

River, realizing that he had just admitted to texting when he shouldn't have been, looked rather sheepishly at the principal.

"Under the circumstances, I fully understand, River. But you know the rule: no texting during class. Okay?" Principal Dreighton pointed to an empty chair. "No need to stand."

River sat down quickly. "Uh, thanks."

Kathryn, who was sitting next to Larsen on the couch, smiled. "River, as Larsen's closest friend, we wanted you to know what was happening. It is wonderful news. Larsen will be coming to live with me."

"Really! Wow! That's effing fantastic!"

Principal Dreighton laughed. "Thanks for not using the actual expletive, River."

"Gee, I never realized how hard it was to have a conversation in front of a principal before. Ha ha. So, what's the story?"

Larsen's face was bright with excitement. "Well, Mrs. Winterstrom and I ran into each other last night at the supermarket, and we talked for a long time. I told her all about my home situation."

Kathryn nodded. "May I interrupt for just a moment, Larsen?"

"Sure."

"River, as many people in this town know, I had a son, Peter, who died many years ago. Like Larsen, he was a fine, young gay man. But he never had a chance to realize his dreams, much less grow into adulthood. Anyway, fast forwarding to the here and now, I have a lovely home with a big extra bedroom, and I am honored that Larsen has agreed to be my permanent houseguest. For many years, I fostered children, and it has always been a very positive experience for me."

Larsen excitedly pounded the fist of his one hand into the palm of his other one three times. "Isn't that great, Riv?"

"Yeah, for sure, but what about your mom? She's just gonna let you leave?"

"It's kind of complicated, but Principal Dreighton and Mrs. Winterstrom have been on about a hundred phone calls this morning. The thing is this: last night, when my mother and Reggie were screaming at me, the neighbors overheard and called the cops. After I left, the police came to the house. They weren't too happy about what the neighbors told them or about what they saw in the house: two loud, sloppy drunks. And let's just say that Reggie Lee White isn't their favorite person. So, after a whole lot of back-and-forth, my mother agreed to let me go and not fight it … especially since Reggie is an ex-con and not exactly considered a good influence for me. He was so drunk, he was bragging to the cops about how my mom fell for him so hard that she let him have his own key after only two weeks of dating. If you call what they've been doing 'dating.'"

River looked at the principal for a reaction, but he just smiled.

"The cards were stacked high against my mother and she knew it. She doesn't want anything to do with me, anyway. And even if she got rid of that loser, she'd still be bullying me every day for being gay. It was easier for her to sign the papers to let me go. I'll be eighteen in a few months, so the expiration date on her parental consent had a short shelf life anyway."

"When are you going to go pick up all of your stuff?"

"My mom agreed to be out of the house for two hours after school. Normally, she'd be gone, but she's off today, too. And the cops told her that if she messes with any of my things, she'll be in trouble."

"Great! So this means you can take the job with my mom."

"Sure does."

River stood up and punched a victorious fist into the air. "Way to go! She'll be so jazzed. About everything. Jess and my dad, too. Even the Mugster. What are you going to do now?"

Principal Dreighton laughed. "I think Larsen is going to have something to eat and finish out the school day. Just like you're going to do, River."

River laughed. "Ha ha. You're a crack up, Principal Dreighton."

Eve's students were surprised when, twenty minutes before the end of class, she asked everyone to put their books away.

"As you all know, especially Larsen Davis, there's been some bullying going on in this school. I think word has gotten around to every single one of you that Jax Reinhardt has been suspended for a week. He's also been required to get some counseling. Let's hope for everyone's sake that Jax comes back with a lot more sense and humanity.

"Now, while I appreciate that Jax has been punished, it would be very inappropriate for any of you to tease him about it, to rub it in, or to bully *him* in any way despite what he's done. Two wrongs don't make a right. It's a cliché, but in this situation, it has its merits."

Antonio raised his hand.

"Mr. Reyes. You want to say something?"

Antonio looked over at his girlfriend, Bianca Torres, who nodded as a show of support. Then he stood up. "Um, I have something I need to say. I was just going to say it to Larsen, but someone very special convinced me to talk to the whole class."

Bianca smiled again and blew Antonio a kiss.

"Okay, then. Come on up to the front of the class. The floor is yours."

As Eve took her seat, Antonio walked nervously to the front of the class. He looked at Bianca, then at Larsen, then at everyone else. "Look, um, like I said, I was just going to talk to Larsen, and to you, Ms. Carrow, but what I want to say needs to be heard by everyone.

"First, I want to thank you for always keeping the conversation real in this class. I mean, you're a sweet lady, and you sure had an SOB for an old man. Most people in your situation wouldn't even talk about the things he did, but you're always down about being open with the truth. And probably, um, you don't want to carry his shame, and that's really good and … sorry, I'm seriously nervous, and, well, no secret, I'm not elegant like …"

Eve smiled. "Eloquent?"

"Oh, yeah, that. Elephant. I mean, eloquent."

The entire class burst out laughing, as did Antonio, who seemed to be breathing easier.

"I think it was the Friday before last, remember, when we were talking about your father, and Jax was starting some sh … I mean, some stuff with Larsen. Then he turned on you, Ms. Carrow, saying that your father was the biggest bully of them all and went into a whole bunch of ugly that he used to lay on Vanesa's sister, Sophia, about Mexicans. Man, I had erased all that from my mind somehow. I'd forgotten that he said we should all be sterilized until we die off. That's real bad. And it hit me so hard in the gut I couldn't even eat dinner that night. The minute I heard that, I felt like a real piece of sh … oh, fuck it, like a real piece of shit raggin' on Larsen for being gay. Made me no better than your old man."

Eve smiled proudly.

Antonio looked at Larsen. "I'm sorry, man. No bullshit. I promise you, I'll never mess with you again. Now, Jax, he's been my friend a long time. He's kind of clued in that I'm not going to be his bully partner anymore, but I can't say how he's gonna be when he comes back to school. But I need to give him another chance, just like I hope you all do with me. Well, that's all I gotta say."

Antonio rushed back to his seat as the class gave him a standing ovation. Bianca got out of her chair, gave Antonio a kiss on the cheek, and scooted back to her seat.

Eve stood and faced the class. "A kiss well deserved. Thank you, Bianca. Antonio, moments like these are the ones that teachers remember forever. I am very proud of you, and I hope everyone in this class is as well."

Larsen raised his hand.

"Yes, Larsen?"

"I just want to say thanks to Antonio. I know that wasn't easy. Means a lot to me. Apology accepted."

"Thanks, man."

Eve walked over to the windows and pulled down one of the shades. "Excuse me. This light is killing my eyes. I didn't want to interrupt Antonio's speech."

River chuckled. "Oh, is that all? Thought something shady might be going on here."

Eve made a face but her eyes laughed. "Oh, River, you can do better than that. … Now, there's just one more thing on my agenda for today. This Friday, I'm told we'll have two new students. Erik and Avalon Martelli. Erik is a senior, so he'll be in classes with all of you, and Avalon is in the tenth grade. Erik and Avalon have a sister, Isabella, but she's in the eighth grade, so she'll be attending the middle school. Therefore, in the spirit of being kind to one another, and knowing how hard it is to fit in, I hope you'll all welcome our new students. That's all I have to say, so you can talk quietly among yourselves until the bell rings."

Chapter 8

"And last but not least on the tour of your new home, this will be your bedroom."

Larsen looked around the large bedroom that was easily two and a half times the size of the room he had in his mother's home.

"This looks more like a studio apartment than a bedroom. I've never had a desk this big, either. Or a sitting area with my own TV. And three windows." Larsen walked around the room and looked out each of the large windows. "What a beautiful view! I'm kind of overwhelmed by everything."

"Well, it's all for you, Larsen. And speaking of windows, you'll find that you'll see the most glorious sunsets if you look out the west window every night. Peter always used to look out at the mountains, and he loved the sunsets because they were all so beautiful, and there are never two exactly the same. But he loved the night sky the most."

"Really. Why?"

"Away from the bright city lights, you can really see some incredible starry nights. The sky there is open, free of light pollution, so the stars seem even more spectacular, closer to you. Peter first fell in love with the sky when he was very young. Nicholas and I would take him stargazing at Joshua Tree National Park. As he got older and realized that he had a gift worthy of sharing with the world, he always used to tell me, 'Mom, someday I'm going to be a superstar.

But first, I'm going to be a desert star.' I laughed and said, 'Well, it stands to reason that you'll be known locally first. And he said, 'Well, of course, but that's not what I meant. I'm going to be the brightest star in the sky so you can always find me.' I didn't analyze his words at the time, but now I wonder why Peter said that. Did he foresee something nobody else did?"

Larsen felt goose bumps. "Wow. So, have you found Peter's star?"

"Oh, I'd love to say yes. When we grieve for someone we love so deeply, we like to believe that miracles can happen. That's human nature; don't you think? I've been looking in the desert sky for years, and the brightest star I see is what I'm quite sure is the North Star. I won't talk myself into believing otherwise. But honestly, Larsen, I believe Peter was just speaking metaphorically, never having any idea that I would survive him and spend years searching for his star in the heavens."

"If I ever see his star, I'll let you know. I hope Peter won't mind me staying in his bedroom."

Kathryn sat on the bed and motioned for Larsen to sit next to her. "When my son first died, I told myself that nobody else would ever set foot in his room. But after a while, I realized that turning Peter's room into a shrine was wrong and unhealthy. This room was meant to be a place of joy as it was when Peter lived here. When I became a foster parent, I had many children live here, and each and every one of them left a happier person. To me, that's the greatest homage I could ever pay to my son's memory."

"You're a smart lady, Kathryn. Peter would be so proud of you. I mean, wherever he is, I know he *is* proud."

Choking up, Kathryn nodded her thanks.

Larsen looked alarmed. "I hope I didn't upset you by saying that."

"No, not at all. Thank you for allowing me to talk about

Peter, and I couldn't be more pleased that you're going to make my house your home. By living here, you make it much more of a home for me, too. Now, did I show you where the dirty clothes hamper is?"

"I'd really like it if you show me where the washer and dryer are. You don't need to do my laundry for me. I can do that myself."

Kathryn laughed. "You are very independent. Sure, I'll take you to the basement after you get settled. I'm going to leave you to unpack, and if you're ready in about an hour, we'll have our first meal at home together."

Larsen reached over and gave Kathryn a hug. "I can't thank you enough for everything."

"It is my extraordinary pleasure."

Kathryn rose and walked out of the room, turning to look at Larsen as she did.

As Larsen looked around the room, feeling a sense of peace he had never known, he heard his phone sound. He pulled it out of his pocket to see who had sent him a text:

Don't U B 4getting who ur flesh & blood mama is boy.

Trying not to let the text rattle him, Larsen felt that this was the closest his mother would ever come to saying that she missed him.

📖📖📖

Larsen caught up with River at his locker.

"Hey, Lars. You look better every day since you've moved into Mrs. Winterstrom's house. It's only been four days, but you look like a dude with a heavy load off his back."

"I feel like one. Especially with Jax being suspended this week. Not sure what to expect when he gets back on Monday."

"Don't sweat it now. Or then."

"I'm not. Trying to focus on all of the great things that have happened. I feel so free. Just put 'Tonight' from *West Side Story* on my cell as my ringtone. Sounds like no big deal, but I couldn't even do that before. My mom had a fit. Said it was 'gay music.' "

"Oh, man."

"Hey, Riv, speaking of moms, I'm meeting yours at the theater after school. She's going to show me around, and then my first day at work will be Monday. She said I might get to be a part of the documentary, too. But she can't promise because it's her friend Lisa's project, not hers. I'm just so happy to have this job … and a new home."

"You miss your mom at all?"

Larsen hesitated and looked down for a moment. "I don't miss being bullied. I don't miss having to hole myself up in that tiny bedroom. I don't miss Reggie White or any of the other men she's brought home. I miss my mom being a mom. But I missed that even when I was living with her. You know?"

"Yeah. I do. There were several years when Jessie and I had a similar deal. But nothing like what you've gone through."

"My mom won't ever make a comeback like yours did."

As Larsen and River stood in the hallway talking, two sophomore boys passed, speaking loudly.

"That must be the new chick in our class."

"Yeah, you must be right. I know it's Halloween and shit, but who comes dressed to school for it? What do you think she's tryin' to be? Looks like her clothes came from her dead grandmother's attic or something."

"You ain't lying, bro. You gonna ask her out?"

"Hell, no. I'd ask yo mama out first."

"Ha! Shut up, fool."

Larsen and River exchanged looks. Listening to the sophomore boys' conversation didn't bode well for how the new student might be treated.

"Hey, Lars. I'm going to go talk to her, okay? Catch you later, dude."

River smiled and walked toward the petite girl with the blue-and-green hair. Dressed unlike anyone at Mystekal High, she wore bell bottom jeans with flowers and butterflies embroidered all over them, a green chiffon blouse with lace sleeves, and oodles of bracelets and necklaces all made from colored beads, crystals, and decorative metal. As River approached, she turned inward, as if she were afraid of what was coming.

"Hi, I'm River. Are you the new girl?"

"Guess so. You'd kinda remember if you'd seen me before. Does everyone in this school stare so much?"

"Some people just don't know what to do with themselves. Don't people stare where you come from?"

"Not like I've been stared at in the whole fifteen minutes I've been here."

"Where are you from?"

"Jersey City. Right across the Hudson River from New York. We've got all kinds of people in JC. From all over. Back in my old school, I didn't stick out the way I seem to be doing here. Oh, my name is Avalon."

"That's a cool name. I like it."

"River is a cool name, too. My mom and dad named me Avalon because they were in Avalon, New Jersey, when they had sex and got pregnant with me."

River grinned as he took in Avalon's surprising information. "Oh, okay. Well, I guess it's good that my mom and dad didn't do the same thing. I might just be plain old 'Bed Dalworth.' Ha ha. Or maybe 'Backseat Dalworth.' Then again, maybe I was conceived in a river. Hmm."

Avalon smiled sweetly. "You're kind of funny. My last name is Martelli, by the way."

Just as River was about to respond, a girl he didn't know walked by, loudly wished Avalon a happy Halloween, then laughed as she continued to walk down the hall.

"Don't pay her any attention."

"Do you think people are going to make fun of me every day? Because this is the way I dress. I'm a freak for the vintage look. Really, I just like being me. I don't care what's in style with everyone else. I'm kind of like a canvas, and my clothes are sort of like what I paint."

"I think you look great. I'm an artist, so I really get what you're saying."

"I am, too. I paint for real. But I had to stop. Things got ugly back home."

Intrigued, River wanted to know more. "What do you mean? What happened back home?"

Avalon looked over River's shoulder. "I think your girlfriend is waiting for you. I don't want to keep you. I don't want to make enemies."

River turned and saw Gina smiling.

"Okay, I'll see you later, Avalon. Maybe we'll be in a class together."

"I don't think so. I'm a sophomore. You're a senior, right?"

"Yeah."

"Then you'll be in classes with my brother, Erik. I should warn you, River. He's kind of angry, so just stay out of his way."

📖📖📖

Henry Sledge enjoyed hearing the collective groan of his students when he greeted them with a rousing "good morning" on Fridays when his was the first class of the day.

"It's great to see your smiling faces this morning. I see we have a new student, Erik Martelli."

Erik, his tall frame hunched in a chair at the back of the class, barely looked up when he heard his name.

"Mr. Martelli, I'd like you to stand and tell us something about yourself, but so that you don't feel singled out, I'm going to ask each one of your classmates to do the same. By the end of this class, you'll feel like you know everyone."

"I don't want to know everyone. Or anyone."

"I'm sorry, Mr. Martelli, you're speaking in a very low voice, and it's hard to hear from the front of the classroom."

Antonio, who was sitting close by, yelled out, "He said he doesn't want to know everyone or anyone."

Henry looked away and spoke softly to himself. "Charming. Just charming."

Duffie Walden, sitting in the first row, yelled to the back, "Mr. Sledge said you're charming."

The class broke out into laughter, but neither Erik nor Henry Sledge was amused.

"Miss Walden, should I find the need for a human parrot, you'll be the first one I engage. But in the meantime—"

"Sorry, Mr. Sledge." Duffie tried to look apologetic, but it was clear to all that she was doing everything to keep from laughing. Finding her suppression of laughter amusing, River couldn't help but laugh to himself.

"Mr. Dalworth. We'll start with you. Please stand and introduce yourself to Mr. Martelli."

River stood up. "Hi, I'm River. I met your sister earlier. She's really nice. Mr. Sledge is married to my aunt Stella. He loves to talk all teachery, but he's more cool than he sounds. I'm an artist and have exceptional intelligence. Ha ha. That's it."

Henry gave River his usual what-will-I-do-with-you look, and Gina giggled while the rest of the class, except Erik, tried not to laugh.

"Moving right along. Miss Walden, your turn."

Duffie stood up. "Hi, I'm Duffie. That's with a D, not a B. I love horses, and I want to go to nursing school. And I want to visit Italy and France when I graduate. Over and out."

Henry took a seat at his desk. "Okay, Mr. Martelli, you've got the hang of it. Your turn. Please stand."

Erik stood up and looked defiantly at his teacher. "I'm here because I need to graduate. I'm not here to make friends. End of freakin' story."

"Perhaps it would be prudent to cease with the introductions for now. I'm sure you'll feel friendlier toward your fellow students as time progresses."

Erik mumbled to himself. "Bullshit."

"Miss Walden, if you'll pass this textbook back to our new student, we shall begin."

📖📖📖

When River walked into the cafeteria, Larsen and Gina were deep in conversation. Looking across the room, he noticed Avalon at a corner table by herself. He could see that the kids were watching her, and he couldn't help but want to make sure she was okay.

"Hey, Lars, hey, Gin. You saved me a seat."

"Sure did." Gina pulled the seat out for River to sit down but noticed he was looking at Avalon.

Trying not to let her disappointment show, she tried to accept the inevitable. "You want to talk to the new girl so she won't feel alone, don't you?"

"Sort of. Yeah. I heard some kids making fun of her this morning. I think she could use a friend. I thought she might be sitting with her brother, but I don't see him."

Larsen swallowed a bite of his sandwich before speaking. "After third period, he headed for the front doors. I don't think he wants to have lunch with anyone. Not even his sister."

"Why don't you go talk to her, River. Larsen and I will have lunch together. We're still getting together after school, right?"

"Sure."

"Okay, then. Go talk to the new girl."

As River walked away, Gina confided in Larsen. "I'm so afraid, Larsen. She's so different, but cute. In the same kind of way that River is. What if he dumps me for her before we really even get started? I don't want him to think I'm a jealous girlfriend. In fact, I'm not even sure we're actually a couple. I don't want to be a bitch like my sister. But between you and me, it's kind of freaking me out."

"I get what you're saying, Gina. But River is being nice to her for the same reason he was nice to me: because he's a good guy and doesn't like to see other kids feeling alone or being the target of other people's stupidity."

Gina looked down at her half-eaten sandwich. "I've kind of lost my appetite. Lars, I'm really glad that you and River became such good friends after he stood up to Jax and Antonio for you. But that's just it; I'm afraid the same thing will happen with that girl. Look at her. Her whole face lit up when River just sat down at her table. Big time. There's enough wattage going on there to light up Mystekal High's football field."

📖📖📖

"Hi, River! I was hoping I'd see you."

"Is everything okay, Avalon?"

"Depends what you mean by 'okay.' A few kids have said hello to me, but I see and hear them whispering about me. One guy asked me where the Halloween party was."

"What did you say?"

"Nothing. Just as he said that, Erik came walking by. The guy took one look at my brother's face and took off. Erik has that effect on people. Guess you've noticed by now. He doesn't want to be here. Can't say I really do, either."

"I hope you'll like it better after a while. And don't worry about the Halloween stuff. Every day is Halloween in this town. We've even had ghosts living in this school."

"For realsies?"

"Yup."

"Oh, wow. Then maybe I won't be so out of place here after all."

"How's that?"

"I'll get to that part in a minute."

"Oh, okay. So … your family just moved here from Jersey City. To Mystekal? Don't think anyone has ever made that particular move in the long and rich history of mankind. Why did you come here?"

"Kind of a messed-up story."

"If you want to tell me, I'd like to hear it. I won't blab it to the school. I know you don't know me, but—"

"You have very trustworthy eyes. And you've been the only person to treat me like a human being today. So, yeah, I guess I'll tell you … if you're sure you want to keep talking to me. But your girlfriend doesn't look happy that you're sitting with me. I notice those things."

"She's with my friend Larsen. He's a good guy. I want you to meet them both. Everything is cool."

"Well, for starters, we didn't move here right away. We moved to Los Angeles. I told you this morning that I was an artist … a painter."

"Sure, I remember. Go on."

"Well, I don't want you to think I'm a witch or anything, but I kind of have this gift where I can paint stuff before it happens. But when I first started doing that, about a year ago, it was never bad stuff. And I didn't know I was painting the future. It started when I painted the neighbors' new dog before they even adopted him from the pound. Stuff like that. Everything was okay until one day I felt compelled to paint this lady lying in the street. The very next day, a dark-haired lady just like the one in my painting got killed by a drunk driver who ran into her … You think I'm a psycho witch, don't you?"

"If you are, then I'm a psycho warlock. I draw dead people. Only when I see them, I don't know they're dead. They just catch my eye, and then I draw them from memory and freak people's shit when they see my stuff."

Avalon smiled. "Awesome!"

"So, how did you end up moving out here from Jersey City?"

The smile on Avalon's face disappeared. "Well, people in our neighborhood found out about my ability to paint the future. I couldn't figure out how they knew, but I'll get to that in a minute. See, after I painted that poor lady, my family started getting death threats from strangers who were calling me the Jersey City harbinger of death. It got really ugly … fast. Do you know what a harbinger is?"

"Hell, yeah. It means you were like a messenger telling people what was gonna happen in the future."

"How did you know that?"

"I'm a walking dictionary."

"Oh, okay. Because I didn't know what it meant before people started calling me that. So, anyway, my mom got super adamant that we had to move. Then, about a week later, she tells my dad that she got a job in LA, so that's where we needed to go. My dad's in the building business, and he had just finished a two-year project, so he agreed … very reluctantly, and only because he didn't have any work lined up right away, and my mom did. She's a fitness instructor. Okay, so my little sister, Isabella, just like me, was not happy to leave all of the friends we've known since forever. But we were all worried someone would kill us all, and we all agreed to move. Meanwhile, and you can't tell anyone this ..."

"I promise. I won't. Not even Larsen or Gina."

Avalon nodded. "Okay, so Erik, who's almost twenty because they held him back in the first grade and then he missed most of his senior year back east—"

"How come? Was he sick?"

"No, he was working part time and wanted to drop out of high school to get a full-time job because his girlfriend is pregnant."

River's eyes widened. "Oh, man."

"Yeah. But my dad was stone-cold set about him finishing high school. Erik was going to stay in Jersey City and live with my aunt and uncle, but then my aunt had a stroke, and it was just too much. Erik couldn't take care of her, his girlfriend, and go to school at the same time. So my dad told him he needed to move west with us, finish high school here, and said then he can go back east and live his life. He is steaming mad being in high school so old, but it'll be better for him to finish. I think he knows that, but he doesn't act like he does. He's just so miserable."

"He must be really unhappy to be here with his pregnant girlfriend back east."

"For sure. Super angry. But it gets worse."

"You sure you're okay telling me this, Avalon?"

"I trust you. If I were still painting, I would probably have painted you and me talking together. You're not like anyone else here. I can see that."

"So, what else happened?"

"When we got to LA, my mom told my dad she was leaving him. Thing is, she already had a boyfriend out here. Met him about six months ago when she came out for some convention. You'll never believe this mess. My dad figured out that it was my own mom who leaked the news to the neighbors about my painting. She was also the one sending the death threats to my family. She orchestrated the entire thing just to get my dad to use some of our savings to move the family to LA. As soon as she got what she wanted, she split on us. She told my dad that her new boss was well connected and she'd ask him to help her find him work because, get this, it was the least she could do."

"Whoa! Why are the coolest people I meet having such bad mom problems? That blows. So, how did you end up in our fair town of desert sand and ghosts?"

"My mom's new boss managed to get in touch with some well-known building contractor in LA. When the guy heard that my dad is an expert in vintage building restoration, he got him a job here with some lady who is restoring a theater. He just started today. This job only has a couple more months to go, but then he's going to be working on some other projects in town."

"Whoa! Hold the cell phone!"

"What does *that* mean?"

"Oh, it's an old-fashioned expression I heard in a 1940s movie. Hold the phone. I just updated it for today's technological times. But it means the same thing. You know, like 'what the fuck?' "

"How come you said that, then? What did I say? What's wrong, River?"

"Is your dad working at the Desert Theater?"

"Yeah, with some lady named Arielle."

"That's my mom!"

"For realsies?"

"Yeah! Hey, is your dad a nice guy?"

"I guess. I mean he's always been the best guy ever. But my mom pulling this major con game on him kinda left him not so happy. And it's left Erik spitting mad, like I told you."

"Uh, yeah. I see that. My friend Larsen over there is going to be working as my mom's assistant. So I guess he'll get to know your dad, too. I hope you don't mind me asking this, Avalon, but your dad isn't looking for a new woman or anything, is he?"

"Heck, no. The way he's feeling right now, I think finding a girlfriend is the last thing on his mind. If I were still painting, I wouldn't be drawing him with anyone. I can just feel it. Why do you ask?"

"Just that my mom is super pretty, and my parents just got remarried two years ago. I wouldn't want anyone to come between them."

"Do they love each other a lot?"

"Hell, yeah. They're lovebirds. Cooing away."

"That's sweet. Well, if they're in love like you say, then nothing will come between them. But you certainly don't have to worry about my dad."

Chapter 9

Larsen walked behind the abandoned paint store, adjacent to the Desert Theater. Behind both buildings was a large expanse of desert, and far in the distance he could see thousands of wind generators, spinning like white pinwheels, right in front of the mountains. The only splash of color was a bright blue truck parked not too far from the back door of the theater. A man, with his long hair in a ponytail and dressed in paint-spattered jeans and a red T-shirt, quickly hopped into it, started the engine, and drove away. Larsen was mesmerized by the way the spinning tires sent sprays of sand into the air as the truck disappeared from sight.

"Over here, Larsen!"

He looked up to see Arielle waving to him from the door of the work trailer and hurried over to her. "Hey, Mrs. D; hope I'm not late for my first day at work."

"Nope. In fact, you're almost twenty minutes early. I hope this wasn't a bad day for you to start. I thought you might have plans with your friends."

"I'm going to help Kathryn give out candy later. That's all."

"That sounds like fun. She's a very special person. I think she's lived in Mystekal longer than most anyone here. She's one of the town's few remaining original residents. I'm so glad you're living with her now, though I'd imagine you miss your mother even under the unfortunate circumstances."

" 'Unfortunate circumstances.' That's a graceful way of saying 'rotten, miserable situation.' "

Arielle nodded as she held the trailer door open for him. "And some would argue that 'rotten, miserable situation' was a graceful way of saying something a whole lot worse."

"Yeah, you're right, Mrs. D."

"Larsen, I hate the way you were being treated, but I'm not going to dis your mom. I don't know her and certainly am not in the know about whatever inner demons she's battling. I'm just glad you're out of the line of fire. And I'm grateful as hell that my family forgave me for some pretty disgraceful behavior. When I think back on the years I was gone, it sickens me. I was another person then. All I'm trying to say is that you shouldn't give up on your mother."

Larsen closed the door to the trailer just as the wind was picking up in the desert. "I'm not giving up on her, but I sure as heck don't have any great expectations, to quote a recent book we read in English class."

"Oh, I love Charles Dickens. He was masterful at creating colorful characters, don't you think?"

"For sure. But I think Mother Nature's been pretty good at doing that, too."

Arielle laughed. "Oh, yeah. Now, are you ready to learn all there is to know about your new job?"

"Are you kidding? I've been ready since you first told me about it."

"I hope you don't mind working in a trailer. As you can see, it's kind of a tight squeeze in here. Two steps in the door and I'm already at my desk. Four steps in and you're at yours."

"I love it, Ms. D. No worries."

"Great! Well, this is my desk. Excuse all of the mess. This is called multitasking." Arielle laughed. "My job here is to oversee all of the work being done. But I'm also in charge of choosing everything related to the decor—you know, finishes, chair fabrics, handles, trimmings, flooring, carpet, bathroom hardware, spigots, basins—a long list. You get the idea. You'll be helping me with all of this, including setting up our grand opening-slash-talent competition in January and getting the school started. So, as you can see, there's plenty of work to be done."

"This is exciting! How much work has already been done?"

"Well, for starters, all 228 seats have been sent to an upholsterer. This theater holds fourteen rows of sixteen and four extra seats in the back. As I told you before, the old paint store will be the site for our new school. That's the easy part. Everything there will be brand new. The restoration of our vintage theater is where the most important work is done."

"I'm psyched! Hey, I see a familiar face under your desk."

Muggins, who had been sleeping, wagged his tail and came out from under the desk to greet Larsen. He jumped on his hind legs, licked Larsen's face, then Arielle's, and went back underneath the desk.

"He's so glad I hired you, Larsen. Being my assistant has been exhausting for the boy."

Larsen laughed heartily. "Well, I promise you won't find me sleeping under your desk. Or at mine."

Arielle chuckled and pointed to a work area with a laptop. "You make me laugh, Larsen. I'm glad you're here. Now, this is going to be your desk. Not an abundance of space, but we just need to stay organized."

Larsen noticed a man sitting at a desk at the other end of the trailer. The man glanced at him briefly, then went back to studying the plans laid out before him.

Arielle motioned for Larsen to follow her and walked to the newcomer's desk. "Gabe, this is Larsen Davis. He's going to be my new part-time assistant. Larsen, this is Gabe Martelli. He's a vintage restoration specialist. He's going to be doing several projects in Mystekal after he finishes work here."

Larsen reached out to shake Gabe's hand. "You're Avalon and Erik's dad, right?"

"Yeah. Guess you met 'em at the high school. My youngest is in middle school. Tough transition from Jersey City. Especially for my son."

Larsen remembered how angry Erik was in science class when Henry Sledge asked him to introduce himself. "Uh, yeah. Nobody likes being the new kid."

Gabe looked uneasy. "It's a lot more than that."

"Oh, sorry. Well, I'll do everything I can to make him feel welcome."

"Don't try too hard. Better that way." Gabe turned back to look at the plans on his desk, and Arielle nodded to leave him alone.

"Well, now that you've had the grand tour of the trailer, how about taking a look at the theater itself?"

Larsen's face lit up. "Absolutely!"

As soon as Arielle walked back to the door and put her hand on it, Muggins came out from under the desk to join her.

Arielle laughed. "An apparent second wind. The Mugster follows me pretty much everywhere."

As they stepped outside, Arielle and Larsen raised their arms to cover their eyes. The wind had picked up considerably. "Let's make a run for it, Larsen. Sheesh, when I mentioned a second wind, I was talking about Muggins' energy. Didn't mean it literally. Oh well, it'll die down. Eventually."

Opening the back door to the theater, Arielle nodded for Larsen to enter. Muggins followed behind him, and she shut the door quickly.

"Whew! You didn't get any sand in your eyes, did you?"

"No, I'm good, Mrs. D. But that's some crazy wind."

Arielle pointed to her left. This breezeway here will take you backstage." She began to walk straight ahead as Larsen and Muggins followed. Right now, we're going down this hallway and that door ahead will take us into the theater.

Arielle opened the door. "After you."

Larsen walked through the door and was awed by the sight of 228 seat frames. "As you can see, Larsen, we have a whole lot of chairs without cushions."

"Yeah, you mentioned they're getting reupholstered."

Take a look at the ornate ceiling. Isn't it gorgeous? Years ago, it was the style to cover all of that up with drywall to modernize it. But we're doing a vintage restoration and everything will be restored to its former glory."

Larsen looked up. "I think the original is so much nicer. Wow, so Gabe's crew is going to get up there and paint all of that? How do they get up that high? Do you have really big ladders and long paintbrushes?"

"Not exactly. They'll be erecting scaffolding right before they're ready to do the job."

"Ha ha. I guess that sounded pretty stupid."

Arielle chuckled. "Not at all. You should hear some of the questions that I asked in the beginning. On second thought, I think I'll keep those a secret."

"Oh, that's not fair. So, how about that chandelier? Is that staying?"

"Absolutely. All of the brass will be buffed and we'll be putting in new glass pieces. You wouldn't believe how many antique light specialists I had to contact to find the right replacement pieces."

"Wow. Even if you found the wrong ones, who would even notice?"

"We would notice. It's got to be right, Lars. Let's see. What else can I tell you? We're going to be getting a new curtain for the stage and a brand-new PA system. All the doors are going to be sanded and revarnished. The floor of the stage will be redone as well. Gabe can tell you much more if you're interested, but as you can see, we've got a whole lot of work to do. Having you here will free me up to do my job more quickly."

"I'll do my very best. Promise."

"I have no doubts … " Muggins ran up the steps to the stage, and began sniffing around the edge. "Muggins, come back here!"

"Where's he going?"

"Probably to sniff out what the workmen had for lunch. They've been sitting on the stage to eat since the seat cushions were taken away. Yesterday Muggins found a piece of roast beef that had fallen out of a sandwich. But he looks like he's expecting to find a whole lot more."

As he watched Muggins aggressively sniffing, Larsen saw the shadow of a person linger behind a back curtain, then leave. "Hey, Mrs. D, I don't think he's looking for food."

Arielle looked surprised. "Sure he is. What makes you think otherwise?"

"Uh … because I just saw the shadow of a guy move behind the curtain. So I figured maybe that's who Muggins is sniffing out."

"Did he have long hair pulled back in a ponytail? That's Raphael, one of our workmen. He's probably just taking last looks for the day. All the men here have kids and came in early so they could leave early to be with them on Halloween."

"Does he drive a blue truck?"

"Sure does. Metallic blue. Just got it this year. Why do you ask?"

"Oh, nothing. Just saw it outside."

Arielle clasped her hands together. "There you go. Mystery solved. C'mon, Muggins, you're not being a very good tour guide. Get your furry butt over here."

Arielle looked perplexed as Muggins, ignoring her, ran to the back of the stage.

"Muggins! Here! Now!"

"Woof! Woof!"

"What in the world are you barking at, boy?"

Muggins, now frantically sniffing, was walking back and forth along the edge of the curtain. "Woof!"

Quickly climbing the stairs to the left of the stage, Arielle went over to him, got down on her knees, and began playfully stroking his face. "What's up with you, crazy dog? Since when do you bark at food?"

Muggins, who was usually overjoyed to receive her affection, was still preoccupied. Grabbing a leash from her back pocket, Arielle attached it to his harness and led Muggins away.

"Lars, I'm taking him back to the trailer. You can also exit this way, too. Just walk backstage and hang a left to the breezeway. You'll end up at the back door."

Still standing next to the stage, Larsen watched as Muggins kept turning his head toward the back curtain as Arielle led him away. He knew Muggins was not barking over a piece of roast beef. He had seen someone, too. Or maybe just smelled someone. But it couldn't have been Raphael. Larsen had seen him drive off just when Arielle had first opened the door to the trailer.

Chapter 10

"Thank you for keeping me company tonight, Larsen. It's been years since I had anyone greet the trick-or-treaters with me." Through the screen door, Kathryn watched the group of six children walk down her driveway. "Well, I think that was the last of them." She closed the front door and walked over to the living room couch. "Have a seat."

Larsen loved the big green plush sofa with the giant throw pillows and fell onto it, his face showing how much he enjoyed the comfort.

Kathryn took a seat on the same couch and sighed. "Happy Halloween, Larsen."

"Believe it or not, this is my first one."

Really? You're nearly eighteen, and this is your first Halloween?"

"Yeah, back where I come from, people aren't real chill about opening their doors to strangers wearing masks."

"My apologies. I shouldn't have said—"

"No problem. Some families were down with it. Not my mom, though. She didn't want anyone coming to the house, and she sure didn't want me dressing up and going out. No options there. I was really surprised to see so many older kids dressing up tonight."

"Well, I think we had our fair share of teens tonight because it's a Friday. Some of them are going to a party after they drop their kid brothers and sisters back home. I'm not an eavesdropper, but I do hear a lot behind that food counter." Kathryn winked.

Larsen laughed. "Oh, that makes sense. Yeah, I bet you see a whole lot of everything, too. After all, that's how we met, although I wish it hadn't been under those circumstances."

"It was what you call a blessing in disguise." Kathryn turned away from Larsen, and he could tell she was upset.

"Are you okay? I said something wrong, didn't I?"

Catching a tear with her index finger before it could tumble down her face, Kathryn managed a smile. "Of course not, Larsen. I was just thinking about this silly fantasy that I had … well, I hate to admit it, but it still haunts my brain."

Larsen wasn't sure how to respond. "Did you want to share it with me, or should I mind my own business? Because I'm real good with that."

"I'd actually like to share. But I'm warning you, it might seem a bit crazy to you."

"Negative, Kathryn. I've seen a whole lot of crazy in my life, and you don't even make the waiting list."

"I like that. Thank you, Larsen. When you mentioned the older kids coming around, that's where my fantasy kicks in. I always dreamed that Peter never really died, but had to pretend he did for his safety and mine, even if it meant never seeing me again. For years after the acc … murder, and even sometimes now, when an older kid comes by, well, I think that maybe Peter is under that mask or makeup and has come home to surprise me. He'd be fifty-five now, and, I know, it's very silly of me."

"I don't think that's silly at all. I've had some really similar fantasies about my dad, like, that he faked his death to get away from my mother. If you knew my mom, that might not seem so unreal."

Kathryn glanced toward the end table where several framed photos of Peter were. "Grief has a powerful effect on people, Larsen.

I used to tell my best friend—she was the neighbor I told you about—that if most people saw their deceased loved ones walk into a room, they'd hug them with tears of joy. I don't believe most people would scream, because in our hearts, we can never really accept that someone is gone. In a way, it's not that surprising if we see them again."

Larsen nodded enthusiastically. "You're right, Kathryn. I mean, if I saw my dad, I'd just throw my arms around him and give him the biggest hug ever, like, one that would last for an hour. And then I'd ask a million questions."

"Exactly. When my neighbor died unexpectedly, I always hoped to see her again, too. In fact, her death was one of the reasons I decided not to retire."

Just as Kathryn had finished speaking, Larsen's cell phone sounded, letting him know a text had come in. He looked uneasy as he pulled his phone from his back pants pocket. The look on his face confirmed his fears.

U been gone less than a wk and already forgot ur blood mama. Don't U be dressin in no drag tonight or showing your Halloweenie to another gay. U don't be shaming me boy. Hope ur new mama is paying 4 this phone b/c I ain't doing it no more.

Kathryn watched as Larsen tensed up and dropped his phone into his lap. Seeing his hands shake, Kathryn took hold of them and squeezed his hands in hers. "I'm sorry, Larsen. I don't know what she said, and I'm not asking. I'm just sorry, son. For whatever it is."

Larsen choked back the tears and tried to make a joke of it as he mimicked a high-powered salesman he used to see on late-night TV shows. "Hey, can't bully your child in person? Want to send that special dis to break your kid's heart or kick him in the ass? No problem! Text bullying is the answer. No extra charges, folks! All included in a monthly package for the low rate of—"

"Oh, Larsen …"

Larsen's heart sank. He watched as lines of anger etched into Kathryn's beautiful face. "Please don't worry about me, Kathryn. And please excuse the sarcasm. It's just my way of … well, you know."

Kathryn sighed, then massaged her temples, as if to ward off a headache. "Of course I worry. No child deserves to be bullied, especially by his or her parent. Not only does my heart ache for you, it hurts for Peter all over again."

Alarmed, Larsen stood up. "Oh, no. I-I didn't realize that living here would make your sad memories even more difficult. I'm so sorry, Kathryn. Maybe I should just go back … to her."

Kathryn patted the seat cushion next to her. "Sit down, Larsen. Please. Absolutely not. You've been here only four days, and you have no idea of the joy and comfort you've brought to me. I am so much happier with you in my life. I hurt for Peter every day. I always have. After all of these years, I still look for his star, but I never find it. I'm seventy-five years old, and I never give up. But like I told you when we first met, I don't fool myself, either. As much as I'd like to see it shining in the sky, I know that's just a silly dream. Will you please sit down again? It would really make me happy."

Larsen sat down beside her. "I just thought … well, I'm glad I'm here, too. My mom said something really ugly in the text. I'd be embarrassed to repeat it. She told me she wasn't paying for my phone anymore, too, but I never expected her to do that. I have a job."

"I can put you on my plan, Larsen."

"But I'll pay the bill, right?"

"You don't have to, son. I want you to save for your future."

"I need to pay for the phone, Kathryn. It's just who I am."

Kathryn grinned. "And that's why I hold you in such high esteem. Because you are a proud man. And you never have to worry about giving me the details of any unpleasantness. Sometimes it helps to get everything out, but in other situations, it only makes things worse."

"Is that why you don't talk about how Peter died?"

"Exactly. The details no longer matter. I try to remember the things that made me happy. And I wouldn't want to hurt …"

"Who wouldn't you want to hurt?"

She paused. "I wouldn't want to hurt anyone else by dragging them into the darkness with me. That's all. Like I said, I try to focus on the good times."

Larsen twisted his mouth. "I wish I had some happy memories to focus on. Well, I do, but they all involve my dad, and he's long gone. But now that I'm living here with you and working with Mrs. D, I'm hoping life will get a whole lot better. I know it will."

📖📖📖

Holding books in one hand and a cell phone in another, Erik looked uncomfortable and angry. "You sure you're feeling okay, baby? Hell, yeah, I miss you. Hang in there. Soon as I graduate, this desert life is history. We'll be a family. Promise. Hey, you got that number I gave you? Don't worry, I got the card in my wallet. Lemme get off this phone and find it. I'll text it to you … yeah, me too."

As soon as he ended the call, Erik reached into his back pocket for his wallet, but not having put the phone away first, his grip slipped, and the contents of his wallet fell all over the hall floor.

Jax, his first day back since being suspended, almost tripped on the fallen items that lay splayed on the floor. "What the fuck! Who the hell are you?"

On his knees, Erik scrambled to pick everything up, but Jax had already nabbed Erik's driver's license. "New fucking Joisey, huh? Ain't that how youse guys talk back there?"

Erik stood up and put his hand out. "Not playin' witchu, motherfucker; give me the license now."

Now standing as well, Jax read the license aloud: "Erik Gabriel Martelli. From Kensington Avenue, Joisey City, New Joisey."

Erik made a grab for his license, but Jax was faster and had turned his back as he continued to read. "What the hell? Says here you're gonna be turning twenty on your next boithday. Coming up soon, too!" Jax roared with laughter. "So what, did you flunk a couple grades? You as dumb as you look?"

With strength Jax hadn't given him credit for, Erik snatched his license out of Jax's hand, stuck it in his back pocket, and with the same free hand shoved Jax against the nearest locker, dropped his books on the floor, then used both hands to push his head hard against the metal door. "Know what mixed martial arts are, motherfucker? 'Cause I'm going to give your ass a demonstration."

Larsen, who had nervously been watching the altercation between his least favorite classmates, edged up to Erik. "Hey, man. You don't want to be doing this."

Keeping his focus on Jax but talking to Larsen, Erik responded forcefully. "The fuck I don't. Now, mind your own business, or you're next. And as I told this douchebag, I don't play."

Speaking as quietly as he could, Larsen whispered in Erik's ear, "I work at the theater with your dad, Gabe. That's your old man, right?"

As Larsen spoke, he noticed that a group of students were watching, and to Jax's dismay, it was obvious that Larsen had come to his rescue. Jax broke away and muttered under his breath to Larsen, "I don't need the faggot police. Fuck you."

Jax hurried away. Quickly, Erik picked his books off the floor, then turned to Larsen. "You threatening me? You fixin' to rat me out to my pops? 'Cause … see, I don't like rats. They run around in sewers and are full of shit."

Larsen's heart was pounding so fast he thought everyone could see it, but he kept his cool. "I'm not going to rat you out to your dad. I just know you want to move on with your life, like we all do, and if you bash Reinhardt's head in, then you'll only end up sabotaging yourself. Is that what you want?"

Erik's eyes met Larsen's. For several seconds, he stared at the classmate who he didn't know to call friend or foe, but really didn't care either way. "Just stay out of my business, and don't say fuck all to my old man about me."

Larsen nodded. "No intention of it. Just there to do my job."

Accidentally on purpose, as he hurried off, Erik gave Larsen a slight warning shove.

Gina, standing nearby, who had been part of the group to witness the action, was just about to approach Larsen when Avalon came rushing over to her. "Yo! Did you see what happened? Someone said my brother was havin' a go at that guy."

"Uh, yeah. I think he was. I'm sure Jax provoked him, but he looked like he was gonna kill him. Not sure how he even had the strength to push Jax against the locker. I mean, Jax is really strong."

Avalon shrugged. "Well, sometimes the peeps with the mixed martial arts background have the edge. Besides that, my brother's got enough anger to power New York City. You know?"

Still not sure how to assess the newcomer, Gina sized up the girl who she feared might have eyes for her new boyfriend. "Not really. So, how about you? Do you use physical force like your brother? Or do you have other ways of doing things?"

Anxiously twirling the rings on her right hand with her left, Avalon took a moment to analyze the situation. "You don't like me, do you? And it's not because I dress different from you or 'cause I might talk a little different. It's because I made friends with River right away, isn't it?"

Gina didn't like the fact that Avalon saw through her so easily. "If River likes you, then I don't have a problem with you."

Avalon put a strand of green hair in her mouth and blew it out with a large puff of air. "Seems like that's the reason you *do* have a problem with me. But for realsies, I'm not here to steal anyone's boyfriend. It was just very cool that he was so nice to me, especially on my first day when most of the people in this school were … and for the record still are … looking at me like I'm the main attraction in some freak museum. Well, maybe I am a freak to some people, but I don't need to see any more eyeballs popping in my direction or bouncin' off my back when I'm walking down the hall. I'm not angry like my brother, but I'm not chill to being messed with, either. River is a cool guy, and so is Larsen. Not sure where you stand, but from the way your face is all twisted up, I'm not sure you know, either."

Gina was surprised by Avalon's honesty. "Well, um, hey, why don't you say what you really feel?"

Avalon laughed. "I got no problem doing that. Where I come from, it's called survival. I'm not a coward."

"Yeah, um, I can see that. Look, I don't want to be your enemy, Avalon. River and Larsen like you, so you're okay with me, too. And I'm cool with your looks. I'm a bit more traditional, but the point is that we all get to make our own choices."

Avalon cocked her head to one side as if to size up what Gina was saying. "So, you don't have a problem with blue-and-green hair?"

"No. Not really. My sister went through high school with a whole lot of purple hair, so I'm kind of used to that. Except my sister is kind of a bitch, and I guess I keep my hair plain ol' blond just so nobody confuses us."

"So you're saying that you're not a bitch?"

Gina laughed. "I sure try not to be. Can't you give me a chance, Avalon?"

"Yeah, I think so. You're all right with me. For nowsies. I'll see you later. I'd better go find Erik and make sure he's not kicking anyone's ass or busting down a wall."

Gina exhaled, then smiled warmly. "Okay, see ya."

Chapter 11

Seeing Larsen close his locker, River hurried to catch up with him. "Hey, dude. I haven't had a chance to talk to you today. Is it true you broke up a fight between Martelli and Reinhardt?"

"Well, it wasn't exactly a fight. Erik was just going to bash Jax's brains in."

"According to the Mystekal minions, you saved your favorite bully from cranial decimation."

"Jax would have preferred to have his skull flattened than to be saved by me. It was probably stupid of me to step in, but I thought about all of the times in my life when people looked away as someone was bullying me, and, well … it felt pretty hypocritical to just stand there … even though it was Jax."

"It's called irony. Anyway, brave move, my man. Hey, let's go outside for a minute where we can talk in private before lunch, okay?"

"Sure, Riv." Larsen walked along the hallway with River until they reached the front doors of the school, then headed outside into the bright sun. The large expanse of desert, with majestic mountains in the distance, was a favorite hangout for the students of Mystekal High, and the large flat boulders, located in eight random spots in front of the school, were considered prime seating for those lucky enough to snare a free one.

Finding the last empty boulder off to the left, River sat down.

"Rest your weary bones that almost got smashed into hopeless fragments of—"

Larsen smiled crookedly as he sat down next to River. "You think I made a mistake?"

"Nah. I wouldn't call it a mistake. But you were lucky, Lars. If those two go at it again, my sage counsel would be to avoid being the meat in a bully sandwich. You catch my drift?"

"Yeah. I hear you. But I had a really good reason for doing what I did. See, the thing is, after your mom showed me the theater on Friday, we went back into the trailer, and I got acquainted with my computer—"

River burst out laughing. "Like what, dude? 'Hey, Mac, nice to meet you.'"

"Yeah, right. Like showing me the websites she uses, setting up an email address for me, going over the programs … that kind of stuff. Anyway, Erik's dad, Gabe, was at the other end of the trailer on the phone with him. He was keeping his voice really low—"

"Ha ha ha. And you were eavesdropping."

Larsen playfully punched River in the arm. "No, man. I just couldn't help but hear stuff, and let's just say that I know Erik can't wait to get back east after we graduate. I knew if he bashed Jax's head in, even if well deserved, he'd mess up his life for good. Really, I was trying to help Erik more than Jax. What's wrong is wrong, Riv. You know?"

Glancing sideways, River could see that a few kids were gossiping about the two of them. Although it didn't bother him, he knew it would upset Larsen, so he angled his body to block the view. "Yeah, I know."

"Sure you do. That's why you're twisting yourself around because you think it'll keep me from noticing that group of dickheads talking shit about us. And you want to protect me because that's who you are. If there's one thing I've learned, Riv, it's that showing bullies that they bug you is the worst thing you can do. They live for reactions, and I'm trying really hard not to give them any."

"Good for you. So, hey, I thought you might stop by on the weekend but I never heard from you. My bad. I could have called, too."

"I knew you had plans with Gina on Saturday, and I took a drive with Kathryn to Palm Springs on Sunday. She wanted to show me the giant Marilyn Monroe statue before it leaves town. It's called 'Forever Marilyn' She's, like, three stories high—that's twenty-six feet high, to be precise—and she goes from city to city. Really cool. Anyway, Kathryn's a special lady. After we walked around town, she took me out for lunch at this bistro and insisted on buying me one of the best meals I've had in ages. Except for your mom's cooking, of course."

River laughed. "Dude, you don't have to be such a gentleman with me and include my mom's cooking. Even if she is your boss now. Ha ha. I'm really glad you're living with Kathryn. She's always been so nice behind the counter, but I never thought any more about her. Wish I had."

Well, you can get to know her now. She's a pretty amazing lady. And she's been a whole lot more lonely than she lets most people know."

"Yeah, you told me about her son, Peter, getting killed for being gay. Kind of amazing she's managed to be such a nice person all of her life. Some people are just plain nasty for no reason. Or at least no reason that anyone knows about. Like Ms. Carrow's old man. He was one mean homicidal bastard. Anyway, I'm glad you spent some time with her. How about your mom? Have you called her since you moved out?"

Larsen looked sorrowfully down at his lap, then slowly lifted his head to answer River's question. "Man, I was going to call her on the weekend. But then she sent me this really ugly text on Halloween night, bullying me right on the phone, and I just wasn't up for any more."

"You don't have to explain to me, Lars. I hear you. You ready to grab some lunch?"

"I am, but before we head for the cafeteria, there's one more thing I think I want to tell you."

River grinned. "You're not sure?"

"Yeah, I think I'm sure. You're probably the one person who will believe me."

Looking around to make sure no one was in earshot, Larsen explained the shadows in the theater that Muggins had been chasing at the back of the stage.

"Did you tell my mom what you saw?"

"Yeah, and she said it was probably this guy Raphael. Only I saw him leave right before your mom called me into the trailer."

"Did you tell her that?"

Larsen looked uncomfortable. "No, Riv. Friday was my first day of work. I didn't think it was cool to tell your mother that I think the theater might be haunted. That would have been kind of extreme, you know?"

"Not for my mom. She's seen a whole lot of ghost action here. But I think she went through even more craziness when she lived in LA with that scumbag producer Jess calls Phony Phil. Mixing with ghosts was nothing compared to shacking up with a Hollywood pig. No offense to my porcine pals, of course. Old Man Carrow slugged Phil with a baseball bat right before he was choked to death. We thought Phil would probably kick the bucket, 'cause he was barely alive when they took him away, but somehow the scumbag survived. He never contacted my mom again, though. I hope he's forgotten her name. Piece of vermin-infested rotting garbage. Anyway, I didn't mean to go off, but just making the point that my mom has dealt with a whole lot more than ghosts. You know?"

"I hear you. But please don't say anything, Riv. Let me just wait and see, okay? Besides, tomorrow her friend Lisa is coming in from LA to shoot footage for a documentary. I don't want to get your mom all freaked out. At least let me wait until that's over with. Anyway, it could have just been some fluke. There could be a very reasonable explanation, like, maybe that Raphael guy forgot something and came back."

"I'm betting on the ghosts."

"But you won't say anything to your mom, right?"

"No, I'll zip it, as my dad likes to say. But I can't promise you Muggins won't say anything. He talks in his sleep. Grrrr. Woof!"

"So, listen, if there are ghosts, do you think they're connected to the stuff that happened in Mystekal a couple of years ago?"

"That I don't know. There are a whole lot of tortured souls from these parts, Lars." River glanced over at the students who were now visibly mocking him and Larsen." Look at those asshats flapping their gums about us as we speak. Messed-up people make for messed-up ghosts. C'mon, let's eat. I'm starved."

📖📖📖

The final bell of the day had rung, and Avalon was already on her way toward the front doors. To avoid seeing the faces of the students staring at her, she looked down at her phone as she walked. All she saw was a leg covered in distressed denim with a blue running shoe at the end of it slicing through the air in front of her like a rogue gate arm. Her phone flew out of her hands and slid down the hallway. Avalon fell to her knees, barely escaping serious injury by breaking the fall with the palms of her hands.

Amid sounds of laughter and cowardly feet running away, she did everything she could to choke back the sobs.

Holding hands, River and Gina had just rounded the corner when they saw her on the ground, wincing in pain. Letting go of Gina's hand, River rushed over to her, kneeling at her side. "What happened, Avalon?"

Seeing River's concerned face, Avalon was unable to hold back her emotion. Still on the ground, now sitting, she threw her arms around River for comfort. "Some punk stuck out his leg and tripped me, and he and his fucking rat pack ran away. Sucker-punching amateur thug juvie idiots!"

As River sat there with Avalon, Bianca, who'd been heading for the front doors from the opposite direction, saw Avalon's phone on the ground, picked it up, and walked over to hand it to her. "I'm guessing this belongs to you. Hey, what happened here?"

River looked up at Bianca. "Some dipshit tripped her."

"Oh, wow. That sucks. Want me to tell Tonio?"

Avalon waved her off. "No, no! I don't want to make a big deal of it. And I really don't want my brother to find out, or he might kill someone."

Bianca looked around. "Oh, yeah. I can kinda see how he might get a little pissed off. Where is he?"

"Probably outside in his car talking to his girlfriend and waiting for me."

Noticing Gina standing alone in the hallway and looking miserable, Bianca nodded and hurried to Gina's side, while River helped Avalon to stand up.

"Hey, Bianca. Where's Tonio?"

"He's outside hanging with his boys. Hold on." Bianca reached into her pocket for her phone, then sent a quick text. "He can wait a few minutes. No drama. What's up with you, *mi amiga*?"

Gina's glance rolled over toward Avalon and River. "Oh, nothing. Just that my boyfriend is playing hero with that zero. Sorry, I guess I shouldn't be calling her names, but I'm just feeling like every time she has a problem, River is there to save the day. I freakin' hate it."

"What happened? Was she lying about someone tripping her? Did she fake all of this just to get River's attention?"

Gina looked embarrassed. "No, some idiots tripped her. She could have been really hurt, and, seriously, my brain understands that, but my heart is gettin' a little jelly, you know? And just earlier today I told her we could be friends, but I'm sure not acting like one. Does that mean I suck?"

Bianca laughed. "No, girl. You don't suck. Hey, if Tonio was playing knight in shining armor to some chick, that would probably chafe my butt, too, even if it were legit. Must be tough being the new kid, especially when you don't look like anyone else. And it blows that she's being bullied, but, yeah, I'm hearing you. I'd like to think I'm a good person and all, but like I said, my hackles would be up for sure."

Gina looked exasperated. "So, what should I do?"

Bianca moved closer to Gina, lowering her voice. "Listen, it's not about dissing Avalon. If you do that, you might as well stick a bow on her ass and hand her over to Riv. No, see, it's about you doing more to make River a happy guy. You hearing me?"

"Are you and Tonio—"

"Hell, yeah, we are!"

"Oh, yeah. Well, of course you are. You've been together for a year and a half or something."

"One year, ten months to be exact. Look, Gin, I gotta run. I'll text ya later, and if you're free, we can have a chat. I definitely think there's a conversation we need to have. Yanno?"

Gina reached over and gave Bianca a quick hug. "Thanks. You showed up at the perfect time. I really needed a friend."

Chapter 12

Larsen tried to play it cool, but he knew that Lisa and her cameraman, Josh, would be arriving shortly from LA. Being a part of a documentary was about the most exciting thing that had ever happened to him. When he received an email from Lisa the night before, asking him if he'd like to be filmed reciting a few lines on stage, after fist pumping the air with a big "Yes!" and sharing the news with Kathryn, he got to work. For the next several hours, he reacquainted himself with a monologue from Shakespeare's *Othello* that he had memorized two years ago.

Arielle watched Larsen as he worked at his computer. Seeing his enthusiasm made her almost happier for him than for herself. "Larsen …"

"Uh … what?" Jumping up in his seat, Larsen's hands flew off the keyboard, and he looked at Arielle, embarrassed by his startled reaction. "Oh, Mrs. D, I'm sorry. I was so absorbed in thought that when you called my name, it was like being awakened from a dream."

"Well, this isn't a dream. Don't you love it? How cool is it that Lis wants you to recite something on stage? I'm a bit jealous. She didn't ask me to recite anything." Arielle mock frowned.

"Uh, well … um … uh …"

Arielle laughed. "Just playing with you, Lars. I don't want to read any lines. I want to make this theater a success, and I want to help dedicated performers of all ages to learn and perfect their craft. Don't mind me; I think I got my sense of humor from my son."

"You mean you think he got his from you."

"Nope. I think I got mine from River. In case you haven't noticed, he's much funnier than I could ever be. But his humor is contagious, and I may have picked up a few tricks along the way."

A knock at the trailer door startled both of them. Arielle burst out laughing. "I think I'm a bundle of nerves just like you, Larsen."

Before she could get up from her chair, Lisa opened the door and rushed over to Arielle, giving her a huge embrace. Josh, a pleasant-looking man in his early thirties, walked in behind her, carrying his camera equipment, and shut the door behind him.

Larsen shook Josh's hand, introduced himself, and watched with joy as the two best friends reunited.

Pulling away from Arielle so that she could take a good look at her, Lisa was so happy with what she saw that her eyes were watering. "Girlfriend, I have never seen you look as fabulous as you do right now, dressed in your jeans and T-shirt. You look younger and more vibrant than when I first met you. How's that possible? Desert air?"

Arielle turned to include Larsen and Josh in the conversation. "First, thanks for the compliment. I think you might be exaggerating a wee beaucoup. But I'll tell you this: being happy with myself, being with a man I love who loves me back, and just trying to be the best version of me I can be has done wonders. The whole time I lived in Los Angeles, I let myself be brainwashed by a horrid man who didn't deserve to know me. I never stopped trying to compete with others, compare myself to others, and, worst of all, please the devil. Ugh! It was a horrible, vicious cycle, and it can age a person fast. I feel so free now. Being with my family again, doing something I love … hey, what can I say? It feels good to be me. And I'm blabbing waaaaay too much!"

Lisa laughed. "I'm so loving this. And, hey, I can outtalk you any day of the week, so you blab away all you wish." Lisa reached over to shake Larsen's hand. "It's a pleasure to meet you, Larsen. Thank you for agreeing to do a little last-minute acting. So much about this project has changed. Let me explain."

"Thank *you* for asking me! And, please, sit in my chair."

Lisa smiled and took a seat.

Arielle was pleased by Larsen's chivalrous instincts. "Yeah, we don't exactly have room for a conference table in this trailer, much less any extra chairs. So, what's the deal, Lis? We're all ears and two bundles of nerves."

"Okay, well, the documentary is no longer a documentary. It's going to be a cable series. Let me fill you in quickly so we can get started. A few weeks ago, Josh and I went back east to film some historical restorations under way in Pennsylvania and Virginia. There was such a wealth of fascinating information, and we'd barely begun. I didn't see how we'd pack it all into a documentary, but we shot a ton of footage anyway.

"Then we started traveling all over the eastern states to visit barn restorations in progress. I never thought I would become such a barn freak. Did you know there are Dutch barns, bank barns, crib barns, round barns, prairie barns—"

Josh laughed. "Are you getting the idea that Lis is a barn fanatic?"

"Oh, stop, Josh. I've always liked barns, but now I'm in love with them. You might say I'm 'barn again.' "

Everyone laughed.

"As my son River would say, 'Good one.' "

Josh persisted. "Lisa's obsession is so bad that she named her new rescue dog Barney."

"Aw, you got a dog. You'll meet mine in a little bit. I asked

Raphael to take him for a walk because Larsen and I were waiting for you. Anyway, Lis, go on with what you were saying."

Excitedly, Lisa continued. "Okay, so we were in Kentucky visiting a crib barn when I got the call that one of our channel's programs was ending immediately. Unfortunately, that's a story I can't repeat. But OMG, what a scandal!"

Arielle twisted her mouth and eyed her friend. "Bullshit. You will absolutely tell me that one later."

With a coy smile, Lisa laughed. "Yeah. I will. You know me too well. Anyway, you know how I'm wired. My mouth is usually five sentences ahead of my brain, but that day they were in sync, and I immediately suggested turning the documentary into a series to fill the slot. This way, we can air one-hour episodes that are much more in-depth than what would have fit into a documentary."

Arielle was beaming. "What a fabulous idea! I so want all the dirt later. Go on, Lis. Tell us more."

"Here's the deal. Today we're not only going to shoot footage of your work in progress, but we're also making a trailer for the series. And that's one of the reasons I asked Larsen to do a bit of acting. What better way to promote a theater than to have a real actor on the stage."

Larsen looked nervous. "I might not be the real actor you need. I don't really have—"

"You're perfect. This is a small town. Nobody is expecting to see a Broadway star on this stage. A future star, yes. Anyway, we'll film today, and Josh will be back as the restoration progresses to film some more. But we'll both be here in January for your grand opening and talent show. I think that will make for fabulous television."

Arielle put one hand to her open mouth and took a deep breath. Removing her hand, she paused and looked at her friend. "I am so ecstatic. This is such a gift, Lis. Thank you. I don't know how you're handling this huge workload."

"Don't thank me, Ari. It's good for both of us. As for the workload, you remember my assistant, Petra, don't you? She's amazing. Except she's got this new love interest in the building who stops by a little bit too much for my taste, but it's no big deal. Oh, hey, moving right along, before I forget, when I was walking from our car to this trailer, I heard the song 'Tonight' playing. Is there a *West Side Story* enthusiast among us?"

Larsen looked shocked. "Uh, me. That's the ringtone on my phone. But nobody has called me today. Besides, if even someone had, there's no way you could hear my phone from outside."

"Oh, it wasn't coming from this trailer. It was coming from the theater."

Arielle shrugged. "Maybe one of our workmen is a fan. Who knew? Speaking of the theater, is everyone ready to get started?"

As Arielle, Larsen, Josh, and Lisa stepped out of the trailer, Muggins, who had been walking in the desert with Raphael, came racing over to her and jumped with excitement at meeting new people.

Lisa flashed a big smile and hugged Muggins as he nuzzled against her legs to greet her. "You are a doll baby. And I apologize for every time in my life when I've referred to some lowlife scumbag as a dog. You're a sweetie, my Barney is a sweetie, and life wouldn't be nearly as sweet without you beautiful creatures in it."

Wagging his tail, Muggins kissed her cheek, ran a few circles, and jumped up to give her a kiss.

"Hey, Muggins, your mama is getting jealous." Arielle leaned forward and patted her thighs, and Muggins came running to her side.

As the five of them entered the theater, they ran into Gabe, who was heading back to the trailer. He nodded hello but did not stop for introductions.

"Ari, who is that guy?"

"That's Gabe Martelli. He's my new vintage restoration specialist. Talented as heck, but not the most talkative guy. Or the happiest."

Lisa looked puzzled. "Well, I'm really going to need him to speak on camera at some point. His expertise will be invaluable to the show."

"Maybe next time Josh comes down to film. How's that? I need to give him some warning. He's kind of broody. Bad divorce, I hear. His wife and family moved out to LA, and she dumped him."

"Oh, damn. That sucks. So he's not originally from California?"

Arielle led her guests from the backstage area, down the short hallway, through the door to the auditorium, until they were all standing in the left aisle of the theater. "Here, Lis, have a missing seat. Why do you ask about Gabe? No, he's not from here. He's from Jersey City."

Lisa laughed at the sight of all of the missing seats, then her face turned a bit more serious. "I just feel so sure I've seen him before."

Josh, who was getting his camera ready for action, addressed his boss. "You probably have seen him before. I have to peel your eyes off every Italian guy who crosses your path."

"My husband is half Italian, in case you've forgotten. And I'm a very happily married woman. I just like to admire the scenery."

"Yeah, okay, boss." Josh picked up his camera. "I'm just going to take a look in the lobby, and then I'll be back in here when Larsen is ready to go."

Larsen looked as if he wanted to faint. "Is it unprofessional of me to say I'm nervous?"

Arielle put her hands on his shoulders and gave them a quick rub. "You'll do fine. You've known the piece for two years. Just give us your best. Stage fright is natural. This isn't live theater, so *this time,* we can do another take."

Lisa laughed. "Or three. Or four. Now, go break a leg."

Larsen smiled and began carefully navigating a path over all of the metal frames where the seats belonged. Arielle yelled after him, "She didn't mean that literally, Lars. Be careful. Do not break any legs."

As Larsen headed to the steps on the right of the stage, Muggins followed swiftly.

"Muggins! Come!" Arielle repeated the command, but Muggins had other ideas. Motioning to Raphael, who had just gone back to work, Arielle pointed to Muggins, then in the direction of the trailer, asking Raphael to take the dog out of the way.

Raphael hurried up to Muggins and took him by the collar, but the dog was not happy.

Arielle turned to Lisa. "He was like this last Friday. Every time we come in here, he doesn't want to leave."

Larsen, now standing on the stage, was trying to find his mark when Josh came down the right aisle and gave him some direction. After catching his breath and calming his nerves, Larsen transformed himself into Othello.

Josh signaled to Lisa that he was ready, and she made the call. "Action!"

Her father loved me, oft invited me;
Still questioned me the story of my life
From year to year—the battles, sieges, fortunes
That I have passed.
I ran it through, even from my boyish days
To th' very moment that he bade me tell it.
Wherein I spoke of most disastrous chances,
Of moving accidents by flood and field;
Of hairbreadth scapes i' the' imminent deadly breach;
Of being taken by the insolent foe

And sold to slavery; of my redemption thence
And portance in my travels' history;
Wherein of antres vast and deserts idle,
Rough quarries, rocks, and hills whose heads touch heaven,
It was my hint to speak—such was the process...

When he had finished, Arielle, Lisa, and Raphael applauded vigorously.

Arielle ran up onto the stage and hugged Larsen. "I expected you to have talent, but you never told me you were *this* good. You're a gifted actor, Larsen. I'm so proud of you. I know you have a passion for musical theater, but just to have this gift alone is a blessing. Wow. Just wow."

"Really? You thought I was good?"

"No, I thought you were fucking amazing. Excuse my French."

Arielle walked to the apron and leaned forward to speak to Josh. "Do you want another take?"

"Yes, please. I'm going to shoot from a different angle."

Arielle quickly left the stage to join her best friend. "Are you as enthralled as I am, Lis?"

"Just blown away. He's brilliant. And with training, he'll be world class. After this next take, Larsen can get back to work, then we'll walk around the theater, and I'll interview you."

"Sounds like a plan."

"Great. Say, Ari, what's up with your dog? He really wanted to get up on stage."

"You know, I think he's a wee bit jealous of Larsen. Muggins doesn't like to be upstaged. You know me, Lis. Doesn't it make sense that I'd get a dog who loves the theater?"

Lisa mulled over what had just been said to her. "Actually, it does. But all kidding aside, my inner voice, the one with the common sense, tells me there's more here than meets the eye."

Chapter 13

Sitting on one of Mystekal High's boulders in the bright morning sunshine, Larsen looked down at the paper in his hands and then looked up. With great intensity, he repeated the process several times. River, standing a distance away, watched his friend with interest and amusement before approaching him.

"Hey, dude. Looks like you're talking to yourself this ante meridiem."

Larsen looked up, using his hand as a visor to block the sun. "Say what, Riv?"

"Ante meridiem. A.M. Before noon." River sat down next to him. "What are you doing?"

Larsen laughed. "I'm working on a new monologue. There's a really cool speech at the end of Salinger's *Franny and Zooey*. I'm just figuring out what part of it I want to memorize. Brilliant stuff."

River opened his backpack and pulled out a poppy seed bagel in plastic wrap and a small container of orange juice. "Hey, my mom said you kicked ass on stage yesterday. Good for you."

"I was lucky, Riv. When your mom's friend Lisa asked me to perform something, I already knew this piece from *Othello*. I was flying high when your mom complimented me so much, but it also made me realize that I'd been neglecting my acting studies. I used to read plays all the time, but then my mom caught onto it, and you can imagine her reaction. She banned me from doing anything 'gay' in her house."

River unwrapped his bagel. "That blows. Speaking of your mother, have you talked to her yet?"

"Nope. What's that on your bagel?"

"Philadelphia Cream Cheese."

"Oh. They don't have any cream cheese in Los Angeles?"

River laughed. "It's a brand name, dude. Get with the program. I'd offer you half, but I'm starved. I'd never make it to lunch."

"That's okay. I had breakfast, and I wouldn't have given you half of mine either. In fact, if we were stranded in the woods, I wouldn't even let you taste my food. Actually, I wouldn't even let you see it!"

River laughed. "Good one. Glad we're on the same page. So, what about your mom? Seriously, you gonna call her?"

"And what? Tell her that I did a monologue from *Othello* and that I'm going to be in a promo trailer on TV? I'm still on such a high from it all; I can't let her bring me down."

"Just call her and leave that part out."

"How come you want me to call my mother so much? You know what she's like."

River, who had bitten off a bit more bagel than he could easily chew, waited a moment before responding. "Oh, I'm just figuring that she might call you and ream you out for not calling her. Just thinking maybe you'd want to stay one step ahead."

Larsen nodded. "Yeah, that's crossed my mind. I gotta think on it. No matter what I come up with, it all leads to the same place: being ripped to shreds. I really wish I could share my good news." Larsen put a bookmark in his copy of *Franny and Zooey* and tucked it in his backpack." Hey, look, Riv. Erik is coming over here. Wonder what he wants."

Wide-eyed, River washed down a smaller bite of bagel with

orange juice.

Erik kicked at the sand as he walked over to his two classmates. He looked anything but happy to be heading in their direction. He stopped just as he reached them and barely made eye contact. He looked first at Larsen. "Sorry for shovin' you the other day."

"Um … it's okay. I just wanted to help, but I should have—"

"Yo, look, I need your help. Both of youse." Erik looked directly at River.

"You need our help? My help? With Jax?"

"Fuck, no." Erik was appalled by the suggestion. "Look, I don't like askin' nobody for jack. But I'm doing this for my sister. Avalon. You two are the only ones in the school who I trust when it comes to her."

River looked alarmed. "Everything okay? What can we do?"

Angrily, Erik pulled a crumpled piece of paper out of his pocket, straightened it out, and then showed it to River and Larsen. Drawn on the paper was a stick figure with blue hair on one side and green on the other. Written in large red letters were the words "GO HOME JERSEY FREAK!"

Erik could see that both Larsen and River were as upset as he was. "Some dipshit taped this to her locker. She was just takin' it down when I came by. If I didn't see with my own two eyes, she wouldn't have showed me. Thinks I get too angry about shit. I don't know who put this fucking garbage on her locker, but you two are the only ones I'm ruling out. Someone needs a lead pipe shoved …"

River, trying to pretend he didn't hear what Erik almost said, reached for the piece of paper Erik held out to him and examined it. "Well, whatever ignoramus did this has obviously not been to Melrose Avenue or any other part of Hollywood. Nobody there would even notice that she looks any different from everyone else."

Erik nodded. "Yeah. Same back home. Pretty much. So, look,

I'm not asking youse to do anything but keep your eyes open, okay? She's not gonna tell you about this, so I needed to do it. I can't be everywhere at once, and I need to know I'm not the only one who's got her back."

River finished eating his bagel and stood up. "It's cool, Erik. She's got a friend in me. Lars, too. We'll watch out for her."

Erik thought for a minute. "And you'll tell me if you find out who did this, right?"

River nodded. "Dude, not if you're going to be wanting to shove lead pipes anywhere."

Larsen agreed. "Yeah, man. I'm not trying to get into your business, but don't you want to go back to Jersey when you graduate?"

"Hell, yeah! I *am* going back to Jersey."

"Then just chill with the bullies. Look, I've been bullied for being gay more times than I can count. I've wanted to punch out a few people, but it's not worth it. Seriously, man."

Erik bit his upper lip as he pondered what Larsen was saying. "I got nothing else to say. Just thanks for being my sister's friends."

Gina had noticed during lunch that River seemed preoccupied and concerned. Every time his eyes scanned the cafeteria, she knew he had to be looking for Avalon.

Bianca, who was sitting with Antonio only a table away, noticed the distress on her best friend's face. Gina wanted to text her but couldn't figure out how to do so inconspicuously. The tension was killing her.

"Hey, Riv. I know you're not looking for Larsen 'cause he just left the table two minutes ago. So, I'm guessing since she's nowhere in sight, you must be looking for Avalon."

"Uh, yeah. Someone kind of did something not so nice to her this morning, so I'm wondering if she's okay. I haven't seen her."

"What happened?"

"I can't really talk about it. I'm guessing she's outside. Do you mind if I go look for her?"

Gina shot a quick look to Bianca to transmit her unhappiness and then put on a happier face for River. "Um, sure. She's your friend. And she's mine, too."

River looked unconvinced.

"Really. We're friends. We even exchanged phone numbers. So of course I want her to be okay. I'll see you in history class."

River stood up, walked over to Gina, gave her a quick kiss on the lips, and smiled. "Thanks for understanding."

As he walked away, Gina, without even realizing it, began to clench her fists as her face tightened. Noticing, Bianca excused herself from Antonio and plopped herself into River's vacated seat. "Please don't tell me he went to look for her."

"Oh, yeah. He did. He said someone did something bad to her, and he has to go see if she's okay. She probably texted him something pathetic to get him away from me."

"I hope she doesn't make a habit of that. Say, Gin, you look like …"

"What, Bianca? What were you going to say?"

Bianca looked uneasy. "Oh, nothing."

"Liar. Tell me. And don't make me beat it out of you because I'm already way too stressed for that."

"Okay, okay. I was just gonna say that you kind of look like your sister right now. You know, all pissed off like you want to kill someone."

Gina looked down at her clenched fists as the color drained from her face. "Oh, shit. I don't want to be like Taylor. I'm nothing like her. But come on, that doesn't mean I like to see some other girl cozying up to my boyfriend."

Bianca leaned in. "Like I told you on Monday. Be a lover, not a fighter. Hey, are you hearing me, Gina? It's not rocket science. It's just showing your guy a little lurve …"

"I hear you. I just wanted to wait a bit. Taylor never waited. I just never wanted to be like her."

Bianca sighed. "Your sister went from one guy to the next just to have someone. You're nothing like that, so don't even go there. Now, listen, you want to keep your guy? Or do you want to make it easy for Miss New Jersey to grab him?"

River had no problem finding Avalon. She was sitting on the farthest boulder from the school, looking off into the mountains. He sat down next to her, but she didn't acknowledge him. River noticed telltale tear stains on her cheeks, and her vacant stare unsettled him. "Hey, Avalon. Feel like talking to a friend?"

After several seconds, Avalon slowly turned her head to look at him. "Nuh uh."

"Erik told Lars and me what happened." River could see the surprise in Avalon's eyes. "Yeah, you know your brother is worried about you when he comes to talk to us. He showed us the toxic waste taped on your locker from the school's welcoming committee."

Avalon reached into her backpack and pulled out another crumpled ball of paper. "Bet you don't know anything about this one."

River looked alarmed. "What's that?"

"Just something I pulled off Larsen's locker on the way to my own. He doesn't need to know about it. Swear you won't tell him, River."

Opening the note, River's mouth dropped open, then he read

it out loud. " 'I hear that that Larsen Davis blows dead cows. But that's not true. I saw one move.' "

River was boiling. "I'm not the violent type, but I swear I'd like to get my hands on whoever is behind this bullshit. I'm not so sure it's not Jax or one of his lackeys. He's already got it in for Lars, and after meeting your brother the other day, well, what better way to stick it to him than to bully his kid sister. But I'm not sure."

Avalon looked into River's eyes. "When I pulled this off Larsen's locker, I heard some snickering around the corner, so I'm thinking that it wasn't just one person involved."

"You know, when an ignoramus decides to throw a bully party, there are always plenty of idiots that are happy to show up. You hear me? And don't worry, I'm not going to tell Lars. I just want it to stop."

Avalon played with the bangles on her arm. "Yeah, like these punk losers are really gonna quit this shit."

"Like Lars told your brother this morning, when you don't react, it's no fun for them. Bullies only enjoy themselves when someone else is miserable. Sort of like how vampires need blood. So, whatever you're feeling, you can't let them see that they've gotten to you."

Avalon sniffled. "Why do you think I'm sitting as far away from school as I can? I hate it here. You and Larsen are seniors. You'll be out of this lame-ass institution in June. I'll be here for another two and a half years. My dad's job is supposed to last just about that long."

"I get how you feel, Avalon. But a whole lot can happen in that time. You just have to focus on something else."

"Yeah? Like what? My mom who tricked my dad into moving to LA so she could dump us for her boyfriend when we got here?"

"I can feel your pain on that one."

"Yeah, well, everything worked out for your parents, but it

will never work out for mine. And don't forget what else my mom did. She faked a hate campaign against me to force my dad to leave JC. Did your mom ever do anything even close to that?"

River had no answer.

"No, of course she didn't. Who cares? She is dead to me anyway. Not only did I lose a mom, I lost my love of painting. My maternal unit made it into something evil. I can't help it that I have this weird gift for painting the future."

"No, of course you—"

"And my dad and my brother are just so angry I barely recognize them, and I have to be like a mother to Isabella. And she's only two years younger than me. She cries all the time because she misses her friends so much. I miss mine, too. Especially my boyfriend."

"You have a boyfriend?"

"Yeah, Anthony. Been with him for a year and two months. But I don't think it's gonna last. Not that he isn't chocolate cake with awesome sauce, but long-distance, high school romances don't exactly have a track record for um ... long ... um ... long... "

"Longevity."

"Yeah, that freakin' word. Fuck it. Whatever."

River stood up and reached out his hand. "C'mon, Avalon. Let's get back inside. I don't want to raise any red flags in Bullyland. Please, will you come with me?"

Reluctantly, Avalon held out her hand to River, who pulled her up. "I hate my life. What's left of it."

"It'll get better. I really wish you'd think about painting again."

Avalon walked alongside River as they headed back toward the main doors of the school. "Did anything bad ever happen to you because of what you drew?"

River thought for a moment. "Hell, yeah. Once my aunt Stella ripped me a new one because I drew her dead boyfriend from twenty years ago. She went totally ballistic on me."

"Wow."

"Yeah, and my dad had to call the cops, and they used the jaws of life to pull her off me when she tackled me with Krazy Glue smeared all over the front of her. It was a tense operation to yank her away before the glue hardened."

Avalon laughed. "You so took a wrong turn into Bullshitland, Riv."

"Well, the first part of it was true."

"I figured that. Whatever. You made me laugh, and that ain't happ'ning too much these days."

"Guess who?"

Gina loved it when River snuck behind her and covered her eyes. She loved the way their bodies felt so close together. "Well, I'm not quite sure who you are, but I can tell you have really handsome hands."

River burst out laughing. "Ha ha. Did you just say I had handsome hands?"

Red-faced, Gina couldn't stop the tears of laughter. "I was going to say that you had really nice hands and that you must be handsome, but it all came out together. That sounds so ridiculous! That's probably the stupidest thing I've ever said."

River was still hysterical when his classmates Jerome and Duffie walked by and said hello. "Hey, Gina just told me I had handsome hands. What do you guys think?" He held up his hands for display.

Gina was still laughing. "You are totally embarrassing me, River."

Duffie was eager to play along. "Wow, River! Mystekal's greatest treasure, and none of us had a clue. Don't you think so, Jerome?"

With a smile on his face, Jerome nodded. "Oh, yeah. Might want to think about having a bronze statue made. Put it in the trophy cabinet in the lobby or something. Hey, better yet, have a larger-than-life statue made and stick it outside the school. Peace out, Riv. Don't let your hands go to your head."

As Jerome and Duffie walked down the hall, River turned to Gina. "You know, I always thought my knuckles were pretty rad, but I just never dared to dream that the entirety of my multifingered extremities would be worthy of such prodigious praise. You know, I've gone through life thinking I'd never be appreciated for all of my gifts, and then a beautiful girl tells me that I have handsome hands, and it completely changes my perspective on life and the role I play in this vast and complex universe. I'm no longer a grain of sand on the beach or the blink of an eye in eternity. I'm a dude with handsome hands."

Gina closed her locker door. "They seriously broke the mold when they made you, Riv. Come on, let me hold one of those handsome hands."

River took Gina's hand in his and walked down the hall toward the front doors of the school. With his free hand, he pushed open the door, and the two walked into the shining afternoon sun.

"Are you going to walk me home?"

"Sure, Gin. I just can't hang today because my dad's off early, and we're going to be looking at art schools."

Gina's face fell. "Are you looking at schools far away?"

"Nah. No farther than LA probably. How about you? Haven't you started planning what you're going to do after graduation?"

"Sure. I'm thinking that I want to learn another language besides Spanish so that I can work with kids. I haven't quite figured out in what capacity, though. But I don't have to make any decisions about my entire life right now, you know? I just need to know where the starting line is."

"That sounds solid."

Gina smiled. The sun's rays felt good on her face, and River's hand felt so comforting in hers. About ten minutes away from school, Gina finally got up her nerve to say what was on her mind. She stopped walking and looked at him. "Hey, Riv. Um … I was wondering if you would come to dinner at my house on Saturday night."

"Sure. Just you and your parents?"

"Uh, actually, just me. My parents are going to LA Saturday morning to visit Taylor. It's one of the rare times I get the house to myself, and believe it or not, I can actually cook."

"Oh, yeah? Can you make tuna casserole? That's the first meal my mom whipped up for us when she came back home."

"Seriously? Is that what you want?"

River chuckled. "Not exactly. I want whatever you want to make. Just not big on fish."

"No way I would make fish. Ever. Maybe some spaghetti with Bolognese sauce or something along those lines. I'm pretty good with Italian cooking."

River put his arm around Gina and squeezed her tight. "Will you let me stir the pot?"

Gina felt every inch of her body go crazy in anticipation. "Absolutely, handsome hands. You can stir to your heart's content."

Chapter 14

Erik leaned against the wall and spoke softly on his cell phone. "Yeah, baby. I'm just sort of watching my sister's locker when I can. It's lunchtime here, and empty hallways are breeding grounds for cowardly scum to do their shit … Yeah, for real. Our mother did enough to traumatize Avvie for life. She was like the hot fudge sundae of destruction, and these douches are tryin' to be the cherry on top."

Hearing footsteps, Erik looked up to see Jax fast approaching with a smirk plastered on his face. "I gotta go. Call you later … love you, too."

Fearlessly, Jax walked up to Erik. "Well, I've been hoping for a chance to catch you alone, birthday boy. You're twenty fucking years old today according to your New Joisey driver's license. And here you are in fucking high school. I hope you're not planning on flunking out again because you really don't want to spend the big two-one here, do you?"

Seething, Erik stepped on Jax's right foot, bearing down. "Yeah, I'm twenty, and how the fuck old are you? Ten? Shouldn't you still be in the fourth grade? Your body may have grown up, but it forgot to send a memo to your brain, asswipe."

Refusing to show fear, Jax continued to torment the newcomer. "So, why don't you come into the cafeteria? I'll buy you a cupcake, and we'll all sing happy boithday to you while I shove the cake down your throat until you choke on it."

Erik had promised himself not to let anyone get the better of him. But he was nearly ready to break his own word as Jax sneered and laughed in his face. "And after you're done singing to me, how 'bout I take a knife and castrate you?"

Jax laughed. "Yeah, right."

Erik put his hands on Jax's shoulders and swung him around until his back was pinned against a locker, once again, only with greater force than the first time. "I think I can perform a little surgery right here in the hall. Won't take me but a minute, desert boy."

Now frightened but trying not to show it, Jax tried to muscle his way loose. "Take your hands off of me, Jersey scum."

Pushing harder, Erik was unrelenting. "I'm gonna teach you a lesson you'll never forget!"

"Nooooooo! Stop!"

Erik turned to find an attractive young woman he'd never seen before. She looked to be just about the same age as he was.

"Break it up, guys. Now. Before you're both really sorry."

The second Erik broke his grip, Jax hurried away, but Erik was intrigued. "And who are you? Like a student teacher or something?"

"I'm the 'or something,' I guess. I'm Jinxsy Patterson."

Erik stared at her. "Uh, yeah. I know who you are. You're Ms. Carrow's daughter, and you own a big piece of this desert paradise. You're my dad's boss. Or at least one of them."

Jinxsy scanned her brain for data. "Okay, you must be one of Gabe Martelli's kids. Did you want to tell me your first name, or should I just do a Henry Sledge and call you Mr. Martelli?"

"Oh, sorry. Erik. Call me Erik."

"Erik. Okay, well, listen, I know all about Jax Reinhardt. He was a sophomore when I was a senior here. He was a bully then, and

I know he's a bigger one now. He just came off a suspension, right? He's treading water by messing with you. But what's your excuse? I'm gonna be really honest, Erik. When I met your dad, he told me that your girlfriend back home was expecting your child and that you're going to be a father. Did I get that right?"

"Yeah."

"C'mon. Take a walk with me to Eve's classroom. We need to have a talk."

Eve and Jinxsy embraced while Erik walked sheepishly into the room and stood by the door. Noticing him for the first time, Eve looked at Erik, then at Jinxsy. "What's going on here?"

With a nod of the head, Jinxsy motioned for Erik to come closer. "Don't be shy. Take a seat. We'll have a little group chat. Doesn't that sound like a blast?"

Having no idea what to make of Jinxsy or her request, Erik tentatively pulled up a classroom chair and sat down, then crossed his arms defensively in expectation.

Eve looked at Jinxsy. "You never do anything without a really good reason, so tell me, what's going on here?"

"Oh, not too much. Only a few minutes ago, I happened to catch Erik just as he was about to kill Jax Reinhardt in the hall."

Eve bit her lower lip as she contemplated her daughter's words. "I see. Is that an accurate assessment, Erik?"

"Yeah. Whatever. Maybe."

Jinxsy turned to Eve. "Gabe Martelli, Erik's dad, told me, on the day that Arielle and I hired him, that Erik is going to be a father in May and that he can't wait to graduate and move back east to be with his family. And to marry his girlfriend."

"Oh, wow. I didn't know that."

Erik looked nervous. "Well, my old man should have kept his mouth shut, but do me a favor and don't broadcast this. I don't need any more bullshit."

Jinxsy cleared her throat. "No, you certainly don't need any more bullshit. Who does need bullshit? I know I don't. So, for someone who doesn't want to ride the bullshit train, why were you hopping aboard with the school bully? Because all bullshit trains end up at the You're Effed station. Is that where you want to go? Do you seriously want to give that guy power over you and your future? Really? Or do you want to graduate and get the hell out of here?"

Embarrassed, Erik put his hand to his forehead and wiped off the beads of sweat. "I want to graduate and go back home."

Eve jumped in. "Then listen to my daughter and stay out of Jax's way. I understand why you would want to respond in kind to someone who is provoking you, but you have way too much to lose."

"Yeah, Ms. Carrow. I hear you. It's just ... uh ... really hard for me to put up with crap. Something in my blood just makes me forget everything that matters and live in the moment. I almost pounded that dick last week, but Larsen stopped me."

"Really? Larsen broke up a fight between you and Jax?"

"Yeah."

Jinxsy looked momentarily confused. "I don't think I know Larsen. Oh, he's the kid Arielle hired as her assistant, right?"

Erik nodded. "Yeah, he's workin' at the theater with that lady and my dad."

Eve smiled. "Well, I'm glad Larsen stood up for you, but in the future, I hope you will both avoid Jax. If he keeps this up, he'll end up getting expelled all on his lonesome."

"I know, Ms. Carrow. Sometimes it's just so hard ..."

Jinxsy laughed. "Oh, don't I know it. You should have known me in high school. I was the warrior child. I still am, but I've grown up a lot. On my seventeenth birthday, I found out that my parents were keeping a major secret from me. To fast forward for a sec, the secret turned out to be that I was adopted. But that night, before I ran off, I had no idea that Eve had given birth to me and the mom who raised me was mentally ill. But that's another story. Anyway, I just knew there was a big secret they'd been keeping under wraps for years. I was so pissed at them that I escaped through my bedroom window and ran out into the desert. Not gonna get into it, but I came way too close to being raped and killed. Seriously. I get what it's like to want to act first and think later. But if you make a mistake, it can be a life changer. Sometimes you just need to chill." Jinksy took a moment to slow herself down. "And FYI, I don't normally divulge my business to strangers, but I'm making an exception here for several reasons."

Eve turned to Erik. "Jinxsy is giving you excellent advice. Listen, I know it's none of my business, but I just need to ask you something. You can tell me to butt out. I'll respect that."

Erik was intrigued. "What do you want to know?"

"This young woman who's carrying your child: are you in love with her, or are you marrying her to do the right thing?"

"I don't mind answering that, Ms. Carrow, because I love Carrie Lynn with all my heart. We've been together for three and a half years. She's everything to me. Yeah, I wanna marry her and be a good husband and father to our child. I would marry her even if she wasn't carrying our baby. How come you're asking?"

"Okay, well, I wouldn't ordinarily share this with my students, but like my daughter, I think I can help. You're also older than my other students and a father to be. That alone makes a big difference."

"What is it, Ms. Carrow?"

Eve glanced at the door to make sure nobody else had come into the room. "I didn't know this until a few years ago, but my mother's parents and my evil father's parents got together and forced them to marry one another when they were both just a bit younger than you."

Erik was stunned by his teacher's openness. "Day-um. Why's that?"

"Apparently my mother's family was desperate to have their only child marry into money, and no doubt my father's family wanted to make sure he married a beautiful woman of their choosing. She came from a poor family, but she was well educated, unbelievably gorgeous, and had a lot of class. The Carrows wanted to control my father's future, and I suppose that's why he spent his life controlling everyone else. Anyway, Jinxsy and I wouldn't be here if that marriage hadn't been forced, but it was sheer hell for my mother. I just want to make sure that it's what you really want."

Without hesitation, Erik responded, "Yeah. It's what I really want."

Jinxsy smiled. "Good. Then you'll take my advice and put your future wife and child's welfare, and your own, ahead of Jax Reinhardt's bullshit. It should be a no-brainer. I know it's easier said than done when someone pisses you off, but you can't afford to mess up. You know?"

"No, I can't. So, what's your deal? Aside from owning half of this town, what else do you do?"

"I'm earning my business degree. Thought it might come in handy just a smidge."

Erik hinted at a smile. "Yeah. For sure. Good choice."

"I'm happy with it. And how about you, Erik? What do you plan to do when you get back east?"

"When I was younger, I wanted to be a corrections officer on Riker's Island. That's until I met a dude who actually was one. When he told me what his average day was like, I was like… whoa, I don't need to be in a chamber of horrors just to make a living. The guy told me that a lot of the officers bring all the anger and rage home with them. I got enough on my own that I'm tryin' to get rid of, you know? My dad is really talented, and he has a whole lot of connections in the building industry. So I'll probably start there and see what happens. But I never want to see Riker's Island. Not as a CO or a prisoner. Enough shit goin' down on the outside."

As the bell rang to signal the end of lunch, Erik stood up and extended his hand to Jinxsy, who eagerly shook with him. "You're okay, Jinxsy. Too bad you don't live back east. You and Carrie Lynn would like each other. I'd introduce youse two. Thanks for being there."

Erik hurried out of Eve's classroom and closed the door behind him. Turning to Jinxsy, Eve's eyes sparkled. "Have I told you today how much I love you?"

Jinxsy stood up and walked over to Eve, still sitting in the chair, and wrapped her arms around her. "I kind of love you, too."

Eve drummed the desk with her forefingers. "Come on, catch me up on everything. First, are you here for the weekend?"

"Yeah, I am. I haven't spent time with Jess in ages, and I want to hang out with you and Grandmomma, too. I'm sorry I didn't tell you I was coming sooner. It was kind of last minute."

Eve looked concerned. "Is everything okay?"

"Yeah, sure. School's fine. My love life is showing promise. I'm cool. You told me in your last email that all of the building projects were on schedule and budget. Anything weird or bizarre to report?"

"Nope. Don't think so, Jinxsy."

"Really? No more ghosts in our fair town of Mystekal?"

Eve cracked up. "No, honey, I'm afraid we're just a normal desert town now."

Chapter 15

"Hey, am I disturbing you?"

Larsen looked up from his laptop to see Gabe standing over him. "No, it's cool. I'm just looking at vintage theater posters. Mrs. D wants to hang them in the restrooms and the lobby. There are so many here, and it's hard to choose. I definitely want to use one or two from the vaudeville era. I just have to be sure not to confuse old movies for theatrical productions, you know?"

"I'm sure you'll do just fine. Listen, I just wanted to thank you for being good to my kids. Erik said you and Arielle's kid are the only ones in the school he can trust. You got their back; I've got yours."

"Sure, Gabe. I like Avalon and Erik. I know he doesn't want to be here, but I can see he's a good guy. And Avalon is sweet."

Gabe was about to respond when his cell phone rang. He pulled it from his shirt pocket and walked back down to his desk at the opposite end of the trailer. He was talking softly, but Larsen was still able to hear him.

"Listen, you need to stop calling me. How many times do I have to tell you that? I've changed my mind about everything. I'm seeing something very different from what you told me … I don't really care. I'm not getting involved in whatever bullshit you've got planned. I want no part of it. You don't need to call me again, or I might just start talking … yeah, well—"

Larsen could see that someone had hung up on Gabe, and he pretended not to hear the stream of expletives that Gabe mumbled as he put his phone back in his shirt pocket.

Gabe walked back to Larsen's desk. "You know where Arielle is?"

"Yeah, she went into the theater to talk to the guys before they leave for the day. Do you need her?"

"No, I just wanted to say good night and wish her a good weekend. Will you do that for me, Larsen?"

"Sure thing."

"Same to you. Thanks again. Well, it's five-thirty, so I'm gonna hightail it outta here. See you next week."

Larsen went back to work, taking screenshots of his favorite posters, including his beloved *West Side Story,* and putting them in a folder to review later with Arielle. About ten minutes later, Arielle and Muggins returned to the trailer. Muggins ran over to Larsen and jumped all over him as if he hadn't seen his friend in days.

"Hey, Lars. How's it coming?"

Larsen laughed as he tried to keep Muggins from licking the entirety of his face. "Fabulous. I'm having the most fun of my life, and I can't believe you're paying me to do this. I'm just thinking how awesome it would have been to see these shows back in the day, you know?"

"Maybe someday we'll produce one of them here. Did Gabe leave?"

"Yeah, he said to say good-bye and that he'll see you on Monday."

"Okay. I can talk to him then. Muggins, get down. Muggins!"

"Don't worry, Mrs. D. We're cool. Just best buddies."

Muggins, with all fours on the floor again, sat down by Arielle's chair and looked up at Larsen.

Arielle shuffled through the stacks of materials on her desk.

"Oh, darn. I can't find that catalog of vintage knobs you ordered from the specialty hardware store for me. Have you seen it?"

"Yeah, it was tucked under your arm when you went into the theater to talk to the guys."

Arielle smacked her forehead with the palm of her hand. "Duh! Of course! What would I do without you, Lars? Do you mind going into the theater and tracking it down for me? I'm sure I left it lying around somewhere."

"Sure. No problem." Larsen stood up, and Muggins did the same.

"Well, I guess you've got company! See you boys in a few."

📖📖📖

Larsen was surprised to find that it was growing dark already. Daylight savings time had ended a few days ago, and that always took some getting used to. He hurried over to the back door of the theater. Once he and Muggins were inside, he stopped to answer his phone only to find that it was not ringing. But the music from the Broadway version of "Tonight" continued to play. Larsen remembered what Lisa had said earlier in the week about hearing the song. It had freaked him out, but he had forgotten about it. Probably because it was too bizarre to comprehend, he thought.

"W-Woof."

Looking down at Muggins, Larsen saw that the dog's ears were perked up, and his tail was up, wagging. "What is it, boy? Damn. I wish you could talk."

Still standing just inside the theater, to Larsen's left, were stairs that led upstairs to the dressing rooms and wardrobe room. Across from him was the closed door with a stairway behind it that led to the basement-level rehearsal area, kitchen, lounge, and set storage. The thought of going either upstairs or downstairs unnerved him. These were not the areas currently being worked on, and he imagined them dead from disuse and dulled from dormant dreams that had nestled in for a forty-year sleep.

Standing by an old board of faded messages, notices, and announcements, contemplating his fears, he noticed that Muggins was a lot more interested in what was happening in the backstage area.

Feeling goose bumps form on his skin, he decided against walking down the breezeway to the stage. Instead, he reasoned that going into the main hall of the theater would allow him to get a look at the entire stage from front to back, as the curtains had just been taken down. Gently holding Muggins by the collar, Larsen walked straight ahead, pulling the dog to the door of the auditorium.

Once inside, he spied Arielle's hardware catalog on the apron of the stage, to the left. Slowly, Larsen began walking toward the steps to the left of the stage. As he walked, "Tonight" became louder and louder.

Muggins ears were now pointing forward. His mouth was opened slightly, and he began to pant. Larsen noticed that his legs were bent, poised to charge ahead. "Who's there, boy?"

Just as Larsen put his foot on the first step, he heard a scream, followed by cries of anguish. As Larsen stepped back, Muggins raced up the steps and toward the back of the stage. Now center stage, Muggins began to sniff frantically, but there was no sign of anyone. The music had stopped, and an eerie silence embraced the theater.

Larsen looked at Muggins. His ears were laid back on his head, and his tail was between his legs. He was shivering.

Looking around just one more time and seeing no one at all, Larsen raced up the stage stairs, ran over to the catalog, grabbed it, and then, with Muggins behind him, walked quickly toward the backstage area. As he passed the part of the stage that Muggins had been so interested in, he felt a distinct chill, as if that one spot was a good twenty or thirty degrees colder than the rest of the theater. But he didn't stop to investigate the reason. Taking a sharp turn to his left, he headed down the breezeway to the back door. Once outside, it was now dark and cold. Hurrying toward the light of the trailer, which seemed to him like finding a port in the storm, Larsen ran until he and Muggins were safely inside.

📖📖📖

"Welcome home, Larsen. Did you have a good day at work?"

Larsen was tempted to tell Kathryn about his end-of-the-day fright, but he thought better of it. His story was so fantastic that he began to wonder if his imagination hadn't played a powerful trick on him. Perhaps his subconscious was acting on what Lisa had said about hearing "Tonight" playing. But if that were the case, how could her mind have known to play the same tricks on her? And why? No, it had to have happened. But that was just it. What had happened?

Larsen took a seat next to Kathryn on the couch. "Uh, it was a really interesting day."

"Was it? Will you share with me?"

"Oh, just that Mrs. D put me in charge of selecting and ordering vintage posters for the theater. Well, I'm going to do an initial selection, and then together we're going to decide which ones to buy. It's just so amazing to even have a part in something like this. To have my opinion matter, you know?"

Kathryn's eyes twinkled. "I do. Your passion for theater reminds me so much of the joy that Peter got from his activities. He started acting when he was just eleven."

Larsen looked over at the framed photos on the end table. "You have so many cool photos of him in costume. And he's smiling in every single one."

"Yes, he smiled a lot. I'll tell you, Larsen, some people go an entire lifetime and never find anything to be passionate about. Peter was born with a passion, just like you. I had some dreams once upon a time, but Peter's death destroyed them."

"I'm so sorry."

"Don't feel bad for me. I've made the best out of the life I have. And I refuse to have the conversation turn maudlin every time we chat about the theater. So let's not do that. Now, how do you feel about ordering in some pizza? After a long week behind the counter, I need a short break."

"Oh, you never have to cook for me! And you don't have to buy me pizza."

"I love cooking for you. For us. It's been a long time since I've had company at dinner. Besides, what I do at the school isn't very exciting. As for ordering pizza, I haven't done that in years. The smallest pizza I can order is way too much for me. Will you let me place an order? What do you like on your pizza?"

"Pretty much anything except anchovies."

"Ha! Peter didn't like them either. Larsen, are you okay? You look a little shaken ... nervous."

Larsen silently chastised himself for letting any trace of the theater incident show. "Uh, no. I'm fine. Really. It's just been a long week. Are you okay? Because now that I look at you, I'm thinking you look a little nervous, too. Or are we both going nuts together?"

Kathryn laughed, then abruptly stopped. "You're very astute. Actually, there is something, and I am feeling a bit nervous."

"Tell me. What is it?"

"Well, when I got home earlier, I noticed this old blue Toyota across the street. And it wasn't the first time, either. It was there on Monday and then again today. The first time I saw it, I didn't pay any attention to it. But today, it was closer to the house. And I saw a woman behind the wheel, and—"

"And you think she's my mother, right?"

"Well, yes, I do. I thought you might notice the car when you came home, but it's parked in front of our neighbor's pickup truck, so it would be easy to miss."

"I'm going to check it out. But I'm going to do it from upstairs where there aren't any lights on." Larsen jumped up, raced up the stairs, and came back within a minute and stood on the landing. "Uh, yeah. That's my mom."

"Doesn't she work on Fridays and Saturdays?"

"Yeah. She's usually off Sundays and Mondays. But sometimes she works on her day off for someone else and then gets a different day off. You know, she switches around. Yeah, that's what she does, and, uh … yeah, so I'm wondering what she wants."

"Most likely to see her son. I'm sure she misses you."

"Yeah, but … sorry, I know I'm kind of rambling all over the place. I'm really nervous. I'm not sure what to do."

"I think maybe you should go out and see her. If you want."

Larsen, still standing at the foot of the stairs, walked over to the front door, opened it, and walked outside. He crossed the street and walked to the passenger side of his mother's Toyota Corolla.

Raylene lowered the window. "She told you I was out here, didn't she? You sure as hell didn't look in this direction when you came home."

"Yeah, Mom. Kathryn told me you were out here. At least she thought it was you."

"Well, seein' a black lady sitting outside her house in an old car couldn't have been too much of a mystery for her now, could it? You come sit in the car and talk to me."

Larsen looked nervous. "Um … are you—"

"Am I what, boy? Don't tell me you think I'm gonna kidnap you or something!" Raylene took the keys out of the ignition and handed them out the window to Larsen. "There. Now you trust me? Come sit in this car with me and stop your paranoid nonsense."

Larsen walked around the front of the car, opened the passenger door, and got inside. His mother was right; he didn't trust her. He held her keys in his right hand so she couldn't snatch them and drive off.

Noticing the way he held the keys irritated her. "You really don't trust me, do you? Why the hell would I do something stupid and take off with you in this car? I got a job to go to. And I don't need any more damn trouble with the police, thanks to you."

Larsen, who could barely meet his mother's intense gaze, thought for a moment before responding. "I didn't get you in trouble with the police. You and Reggie did that on your own."

"Don't you be dissing me and my man."

"Oh, so I guess you're still together."

"Of course we are. You think Raylene Davis can't keep a man? Yeah, we're still together despite your efforts to break us up."

"I never tried to break you up."

"Don't lie to me, boy. You made up that story about Reggie's dead wife being alive. You know, in this day and age, it's not very hard to find out what's true and what's not. The lady passed away years ago. Just like he said. So why don't you tell me why you made that story up?"

Telling his mother what he now believed to be the truth, that Martha Joy was a ghost, was not something he would even think to attempt. He would just have to let her think he'd been lying.

"Mom, how come you're here?"

"I'll ask the questions. How come you haven't called your mama since you moved into this big house with this old white lady?"

"Well, I was gonna call you, but then a week ago, on Halloween, you sent me that text. That was pretty nasty, Mom. Mean. Why would I want to call you after that?"

Raylene had no intention of answering the question. "What are you doing with your life now that you're livin' the high life? And

I hope you got my message that I ain't paying your cell phone anymore."

"Yeah, I got it, Mom. It was in that charming text you sent me on Halloween. I don't need you to pay it. I have a job."

"Oh, helllllll no! Don't tell me you went and took that gay job!"

"It's not a gay job, Mom. It's just a job. I work in a trailer behind a theater with River's mother and a guy who's a vintage restoration specialist. I'm actually learning something about building restoration. That's not gay, is it?"

Raylene looked pensive. "Well, no. Not that part of it. I suppose that's a good part. Depends on the guy you're working with. Does he bat for your team?"

Larsen clenched his teeth. "No, he's straight. He's got three kids. Two of them go to Mystekal High. The other one's in the middle school."

"What do you do on this job?"

As much as he wanted to share his enthusiasm for selecting vintage theater posters, Larsen knew his mother wouldn't want to hear about it. "Well, I help Mrs. D coordinate everything having to do with the renovation. It's her job to choose all of the materials that will go in the theater, right down to the hardware. I get samples and catalogs for her. I run errands. That kind of stuff."

"You go to hardware stores?"

"Yeah, Mom. Why?"

"Maybe you could get a job there instead. With some manly men."

"Mom, I didn't get into this car for more gay bashing. If that's all you want to talk about, me being gay, then I'm going back into the house. I'm not going to apologize for who I am or what I do. I have a really good job, and I'm learning a lot of great skills. I'd think you'd be happy about that."

" 'Spose so."

"So how come you're not working tonight? Did you switch with someone?"

"Yeah, Mr. Nosy. I did. Reggie Lee is taking me to Palm Desert for the weekend. A fella he works with got him a complimentary room at a spa resort. So I'm off to have a good time, and I wanted to see my son before I left. I worked last Sunday for a girl, and now she's taking my shift. Anything else? Speak now, boy. What else do you want to know?"

"Just wondering if we could ever have a conversation without my sexual orientation being a part of it."

"Oh, damn. Don't be mentioning sex to me. If you go find some nice girl to get it on with, you can tell me all about that, and I'll be one proud mama."

"Really? So what if I were straight and didn't use any protection and got a girl pregnant or caught an STD? Would that make you proud?"

Raylene's response was barely audible. "Be better than this."

Larsen wiped a tear from his eye with his wrist while his hand felt sore from having Raylene's car keys in his grasp. "Here, Mom. Here are your keys. I hope you and Reggie have a great weekend."

"You cutting out on me already?"

"If you ever decide to accept me for who I am, let me know, okay?"

As Raylene squinted her angry eyes, Larsen got out of the car, shut the door, and ran behind the car and back into the house.

Chapter 16

"Wait, Riv! Don't eat that yet!"

River looked down at the plate of spaghetti Bolognese Gina had placed in front of him. "Okay, I'll bite. I mean, no, I won't bite. Why not?"

Gina giggled. "I forgot to take the bay leaves out of the sauce. They're just for flavor, then you discard them."

Reaching for the only visible bay leaf he could find, River plucked it out of the pasta. "Are you telling me that I can't eat this? Because I've had my eye on this sucker for at least ten seconds. Look at the succulent juices dripping from this leaf."

"Bay leaves don't have juices."

"Exactly! That's what makes this one so special. And here you are, trying to deny me the pleasure of savoring this …um … leaf."

Coyly, Gina looked into River's eyes. "I wouldn't want to ever deny you any pleasure."

River reached out through the candlesticks on the table and grabbed Gina's hand. "You mean that, baby? You don't want to deny me any pleasures?"

Gina smiled crookedly, trying not to let her nerves get the best of her. "That's right."

River caressed her hand. "That's so sexy of you. And that's exactly why I'm going to eat this bay leaf." Before Gina could say another word, River popped the leaf into his mouth and began chewing.

"O ... M ... G! I can't believe you're eating that."

Trying not to laugh, or choke, River chewed the leaf as best he could and then swallowed it. "Yum. Bay leaf Bolognese. You're the best cook ever!"

"Oh, no, you are so not going to tell people I made bay leaf Bolognese for you, are you? I'm still trying to forget I said 'handsome hands.' So, how was it?"

"Crunchy, for one. And kind of sharp. As in pointy. But the tomato sauce helped it to go down easier. I think I'm going to have to wash this delicacy down with water." River picked up his glass of water and drank nearly all of it at once.

Gina blushed. "Will you please eat the meal I did make for you? I want to know if you like it."

"I'm sure I will. I told you, I'm fine with anything but fish."

"I'm not that big on seafood either. Were you forced to eat fish as a kid or something?"

"Nah. My parents never forced me to eat anything. But when I was a little kid, we went for dinner to the home of these people who worked with my dad. Me, Jess, Mom, Dad, and Aunt Stella. Anyway, the lady served us this big fish on a platter. She decorated the plate with lemon wedges and parsley. Oh, yeah, and cherry tomatoes. But the fish still had this big freakin' eyeball in it. I swear the damn thing winked at me."

"You're so funny, River. It did not."

"Well, it completely freaked me out. Now, in case you hadn't noticed, I kind of say what's on my mind, and I was even worse when I was a kid."

"Oh, gee, I never noticed."

"Ha ha. Yeah, right. So, anyway, I blurted out that the fish was staring at me and said that there was no way I was eating it. My parents were real embarrassed, Aunt Stella didn't care, and Jess felt the same way I did. The lady was so eager to be a good hostess that she took this big spoon out of the bowl of vegetables and just scooped the eyeball out."

"No way!"

"Yes way. Only it fell off the spoon right into my mom's glass of red wine. Mom screamed and knocked the wine glass over, ruining the lady's new tablecloth. Then Jess started screaming and knocked over Dad's wine. Then I started screaming, and I was so freaked out that I yanked the tablecloth off the table. Oh, man. Plates and food were flying everywhere. The one-eyed fish flew into the air and got stuck in the chandelier. The lady wasn't too happy by that point. She ran into the kitchen, grabbed a meat cleaver, and chased us all out of the house, calling us uncultivated lowlife plebian scum. So, that's kind of why I don't eat fish."

"You are so full of shit, River. But that's hysterical. What makes you even think of things like that?"

"I like to make up eyeball stories." River twirled the spaghetti around his fork and tasted it. "Hey, this is actually really good."

"Of course it is. What were you expecting?"

"I wasn't thinking about the food. I just like being with you. And by the way, the fish story is partially true. The lady did scoop out the eyeball. Just the rest of it … um … maybe not so much."

Gina daintily wiped the sauce from her lips. "You're the most different guy I've ever met."

River was embarrassed. "I'm just me. This is really good. I like the salad you made, too."

📖📖📖

Gina adjusted the dimmer switch in the living room and turned the lights down low. She put a couple of CDs into the changer and sat down on the couch next to River. She rested her head on his chest and was ecstatic when he put his arm around her and pulled her closer.

"Thanks for that amazing meal. Believe it or not, I do know you went to a lot of work making that. The pasta was fantastic. Those cannolis were delish."

Gina looked up at River. "I have a confession to make."

River laughed. "Does it have anything to do with Stinelli's Bakery?"

"How did you know where I bought them?"

"Hey, this is Mystekal. We don't have any bakery wars going on here. My aunt Stella loves that place."

"You're just such a been-there, done-that guy. I mean, I really have to think hard to find something you haven't tried before."

River stroked Gina's hair. "Yeah. You just might, sweet thing."

"How about this?" Gina turned to face River, folded her arms behind his neck, and then pulled him down. In one fluid movement, River was on top of her, kissing her deeply.

As his tongue slowly explored her mouth, Gina could feel his arousal, and every part of her tingled as she experienced something she'd only dreamed about before.

Raising himself up, River started to take off her top, but Gina did it herself, with far greater ease. As she threw it onto the floor, River unhooked her bra and tossed it in the same place. Then, as he lovingly kissed her breasts, running his tongue over her nipples, Gina wrapped her legs around his waist. "This is just the best feeling ever, Riv. Can we stay like this forever?"

Slowly thrusting himself against her body, River began to imagine how good it would feel to be inside her. "Hey, Gin, you got a bed, baby?"

Gina could barely catch her breath. "Yeah, let's go."

Never taking their eyes off one another, they got off the

couch and walked together into her bedroom, where Gina finished undressing herself as River watched, fixated on every inch of her. "You're so beautiful. Wow, you're just amazing!"

Naked, Gina sat on the bed. Rolling her tongue over her top lip, she slowly unbuckled River's belt as she felt him react. Just as she was about to pull him out, completely unaware of her own words, she murmured softly, "From now on, I'm the only girl you're ever going to need to think about. Ever."

Surprised, River gently pulled her hand away and looked at her. "Wait a min—"

"Don't worry, I have condoms. They're in the back pocket of my jeans." Gina pointed to the floor, where her discarded pants lay.

River took a deep breath and sat down next to her on the bed. "Baby, what is this about?"

"Nothing, Riv. Nothing. I was just mumbling to myself."

"No, I don't think so."

"What else would it be? Don't you want to be with me?"

"More than anything. In case the augmentation of my male anatomy didn't give me away, that would be a yes."

Gina smiled, reached up, and stroked his hair. "I always wondered if you'd make jokes during sex."

"Hey, I'm still me, baby."

"Then can we get back to where we were? Please? My bed is super comfy."

River put his hand on her knee. "Gin, what did you mean when you said you're the only girl I need to think about?"

"Nothing, Riv. It was just one of those things people mutter during sex, you know?"

"Actually, it sounded like you meant something more specific. This isn't about Avalon, is it?"

The look on Gina's face answered River's question, and as disappointment washed over his face, Gina knew that the night of sex she had planned was over. But she wasn't giving up without a fight.

"Can't we just forget all of this and get back to what we were doing? It felt so good. I can make you feel even better. Let me show you."

"Did you plan this because you think Avalon's your competition?"

Gina looked down, not wanting to meet his gaze. "Yeah. Sort of."

River put his hand under her chin and lifted her face. "First of all, Avalon's not your competition. She's just a friend, and I don't like her that way. And you know what else? She doesn't like me that way, either. She's got a boyfriend back home. And she misses him a whole lot."

"Really? She does?"

"Yeah."

"Well, maybe she's missing him so bad that—"

"Don't say that, Gina. She's never hit on me in any way. I'm telling you the truth."

"Okay. Well, forget about her. It's just you and me here."

"I would love to be with you, sweet girl. But I don't think this is what you really want. You told me on our second date that it was really important to wait a while, remember? And I told you I was cool with that. And now everything's changed, and I think it's because I left the cafeteria on Wednesday to look for Avalon."

"Riv, I just want us to be solid. Like a real couple. Like Bianca and Tonio, you know?"

River looked surprised. "What do they have to do with any of this? Wait … did Bianca talk you into this?"

Again, Gina lowered her head. She couldn't bear to look him in the eye.

River got up from the bed and began to pick her clothes off

the floor. "Put these back on, okay? This isn't our time. As much as I wanted this, too, I knew it was too soon. Let's just do it for the right reasons. We don't need to initiate ourselves into any club. What other people do is their business, you know?"

Gina slipped her jeans on, not bothering with her underwear, and put on her shirt. "I'm so embarrassed, Riv."

"Don't be. I'm glad it happened. I've got the best images in my head now, and I know what I've got to look forward to. C'mon, sweet baby, let's go back into the living room. I'll tell you another eyeball story."

"So, after the scream, I heard someone crying. It sounded like they were in the worst pain ever. And then everything just went quiet. Muggs and I were completely freaked."

River smiled at the Kalifornia Kafe server as she put the lunch on the table, then returned his focus to Larsen. "That's mind-blowing. You didn't see anyone or anything?"

"No, like I told you, on my first day of work I saw that shadow moving backstage, and then on the following Tuesday your mom's friend Lisa said she heard 'Tonight' playing. Then on Friday, this happened."

"So, what did my mom say when you told her? And how come she didn't tell us?"

Larsen took a sip of his drink. "Riv, are you kidding me? No way I'm telling your mother this. That's one of the reasons I asked you to meet me here for lunch … besides the fact that I like that we can sit outside here. I didn't want anyone at your house to overhear me telling you this stuff."

"My mom has working ears, but she can't hear through walls."

"It's not just that. I mean, she sees me all week, and I don't want her to get sick of my face. Just don't want to wear out my welcome."

River paused to chew the bite of sandwich in his mouth. "That's the real reason you didn't want to come over, isn't it? Why do you always think you're gonna wear out your welcome?"

Larsen looked down as he picked up half of his sandwich and mindlessly tugged at a piece of lettuce sticking out between the two pieces of bread. "Well, I kind of wore out my welcome in my own home."

"That's different, dude. Bad different. And not exactly what happened. Anyway, don't you think my mom should know what's going down at the Desert Theater? She's not a virgin to ghost action. Trust me, she's a believer."

Larsen emphatically shook his head no. "That's not what I'm worried about. Your mom is busting her butt for this theater. She's putting her whole heart and soul into it. What's she supposed to do if I go tell her some mess like that? 'Hey, Mrs. D, the Mugster and I heard this screaming and wailing in the theater Friday night after everyone was gone. I'm pretty sure the theater is haunted.' No, not doing that. I told you, Riv, she knows about the shadow, but she just figured it was Raphael. And she heard her friend Lisa mention hearing the song playing, but she probably just assumed it was coming from someone's car, if she even bothered to think about it at all. She hired me to help her get a job done, not stand in the way of it. But I had to spill my guts to someone, so tag, you're it."

"I'm glad you clued me in. I hear ya. I know the theater has to be finished by early January for the talent competition."

"Yeah, she's arranging to have all kinds of people come in from LA and all over. Not to mention that the competition is going to be filmed for a TV show. There's no way I can let anything slow down the works. We have to finish on schedule."

River twirled his straw in his drink as he thought about what Larsen was saying. "Well, what if the next thing happens when my mom is with you? What if the ghost starts wailing right in front of her? 'Hellllp! Waaaaaaah!' Then what?"

"Then I'll deal with that as it happens. I'm too busy with 'what is' right now to freak over 'what if.' Promise me you'll keep your mouth shut."

"Yeah, I will. Anything else I should know?"

Larsen raised his glass to let the server know he needed a refill, then nodded thanks. "Oh, just that my mom was sitting out in front of Kathryn's on Friday night. She had been there the previous Monday, too."

"Like what? Spying on you?"

"I guess. Kathryn told me there was a lady in a blue Toyota outside, and she figured it was my mother. Kind of made my stomach flip even hearing that. But I went outside, got in the car with her, and it took only seconds for the gay bashing to begin. I told her that I wasn't going to listen to that, and I left. I'm sure she got over it. She was on her way to some spa resort with Reggie. So, listen, enough about me. How did your dinner with Gina go last night? Wasn't she going to cook for you?"

River paused before responding. "Yeah, she did. It was great."

"Great, huh?"

"Yeah."

"Hey, I'm sorry, Riv. I can tell there's something you're not saying, and, seriously, I'm not trying to pry it out of you."

"Thanks, dude. It's just that this relationship is still pretty new for both of us, and I'm falling for this girl more and more. We almost went somewhere a little too quickly. Get my drift? Not that I didn't want to take the trip, but the reasons were all wrong. I don't want to eff this up. You know?"

Larsen gave River a knowing look. "I've been there."

River looked embarrassed. "Oh, shit. I never even asked you if—"

"I understand. I'm just glad you wanted to be my friend."

"Wait, Lars. No, you shouldn't understand. Because all along I'm talking to you about Gina, and I never asked you if there was anyone in your life. But if you had been a straight guy, I'm sure I would have. I don't like to think that I was such an idiot. Honestly, I didn't even realize it until just now. I'm sorry, dude. My bad."

Larsen looked down the street at the people who were lining up for the Mystekal Sands Theater. "Wow, there must be some good films playing there. That's a big matinee crowd for this small town."

"Are you changing the subject on me?"

Larsen hinted at a smile as he turned back toward River. "I know you never asked me about my love life, but I knew that if I wanted to tell you, you'd be cool with it."

"Yeah, I am. So … is there someone?"

"There was. Before we moved here I met this guy, Chaz, who lived down the street. I was a junior, and he was a senior. His parents were pretty accepting, so we didn't have to hide in the shadows to spend time together. We just hung out at his house and sometimes went into Palm Springs together on the weekend. Things were going okay for us, better than okay, and then, on the exact same day I realized just how much I cared about him, my mom ran into his mom at Trader Joe's, and everything hit the fan."

"That's how your mom found out you were gay?"

"Hell, no, Riv. She always knew that. But she had this idea in her head that as long as I just *thought* I was gay and wasn't in any actual relationship, she could straighten me out when the right girl came along. So, when the right guy did come along … or so I thought … well, that was all she needed. She was on the computer that night looking for a new town to live in."

"What if you had met someone here? What would you guys

have done? Moved again?"

"Wouldn't surprise me. You know why she picked Mystekal? Because it's smaller than the other towns, and she figured the chances of me finding anyone would be slimmer. Well, she was right. There's nobody here I'm interested in. And that's actually okay because I'm concentrating on my job and my future. I need a clear head. For now. Holy shit, Riv!"

"What, dude?"

"You know that clear head I was talking about? It's like San Francisco fog rolled in just about now."

River saw Larsen staring intensely at the Mystekal Sands Theater. "What, is your ex, Chaz, down there?"

Larsen looked surprised by River's question. "No. Look. Can't you see her?"

"Who? Gina? Is she here with someone else?"

"Chillax! No. Quick. See the lady there with her hair up and a white flower in it?"

River's mouth dropped open in sync with his bulging eyes. "That's the lady you met inside. The one I saw crying later on. The one who we looked up on the Internet who got killed when your mom's new boyfriend drove his big rig into her. Um … Martha something."

"Martha Joy!" Larsen jumped out of his seat and ran down the steps of the café, then down the street toward the theater. He had nearly reached the last person in line when he saw Martha Joy standing about two feet apart from the line of moviegoers. She turned, smiled brightly at him, then disappeared into the crowd. Five seconds later, Larsen had reached the very spot where he had seen her go, but there was no trace of her and no way she could have made it inside that fast … had she been a living, breathing person.

Chapter 17

"TGIF, huh, Mrs. D?"

Arielle laid her head back against her chair and closed her eyes for several seconds. "Today *is* Friday, but I'll be working through the weekend. Tomorrow I'm going to Palm Springs to meet a friend of mine who's in for the weekend. She's been managing a theater in LA for over ten years and has promised to share her trade secrets. Sunday, I'll be hanging out here in the trailer. No rest for the weary. The show must go on."

Larsen spun around in his chair. "But you're exhausted! You've been here for nearly twelve hours today. And you've been pulling long days like this all week."

"Believe me, I know. My mirror knows. When I got up this morning, I screamed when I saw my own reflection. Then my mirror cracked."

Larsen laughed. "Yeah, right. Well, I think you look beautiful. And don't worry, there's only one month to go before the opening and the talent competition."

"Exactly! Why do you think I'm working seven days a week? How long have you been working with me? I think I've lost all track of time."

Larsen did the math in his head. "Let's see. I started on Halloween, so today it's been five weeks. I never thought first jobs were supposed to be as epic as this one is."

"You've been a godsend to me. Hey, while we have a few minutes, tell me: how are things with you personally? Have you seen or spoken to your mother?"

Larsen's happy face disappeared. "I haven't seen her for a month since Kathryn told me she was sitting outside in her car. She texted and asked me if I would have Thanksgiving dinner with her at a restaurant and then an hour later told me that she couldn't do it because 'her man' wanted her to go somewhere with him. Nice, huh?"

"I'm sorry, sweetie. Well, her loss was our gain. I'm so glad you and Kathryn joined us for dinner. It made it that much more special. Listen, I need to ask you something."

"Sure. Go for it."

"That guy at school, Jax, the one who was bullying you and then Erik, has he left you alone?"

"He has other people doing his bully work now. I haven't said anything to anyone, but I saw Jax handing notes to this sophomore kid. Then, a few hours later, the notes show up on my locker and on Avalon's. I took them down and threw them out. Really ugly stuff, Mrs. D. I told Gabe and Erik I'd watch out for Avalon, and I have been. I just didn't want to give Erik anything more to be upset about, so I kept it to myself. The things Jax wrote about Avalon and me were really ugly. I try not to let the words of an ignorant person hurt me."

Arielle's face tightened in anger. "I despise bullies. This Jax kid, he doesn't happen to have blond hair, does he?"

Larsen looked surprised. "Yeah, actually, he does. How did you know?"

"Damn."

"What's up, Mrs. D?"

"There have been two times in the past two weeks when I thought I saw a blond kid backstage. Both times I went looking for him, calling after him, but I couldn't find anyone. Maybe my mind is just playing tricks on me. But I was really worried he'd come here looking for you to start some trouble."

Larsen looked intrigued. "Have you seen or heard anything else unusual?"

Arielle laughed. "Well, I do see my son every day. Does that count?"

"That's so funny. But really, anything unusual here?"

"Why do you ask? Have you?"

Larsen panicked. "Oh, no. I'm just trying to figure out if it was Jax."

"Well, there was one night when I was here late, and I thought I heard someone crying. But it was really windy outside, and the wind has many voices. Now that I think about all of these incidents, every single time I've seen or heard something unusual, Muggins has, too. But you know how hypersensitive dogs can be. They often bark for things only they can hear. Well, I'm freaking myself out, so let's change the subject. I have some pretty exciting news for you."

"I'm always a sucker for good news."

"I know you've been wondering about that footage that Lisa and Josh shot last month of you doing your Othello bit on stage."

"I've been dying to ask, but I didn't want to seem too eager or anything."

Arielle looked through a stack of receipts as she continued to talk. "Lisa was just waiting to combine that footage with what they shot yesterday with the reinstallation of the seats. She's going to edit it this weekend, and the promos will air next week on both the station Lisa works for and their sister station. Both stations are national, too."

"That's fantastic! I forgot the seats are going back in. I was working on the media kits and programs for the past week and haven't even been in the theater."

"No, you haven't. That's right. I'm sorry, Lars. You have to see them. They look more beautiful than I imagined. The craftsmanship is exquisite. Listen, there's a sleepy boy under my desk who could use a walk. Take him out for me and then go into the theater. Gabe's there. He'll show you everything. It's so exciting!"

Larsen jumped up from his seat as Muggins simultaneously came out from under Arielle's desk without being called. "You're such a smart boy. Come on. Let's go."

📖📖📖

Gabe smiled proudly as he looked at the seventy-six seats that were back in their original setting. "So, Larsen, what do you think?"

"I think these look incredible. Did you say that all of them should be in by next week?"

"That's right. The guy who did this work, Joey, is an old friend of mine from Jersey. I knew he wouldn't disappoint Arielle. Yeah … feel really good about this."

Larsen looked at Muggins. "What do you think, boy?"

Preoccupied, Muggins seemed interested in everything but the refurbished theater seats.

"Wow, Gabe. This must have been quite a job."

"You bet. All of the old upholstery had to be stripped and each chair disassembled. After that was done, Joey stripped and sandblasted all of the metal and iron pieces to get the paint off. Said he found over a hundred pieces of petrified chewing gum."

Larsen made a face. "That's awful. Why can't people just wait until they find a trashcan?"

"Ah, some people just suck. You know that. Yeah, people can suck real bad."

"Grrrr."

Taking a quick look at Muggins, Larsen knew he had seen or heard something unusual. "What is it, boy?"

"Ah, don't pay the dog no mind. Every time he's in here he's growling or woofing. It's what dogs do."

Larsen looked curiously at Gabe. "Yeah, I know what dogs do, but, um, the last time I was in here alone with Muggins, I not only heard a song from *West Side Story* playing, I heard a loud scream followed by this really intense wailing. That was about a month ago. I spend most of my time in the trailer, so if there's weird stuff going on in here, I don't see too much of it."

Larsen watched as Gabe's face reddened. "But somehow I'm thinking you're seeing it."

Gabe looked panicked. "You didn't tell Arielle about any of that, did you?"

"Uh, no. I didn't want to upset her. But now I'm wondering if she's seen or heard things."

Lowering his voice, Gabe moved closer to Larsen and looked him squarely in the eyes. "Listen to me. I've trusted you with my kids, so I'm gonna trust you with this. Don't ask me any questions. I'm just telling you that people like to play mind games to mess with other people's heads. Things aren't always what they seem to be. I'm just sayin'. I've been racking my brain since I got here tryin' to figure out how they've rigged this place, and for the life of me I can't find squat. But I will. I've had enough crap pulled behind my back for a lifetime. So whatever you think you see, you only tell me, okay?"

Larsen looked confused. "Who are the people playing mind games?"

"You're a good kid. But what part of 'don't ask me any questions' didn't you understand? I'm heading back to the trailer. You stay here a while if you want. Sorry I don't have time to give you a walking tour of all we've done, but you can see for yourself. Okay, kid?"

As Gabe hurried out of the theater, Muggins' interest in the backstage area grew tenfold. But unlike the previous times, Muggins seemed afraid to approach the stage, but his eyes remained fixated on it, and his tail wagged nervously between his legs. Larsen followed the dog's gaze and was startled to see the faint image of what looked like a young blond man in distress, crying for help.

Larsen knew immediately that this must have been the same person Arielle had mentioned, but this kid looked nothing like the muscular, taller Jax. He had no idea what Gabe had been talking about, but the person he was looking at was definitely not a trick or a mind game. Though the teen wasn't speaking, Larsen found himself able to communicate telepathically with him. He wasn't able to make out any words, but he knew the boy was crying for help. Only Larsen couldn't figure out what kind of help he needed. And he knew one other thing: if he tried to approach him, he would disappear, the same way Martha Joy had disappeared into the crowd, because like her, he, too, was a ghost.

📖📖📖

"Hey, dude. I'm glad you could come over today. So, look, tell me more about what happened yesterday. Sorry I had to hang up on you. Gina was freaking out about something, and I had to calm her down."

Larsen sat back in Mick's armchair. "Hope everything's okay. You two still are going strong, right?"

"Hell, yeah. Stronger than ever. It wasn't about us. Her sister, Taylor, is like this volcano that erupts every two months. You ever hear of Mount Vesuvius?"

"No. Should I have?"

"It's an active volcano on the west coast of Italy. Never mind. Anyway, Gina's parents dealt with Taylor's latest crisis … for now.

So, go back to what you were telling me last night. You said that my mom thought Jax was hanging out at the theater, Gabe told you someone was playing mind games, and you saw a blond-haired guy ghost who needed help. Did I get that right?"

"That's right, Riv. I've been going over it all a million times. First, I'm convinced that your mom has been seeing the same kid I have. Only neither of us have seen him clearly enough to make out his face, but I can see he's nowhere near as tall or as muscular as Jax. But your mom has never seen Jax, so she just figured he might be lurking around trying to bully me away from school grounds where he can't get into trouble or something."

"Yeah, Lars, but if she thought that was Jax, why wouldn't she say anything to him? No way my mom would just let him hang in the theater. My mom is tough. She can kick ass! Seriously."

"I asked her the same thing when I got back to the trailer, after Gabe went home. She said that when she saw him, he was way backstage. She did yell after him, but both times she just assumed he left through the back of the theater because she scared him off."

"And what do you think, dude?"

Larsen looked around the Dalworths' living room to make sure nobody was around. "I think that ghost I saw lives backstage."

River contemplated what his friend was saying. "Okay, so what's Gabe Martelli going on about?"

"I don't know, Riv, but I think that's an entirely different scenario. Remember I told you about a month ago that I heard Gabe on the phone in the trailer? Well, someone was on the other end telling him to do something, and he was saying that things were going really well, and he had changed his mind and wasn't going to do whatever."

"I hope nobody's trying to hurt my mom."

Larsen was concerned. "Well, I think if he thought your mother was in danger, for sure he'd do something about it. But when he was talking about people playing mind games, I got the idea that someone was trying to get Gabe to pull some shit, and when he refused, they were doing it themselves. Only Gabe can't seem to find any trace of foul play."

River laughed. "Foul play? You sound like somebody in a cop show or a murder mystery."

"Get real, Riv. With all of the weird things you say, you're really gonna get on my case for saying 'foul play'?"

"Damn, I hate when you make a valid point. Go on with what you were saying."

"Well, I think that whatever Gabe is worried about has to do with real-life human beings. And for the sake of your mom and the theater, the sooner we figure that out, the better. I think Gabe is seeing and hearing stuff, too, but he's ignoring it because he thinks it's some kind of setup."

River lay back on the couch, taking in all that Larsen had just told him. "That's some theory you've got going on."

"Yeah, well, guess what? I think I'm right."

"Listen, I'm not meeting Gina until eight o'clock. My mom has been asking me to come by and see the progress on the theater. I told her I'd try to do it this weekend. I was going to go tomorrow, because she's meeting some friend in Palm Springs today, but maybe it's a good thing she won't be there. I think you and I should go by this afternoon. Gabe's off, right?"

Larsen nodded. "Yeah, for sure. He told me yesterday he was going hiking at Indian Canyons with his kids. Okay, Riv, so why do you look like you're hatching a bigger plan than you're letting on? The look on your face is telling me to beware."

"Nah. But I just remembered that the Jinxster is in town this weekend. She and Jess are going around town taking photos. Jess is doing something for her photojournalism class, and Jinxsy wants to develop a photo history of the new Mystekal. Anyway, I'm gonna call

Jess and see if they'll meet us. If there's a ghost in that theater, we'll find him. Take that to the bank, dude."

Chapter 18

Jessie and Jinxsy had just pulled up in Jinxsy's car when they saw River and Larsen approaching the back of the theater.

Jinxsy jumped out of the car and ran over to River, giving him a big hug that he happily returned. "Haven't seen you in forever, Riv."

"It's only been three months since our last visit. But I know you have been suffering unbearable pangs of yearning since that fateful day you left Mystekal to get your business degree. I warned you being apart would be painful, but you chose to ignore me, and now I see the lines of distress etched all over your youthful visage."

"What a truckload of BS. If you're seeing 'lines of distress etched all over my youthful visage,' it's because my face also serves as a bullshit meter, and it is totally on overload right now. But I'm happy looking at your face. Sorry I missed you on my last couple of visits home. Life is hectic, to say the least. And seeing how you were a part of my life almost every day for so many years, well, I guess three months is a long time … or maybe not long enough."

"Ha ha. You know you love me, Jinxster."

Jinxsy smiled and winked at River.

Just as Jessie had joined the group, Jinxsy turned to face Larsen. "Hi, I'm Jinxsy Patterson. I've heard so much great stuff about you, Larsen. Thanks for working here and helping to bring the theater alive."

Larsen reached out to shake her hand. "I can't even tell you how much I appreciate having this opportunity."

River exhaled. "Nice choice of words, Jinxster. About bringing the theater alive. That's the thing: I think it already was!"

Jessie brushed a strand of hair out of her eyes that the wind had blown in her face. "Like I told you when you called, Riv, you were on speakerphone, so Jinxsy heard everything. Lars, it sounds like you're convinced the theater is haunted."

Larsen looked uncomfortable. "Uh, yeah. Kind of."

"Don't worry too much because Jinxsy, River, and I are all ghost veterans. We'll figure out what's going on … maybe."

"I hope so. Did River tell you that I actually met a lady ghost who lives at the Mystekal Sands movie theater? She's the dead wife of my mother's new boyfriend."

"Say what? No, I sure didn't know that. Wow, Jinx; looks like you've inherited more than just a town. Seems like you've got some former residents, too." Jessie turned back to Larsen. "So, when you say that you met her, does that mean you actually had a conversation?"

"Yeah, I did. Inside a dark theater. Not too long after Riv and I first became friends. I had no idea she was a ghost until I found out later that she died. And then, about a month ago, Riv and I were having lunch at the Kafe, and I saw her outside the theater sort of hanging out near all of the people waiting in line. By the time I got to where she was, there was no sign of her."

Jinxsy shook off a chill and began walking toward the back door of the theater as she motioned for everyone to follow. "I just can't help but wonder if there's any connection to everything that happened here two years ago. I mean, could that lady and this male ghost that Larsen and Arielle have seen in the theater be connected to my biological dad living as a ghost in the high school for all those years?"

Jessie looked overwhelmed. "My freakin' head hurts. Reminds me of when my dad brought us this thousand-piece puzzle to put together when we were kids. I thought we'd never do it. But to answer your question, I think it's very possible, Jinx. It's just all so weird. It was hard enough to believe everything that I witnessed with my own eyes two years ago. And now to think that it's all starting up again …"

River looked startled. "It has, Jess … damn, I hear it. Holy shit! Listen, it's the song Larsen was telling us about: 'Tonight' from *West Side Story*. It's so clear."

Larsen put his hand to his mouth, but he couldn't suppress his laughter. He reached into his side pants pocket and pulled out his ringing phone. When he saw the caller ID, he laughed heartily. "I definitely heard the song playing, and so did Lisa, but what you're all hearing right now is my phone. It seems that River just butt-called me."

Jinxsy and Jessie exploded into laughter. Embarrassed, River reached into his back pocket and pulled out his phone that indeed was ringing Larsen's number. "I did that on purpose. Just to get everyone ready for the real thing."

Jinxsy was the first to call him out. "More bullshit. You so hate that you did that. I know you, River Dalworth. And jokes are never funny if they concern you and you didn't initiate them. Hey, it's okay, my adopted little brother; we all have chinks in our armor."

📖📖📖

Larsen, who had the keys, unlocked the back door of the theater. "I'd say 'Ladies first,' but in this case, I'm thinking you two would rather have River and me go in first."

Jessie, who looked more nervous than Jinxsy, stood the farthest away with her camera hanging around her neck. "You're a true gentleman, Larsen. Yeah, please, you guys go in first."

Larsen entered first and flipped on the lights that illuminated the immediate area. Seconds later, River, Jinxsy, and Jessie followed behind him. There was complete silence as everyone stood in place and looked around, each set of eyes scanning in nervous anticipation.

Jinxsy was focused on the faded message board on the wall. As she squinted, she tried to read one of the notices that had nearly faded. Suddenly, she let out a harrowing scream. Before anyone could ask her what she saw, the answer came in the form of River, holding his stomach and howling with laughter.

Jessie playfully pushed her brother's shoulder with her hand. "What did you do to Jinx, numbnuts?"

"He pinched me on either side of my waist. Scared the crap out of me."

"I swear, Riv. No matter how old you get, you're still going to be my little brother. And let me tell you something else, numbnuts. You're going to *have* numb nuts if you keep it up."

River was still laughing. "Oh, yeah, Jess. What are you going to do?"

Putting her hands on her hips, Jinxsy positioned herself in front of him. "She's just gonna hold you while I take a red hot fire poker to your manly parts."

Larsen winced. "Ouch."

Having calmed down quickly, Jinxsy laughed. "Just like I said outside, Riv, you have to be the one pulling the joke, don't you? Boy, it didn't take you long to prove me right. Just can't help yourself."

"Hey, we're ghost hunting here. A little levity is in order."

Jessie took the lens cap off her camera, turned it on, and started taking photos of everything in sight. Jinxsy resumed trying to read the discolored notice, while Larsen and River ventured a few yards down the breezeway to see if anything unusual was going on.

Larsen turned to River. "I wish Muggins was with us. He always knows when something is happening."

"Yeah, I thought of that, Lars. Mom took him to Palm Springs because they're real dog friendly there. He's her bodyguard. Ha ha."

"I know. He adores your mother. Well, we're on our own today. Let's go back to the girls. I want to see if Jinxsy was able to read anything on that old notice."

Jinxsy looked excited. "I can see a little bit of it right here." She pointed to some type that was larger than the rest. "Look, it says 'West Side Story.' They must have produced that show here. That would explain why Lisa and Larsen were hearing the song 'Tonight.'"

Jessie didn't seem convinced. "It doesn't really explain anything. I mean, that's quite a leap from knowing they did a show here to hearing the song play by itself decades later. You think?"

"Well, yeah, Jess. But we're still a step closer. So, listen, Larsen, exactly where were you when you saw that guy? Were you back here?"

"No, I was in the main hall of the theater, and I was looking back this way. At kind of a distance, you know? Do you want to go out into the theater? You can see some of the new seats that were put in, and then you'll also have the same vantage point I did. Hold on; I'm just going to go to the light booth so nobody is ghost busting in the dark. Wait here. I'll be right back."

Jessie looked panicked. "Where's the light booth?"

"It's just off the lobby, to the right. Once the work is finished, we'll be entering from the front door, so it won't be such a long walk to turn everything on." Larsen grabbed a flashlight that was hanging on the wall. "I'll be right back, guys."

Leaving everyone behind, Larsen opened the door to the theater and walked up the aisle toward the stairs. He had never been alone in there before, much less in the dark. All he could see was the path in front of him. Halfway to the light booth, he stopped and listened. He was so sure he heard something, but he couldn't identify the sound. He wanted to turn around and shine his flashlight onto the stage, but he felt it would be rude and hurtful to anyone who might be there. Being anything less than a gentleman, even to a ghost, was not acceptable.

Pointing the flashlight to the floor, he stopped, slowly turning toward the stage. Very faintly, he heard what sounded like a cry for help. But once he was fully turned around, he couldn't hear anything but his own heavy breathing. Turning again, pointing the flashlight ahead, Larsen hurried toward the house entrance doors and out into the lobby. Once there, he opened a black door in the corner of the lobby, where he climbed a small set of stairs to the light booth. After switching on all of the lighting, he took a deep breath, but his heart was still pounding. As he returned the same way he had come, once inside the theater, he saw River, Jinxsy, and Jessie coming through the door.

"Hey, dude. Took your own sweet time! We were wondering if the lights were gonna go on at all. It was like the darkness swallowed you up. Or maybe something else."

Jinxsy was in awe as she looked around. "Wow. I was only here one other time, before any work was done, and I'm just blown away by how amazing everything looks. It's gorgeous."

As she began snapping photos of everything, Jessie agreed with her bestie that the work was incredible. "It's just like Mom described it. Top-notch craftsmanship. So, hey, Larsen, although I hate to agree with River, it did take you kind of a long time to get to the light booth. Any reason?"

Larsen wasn't sure if there was anything to tell. Maybe he heard something because he was expecting to do so. If he told the others, they might hear the same thing merely by the power of suggestion. "No, nothing unusual. I was just walking really slowly because the new carpet isn't in yet, and as you can see, there's a whole lot a person can trip over here. So, be careful, everyone. Go take a look at the new seats. They're beautiful."

Larsen stood in the aisle, watching the stage, while Jessie continued to take photos, Jinxsy inspected the seats, and River decided to walk up onto the stage. Swallowing the lump in his throat, Larsen watched as River slowly walked around the stage, then stopped. Jessie and Jinxsy were too busy observing the rest of the theater to notice, but to Larsen, it was clear that River was hearing or seeing something out of the ordinary.

River turned to Larsen, raising his voice so as to be heard clearly from the distance between them. "Man, it's freezing here. Right on this spot. How come?"

Larsen hadn't thought of it since the day he went in the theater to find Arielle's hardware catalog and Muggins had become transfixed by something on the stage that Larsen couldn't see. As he had run across the stage to the back, he remembered feeling a chill in the very spot where River was standing. He had forgotten about it and never mentioned it again.

"Aren't you going to answer me, dude?"

Shaking his head no, Larsen just stood there. He didn't know what to say.

River continued to stand in the same spot and look and listen. Once more, he turned around to talk to Larsen. "Someone's crying."

Jinxsy, who had finished looking at the seats, was now watching the exchange between the two friends. "Are you for real, Riv? Do you honestly hear someone crying?"

"I not only hear someone, but now I see someone. Man, he's really upset."

Jinxsy headed toward the stage. Just as she got to the stairs, River made an announcement. "He's gone. I can't see him or hear him anymore."

Looking disgusted, Jinxsy headed back toward Jessie, who had been in a world of her own with the camera. "You know, I think the guy that Riv heard crying and happened to see for only seconds was the same one who pinched me. In other words, I call bullshit." She turned to River. "Obviously, I know ghosts exist. I met my own father after he died. But that doesn't mean that I'm gonna swallow every line of nonsense out of your mouth."

River looked frustrated. "I'm not lying, Jinx."

"Yeah, sure."

"I'll prove it to you."

Jinxsy's curiosity was piqued. "How are you going to do that?"

"I'll draw the dude."

Jinxsy looked at River, then at Larsen and Jessie. "I'm sorry, I don't see what that proves. You could draw anyone and say that's the guy you saw. So don't bother."

Jessie grabbed her friend by the arm. "No, let him do it. For sure let him do it."

River looked at his sister. "You want me to draw him?"

"Yup, I sure do. I've got to do something right now. But Jinxsy and I will be at the house in about an hour. When you're done drawing the guy, meet us at home. Okay?"

"Yeah, sure, Jess."

Whispering something frantically in Jinxsy's ear appeared to change everything. Jinxsy was now her usual animated self. "Yeah, draw that guy like Jess said. We'll see you soon."

As the girls rushed out of the theater, Larsen and River exchanged looks.

"Hey, dude. I really did hear someone crying."

"I believe you, Riv. I think I did, too."

Chapter 19

Sitting next to River on the couch, Larsen looked on with amazement as he watched his best friend come close to finishing the drawing of the figure he claimed to have seen at the theater.

"I didn't realize you drew so fast, Riv. Wow, I feel like I've got a front row seat to genius."

"That's pretty much the situation any time you're around me, Lars. Ha ha."

"Can I amend that compliment? In fact, can I take it back completely?"

"Nope. My ears have already soaked in your words. I'm a genius."

Larsen laughed. "Not the most humble one I've ever met, though." Watching River fill in the features on the face, Larsen started to feel anxious. He was no longer in a mood to joke around.

River looked up. "Man, where did you go, Lars? What's the matter? Hey … this guy looks familiar to you, doesn't he? He's the same guy you saw."

"Maybe."

"By the look on your face, 'maybe' means 'hell yes.' Anyway, I'm almost done. The girls should be here soon. They've been in the backhouse since we got here. Wonder what they're doing."

"They're coming in now. I can hear them." Larsen turned around and saw Jessie and Jinxsy entering the house through the kitchen door.

Without stopping, River continued to add the last touches to his sketch. "Good, because I'm done. Perfect timing."

Glancing over to see the finished work, Larsen felt numb as he looked at the face of the boy in the sketch.

Jessie and Jinxsy came into the living room and walked right over to the couch. "Well, I'm glad to see you've been drawing, lil bro. Have you finished?"

"Yup!"

Jinxsy held out her hand. "Can we see your sketchbook, Riv?"

"What's it worth to you?"

"If there was ever a time not to mess with me or your sister, this would be it."

Jessie nodded in agreement. "Seriously, hand it over."

Seeing the complete lack of amusement on both girls' faces, River handed them the sketchbook and watched as their faces paled in unison.

"Holy 'effin shit, Jess!"

Astounded by what she saw, Jessie had no words. But River did. "Okay, now this is getting weird. Lars looks at my drawing and goes quiet, but I can understand that, because he's seen the dude. But you two haven't. In fact, you didn't even believe me. So what gives with the pale faces and open mouths here? You look like you're gonna faint, Jess."

Alarmed, Jinxsy took hold of Jessie's arm to steady her. "C'mon, Jess, sit here in your dad's chair."

Jessie sat down in Mick's armchair and took a deep breath to calm her nerves.

Impatiently, River stood up. "Okay, cut the suspense routine. I showed you my drawing; now it's your turn to explain why it's freaking you the fuck out!"

Jinxsy took a seat in Arielle's chair. "Tell them, Jess."

"Okay, well, while Jinxsy was looking at the refurbished chairs, and you guys were looking on the stage, I was playing crazy woman with my camera. Riv, right after you said you heard someone crying, you said that you could see the guy. Well, at that same time, a moment after I clicked the shutter release, I thought I might have seen someone, too."

River looked surprised. "Really?"

"Yeah, but in a fraction of a second, I couldn't be sure of anything. I didn't want to stop and see what I'd taken because I was afraid I'd miss something even if I stopped for fifteen seconds to fiddle with my camera. So I just kept snapping away."

Larsen was curious. "How come you didn't say anything?"

"Like I said, Lars, I wasn't sure if it was anything at all, or if just being there on a ghost-hunting mission made me feel like I had. I was afraid that if I spoke up, it might influence someone else, you know?"

Biting his tongue, Larsen looked guilty. "I know exactly what you mean. The power of suggestion is … um …"

Comically, River raised his eyebrows. "Powerful?"

Everyone laughed, but a second later, the mood was serious again. Larsen continued talking. "Yeah, right. Powerful. Anyway, yesterday, like River told you, I was in the theater and saw this guy. He didn't speak to me, but he was telling me, sort of telepathically, that he needed help. He looked so desperate. Then he just disappeared. Today, when I was going to the light booth, I thought I heard that wailing again. But unlike yesterday, I didn't see him. If I had been positive that I really heard someone, I would have spoken up. Just like you, Jess, I didn't want to bias anyone else's perception. So I kept quiet."

Jessie looked at Jinxsy, who responded with a go-ahead nod. "Okay, boys, so here's the thing. Jinxsy and I were just at my place looking at all of the photos I took. At first, I couldn't find anything unusual, but then I found a few of the stage photos that had distinctly different light patterns from the others. They looked like streaks. I imported them into Photoshop, then I changed them into black and white, adjusted the levels, played with the hue, saturation, and contrast, and, well, that changed everything. Here, take a look."

Jessie reached into her back pocket and handed the boys a piece of paper that had been folded in four. Upon seeing it, River looked animated, while Larsen appeared dizzy.

"See, Riv? See, Lars? The guy in the drawing is the same one in the photo. It's very washed-out looking, but you can see without a doubt it's the same guy."

"Wow, Jess. Freakin' amazing! Hell, I'm freakin' amazing, too. I drew the dude dead on." River looked at Larsen, expecting him to make a wisecrack about River's lack of humility, but Larsen looked as if he were frozen in place.

Jinxsy stood up and began pacing the room. "So, as you can see, we've got a match. Now we just have to put our heads together and figure out who this guy is."

Larsen's eyes focused on Jinxsy, while his body remained motionless.

Noticing, Jinxsy sat down again. "That won't be necessary. Will it, Larsen? You know exactly who this guy is, don't you?"

"Yes, I do."

"C'mon, dude. Tell us."

"Now that I've seen your drawing, Riv, and your photo, Jessie, there's no question who it is. I look at the guy's photos every day. I live in his house with his mother. That's Kathryn's son. That's Peter Winterstrom."

"Man, Lars, how come you didn't mention this guy before?"

"Riv, you already know that I'm living at her home and that she had a gay son who died when he was fifteen. I didn't want to go into any more detail out of respect for Kathryn. I didn't see the need to repeat it. The poor lady has been grieving for forty years."

Jinxsy looked incredulous. "Do you know how he died?"

Uncomfortably, Larsen looked around. "I'll tell you the little bit I know, but we have to make a pact that nobody repeats anything. Riv, you can't share this with Gina or anyone else, and Jessie and Jinxsy, you can only discuss it with one another. At least for now. Is that a deal?"

Everyone agreed to Larsen's terms in unison.

"Well, all I know is that Peter was gay and loved the theater. Unlike me, he had this beautiful baritone voice, a boyfriend he was madly in love with, and a mother and a father who were very accepting. But Peter's boyfriend's family was even worse than my mom. Way worse. His dad threatened them both all the time, so Peter's dad told him only to see each other in secret.

"Kathryn said that the boyfriend's father staged an accident to kill Peter and his own son. Only his son lived, and Peter died. At the time it happened, everyone thought it was an accident. I'm not really sure if Kathryn and her husband did, but years later, Kathryn said she found out for sure Peter had been murdered. She never talks about the details. It hurts her too much, and she doesn't want to be a downer. She still misses him like crazy."

"Damn, dude. Maybe the guy wants to see his mother. She sure would like to see him. Maybe we should take her to the theater, and then he can go into the light, like Jinxsy's dad, Tommy, did."

"No, Riv. It's not that simple. We're not going to do anything at all until we know a whole lot more. Telling Kathryn that her son is a ghost in the theater could kill her. I'm not doing that, and you're not either. You guys have to trust me. I know her better than any of you do."

Jinxsy held up a hand to calm Larsen. "It's okay. We're not saying a word to anyone. Not even Arielle. What we are going to do is put together a reconnaissance mission to find out as much as we can. Then, we'll go from there. Larsen, since you live with Kathryn and know her, you have the final say. We're not going to ever do anything without your permission. And that's a promise."

"Thanks, Jinxsy." Larsen looked at River and Jessie for their assurances, too.

"Promise, dude. Everything the Jinxster said."

Jessie nodded. "Promise. Now, let's figure out what to do."

Larsen looked pensive. "I'll tell you all this: the only way that I'll know for sure what to do is to make contact with Peter. If he wants to see his mother, I'll arrange it."

"Well, this is a nice surprise! I've got four of my favorite people together in my living room at once. Is there a special occasion I've forgotten about?"

Jessie got up and gave her mother a hug as Muggins ran in behind Arielle and greeted everyone individually. "Hey, Mom, you've been bugging us to come see the theater, so when we ran into one another here, we thought today was a perfect time to go see it. Jinxsy and I already had the day set aside for taking photos around town, so it all worked out."

Jinxsy jumped up from Arielle's usual seat and motioned for her to sit down, which she did. Jinxsy took a seat on the couch next to Larsen. Muggins had finished greeting everyone and went into the kitchen to get a drink of water.

"I hope you're not upset, Mrs. D. I hadn't planned to give the grand tour in your place. Sorry. Don't worry, though; I turned off the lights and locked up the theater before we left."

"No problem, Larsen. I would've loved to have been there with all of you, but I am just happy my kids finally paid the poor theater a visit. Tell me, what did you think? River? You first."

"It's dope, Mom. What a transformation so far."

"We're getting there. Gabe assures me we'll be done by January eleventh, which you all know is the date of the grand opening and talent competition. Jess?"

"I think that you are putting your heart and soul into this theater, and that's why it's every bit as beautiful as you are."

"Aw, Jess. That's so sweet."

"Hey, Mom, sounds like she wants something, doesn't it?"

"My daughter just gave me the most amazing compliment, and we'll leave it at that. Love you, too, Riv. Smart-ass. I wonder where you get that from. Oh, yeah. Mars. So, Jinxsy, it's your theater! Are you pleased with what you saw?"

"Are you kidding? I couldn't have asked for anyone better to manage this project. It was just meant to be. Can't wait to tell Eve tonight when I have dinner with her. She might come by tomorrow if she can."

Muggins came back from the kitchen and jumped in Arielle's lap with a thud. "Oh, Muggins, you do love me, don't you, boy?"

"Hey, Mrs. D, how did things go in Palm Springs? I thought you said you were going back to the theater after you met your friend."

"I had the best time! My friend, Virginia Barnett, was telling me some of the most hysterical stories about running a theater. I hope none of them ever happen to me. But it was wonderful. I was so happy to see her again, and she gave me some really valuable information. I was going to go back to the theater, but when my hunky husband called and said he was getting off work early, I changed my mind. I need a nap, a shower, and a romantic dinner much more than a few more hours in the trailer."

"Ha ha. Keep going, Mom. What do you need after that?"

Arielle smiled. "None of your business, that's what."

Although he was making a joke about his parents' sex life, he couldn't help but flash back to the night he and Gina came so close to being together. They'd talked about it since and enjoyed telling one another their secret fantasies. But Gina wanted to wait until she knew it was right without having to think about it. And River knew it would be way better for both of them without any regrets.

"Sorry, Mom. Old habits die hard."

Arielle laughed. "Well, now that you have a girlfriend, maybe I should … never mind. I don't want to know. I absolutely do not want to know. Just be careful."

River turned a lighter shade of crimson as Arielle quickly shifted the focus from her love life to his own.

"So, Mom, what else is new?"

Arielle scratched Muggins on his neck and gave him a kiss. "Go to your bed, boy. Mama needs a break, okay?"

The dog jumped off her lap and began walking away. He stopped, turned to Arielle as if to protest, then kept on walking until he reached his bed and curled up on it.

"Okay, now that I'm no longer pinned down by my canine son, I have some news." Arielle looked directly at Larsen. "I spoke to Lisa a while ago. She and Josh are working on the promo trailer late this afternoon. They're going to finish up tonight, and on Monday morning, the file will go off to the station. The first airing will be Monday night at 7:17 on the sister station. It's the one that airs a lot of family and women's programming."

Larsen was stunned. "So it's true; I'm making my national TV debut on Monday night."

"You so are, Lars. And I thought maybe you and Kathryn would like to come to dinner; we can all watch together. I can't cook for everyone now with my schedule, but we'll order pizza, and I'll make a big salad. It wouldn't be the same without you and Kathryn."

"When I talk to her tonight, I'll ask. I'm sure she'll be up for it."

"Jinxsy, will you be able to make it?"

"I don't have to be in class this week until Tuesday afternoon. So, yes. And I'll bring Eve and Madeleine if that's okay."

"Wonderful. I haven't seen your mother or your grandmother in quite a while."

Jinxsy smiled. "It will be great for all of us to be together."

Arielle smiled but looked distracted. "Lars, you haven't had any problem with Jax or any of his friends, have you? I just want to make sure they're not hanging out at the theater trying to bother you. It's been on my mind ever since I saw that kid."

"Oh, don't worry, Mrs. D. I think I saw him the other day. I'm pretty sure he's just someone from the neighborhood. I found out that Jax works at a gym after school. Anyway, Jax looks nothing like that kid."

Arielle smiled. "Well, that's a relief!"

Chapter 20

"Are you nervous about your television debut tonight?"

Larsen turned around in his chair to answer Arielle. "Yeah, I guess I am, but more than nerves, I feel like I'm in a dream. My life changed so much for the better since I met your family and Kathryn. I've still got some pretty big problems, especially where my mom is concerned, but I am kind of amazed when I think about how things turned around for me. I know a whole lot of kids are out there feeling like life is gonna suck forever. I wish I could tell them all not to give up hope."

Arielle grabbed a couple of folders and filed them in the drawer to her right. "You know, Lars, I think one day you'll get a chance to help others just by being who you are and living a good life. I think you're pretty fabulous to even be thinking about other people right now. By the way, Kathryn is coming with you tonight, isn't she?"

"Oh, yeah. I guess River told you she wasn't feeling well. When I got home on Saturday, she had a fever. She stayed in bed most of the weekend, but by last night, she was doing much better. This morning she told me she was back to her old self."

"Great. I look forward to seeing her. Do you know where Gabe is? When you were out walking Muggins a little while ago, his private line rang three times. Every time I picked it up, someone hung up on me. I hope there's no problem with any of his kids. I tried calling his cell, but it went straight to voicemail. Maybe that's why they were calling the landline. I was going to tell him when he came back to the trailer, but I'm thinking you should go into the theater and let him know in case it's important. I get the feeling someone is anxious to speak with him."

Larsen jumped out of his chair and had his hand on the trailer door within seconds. "Sure, I'll go right now. I'll tell him."

Arielle blinked her eyes in astonishment. "You're a great worker, Lars, but I've never seen you move that fast. You look like a film that's been sped up!"

Larsen realized that his desperation to get into the theater again was showing. "Oh, yeah, I guess I'm a little wired. I'm just really nervous about tonight. Apparently more than I thought."

📖📖📖

As he hurried to the back door of the theater, he wished that he had taken Muggins, but he couldn't think of any excuse for the dog to accompany him just to deliver a message. He felt an odd chill in the air. The sky was getting darker every day, and even though it was only four-thirty, it looked and felt later.

Seeing Raphael standing by his blue truck, Larsen knew he was done for the day and hoped the other two men had left as well.

Larsen found Gabe in the main hall of the theater, inspecting the latest seat delivery. "We've only got seventy more seats to put in, Larsen. Then we're ready for a full house. SRO. Do you know what that means?"

"Sure. Standing room only."

"Right. I forgot you know your theater lingo. You here for any particular reason, or did you just want to see today's progress?"

"Actually, Mrs. D sent me. When I was walking the dog, your private line rang three times."

Gabe looked nervous. "Okay. So, is that all that happened? The phone rang three times?"

"Well, not really. Mrs. D kept picking up, and someone was hanging up on her."

"Bastards. Son of a …"

Larsen tried to pretend he hadn't heard Gabe's mumbled response. "Yeah, so, um, she was worried that since your cell phone went to voicemail that your kids might be trying to reach you."

Reaching into his pocket, Gabe pulled out two phones. "Between you and me, Larsen, I've got two phones. One is just for my kids. I'm here twenty-four / seven for them. This one is for business, and sometimes when people are fucking with me, I need to turn it off. No need to repeat anything I've said."

"I won't say anything."

"Good. I'm going outside to make a call or two. Then I'm going into town to run an errand. I'll be back in about a half hour to lock up. You let Arielle know that."

As Gabe walked away mumbling expletives under his breath, Larsen looked around, then slowly walked toward the stage. The closer he got, the colder he became. His nerves were so rattled that when he heard "Tonight" playing softly, coming from the back of the theater, he thought his ears were deceiving him. As he exhaled, he noticed he could see his breath. "Peter? My name is Larsen Davis. Are you here, Peter Winterstrom?"

The air got colder and the music louder, but Larsen couldn't see anyone.

"Don't be afraid, Peter. I live with your mom, Kathryn. She took me in because my own mother bullies me for being homosexual. They call it being gay now. I hope you don't mind I've been living in your room."

There was no response. After about a minute, Larsen noticed that Peter's outline was forming on stage. "I can almost see you. I want to help you. I know you're in a lot of pain."

Slowly, the features on Peter's face began to fill in. Larsen watched in wonder. "Can you tell me how I can help you?"

Peter raised an arm, as if he were reaching out, and the music began to subside. Larsen could now see Peter's face clearly enough to know that he had been crying. "You haven't been crying for forty years, have you?"

Larsen understood that Peter was saying yes, and it made his heart hurt in a way he had never experienced before. "Your mother has never stopped missing you. She told me that she's been looking for your star in the sky."

Hearing that, Peter collapsed to the ground and appeared to be burying his face in his hands. Suddenly, his sobs were audible as they grew in intensity.

"Oh, I'm so sorry. Do you want me to bring your mother here? I'm sure she'd—"

"Yo, Larsen. You still in here?"

Larsen turned to see Gabe, red-faced, back in the theater. "Left my goddamn wallet on one of the seats. What's wrong with you?"

The stage was empty. Peter was gone. Larsen's face fell.

"Why're you lookin' like that? Don't tell me you've seen or heard something."

"Uh, like what?"

"Like anything that isn't normal for this place. I'm not gonna go into detail. I told you there are people out there playing mind games. So if you saw something that wasn't quite right, you'd spill, right?"

Larsen had no idea who Gabe was talking about, but he knew Peter was the real thing, and he wasn't about to share anything that had happened. "I haven't seen anything."

"Good. Now, get the hell back in the trailer. You just came in here to give me a message. What are you standing here for?"

"Um … just daydreaming about being on stage someday. Thinking about the talent competition. You're right; I need to get back to the trailer."

Gabe sighed in frustration and gestured for Larsen to go ahead of him. "I guess it's good to have dreams, kid. Just don't forget that they're meant to be broken." On his way out, Larsen looked mournfully at the stage; discouraged that the opportunity had been lost, but hoping that Peter would reappear soon.

◍◍◍

By the time Arielle, Larsen, and Muggins reached the Dalworths' home at six-fifteen, Mick, Jessie, River, Jinxsy, Eve, Madeleine, and Kathryn were already assembled. Extra chairs and snack tables had been set up in the living room, and a buffet dinner had been arranged on the dining room table except for the pizza.

Larsen was eager to talk to River, but he was far too polite not to make all of the necessary greetings first. "Hi, Jinxsy. I'm really glad you were able to make it."

"I am, too. Hey, obviously you know my mother, she's your English teacher, but this is Madeleine, Eve's mom and my grandmother."

Eve smiled warmly. "Hey, Larsen. This is a great occasion. We're all so proud of you. I just might have to ask for an autograph before the night is over."

"I'll sign my next English paper. How's that?"

Eve laughed. "Fair enough. If you'll all excuse me, I have a quick phone call to return."

"Sure, Ms. Carrow."

Eve smiled and walked away as Madeleine reached out to shake Larsen's hand. "It's such an old cliché, but I really have heard wonderful things about you. I've known Kathryn for many years. She's a special lady and I'm so pleased that you have a home with her. No doubt you're a shining star in her life."

Larsen gulped as he thought about how much the mention of a star had pained Peter. "She's the star in my life."

Kathryn, upon hearing the conversation, smiled and then made a face. "You wouldn't be trying to embarrass me now, would you, Larsen?" As she burst into laughter, Larsen realized she was kidding.

Impatiently, River walked over to join the group for a brief moment. "Hello again, everyone. Sorry to bust in here, but I need to talk to Lars. Oh, and my dad just told me the pizza guy called his cell. Our dinner should be here in just a few minutes."

Kathryn's eyes lit up. "I love pizza. I hope you ordered at least one pie with extra anchovies. My housemate here loves them."

Larsen made a face and then chuckled when he realized Kathryn was teasing him again. "You just got me twice in one minute."

Her eyes twinkled. "Being seventy-five doesn't mean I don't have tricks up my sleeve."

"Good one, Ms. Winterstrom." Eagerly, River yanked Larsen away and off into a corner of the living room. "So, I got your text. You said that you saw Peter and would explain the rest later."

"Yeah, I did. I introduced myself and told him I wanted to help him. The poor guy has been crying for forty years."

"That's really sad. What else did he say?"

"He didn't say anything. I just asked him a question, and I could hear him say yes. You know, sort of telepathically. I could hear him the same way I hear you now. I asked him if he wanted me to bring his mother to the theater."

"Great! What did he say?"

"Gabe came in looking for his wallet, and Peter disappeared. I was so bummed. It was really embarrassing, Riv. I mean, I supposedly had come in to give Gabe a message, and I'm still there five minutes later, staring into space. I had to leave when Gabe told me to get back to the trailer."

"Did Gabe say anything else? You know, has he seen anything?"

"I'm sure he has, Riv. But all I know is that he thinks whatever he is seeing is an illusion created by some not-so-nice people."

"I hope my mother's not in danger!"

"We'll get to the bottom of it. I'm so on it."

Chapter 21

"And we've got three minutes until show time!"

Larsen looked around at everyone, whose eyes were all on the TV. "You're making me nervous, Mrs. D. I feel like I have to perform live in three minutes."

Arielle laughed. "You mean in two minutes and forty-five seconds."

Mick put his arm around his wife. "I have it on great authority that your Othello rocks. Nothing to be nervous about."

"Well, honey, he is going to be performing live at the talent competition in one month and two days."

"Ha ha. Dude, welcome to the family. My parents only mess with people they love." River pulled his cell phone out of his pocket and snapped a photo of Larsen. "I love the look on your face. I'm calling this one 'Stupefied.' "

Jessie laughed. "Sounds like something I used to call you, numbnuts. Only it didn't have that many syllables in it."

Kathryn pointed to the screen. "Look; here it is!"

Everyone watched as the promo trailer opened up with a velvet-voiced announcer explaining that the Desert Theater in Mystekal, California, was undergoing a complete renovation. The announcer introduced Arielle as the project manager, and there was a shot of her giving a tour of the lobby and then going through the main entrance doors to the theater. After a brief explanation of how the show would focus on the vintage restoration from start until the grand opening and talent competition, the scene switched to Larsen, fully in character, standing on the stage.

As the group watched the close-up footage of Larsen reciting his monologue, Arielle was the first to gasp in horror. Behind Larsen stood a young woman in a flimsy white gown, putting her hands to each side of her head and letting out a blood-curdling scream.

"What the hell! Who is that?" Arielle turned to scan the stunned faces in her living room. "Does anyone know what's going on?"

Jinxsy, Jessie, Larsen, and River exchanged looks, but everyone was at a loss. On the TV, the woman behind Larsen finished screaming and faded into nothingness as the promo ended.

Arielle almost jumped when her cell phone rang. She turned to Mick. "It's Lisa. Maybe she knows something. I'm going to take this in the kitchen. She hurried out of the room.

Everyone expressed shock over what they had just seen, then focused on Arielle when she returned a minute later. "Okay, people, that was my friend who produced and edited this trailer. She has no clue what the screaming woman was doing there. All Lisa knows is that woman wasn't there on Saturday night when she finished the promo. She's freaking the eff out, and she's on the warpath right now to find out what happened. You're all welcome to hang out here to see what she turns up. Larsen, I'm so sorry, sweetie. I hope you know I had nothing to do with this."

"Oh, Mrs. D, I know you didn't. Believe me, that never entered my brain."

"Good. Well, there's got to be a good explanation for this nonsense, and I sure as hell am going to figure out who's behind it."

Forty-five minutes later, everyone in the Dalworths' living room was still trying to make sense of what had happened. Arielle, desperate to hear back from Lisa, clutched the phone, unaware that she was looking at it every few seconds.

"Watching the phone doesn't make it ring, honey."

"I know, Mick. I'm a complete wreck. I don't have a clue what that insanity was. I just wish Lisa would call with some answers."

A loud knock at the door rattled Arielle so much that the phone flew out of her hands and into Mick's. Everyone else was startled as well. "Riv, you want to see who that is?"

"Uh, yeah. Sure, Dad."

River opened the front door to find a forty-something African American woman scowling at him. "So you must be—"

"Mom!" Panicked, Larsen stood up and ran over to Raylene as River moved out of his way. "What are you doing here? Seriously?"

Raylene scanned the room. "Well now, looks like you got a damn party going on here."

"Do you want to sit down, Mom? Here, you can have my seat. Right over here."

As Larsen motioned to show his mother where to sit, she took a swipe at his hand and pushed it away. "I'm here to take a stand, and that's what I'm gonna do. What fool sits down to take a stand?"

River watched nervously as he saw beads of sweat form on Larsen's forehead. In an instant, he understood why Larsen had said his mother was worse than Jax could ever be.

"Really, what are you doing here? Let's go outside and talk."

"Oh, hellllllll no!"

"Please, Mom. I won't leave this time no matter what you have to say, okay?"

Instead of responding to Larsen, Raylene turned toward the others in the room. "I'll tell y'all what I'm doing here. I'm a hard-working woman enjoying my night off, and I turn on the TV to watch a romance movie and relax. At commercial time, I almost got up from the couch to pour me another drink when what do I see but the damn Desert Theater on the screen." Raylene looked at Arielle. "And I see you, the woman who hired him. You weren't cursed with a homo son, so you go hire mine to do your gay work."

Arielle wanted to respond, but no words came out. Kathryn stood up. "I won't tolerate this! You stop this instant."

Narrowing her eyes, Raylene shifted her focus. "I'll get to you in a moment, old white lady playing mama to my boy. You just wait your turn."

Watching Larsen plead with his eyes, Kathryn reluctantly resumed her seat, barely able to contain her anger. Madeleine, who was sitting next to her, put a comforting hand on top of Kathryn's.

"All these years knowing my boy was a queer have been hard enough on me. I've been ashamed and embarrassed. No man wanted to stay in the damn home with a gay in the next room. I only brought them home to try and give my boy some manly role models, but that sure as hellllll didn't work. Least I finally got a man to stay. Next thing I know my son doesn't want to live with me anymore. If that weren't enough of a punch in the gut, what the hellllll does he do next but publicly humiliate me by making a spectacle of himself on the TV. And the announcer man says he's gonna be up on stage again, in January, in front of a packed house next time. Well, I'll be damned if I'm gonna let that happen." Her eyes black with anger, Raylene went face to face with Larsen. "That there embarrassment on the TV is all I'm gonna take!"

Trying desperately not to fall apart in front of everyone, Larsen panicked as he attempted to explain. "We don't know what happened, Mom. Mrs. D's friend who produces the show is doing everything she can to find out. That screaming woman wasn't supposed to be a part of the promo. I'm so sorry you're embarrassed. I am, too. We all are."

"Tell me you're joking! That screaming banshee is the only one with any damn sense. No wonder she covered her ears and screamed. She didn't want to hear a gay boy read Shakespeare any more than any sane person wants to see one play Romeo. Or Superman. Batman. Then again, a lot of them superheroes wear tights, so you really don't know anymore. All y'all are infiltrating the planet."

Madeleine's calm touch could not keep Kathryn in her seat. She got up and walked over to Raylene. "I understand how it feels to take a stand. Now, you watch real good, because this old lady is going to show you how it's done." Kathryn turned to look at Larsen, whose eyes had welled with tears. "Please sit down in my seat. I need to talk to your mother. And know that I'm very sorry it's come to this."

Larsen nodded and took a seat next to Madeleine, who immediately put a comforting arm around him.

Kathryn now stood face to face with Raylene. "This March sixth will mark forty years, Mrs. Davis, forty years since my fifteen-year-old son, Peter Nicholas Winterstrom, was murdered by a madman."

Everyone, including Raylene, looked shocked at hearing Kathryn's words. "My son, just like yours, loved the theater. God had gifted him with so much talent. He was a brilliant actor and had a voice that stopped people in their tracks. That's right. Nobody could hear my Peter sing and continue about his or her business. His voice was powerful and mesmerizing. But it wasn't just his talent that most people loved; it was his exuberance and his love for life.

"It's tough as hell even in these times for young men and women who are homosexual. They can't change just because some people are uncomfortable with their sexuality. If the world suddenly flip-flopped and being heterosexual was deemed wrong, could you change, Mrs. Davis? Could you make yourself be attracted to women because society wanted you to be?"

"That's the damn stupidest thing anyone has ever said to me. Ain't no secret that Raylene Davis likes herself some—"

"Mom!"

"Oh, hush up, Larsen. Ain't nobody in this room doesn't know what the helllll I mean."

Kathryn was relentless. "You can articulate any nonsense you want, Mrs. Davis. My train has been coming down the track for a long time, and you're not going to derail me. Now, you listen!"

Raylene, surprised by the rise in Kathryn's voice, stepped back. "You ain't got nothing to say to me."

Taking a moment to inhale deeply, Kathryn steeled herself to continue. "Maybe you missed what I first said about my son being murdered by a madman. That's right, he had a boyfriend who he loved dearly. They were meant to be together. But this boy had a very evil father who hated homosexuality even more than you do. When his many attempts to separate the boys failed, he devised a plan to not only kill my son, but also to kill his own. Can you imagine that? People with a lot of money can do most anything they want. It was nothing back then to fake an accident, especially when you've got the police department on your payroll.

"They said Peter died when a metal crate in a warehouse fell and crushed his skull … I hope he died right away … I hope he didn't suffer the way I have all of these years. Deep in my heart, I knew it wasn't an accident, but there was nothing I could do to prove it. The grief was so unbearable that my husband disappeared after a couple of years."

"Probably because he was gay like your son."

Kathryn's eyes flared with rage. "You hush, woman!"

"I'm just telling you the truth. We don't know each other, but you can't tell me that in forty years you haven't considered that was the reason."

A long, silent pause ensued. Kathryn looked within herself, while everyone else looked at her, and at each other.

"That's quite an offensive thing to suggest, Mrs. Davis. But when you have nearly forty years to wonder about something, you do look at it from every possible angle. And I did. But no, I did not conclude that my husband was gay." Kathryn's angry voice softened. "You've got a wonderful son in Larsen. He's bright, talented, polite, funny, ambitious, loving, and so much more. And you're ashamed of him because he is openly gay and proud of the man he is. Do you have any idea how lucky you are, how blessed you are, to have this wonderful young man alive and well here in this room with you? He has dreams, wonderful dreams. And I know he's going to fulfill them, with or without you. I hope you decide to be a part of his life. It gets real lonely without your only child. Believe me, I know. You should be his biggest cheerleader."

Raylene looked into Kathryn's eyes. "I'm sorry you lost your boy. Guess that kind of explains why you want mine. But I'm sorry; you won't find me waving any damn pom-poms in the air. I'm outta this mess." Turning to Larsen, her voice cracking, Raylene uttered the unthinkable. "You're dead to me, son. Now I'm gonna go home and have me a damn drink."

📖📖📖

Everyone was still as Raylene let herself out the door. When the sound of her car driving off was heard, Larsen let the tears fall silently down his face. He looked at River and knew by the devastation on his face that he was heartbroken for him. He knew all of the people in the room felt the same way.

He stood up as Kathryn walked toward him, then burst into tears and buried his head on her shoulder.

Kathryn held him for a long minute while he cried. "Come on, son, sit down."

Arielle jumped up and grabbed a box of tissues and handed them to Madeleine to pass to Kathryn. Everyone in the room was dazed. Even Muggins got off his bed and came over to Larsen, rubbing the side of his head against Larsen's leg.

Larsen looked at Arielle. "I guess what I said about my life turning around was just a bit premature."

"Oh, no, honey. Your life is going to be magnificent. I'm not going to pretend that what just happened wasn't devastating and horrible, but I'm never going to believe that your mother meant what she said. Your life *has* turned around, and you've brought so much into all of our lives. We're all better for knowing you."

Kathryn handed Larsen a tissue, which he squeezed in his hand, but he didn't bother wiping his tears. Glancing around the room, he spoke aloud to no one in particular. "She's so evil. She's so filled with hate. I've never done anything to embarrass her except be me. I can't change who I am."

Kathryn took his hand in hers. "No, you cannot change who you are. Your mother is not evil. She's fighting her own demons. Like Arielle said, I want to believe that she'll conquer them. Those were very ugly words she spoke, though. Nobody here will dispute that."

As Eve's own memories came rushing back, she began to tear up. "I agree with Kathryn. Your mom has deep-rooted issues, but she wasn't born evil, not like my father. He was the cruelest, meanest man I ever knew." Her pained voice grew louder. "If you want to know what being born evil really means, look up Ernest Carrow in the dictionary of life. I'm sorry; I don't mean to diminish your pain. How selfish of me. It just triggered—"

Jinxsy got up and put her arms around Eve, who smiled as she felt her daughter's loving touch.

"It's okay, Ms. Carrow. Really. If I were you and heard everything my mom just said, I'd be having the same flashbacks." Larsen turned to Kathryn. "I know this is really hard for you, but when you were talking to my mother and telling her about Peter, you said that he died in a warehouse."

River, Jinxsy, and Jessie all looked at one another quickly as they realized why Larsen was asking.

"That's what I said, Larsen. But Peter didn't die in a warehouse."

River whispered to Jessie. "He died in the theater. Definitely."

"I know, Riv. But we can't say we know anything about it."

Larsen, unclenching his fist, took the tissue he had been holding and wiped his tears. "I shouldn't have asked about Peter, because I know you don't like to talk about the details. I was just …"

Responding to Mick, who was holding up a bottle of cognac, Kathryn nodded yes to the offer of a drink, which he poured and passed to her only moments later.

"This is just what I needed. Thank you, Mick. Larsen is right, my friends. I have never liked to talk about the details because doing so only made the pain deeper. The truth is, the details made everything all too real. I've been living in a fantasy world hoping that someday I'd see my son alive again. It's kept me sane. But after what happened today, and hearing what Eve had to say, I think it's time I tell you all the story of Peter's death."

Eve looked confused. "I'm not sure what I said that had anything to do with Peter, but you shouldn't disclose anything that you want to be kept private."

"I think I need to. You're all here for a reason; I believe the time has come. Unless someone here would rather I didn't say anymore."

River looked explosive. "No, please. We really want to hear about Peter."

Arielle and Mick looked curiously at their son.

Kathryn handed her drink to Larsen, then folded her hands together and said a silent prayer. "Well, you all know who Peter was. There's nobody in this room who hasn't heard about his talent and his passion for life. As much as I like to brag about that part, I'll move on to the things you don't know.

"Peter met his boyfriend when he was fourteen, and there was an instant and magnetic attraction. They both used to say that destiny brought them together in a small desert town. Nicholas, my husband, accepted Peter's homosexuality as I did. We knew early on who he was, and when he told us, we were actually grateful that he hadn't felt the need to live in the closet. Back in those days, and even in today's times, there are still men and women who are not comfortable coming out to the world. It is not for us to judge them either way.

"Anyway, Peter and his boyfriend saw each other for nearly a year before the boy's father found out. Now, there was an evil man. He threatened his son, he threatened our son, he threatened us, he tried to bribe us, and on and on. As time passed, his words and his threats got more ugly and more desperate. One day, Nicholas told me that he feared this man's anger knew no bounds."

Eve put her hands to her mouth. "Oh, my! He sounds as evil as my father."

Larsen handed Kathryn's drink back to her and she took a sip. "As I told Mrs. Davis, it will be forty years ago on the sixth of March that Peter was killed. We were told that the boys broke into a closed warehouse and were snooping around when a crate fell and killed Peter, narrowly missing his boyfriend."

So immersed in Kathryn's tale, Arielle didn't even bother reading the text message from Lisa that she heard come to her phone. "That's horrifying. You were so right when you told Larsen's mother how blessed she was to have her son alive and well and in this room. I know that's how I feel."

River looked at his mother. "Thanks, Mom."

"I'm sorry, Kathryn. I didn't mean to interrupt you."

"I'm glad you did, Arielle. Telling a story like this one, having an extra moment to breathe is a much-needed thing. Anyway, as you can imagine, it was the most horrifying news any parent could receive. We were inconsolable and certainly not permitted anywhere near Peter's friend ever again. We weren't able to ask him a single question. I didn't know what had happened, but I knew what hadn't happened. These were two wonderful boys. They didn't break into warehouses to snoop around or steal. They spent their time together in the Desert Theater, where Peter was set to appear in *West Side Story* as one of the Jets."

Surprised, Larsen looked over at River, Jinxsy, and Jessie, and then turned to Kathryn. "I wouldn't be surprised if his favorite song was 'Tonight,' just like mine."

"You're right, Larsen. It was. He loved that song, especially the line about the minutes seeming like hours, and the hours going so slowly ... he said they were words he could relate to in difficult times."

Trying to disguise his stunned reaction, Larsen asked another question. "Was his boyfriend in the show, too?"

"No. There's no way his father would have allowed that. He kept very quiet about his interests because he thought the theater was one place they could meet safely. And for a while they did.

"On that fateful day, a Saturday, the cast had finished an early rehearsal, and Peter and his friend, with permission, stayed behind just to spend time together. Peter worked at the theater, cleaning, so he had keys and access. Everyone there was very sympathetic to the boys' situation."

Kathryn's voice began to waver, but she fought to tell her story. "When we were told what had happened, after making it through the shock and horror of the news, we didn't believe it. Not any of it. And despite our protestations, despite imploring the police to conduct a full-scale investigation, it was ruled an accident, and the case was closed. Tighter than a drum. I was exhausted by that point. If I thought my continued pleas for justice could have brought my son back, I would have gone on fighting the law forever.

"It wasn't until this murderer died that I found out what had really happened. At the Desert Theater, downstairs, there is a rehearsal space about the size of the stage. Over the years, unused sets have been stored on one end of the large room. There's a lounge area off to the side, as well as a kitchen area and bathrooms. I hope you can all follow me. Now, there was a young man, an actor, who played the role of Tony. That horrible day, he and his leading lady, who played Maria, decided to extend their rehearsal time, as they often did. The two actors stayed downstairs while Peter and his friend hung out on the stage. They often enjoyed reading lines from some of the most popular plays of the time.

"When the young actor heard a loud crash upstairs on the stage, he told his leading lady to stay put, and then he rushed upstairs to see what had happened. That's when he saw the boy's father telling his goons to 'move the dead faggot' ... meaning my darling Peter ... to the warehouse and make it look like a crate had fallen on him. What really killed Peter was a piece of strip lighting. For those of you who don't know, they are very long, heavy units that hold multiple lamps in different colors. I'm sure you've all seen ... oh, who cares, this boy's evil father had his goons climb up on the catwalk above the stage, unsecure the lighting, then drop the unit on top of the boys. When Peter was struck and killed, the bastard ran out onto the stage and said to his son, 'That was meant for you, too!'"

Arielle cried out and covered her face, while Mick tried to calm her.

Kathryn paused and took a sip of cognac. "Is it all right for me to continue?"

Looking up, Arielle gave the go-ahead. "Yes, please, Kathryn. I'm sorry. We want to know. We want you to get rid of the awful secrets you've been carrying around."

"Okay then." Kathryn took another sip. "As I said, it wasn't until after the murderer died that we learned the truth. It was then that the actor, Jamison, felt safe in telling me what he had seen and heard. He said that when he realized what was happening, he went downstairs and grabbed the young lady, and they hid behind the scenery for many hours. He was petrified of being discovered by this wretched man or one of his hired hands. He didn't even tell his costar what he had seen. He only told her to trust him. He didn't want her to have the burden of knowing. For years, he was racked with guilt because he never came forward as a witness. He knew the son would never speak up because his father threatened him immediately after the murder."

Larsen looked curiously at Kathryn. "I still don't understand why he didn't speak up, especially knowing the murderer's son could never do so. His testimony could have put those guys away for life."

"Oh, Larsen, it was no secret that the boy's father had control over the town. Jamison was afraid that if he spoke up, he or his family would be killed. It had already been ruled an accidental death, despite the fraudulent crime scene, and he did the right thing. I'm glad he kept quiet. I would have hated for anyone else to die at this monster's hands. It would have never gone to trial. Maybe today. Not back then."

Eve looked at Kathryn in amazement. "This man sounds exactly like my father. Born evil."

Kathryn took a long pause before responding. "Ernest

Carrow wasn't born evil, Eve. In fact, he was a charming young man. He was Peter's boyfriend."

Chapter 22

Eve and Madeleine stared at one another in mind-numbing disbelief. Kathryn, knowing she had unleashed a shocking truth, bent her head, worried about the impact that her revelations might have had on those she cared about. Larsen tried to comfort Kathryn as she had comforted him. "Everything will be okay, Kathryn. I think everyone here is happy to know the truth."

Kathryn looked forlorn. "I hope so. These shocked faces I'm looking at say otherwise."

Larsen looked soulfully into her eyes. "You've told me so many times how important truth is. And you've told me how destructive lies and secrets can be. Just because people are shocked at the moment, including me, doesn't mean you didn't just do a wonderful and brave thing."

With a faint smile, Kathryn reached over and gave Larsen a hug. "You have wisdom beyond your years. I'm so very proud of you. Thank you for saying that."

Looking helplessly at her best friend, Jinxsy tried to process the surreal and staggering disclosure. Jessie merely shrugged as she mirrored her best friend's incredulity.

River looked at everyone in the room, then at his parents. "Wow; who saw that coming?"

As she took her mother's hand in hers, Eve looked into her eyes. "You were married to him. You had a child together. Didn't you ever suspect?"

Madeleine tilted her neck back and looked at the ceiling. "Good Lord! How in the world did I not know!"

Jinxsy looked at Kathryn. "I'm very grateful to you for telling us the truth. Maybe now I finally have the whole story of where I came from, and maybe now we can all make a bit more sense out of the past. How come you never told anybody before tonight?"

Kathryn looked devastated as she saw the distress on Eve's and Madeleine's faces. "If Ernest Carrow had been guilty of anything besides murdering Eve's true love, Tommy Ribellio, I would have told the truth after his death. I would have explained that he was the victim of heinous abuse. But I couldn't, because despite what Ernie endured at the hands of his father, Willard, he had no right to kill Tommy or try to kill anyone else. I had no sympathy for him. My own child was brutally murdered, and I've never hurt a soul. Not intentionally. Ernie had no right to do the things he did. Just because you understand someone's reasons for being evil does not mean you can accept them. Murderers do not get any special dispensation in my book.

"Yes, Ernie grew up to be an awful man. I think I was the only person in Mystekal he never threatened because he knew I understood his anger. He knew that I would never tell anyone. He gave me a job and told me it was mine as long as I wanted it. But it was understood that I was never to say a word. Believe me."

Madeleine began furiously wringing her hands. "I should have known. Oh, I should have known. You're an idiot, Madeleine! You're a bloody idiot!"

"Momma, stop berating yourself. Please. You told me that your parents forced you to marry him because they were poor and wanted you to have money."

"Oh, Evie, they wanted social status for themselves. I would have done just fine for myself, but Willard handpicked me for his daughter-in-law, and they were easily seduced by his wealth and power. I was seventeen, for goodness sake. I remember overhearing Willard talking to my parents. He said I was the most beautiful young woman in town."

Larsen looked repulsed. "My mother used to point out pretty girls to me all the time. And she was right: they were beautiful. I always agreed with her. Then she'd ask me why I didn't want to ask them out. I'd tell her that she knew why, and she'd just give me a nasty look and say mean things. But, yeah, I understand that kind of thinking. It's ignorant, but some people think a good-looking person of the opposite sex is the best cure for homosexuality."

When Larsen finished speaking, Eve turned back to look at her mother. "I don't want to get personal in a room filled with people, but I was born, so obviously—"

"Three times, Evie. That's right. Three times and three times only. That's all it took for me to get pregnant, and Ernest never touched me again. He just grew meaner and more resentful by the day. I've been in denial. It's all so clear to me now. Of course! Why didn't I see it then? Once he had convinced his father he was a now a straight man and that his youthful homosexuality was nothing but a childhood disease he'd been inoculated against, his father's fortune would be his someday. There was no reason to try to love me."

Kathryn nodded in agreement. "That's exactly what happened, Madeleine. Hindsight is twenty twenty."

"You're so right, Kathryn. I feel so silly saying this now, but it never occurred to me that Ernest might be gay. I thought he was an arrogant rich kid forced to marry me as some kind of arm candy or trophy wife, although at seventeen I didn't couch my thoughts in quite those terms. I tried to make it work because my parents relentlessly pounded it into my brain that it was a match made in heaven and I was 'so lucky.' " Madeleine turned to face Eve and Jinxsy. "The only reason I don't regret what happened is because you two are here."

Jinxsy looked at her grandmother. "You haven't said a thing about Willard Carrow's wife."

"Bernadette. There is nothing to say about Bernie Carrow except that she named her son Ernie so it would rhyme with her name. That was the only decision that poor woman was ever allowed to make in her life."

Kathryn nodded. "That's very true. Bernadette was a sad soul. She rarely smiled, and the only friendships she had were for show— you know, dinner with the local minister and his wife. She was never allowed to be alone with anyone, and she was forbidden to make eye contact with me."

As the conversation went on, Kathryn and Madeleine continued to put together the pieces and make sense out of the past. Arielle, like everyone else, was riveted by the stories. Then she remembered that Lisa had texted her.

Quietly, she slipped out of the living room and into the kitchen, placing the call as she walked.

"Lis, it's me. Sorry, it's been a wild night here. I couldn't get back to you right away. Do you have any news? Tell me you do."

"Hang tight, Ari. I'm really close, but I can't verify anything until I get more information tomorrow. When I do, I'll text you. Leave the trailer to call me back. Take a ride somewhere. Or just sit in your car. Whatever. Just make sure you speak to me in private. Love you, girly. We'll talk then."

📖📖📖

"Hey, Mom. Were you talking to Lisa? Did you find out anything?"

"Yes and no, Jess. But I think she's going to have a lot to tell me tomorrow. I just have to be patient. Not my strong suit at the moment. Larsen, don't worry. Lisa will get to the bottom of this very quickly."

"Of all of the stuff I worried about, the things that happened tonight were never on the list."

Mick got up from his chair and stretched. "They never are."

River was curious. "What were you worried about?"

"That nobody would think I was any good."

Arielle made a sad face. "You were wonderful, Lars. Unfortunately, a person or person(s) unknown decided to upstage you."

Madeleine turned to Larsen. "I'm so sorry that your mother saw it and reacted in the awful way that she did. For my family, something positive came out of this. We have much greater understanding of the monster who brought us so much grief. But I despise the fact that it was at your expense."

"No, don't be. I'm not going to lie. I'm a wreck right now. But I believe in fate, and I think it was meant to be that Kathryn was finally able to talk about what happened to Peter. More than you know." Larsen looked over at River.

Kathryn stood in front of Madeleine and Eve. "Before we all say our good nights in a moment, there's one more thing I think is worth mentioning. It won't bring Tommy back, but it may bring greater clarity. Eve, I don't believe Ernie killed Tommy because you became pregnant. That was just an excuse. I believe he killed Tommy because he couldn't stand for anyone to be so much in love when it had been denied to him. I think he killed Tommy out of jealousy. His true love was dead, and nobody else deserved to have what he didn't. Not if he had any say. Well, a murder is a murder. I guess the reasons don't really matter. I'm probably just rambling now."

Eve put her arms around Kathryn. "No, that information helps. Knowing the truth, even when it's ugly, is a good thing. I always tell my students that when people don't have answers, they make them up because we all have such a strong desire to have life's mysteries explained. You've helped my family tremendously, and I hope you feel much freer by releasing the secrets you've been keeping for forty years."

"Yes, I do. Thank you. My worries are with Larsen now."

Larsen looked compassionately at Kathryn. "Don't worry too much, okay? Things with my mom are the worst ever. But I have more supportive friends than I've ever had in my life. That's got to count for something, right?"

Chapter 23

Gabe was fidgeting with his desk drawer when Arielle and Muggins got to the trailer at ten o'clock. Muggins took his usual spot on his bed under her desk, and Arielle noticed that the dog didn't offer his usual good-morning greeting by running to the end of the trailer.

Putting up his hand to greet her, Gabe didn't say a word. Arielle was just about to ask him what he thought of the promo whodunit, when something told her to wait for Lisa's call. "Good morning, Gabe. I hope you got my text. I went to Palm Desert to pick up the hardware for the restrooms. The packages are in my car. I'll go get them in a bit."

Gabe glanced at her sideways, avoiding direct eye contact. "Not gonna need them until tomorrow. Not a problem. Getting the rest of the seats in will be today's priority."

"Yeah … right. Well, I'm just letting you know." Arielle turned on her computer and tried not to look at Gabe while she nervously waited for it to boot. Lisa had said she'd text her, but Arielle hoped that maybe she'd sent an email with more information.

Out of the corner of her eye she watched Gabe. He was working almost too quickly with an intensity unlike any she'd noticed before. Twenty minutes into reading her emails, she heard a notification on her phone. Seeing the text she was waiting for, she hurried out of the trailer to her car, jumped inside, and called Lisa.

"Hey, Ari. That was quick."

"Quick? It felt like an eternity between last night and now. Please tell me you've solved this miserable mystery. My heart can't take it."

"I've solved it all right, pretty much, but you're not going to like it. Steel yourself, girlfriend."

Arielle leaned back in the car seat and took a deep breath. "I'm ready. Let me have it."

"Okay, you remember the first time we came to Mystekal to film. I think I'd mentioned to you that a guy who worked in the building was visiting my assistant, Petra. I told you it was a bit much, but I was being cool about it."

"Uh ... yeah, I think I do remember that. It didn't seem too significant, so I haven't thought about it since."

"Ah, well, turns out, it was very significant."

Arielle grabbed the steering wheel with her free hand as if it were Lisa's arm. "In what way?"

"Do you remember when I first called you about this project and I gave you some dirt on your ex? Remember I told you Phil works in my building?"

"Yes, I do. But slow down; I'm confused. Are you saying he's been disguising himself to see Petra?"

"Oh, no! Not enough makeup in the world to disguise that mug. Ugh. Phil hasn't been seeing Petra. For one, he's hot and heavy with his new girlfriend, Candace. Found out via Petra that's the name of that blonde he's been seen around town with."

Arielle scrunched up her nose as if a bad odor had invaded her car. "Ugh, I remember. Go on, Lis."

"She has some kind of workout show he's producing. Anyway, forget about her. The person of interest here is Daniel Clemmons, Phil's assistant. He's the one involved with Petra."

"Are you serious? Phil's assistant has been hanging out in your office every day?"

" 'Fraid so, Ari. Let me backtrack to last night. I was so wired up after what happened that I was still online around two a.m. I was just about to shut down my email when one comes in from a guy named Edgar Benson."

"That name rings a bell, but I can't place him."

"He's a B-movie director. He's known for doing mostly horror flicks. Anyway, his wife was watching that romance movie on our sister station last night, and at the commercial break she was rather startled to see a clip from her husband's film smack in the middle of the Desert Theater's promo trailer."

"Is she one hundred percent sure it's from his film?"

"Think so, Ari. She was the actress who did the screaming."

"Wow …"

"Yeah. Wow. Anyway, Edgar was polite in his email but wanted to know how the hell footage from his movie ended up in my station's promo trailer. I wrote back and told him I didn't have the faintest idea and was looking into it. Then I went to bed. Got up this morning, grabbed my shovel, and started digging. Two hours ago, I get a call from him. At first, he has a not-so-friendly accusatory tone in his voice. He said he read my email, and it was hard to believe I didn't know anything. Know why? This is rich: because he knows that the production manager from said film, Phil Hodges, used to work with my husband, Ross Finlay."

"Oh, man. What did you say, Lis?"

"You mean after the F-bombs stopped flying out of my mouth?"

Arielle managed to laugh. "Yeah, then."

"I told him that Ross and I had cut all ties with Phil over two years ago and that he just happened to work in the same building I did. I told him that the fog was lifting, but I needed to investigate and would get back to him ASAP. Meanwhile, Petra is shoving a note in my face to let me know that Sam Olson from the corporate office is on the line demanding to speak to me immediately. I put that fire out for the moment and went to speak to Petra."

"And what was she doing? Playing dumb?"

"Believe it or not, she had nothing to do with it. Not directly. Poor thing. She's actually been sleeping with this Daniel guy, thinking she had a hot new boyfriend, and the entire relationship appears to be a farce. We're guessing Daniel has been paid by Phil to see her. I was wondering how he managed to take her to extravagant restaurants on an assistant's salary. Not to mention the flowers and other gifts he was giving her.

"Petra should have kept her mouth shut about my business, but since she and Daniel had similar jobs, his keen interest in my work didn't seem all that suspicious to her. And nothing was really top secret, either."

"Okay, so didn't Petra know the name of his boss? She's been working for you for years. She would have had to recognize the name."

"I asked her that. He just said he worked on whatever health and fitness show Phil produces. There are a lot of people who work on that show."

"So what happened next?"

"On Thursday, Petra happens to mention in passing that Josh and I would be working on Saturday to edit the promo here in the office. Later that afternoon, Daniel asks for her car keys so that he can leave a special gift for her in there. She thought that was so flippin' romantic that she gave them to him. Clearly, he went and made a copy of our office key, then bought a teddy bear to stick on her passenger seat to keep the ruse going."

"Have either one of you confronted Daniel or Phil?"

"No, not yet. Thinking about what to do. I have a locksmith here at the moment taking care of one problem. Anyway, my guess is that Daniel gave the key to Phil, and when he saw Josh and me leave, he came into my office, stole the flash drive from my computer, downloaded the file to his own, worked his revolting magic on it, then replaced the file on my drive. And I come in here yesterday morning and merrily shoot the file off like a damn fool."

"Are you kidding me? I feel sick to my stomach. Phil must have done this to try and sabotage my work! Why would he do something so stupid like that? Even he's capable of better tricks than the one he pulled. This is so childish. He wants revenge; I know it. He blames me for ruining his movie career. He's out to get me, and he's not going to stop until he gets what he wants: my total destruction."

"Ari, I need to think about this. Just hang on. Listen, there's one more thing I need to tell you."

"Holy hell. There's more?"

"Yeah. Um, that first time I was in Mystekal, I told you that Gabe looked familiar."

Arielle felt a tingling sensation as goose bumps formed on her arms. "Uh, yeah."

"I remembered where I've seen him before: at the coffeehouse in the lobby of our building. He was in some heavy convo with Daniel."

📖📖📖

When Arielle returned to the trailer, she found Gabe sitting at his desk looking very angry and agitated. He was so lost in thought that he didn't hear her come in. Not wanting to startle him, she walked slowly over to his desk.

Just as she approached, he put a cup of coffee to his lips. Seeing Arielle standing there, he put the cup down so quickly that a fair amount of coffee spilled on his desk. Cursing, he blotted the wet spots with tissue, then looked disgusted as they turned to soppy mush in his large, muscular hands. Finally, he looked up at Arielle. "Sorry, I'm a bit jittery today. On my third cup of coffee. Bad idea. Just didn't get enough sleep last night."

"Really? Any particular reason?"

"Well, uh ..."

"I take it you watched the promo trailer."

Flustered, he picked up a stapler from his desk to give his trembling hands something to do. "Yeah, I saw that nightmare. Watched with my kids."

Arielle stood there, trying to gauge his guilt or innocence. "Gabe, come sit at Larsen's desk. We need to have a chat. Okay?"

She noticed as he swallowed a lump in his throat, then put the stapler down and rose to follow her back to the other end of the trailer. Fumbling with Larsen's chair as he pulled it out from under the desk, he sat down, trying to give Arielle his very best impression of a man with few worries.

Arielle looked at Gabe for several seconds before speaking, noticing that he got more nervous with every moment that passed. "Gabe, it's very interesting to me that you saw that trailer, with a woman in a white dress screaming as Larsen recited from *Othello*, and it wasn't the first thing you mentioned to me this morning. Or the second. Or the third. Why in the world weren't you eager to discuss it? Didn't it flip you the fuck out the way it did me?"

"Yeah, of course. As for this morning, well ... you looked really upset, and I figured maybe I should leave you alone. I thought you'd talk to me when you were ready. Just like we're doing now."

Arielle smiled sweetly. "Gabe, no disrespect intended, but that's bullshit, and you know it."

Gabe sighed heavily and said nothing.

"Cat got your tongue? I get it. You don't really want to say anything to me until you figure out how much I know. Am I getting warm?" Arielle grabbed her bottled water and took several long gulps. "Gabe, you're tops in your field. You came highly recommended. That's why I hired you. And I know you're supporting three kids. I'm assuming that you want to keep not only this job but also the ones you were hired to do when we're finished here. Just speak up at any time and let me know if I'm on the right track. Before the end of the year would be good."

"You're right. I want to keep my job. I need to keep my job. My family will go down in flames if I don't. My kids need me more now than ever. You know I'm recently divorced, and you know my wife tricked me into moving to Los Angeles just so she could dump me when we arrived."

"Right. I do know all of that, and I'm very sorry." Arielle picked up her key ring and began playing with it. She noticed that whenever she stopped talking, Gabe appeared even more agitated. After two long minutes of silence, she put the keys down and looked into his eyes. "So why don't you start by telling me what I don't know? How about that, Gabe? Do I sound like a happy woman to you? I hope not. In fact, I'm a really pissed-off woman who has zero tolerance for bullshit right now. So why don't you start by telling me how you know Daniel Clemmons in Los Angeles. And don't even think about saying you don't, because I know that you do."

"Aw, shit. Arielle, I know this looks bad, and I'm not entirely innocent, but I didn't do anything. I had nothing to do with that promo trailer, and I've done nothing to compromise the integrity of this renovation. Well, not really."

"What the hell does 'well, not really' mean?"

"Will you let me explain everything without cutting me off or firing me before I finish? Please, Arielle. Can you do that?"

"Absolutely. Believe me, it would be disastrous for me to lose you. But if you deserve to be fired, you will be. So start talking."

"All right. You know that work had dried up in Jersey City, or so I thought, and my wife found herself a job in Los Angeles.

She'd been out here at some convention and apparently made some connections. Yeah, she connected, all right! Whatever. Anyway, I had no desire to leave Jersey City. I've lived there all my life. It's my home. I know people and knew something would turn up soon. Meanwhile, my older girl, Avalon, the one your son knows, has this gift for painting things before they happen. Yeah, I know, it's freaky and all that, but if you knew my girl, well, it wouldn't surprise you. She's different and just about as wonderful as a kid can get.

"So, uh, one day she paints this lady lying on the street, and the next day a lady gets hit by a car. The scene was pretty much as Avvie had painted it. Before you know it, we're getting phone calls, death threats, and all kinds of shit saying that my girl was the devil and we needed to get the hell out of Dodge. My daughters were scared out of their mind, so I finally gave in to my then wife and said yes to Los Angeles. When we got to the City of Angels, she dumped me within forty-eight hours."

"Are you serious? In two days?"

"That's right. And that's when she clues me in that she's had a boyfriend there the whole time. She conned me into moving the family there because I 'owed' her. She raised my kids. What the hell does that mean? Who does she think has been supporting the fam damily for two decades! Next thing I know, I get a call from a Good Samaritan in JC telling me that my wife was the one who initiated the hate campaign against our own daughter."

"What the … That's horrible! Why would a woman traumatize her own child like that? The entire family? That's crazy, Gabe."

Gabe's face reddened, and Arielle could see that he was getting angry all over again. "Why? Because she wanted to be with some son-of-a-bitch more than she loves our kids, that's why. She's tried to tell my kids that it was for their own good that she told a little white lie to bring the family to California, where they'd have a better life. Have you ever heard such a damn crock?"

"No. And I'm guilty of some pretty twisted rationalizations myself, but nothing that bad. So, what happened next?"

"She tells me that the least she can do is find me a job. Turns out her new employer is also her new boyfriend, and he knows a lot of people, including some restoration specialist in Los Angeles, Winston Blane. He's also an old friend of yours, right?"

"Yes … I've known Win for several years. He's the first person I called when I was hired to renovate the theater. He said he didn't know you personally but that you had an impressive work history and impeccable references. There was no reason to ask him anything else. Go on."

"Okay, my ex introduces me to Daniel Clemmons, who she says is a coworker of hers, and he'll introduce me to Win. He does. Win tells me you had called him for referrals, sends me down here, and you hire me on the spot. When I go back to LA to pack my stuff, again, Daniel tells me there's one caveat: he says that he needs me to plant some clues around this place so that you'll think the theater is haunted. He doesn't give me any reasons why, but he tells me that you left your husband and kids once and moved to LA, where you found another man."

Arielle looked nauseated. "A part of my history I would gladly erase from the annals of time if I could."

"I'm sure. So, I'm really pissed off with my soon-to-be-ex, and I'm not really thinking clearly. All I want to do is support my kids. When Daniel tells me that you're a woman who left her family, well, I'm throwin' you in the same mud pile with Candace. I figure you're already dirty, so what's the big deal if I do what the guy says?"

"And then what, Gabe? What did you do?"

"Nothing, Arielle. I'm a guy who grew up on the streets. Yeah, my senses went on vacation when Candace pulled all the shit she did, but once I got here, I saw you were a good woman. I found out you'd remarried your husband and were very much in love."

"Yes. Even more so than when I first married him."

Gabe smiled in acknowledgment. "I saw you were a good woman and that you had the same passion to restore this place as I did. Then the first day of school my girl gets bullied, and it's your kid who's got her back. I'm telling you, there was no way I was going to do jack to hurt you. And I told Daniel that."

"I see. And what did he say?"

"He and some other guy kept threatening me. They said they were going to tell you what I had planned to do, and I threw that back in their faces. Those dim wits aren't the brightest bulbs. I kept calling their bluff, but the threats kept getting uglier. Then shit started happening around here, and—"

"Whoa. Wait a minute. Rewind the tape. Did you say your wife is named Candace? Is she an aerobics instructor? Does she have a little show on another cable network? Is her boss the guy she left you for?"

"Yeah. That's her."

Arielle lay back in her chair and screamed, "Holy shit!"

Muggins came out from under the desk and looked at Gabe to see if he'd done anything worthy of a growl. "It's all right, boy. Go back under Mommy's desk. Go on." Muggins looked at Arielle, then at Gabe, as if to warn him, and curled up again on his bed.

"Gabe, do you swear to me that you have told me everything and left nothing out?"

"On my children's lives, Arielle. And I don't get any more serious than that."

"It's all making sense now. The bastard that your wife is shacking up with, the one she dragged you all out here to be with ... he's my ex. His name is Phil Hodges."

Gabe pondered the information. "Jesus! Damn her. Damn them. Yeah, that's right: Phil. She wouldn't tell me his name, but I heard Daniel calling some guy named Phil on the phone when I was coming back from the men's room in the coffeehouse. He didn't think I'd heard him. I didn't think anything of it. He could have asked for Tom, Dick, or Harry. What the hell did a name mean to me?"

"Listen, Gabe, Phil Hodges is the scum of the earth. He fits every cliché about Hollywood slime you've ever heard about, and he blames me for ruining his career."

"I thought he was a hotshot producer at the cable network."

"Oh, he very well may be. But he used to be a hotshot movie producer and lived an entirely different life. I'm sure his current situation may look appealing to many people, but he's not the least bit happy with it. He's living in a two-bedroom condo in Hollywood when he used to have a six-bedroom house in Bel Air. That's where I lived with him. Believe me, Gabe, Phil destroyed his own career by being an abusive prick, but men like that don't take personal responsibility. They're not like you. So, not only is he now with your ex-wife, but he tried to use your anger against her to hurt me. Are you following all of that?"

"I sure as hell am. Arielle, I'm really sorry. Believe me, I've been trying hard to keep them at bay. I just wish I knew how they were getting in here to do everything. I know Larsen's seen something, but he's not talking."

"Wait; you said something a minute or so ago about how things started happening around here, and now you're going there again. What are you talking about? What is Larsen not talking about?"

Gabe leaned forward and lowered his voice. "I have no idea how they're doing it, Arielle, but I'm positive they're the ones who messed with the promo—"

"Yes, I know. My friend Lisa has pretty much confirmed that."

"Well, I'm trying to tell you that they're getting in here somehow, and I'll be damned if I know how. I've watched Raphael and the other two like hawks, and it's not them. I've checked every nook and cranny of this place and come up with nada. I'm telling ya, it's keepin' me awake at nights."

"What is it that Raphael and the guys aren't doing and someone else is doing? Don't keep me in suspense."

"Making it look as if this place is haunted, that's what. Making a blond kid appear and disappear. Playing that song from *West Side Story*. Making the stage cold. Making crying noises come outta nowhere. They're clever. I've tried to stop them. I thought I was a smart guy. But for the life of my kids and me I can't figure out how they're doing it. Guess they're not as stupid as they sound most of the time."

Arielle took a few more sips from her water bottle. "Thank you, Gabe. You can go back to work now."

"Is everything okay with—"

"Please, Gabe. Just go back to work."

Chapter 24

"So, Lars, there you have it. That's everything I know, from my horrid ex tampering with our promo trailer to his new girlfriend and Gabe's ex-wife being one and the same."

Larsen scratched Muggins' neck as the dog cozied up to him. "I would have never figured all of that out if I lived a hundred years. Just like Shakespeare wrote in *As You Like It*: 'All the world's a stage, And all the men and women merely players. They have their exits and their entrances; And one man in his time plays many parts …' "

"You're quite a fan of the Bard."

"Yeah. My English teacher at my last school was a Shakespeare freak, lucky for me. And now I'm a bit of one, too."

"Golly gee, that's interesting, Lars." Arielle's voice grew more sarcastic. "And you know what? I'd be even more interested if I weren't so busy here and if there wasn't a big piece of this story that you know and I don't. So before Gabe comes back—"

"I'm so sorry, Mrs. D. I really am. We just didn't want—"

"We? Did you say 'we'?"

"Um …yes, I did."

"Lars, you know I adore you, but I'm not really happy that you've been hiding the truth from me about the goings-on at this theater. By 'we,' I'm assuming you mean you and Gabe, right? You and Gabe decided not to tell me about the unusual things you've seen, despite the fact that you know I've seen someone, too. You even told me you thought it was someone from the neighborhood.

Was that what you believed, or was that meant to throw me off track? Because I don't like being lied to, Lars."

Becoming emotionally distraught was the last thing he wanted to do, but Larsen had been on edge ever since his mother's surprise visit the night before, and he was a lot more fragile than he cared to admit. As a few tears rolled down his face, he quickly wiped them away with his hand. "I hate myself right now. You've been so good to me; I'd be lost without you. And, no, I didn't mean Gabe and me."

Arielle folded her arms and stared at Larsen. "Then real quickly, you'd better explain who the 'we' includes."

"Um, River, Jessie, and Jinxsy. And, yeah, Gabe told me not to tell you that people were messing with things in the theater. He just didn't want to upset you."

"I'm up to date on Gabe's rationale, but I'm clueless about yours. So, my kids and Jinxsy knew about this, too. And that's the real reason you were all together at my house on Saturday, right?"

"Yeah … sorry."

"Jinxsy owns this theater, I don't, so let's leave her out of this for the time being. Give me one good reason why you and my children made a mutual decision to keep me in the dark about the fact that people have been gaslighting me, perhaps all of us, into thinking this theater was haunted."

"Gaslighting?"

"Oh, sorry. It's actually a word that originates from a 1940s film called *Gaslight.* It's when you manipulate a person's environment to make him … or in this case, her, think that she's going insane."

"Oh, yeah. I've actually heard that before."

"Good. Now, can we return to our regularly scheduled question?"

Noticing that his hands were trembling, Larsen put them in

his lap, hoping his anxiety would be less obvious.

"Lars, I'm sorry. I've been sarcastic as hell all day today. No one has been spared. I'm just all out of patience. Now, tell me why I wasn't allowed to know that someone's been sneaking into this theater to create illusions, delusions, or whatever the hell it is they've been doing to make me, and perhaps everyone else, think this place is haunted."

"Mrs. D, Gabe is the only one who thinks that someone is coming in here to mess with you."

Arielle ran her fingers through her hair and dug them into her scalp in frustration. "What do you mean Gabe is the only one who thinks that? If that's true, and I believe you're telling me the truth, just what is it that you, River, Jessie, and Jinxsy think? And please, Lars, no long dramatic pauses here. Just answer my question. Right now."

"We think the theater is haunted for real, Mrs. D."

"Say what? Are you kidding me?"

"Why do you think that Gabe told you he's turned this place inside out and can't find anything? Because there's nothing to find. We just didn't want to freak you out or distract you from your work until we knew what we were dealing with."

"And do you know what or who you're dealing with?"

"Yes, we do. And it's really ironic, but my mother's visit on Saturday is indirectly responsible for us knowing much more."

"How in the world could that be?"

"Because when Kathryn got so angry with my mom, she told her about Peter. And then after she left, Kathryn told us all the horrible way Peter was killed."

Arielle covered her face with her hands. After a few seconds, she folded her hands in her lap and looked up at Larsen, her face as pale as a ghost. "Peter was killed in this theater. Of course. So he's the blond boy I've been seeing."

Larsen nodded. "That's right, Mrs. D."

"Does Kathryn know?"

"Oh, no. I didn't want to tell her until I was able to contact Peter and ask him if he wanted me to bring her here."

"Did you try?"

"Yes. I actually connected with him yesterday. Remember when you asked me to give Gabe a message, and I got up so quickly? It's because I was really eager to find Peter. After Gabe left, Peter appeared to me, but then Gabe came back unexpectedly, and Peter disappeared."

"My head is spinning. Look, I'd like you to have dinner with us tonight so we can discuss everything and figure out what to do next. But right now, you need to get back on the computer and get the rest of that invitation list put together. And I've got a million and one things to do. Ghosts or not, the show must go on, and we've got a deadline to meet."

"Sorry, Mom. I was just so freaked when the photo that I took matched River's drawing, and it seemed kind of selfish to worry you until we had some idea of what was going on. We kept it a secret for your own good."

"Oh, Jess, get real."

Jessie, sitting cross-legged in her father's armchair, looked embarrassed. "I'm sorry, Mom. That's the truth."

"Are you serious? For my own good?"

River laughed. "Ha ha, Mom. You and Dad used to say that to us all the time as kids. 'It's for your own good.'"

"Riv, that's a cliché reserved for parents only. You're not allowed to say 'It's for your own good' until you have kids of your own."

"Good one, Mom."

"I feel really bad, Mrs. D. I let you down. I hope you'll forgive me."

"Lars, I'm over it. Besides, I know you were between a rock and a hard place. No more secrets, okay? I'm a big girl. Now, before Mick comes home, let's figure out how to handle this."

"Ha ha. Are you gonna keep Dad in the dark for his own good?"

Larsen wanted to laugh but was too afraid to do so.

"You're more fun than a barrel of monkeys, Riv. I have no intention of keeping any of this from your father. Now, am I up to date on absolutely everything? I've told all of you everything I learned from Lisa and Gabe."

Jessie wriggled uncomfortably in the chair. "Mom, I sure hope that Phony Phil creep isn't stalking you or something. I despise that scumbag. Even thinking about him makes me sick."

"I hope he's not either, Jess. But now that Gabe knows who he is, Phil had better not even think about coming to the theater or messing with me, much less Gabe. You know what really kills me? Gabe told me this afternoon that Phil wanted Candace to live in LA with him, but not enough to move her there. No, she was only welcome if she could pay her own way. That's how expendable the douche bag's women are. She could easily have been replaced, and eventually I've no doubt she will be."

Jessie gave a look of disgust. "Why didn't Candace Martelli just leave on her own and let her family stay in Jersey City? Why did she do all of those horrible things and then drag her family to California just to leave them?"

"I don't know the woman, Jess. But I'd assume it's so she could still see her kids when she wanted. Of course, now none of them will speak to her, so that didn't exactly work out too well, did it?"

Larsen looked pensive. "I'm trying to figure out if she's worse than my mom. At least my mom is upfront about things. But that sure isn't saying very much. Sorry, I don't mean to keep talking about her."

"Hey, dude, how can you not think or talk about her? It's all right. We all feel bad, not only after what happened last night, but what's been happening. You don't deserve any of that."

"Thanks, Riv."

"Okay you three, is there anything else I need to know before we put our heads together to figure this out?"

Larsen raised his hand. "Permission to speak from the couch."

"Ha ha. Dude, we're not in school."

"Lars, maybe someday when you have spare time you'll teach my son to be as polite as you are. You're very sweet, but you don't need to be so formal. Now, what did you want to tell us?"

"I would have told you on the car ride over here, Mrs. D, but you were on the phone with Lisa."

"There's more, Lars?"

"Yeah. I went into the theater around four o'clock. The guys were cleaning up in the lobby, and I was hoping to make contact with Peter in the main hall. I walked down to the stage and called to him. After about a minute, he appeared, but he was very faint, meaning I could barely see him. Then, just as I was going to speak to him, he totally disappeared."

"Ha ha ha."

"What's so funny about that, numbnuts? "

"I was just thinking, Jess. Maybe someone spooked him. Ha ha. Can ghosts get spooked?"

Arielle, Jessie, and Larsen laughed.

"So what did one ghost say to the other?"

Jessie rolled her eyes. "I'm afraid to ask."

"You look pale, dude, like you've just seen a person. Ha ha. 'Knock knock.' 'Who's there?' 'Boo!' 'Boo who?' Ha ha."

"Hilarious. Are you finished? Or will your father and I have to take you back to Mars when he gets home? What's the plan here? Larsen, you know Kathryn better than any of us. How do you think she'd respond to this news?"

"Well, Mrs. D, I've given that a whole lot of thought. First, I don't think she should know anything until I can find out what Peter wants me to do. Wow, I can't even believe I'm having a normal conversation about talking with a ghost, but I guess I am. For starters, I do think Peter is scared. I guess after spending forty years as a ghost and only fifteen as a person, he might be scared to do anything. You know how some people are really afraid of change? Well, maybe ghosts get the same way. I'm just rambling. Sorry."

"How do you think Kathryn would react to seeing her long-dead son again? As a ghost! I wouldn't want her to have a heart attack."

"Don't think so. She's been looking for him for forty years. I think she'd be really glad to find him. She told me once that most people never really accept that someone has died, so if we see our deceased loved ones, we're more likely to experience joy than fear. Those aren't her exact words, but you know what I mean."

"It's called paraphrasing, dude."

"Oh, right. Gee, it's great to have a dictionary as your best friend."

Arielle sat straight up in her chair. "Oh, wait. I have news. Lars, you couldn't hear my conversation with Lisa because I had ear buds on, but it seems like Phil's ridiculous little caper got a whole lot of people talking about our theater. In fact, having the screaming woman in the trailer brought more publicity than we ever dreamed, so much so that some people even accused Lisa of doing it as a publicity stunt. She's set the record straight on that, though. Anyway, as embarrassing as that was, it's been getting news coverage all over the country. You're famous, Lars, and so is our theater. And the director, Edgar, is now thrilled because his old film is getting renewed interest. And because of Phil's silly sabotage, we're going to get double or triple the media coverage on opening night."

Jessie looked disgusted. "I'm glad it backfired on him, but I just hope that doesn't make him even angrier. This all may be good news for the theater, but it's bad news for Phony Phil, and you know he is not gonna like it. I'm scared. I just hope he doesn't come after you again."

Arielle's excited tone ceased immediately. "I hope not, Jess."

📖📖📖

"Happy hump day, handsome hands."

River closed his locker and spun around to face Gina. "Oooo. Humping. That sounds like a great idea."

Gina pressed her body gently against River's until his back was up against the locker, then whispered in his ear, "I'm feeling more and more like it's gonna be right for us really soon. And when it is, you will be the first and only person I tell."

River ran his hand through her blond locks. "You're so sexy, baby. You're my favorite fantasy."

Coyly, Gina looked up at River. "I love hearing that. Riv, what happens after we're together? I'm afraid I won't be your favorite fantasy anymore because you'll already know what I have to offer."

Putting his lips to hers, River kissed her deeply, something he had never done before in the hallway of Mystekal High. When he was done, he looked into her twinkling blue eyes. "What makes you think that I'll stop fantasizing about the next time? Or replaying the memories in my head—over and over again? No commercials. Just you and me on the love channel broadcasting directly from the hippocampus. Ha ha."

"The hippo campus? Say what? Is that where hippos go to college?"

"No, it's the part of the brain where our memories are stored."

Gina laughed, then got serious again. "So you really don't mind waiting a bit longer?"

"Hey, Gin, I could take you somewhere and make love to you today because I want you so bad. And I know you want me. But I know you have your reasons for waiting."

"I just can't be like Taylor. She gave it away like Halloween candy. Probably still does. My sister is a mess. I just don't want to be Mess Junior."

River wrapped his arms around Gina and held her close. She felt every cell in her body shiver with excitement. "Hey, just because I'm a guy, that doesn't mean that I'm always ready to be with any girl. You're the only girl I have any desire to be with. And that desire is getting bigger all the time, so I'd better chill because I can't go to class with my desire showing. Ha ha."

Gina looked to her right and left to make sure nobody was watching them and grabbed River to feel him getting hard. "Oh my, did I do that?"

River laughed and pulled away. "Damn, girl. We're at school. I'm gonna have to think of someone really ugly to make this go down again."

"You're so funny. Nobody has ever made me laugh the way you do. So, are you thinking of someone ugly?"

"Nah. I'm thinking of how embarrassing it would be for someone to see me. That seems to be doing the trick. Wow; what a way to start the day!"

Just as Gina was going to give him a quick kiss, she saw

Avalon hurrying down the hall toward them with a look of urgency on her face. Feeling every muscle in her body tighten, Gina tried not to let her feelings show.

Looking frazzled, Avalon first addressed Gina. "I'm so sorry to interrupt. Please don't be angry with me."

"I'm not angry with you, Avalon. We're friends, remember?" Gina felt as if she were going to choke on her own words. Liver and onions tasted better in her mouth.

"River, I really need to talk to you. I know we've only got seven minutes before first period, but can I steal a few of them? Sorry, Gina."

"Like I said, Avalon, no problem. See you in class, Riv." Gina gave River a quick peck and hurried away, hoping he hadn't noticed how annoyed she was.

"Hey, Avalon, are you okay? You look like you've come a little unglued."

"Well, that would be pretty accurate. There are two things. First, last night my dad was colossally upset. He didn't want to talk about it, but he said something happened at work, and he's afraid your mom might can him, even with the grand opening of the theater being only one month away. Riv, do you know anything about this? Because if you think your mom is going to fire my dad, can you please beg her not to do it? We'll be so doomed if that happens. I mean, we'll be totally fu—"

River put his hands on her shoulders. "Calm down, Avalon. Your dad isn't going to get fired because of anything that happened. My mom worked it out with him. I wouldn't bullshit you about this. And if she were thinking about it, I'd grovel and beg until she changed her mind."

"For realsies? You'd do that for me? You don't think she's gonna ax him?"

"No, I don't. I won't even make a joke about it because I can see how upset you are. What else is bothering you?"

"Well, you already know that someone is leaving nasty notes on Larsen's locker and mine. I've found several, but I'm sure there's been more. I know that my brother and Larsen have taken them off before I could, and I've done the same thing when I've seen anything taped to Larsen's locker. The nasty notes are always folded, too, you know, so someone walking past, like a teacher, won't take them off."

"Has there been a new development?"

"Yeah. Today Erik and I came to school a little early. He stayed in the car to leave a voicemail for his girlfriend, Carrie Lynn, and I headed into school. So, first I go right to the girls' room. About five minutes later I'm on my way to the locker, and I finally see the kid who's putting up the notes. He's this sophomore named Kenny Milano who I've seen hanging with Jax. I'm pretty far away, so I wait until he's done, and just as I was going to say something, I saw Erik coming from the other end of the hall. We both saw the same thing from two different directions."

"So, what happened? Did Erik go after him?"

"Oh, he was definitely going right to him, but when he saw me, he just let the kid walk away. But he said he was going to deal with him at lunch."

"Oh, shit."

"Riv, I swear, I'm not asking you to get in the middle of a fight or anything, but just keep your eyes open, okay? If my brother touches that kid, he's going to destroy his own future. I just can't let him do that."

"Hey, it'll be okay. Try not to worry. Your dad's job is safe, and I'll keep an eye out for your brother. See you later, Avalon."

Chapter 25

Gina had been stewing all morning about how Avalon was stealing her precious time with River. At lunch, when she noticed that River kept scanning the cafeteria for someone, she felt even more resentful of Avalon. Bianca, sitting at the same table, gave Avalon a quick smile to remind her best friend to do a better job of hiding her feelings.

But Gina was determined to find out what was on her boyfriend's mind. "Hey, Riv. You looking for someone?"

"Oh, yeah, Gin. Actually, I was wondering if Erik was here."

Bianca piped up. "He's right there by the door, staring at someone. He's half-hidden by the pillar. See him? He's wearing the New York Mets T-shirt."

"Oh, yeah. Thanks." River watched as he saw Erik leaning against the wall by the door, staring intently at Kenny Milano, who didn't notice him at all. As Kenny rose from his seat, Erik stood up straight, and River had no doubts Erik would follow him out the door.

As Kenny left, then Erik, River excused himself and left his half-eaten lunch on the table.

"What the eff? Where's he going? Did Avalon ask River to babysit her twenty-year-old brother? Give me a break! Why doesn't that girl get her own knight in shining armor and leave my boyfriend the fuck alone?"

"Gina, calm down. You are getting yourself way too worked

up over this. River only has eyes for you. Now, don't blow it by acting like a jealous bitch. Or worse—like Taylor."

📖📖📖

As soon as River left the cafeteria, he saw that Erik had caught up with Kenny. He was pleased to see that Erik didn't have Kenny in a chokehold, but Erik clearly looked angry. Not wanting to interfere, River pulled out his cell phone, leaned against the wall, and pretended to be talking to someone.

Forty yards away, Erik jumped in Kenny's path to keep him from turning the corner and going outside. "Yo, kid. You seem like you're in a hurry. Where you going?"

Kenny stammered. "Uh … just going to meet my friend outside."

"Oh, yeah. Your friend got a name?"

"Yeah."

"Why don't you tell me what it is?"

Kenny tried to toughen his stance. "What's it to you? You don't need to know my business."

Erik got in his face. "Listen to me: I'm not the kind of guy who sticks his nose into other people's business because, see, I don't give a fuck what other people do unless they fuck with me and mine. Then, Kenny boy, it's a whole new ballgame. And right now, you're up to bat."

Kenny sneered at Erik's New York Mets T-shirt. "I'm a Dodgers fan. Dodger blue all the way."

"You're gonna be black and Dodger blue up the ass and in your face if you don't shut up. Do I look like I give a fuck?"

Kenny looked down at his shoes. "No. Not really."

"Now, you gonna tell me your friend's name?"

"Yeah, okay. It's Jax."

"Like in Jax Reinhardt?"

"There's only one Jax in the whole school, and you seem to know it, so why are you asking me?"

"You're a real smart-ass, aren't you? I've got some questions for you, and you're gonna answer them, hear me?"

"I don't even know you."

"And unless your nose doesn't want to make the acquaintance of my fist, you'll talk to me. Those notes you've been taping up on people's lockers when you think nobody's watchin', are you doing that for Reinhardt?"

Kenny tried to hide his mounting fear. "Uh, maybe."

"Is he paying you to do it?"

"No way!"

"Is he threatening you if you don't do it?"

"No, man, he's my friend."

Erik got closer to Kenny the second he saw him looking to get away. "Really. That senior punk just can't get enough of your sophomore punk ass. You expect me to believe that?"

"We're friends, man."

"Were you friends before you started taping notes on lockers?"

Embarrassed, Kenny didn't respond.

"Answer me, punk! Tell me, did you just become friends when he asked you for a favor?"

"Yeah. So?"

"Why the hell do you want to be his friend?"

"He's cool."

"What's cool about him?"

"He drives a black Stang, works out at a gym, hangs with the cool kids ... he's just cool. Whatever."

Kenny tried to move away again, and Erik blocked him once more.

"So, you think Jax is gonna still be your friend when he's done using you? Do you? Because I'm here to tell you he's not. Now, I've got another question for you."

Kenny wiped his sweaty palms on his pants, hoping Erik wouldn't notice.

"Do you read those notes you tape up on people's lockers?"

"Yeah."

"So let me get this straight. You know what garbage is in those bully letters, and you don't give a rat's ass. As long as you think that dick is your friend, you'll do anything to hurt anyone."

Kenny began to tremble. "They're just notes, man. Sticks and stones will break my bones and all that names-will-never-hurt-me stuff. People get over words."

"Is that fucking so? Aren't you a goddamn scholar. Did you know that Avalon is my little sister?"

Erik glared at Kenny, watching how his eyes bulged upon learning Erik's identity.

"Oh, shit. You're Erik Martelli."

"Oh, shit, that's right, little dick. So, where were we? Oh, yeah. You were saying people get over words. I guess you think my sister's gonna get over being called a freak, a Jersey whore, a blue-and-green piece of rotting cheese, and all of the other shit on those notes? And I guess Larsen Davis is supposed to forget someone saying he blows dead cows and all of that other homophobic crap?"

Kenny took a step back as Erik took one forward. "I don't know. I guess."

"You fucking guess, do you? Say, Kenny, you look like you've got a bad skin thing happening. How long has that been giving you trouble, Acne Boy? Looks like someone tried to put a fire out on your face with an icepick. Hey, Crater Face, how's life on the moon? Is that shit contagious? Was there a zit epidemic and someone forgot to tell me? Hey man, I hear some cons escaped from the local prison.

When did you break out?"

Erik could see the hurt in Kenny's eyes. "I can keep going. I got lots more where those came from. You think you're gonna get over these words by tonight? Tomorrow? Because I can see on your face that they hurt."

Kenny relented. "Yeah, okay. So maybe words hurt."

"You know what words are gonna hurt you the most?"

"No ..."

"When Jax Reinhardt tells you to fuck off because he's used you up like a dirty old rag. That's gonna be pretty humiliating. I sure wouldn't want to be the chump who lets a guy like Reinhardt use me like that. No, I'd want to walk away before anyone got the chance to make a fool out of me."

Kenny considered Erik's words.

"So, Kenny, do your parents know you've been hanging out with Jax?"

Kenny choked back the tears. "My dad died two years ago. It's just my mom and my little sister, Kasey."

Erik's tone eased considerably. "So, you got a little sister. How old is she?"

"Twelve."

"No kidding. I've got a kid sister who's twelve. Isabella. She's in the middle school. I'll bet she's in the same class with your sister."

Erik could tell by the look in Kenny's eyes that their sisters were acquainted. "So, what if someone put notes on your kid sister's locker calling her the kind of names Jax has been calling Avalon? Would that be okay with you?"

"Hell no! I'd punch the crap out of them." Kenny stepped back, realizing what he'd just said.

Erik stayed put. "Chill. I'm not going to touch you. But you know what? My first instinct was to break you into little pieces just for taping that shit on the lockers. But my life has been fucked up enough, and I don't need to make things worse for myself or the people who love me. Now, you can stay friends with Jax Reinhardt if you want, but I'm telling you he won't stay friends with you. He's not your friend now." Erik raised his voice to make a point. "The dick is using you. Got that?"

"Yeah. I hear you."

"You sure?"

"Yeah."

"Good. And I'm never, ever gonna catch you thinking about playing courier for a bully again, right?"

"No, I hear you. I'm gonna tell Jax I can't do it anymore."

"Okay, well, if you do that, and he gives you any trouble, you come find me. I'll be your friend for real. You know that the only reason Jax is messing with Avalon is to get to me, right?"

"No, I didn't know that."

"Time to grow up and man up, kid. Okay? Now, go take care of business. I'm gonna believe you're a man of your word."

"I am. You'll see."

"Good." Erik turned to leave, but Kenny called his name.

"Yeah, what is it?"

"Just wanted to say thanks and all. Deep down, I kind of knew you were right, but I thought I could make him like me for real. You're actually a good guy. Someday some kid is gonna be real lucky to have you as his dad."

As Kenny walked back toward the cafeteria, Erik swallowed the lump in his throat and spoke softly to himself. "Thanks, kid. You just made my day."

River rushed back into the cafeteria and took his seat again. "Miss me, baby?"

"Yeah, Riv. Where did you go?"

"I didn't go anywhere. I was just outside the door. Had to make some calls."

"Really, you got up in the middle of eating your sandwich to make some calls?"

Bianca knit her eyebrows to warn Gina not to ask River too many questions.

"Yeah. Just some family business. No biggie. Thanks for not throwing my sandwich out."

Bianca stood up. "I'm gonna go catch up with Tonio. See you two in class."

"Catch you later!" Gina looked doe-eyed at River. "I'm glad you came back."

River looked puzzled. "Of course I was coming back. Why do you even say that? Baby, is this about Avalon coming up to me this morning?"

Gina silently chastised herself for letting her jealousy show. "Sorry, Riv. I just worry ..."

River wolfed down the rest of his sandwich, put the plastic wrap and his napkin in the brown bag, and made a ball of it. "Avalon's not trying to come between us, Gin. She had some real serious things on her mind, and believe it or not, there was a good reason for her to talk to me. I'm not going to blab about what she tells me in confidence. Okay? Are you cool with all that?"

Gina moved her chair around the corner of the table until she was next to River. After gently touching his face, she kissed him softly on the lips. "I'll get it together. I promise."

"Okay then, baby, we're good." As River gave Gina a kiss, all she could think about was the great conversation they'd had first thing in the morning before Avalon came along and messed everything up.

Chapter 26

Larsen took a long sip from his water bottle. "You know, Riv, I love looking out at the mountains. We live in a really pretty part of the world. But sometimes this year-round heat really gets to me. It shouldn't be so hot when winter is two weeks away."

River sat down next to Larsen on the boulder and looked out at the desert scenery. "Yeah, I know. My dad was saying last night that in 1995, it was a record 123 degrees on Christmas Day."

"Wow!"

"Yeah. Santa Claus sweated off so much weight while delivering presents here that his reindeer didn't recognize him when he got back on the sleigh. But it made it a whole lot easier for him to get down the rest of those chimneys. Ha ha. And I'll bet Mrs. Claus was—"

"You're a trip."

"Well, the first part is true."

"My parents are from Chicago. I was born there, you know. We moved out to California when I was about five. My dad used to tell me about some really brutal winters. As bad as they sounded, I wouldn't mind checking one out right about now. He used to tell me all kinds of stories—not just about Chicago, about being a jazz musician and traveling through Europe in his early twenties. He played the trumpet. Paris was his favorite city, and he stayed a whole year there. After that gig was up, the quartet he was in went to different cities, like London, Berlin, Nice, and lots of smaller places most people have never heard of. When he would tell me stories about his early life, I would feel like I'd seen a whole lot more of the world. He was a great guy. I really miss him."

"How come you hardly ever talk about him?"

"Probably because my mother used to get upset when I mentioned him, so I just stopped. I guess I've been programmed, like a robot or something. But I think about him every day of my life. Hey, where's Gina?"

"Bianca's mom picked them both up about five minutes ago. They're going into Palm Springs to do some Christmas shopping. Anyway, I wanted to meet you out here, away from everyone, because I was wondering if you're going to try to contact Peter today."

"I'd really like to, Riv, but I think it's going to be nearly impossible right now. The work being done inside the main hall is crazy. And they're refinishing the stage."

"And what? You're afraid Peter's going to slip on some varnish or trip over equipment?"

"You're too much, Riv. Get real."

"Why? That's no fun. Kind of ironic that I'm talking about a ghost, and you're asking *me* to get real."

"Yeah. That is kind of weird. What I'm trying to say is that there are a whole lot of people around, not just the guys who work there regularly, but the air-conditioning guys, too. There's no way I can be alone to see if Peter will talk to me. And the regular guys are working OT to make sure we're ready to go before the deadline. You know your mom; no way she's letting it go down to the wire. I'll try to contact Peter first chance I get. Might not be for a week or two. Believe me, I want to help Peter and Kathryn in any way I can. I'm not exactly an expert in this. In fact, I'm clueless. It's not like there are a lot of people I can ask for advice. Hey, heads up. Here comes

Avalon."

Avalon hurried over to where the boys were sitting. They both stood up as she approached. "Hey, you two. Riv, I just wanted to thank you for being my friend this morning. I haven't seen my brother. I was just wondering if you knew what—"

"Hi, uh, can I talk with you guys for a minute?" River, Avalon, and Larsen were surprised to see Kenny standing before them. "Look, um, Avalon, I don't know if you're aware, but I had a talk with your brother—"

"Oh, no! He beat you up!"

"No—"

"Your nose is bleeding like crazy. Looks like someone slammed you head first into the ground. You've got sand and dirt stuck all over your bloody face, and unless you've got a nose that dispenses cherry sauce, I'd say it's bleeding pretty serious. " Avalon reached into her bag. "Here's some tissues. Sorry. I don't have anything else."

"Sit down, dude. You look a little dizzy."

Kenny took River's seat on the boulder and dabbed his bloody nose with the tissue. "I don't deserve any of you to be nice to me. I just wanted to say to Avalon and Larsen that I'm really sorry. I should have never put those notes on your locker. I was an idiot doing that just because I wanted some jerk senior to be my friend."

Larsen looked uneasy. "I appreciate the apology. Can't wrap my brain around why you even wanted a friend like that, though. Just hope you learned from it. For the record, your apology doesn't make the ugly words go away. But thanks for saying you're sorry."

"Thanks, Larsen. Do you hate me, Avalon?"

"No, I don't have room for hate in my heart. I don't want to be like the people who hate on me. I've seen this kind of thing before where an older bully gets a younger one to do his shit for him. My dad calls it 'bully by proxy.' Anyway, I feel pretty much like Larsen does. I don't have much more to say about it. Just that I'm sure as hell not gonna try to make you feel better just because Jax put you up to it. You knew damn well what you were getting yourself into, so you handle that mess yourself. I'm not gonna clear your conscience for you. You deal with that. 'Nuff said, Kenny. So, did my brother punch you in the face?"

"No, he really didn't. Jax did. Your brother was right: Jax was just using me. Erik said he wouldn't have anything to do with me if I stopped doing his dirty work. I knew he was right, but I didn't think Jax would punch me and throw me on the ground when I said I was done taping up notes. Once he had me kissing the sand, he kicked me a bunch of times in my hips and my shins. Called me a yellow-bellied coward and a piece-of-sophomore shit. And a whole lot more I won't repeat. After what I did to you guys, I deserved it."

Avalon reached out for Larsen's water bottle and poured some water on the last few tissues she had found. "Here, wipe off your face. Maybe you should go see the school nurse. As for Jax, he's an expert in being a coward; he just doesn't know it."

Kenny wiped his bruises with the soggy tissues. "I'll be okay. Like I said, I deserve it for being so stupid. Here's the thing, though. I kind of think your brother might have been following me from a distance after school, and he might have seen Jax beating on me. He told me that if Jax bothered me, he'd be my friend. So, um, I don't want him to get into trouble with anyone on my account. He was really harsh with me at lunch, but I deserved it. He's really a cool guy. I couldn't bear for him to … Erik!"

Erik sauntered over to the quartet. "The bastard got you good."

"Yeah, Erik. He was no friend. Just like you said."

Avalon looked frightened. "You're not going to do anything to Jax, are you? Our family has enough problems. Please."

"Nope. I don't do dope, and I'm not messin' with that one.

Karma took care of his ass."

Larsen took another long drink from the water bottle Avalon had returned to him. "What do you mean, Erik?"

"Who's the chick that gets a ride home with the principal? Do you know, River?"

"Sure. That's Simone Dreighton, Hal Dreighton's daughter. She's a junior."

"Well, she got video of the whole thing with her phone, and her BFF took some from another angle. Jax is on probation, right?"

"Wow, dude! He so is. Looks like it's expulsion time for Reinhardt."

Larsen hinted at a smile. "Oh, well."

Erik took an arm and pulled Kenny up from the boulder. "C'mon. I'm taking you inside to clean up. You're not going home to your mother and sister looking like roadkill."

Kenny smiled and turned to Avalon. "Am I what you call a 'hot mess'?"

Avalon laughed. "Afraid not, Kenny. Not even close. Just go inside with my brother."

"Okay. See ya. And, hey, for the record, I think you're the prettiest girl in school."

Erik made a face and yanked him away. "Don't even think of looking at my sister that way. I'm serious. I said I'd be your friend if Reinhardt messed with you. I don't want your punk ass for a brother-in-law. Get a grip. Come on. You look like shit, man."

📖📖📖

"I won't make the mistake of saying TGIF again, Mrs. D, because I know you're going to work on the weekend."

Arielle sighed as she looked through the stack of paperwork on her lap. "I'm going to work tomorrow until four, and then I might come in Sunday afternoon for a few hours. I need to rest, and I most definitely need time with my husband."

Larsen, who was busy assembling press kits and putting them in envelopes, worked steadily as he spoke. "Is everything on schedule?"

"We're slightly ahead of the game, but I don't want to say that too loudly. I don't want to jinx anything."

"I'm almost done with these press kits, and then I'll get the invitations finished. I think you'll be able to mail everything in the morning. I know the post office is open until noon on Saturday. I'll stay until everything is packed and ready to go, okay?"

"Would you, Lars? That would be so helpful. Besides, if you do work late, maybe you'll get a chance to contact Peter. On second thought, I'm not sure how long Gabe and his men are working tonight. And since we're dealing with a ghost, well, you can't exactly make an appointment to see him."

"I've thought of that. I wish I could."

Arielle paused to think. "He must've been living in this theater for forty years. All by himself. Wow, that's some serious loneliness. I wonder if ghosts feel the passage of time the way we do."

"I don't know. I just hope he's still here and wants to talk to me."

"I think so, Lars. I haven't had a chance to tell you this, but I think I heard Peter backstage this morning."

"Really? What happened?"

Arielle peered toward the end of the trailer to make certain that Gabe wasn't there. "Well, I was looking for Raphael and walked through the breezeway to the backstage area. I started to feel goose bumps on my arms and a chill. Then I heard this very soft crying. A week ago, before I knew the truth, I would have just ignored it. But I know it was Peter. I wasn't sure if anyone else was around, so I softly called out to him."

"Really, Mrs. D? What did you say?"

"I told him that my name was Arielle and that I worked here. I explained we were preparing to open the theater to the public again on the eleventh of January. I felt kind of silly giving a date to a ghost, but, strangely, I don't quite think of Peter that way. I think of him as a lost boy who never grew into a man. I told him that you worked for me and that you were going to come talk to him again when nobody was around. I told him we all knew and loved his mother and wanted to help and that she knew how he really died and was able to release the burden of her secret just a few days earlier. As soon as I said that, he started crying again. Lars, I wanted to reach out and comfort him the same way I did River when he was little, but I couldn't. Then I heard Raphael calling me, and I felt Peter's presence leave instantly."

"At least you were able to talk to him. I'm happy about that."

"Me, too. I hope I'm not making the mistake of assuming you're okay with all of this, because helping a ghost is not in your job description. If in any way you're not comfortable, you can back out. I'll find a way to help him myself."

"No way! I feel like I know Peter through Kathryn. He's like an older brother who died. Besides, ghosts are a lot easier to handle than bullies."

"Oh, speaking of which, River told me what happened on Wednesday afternoon. Last night he mentioned that there's an expulsion hearing with the local school board next week."

"Yeah, so we hear."

"Lars, I appreciate that you're willing to stay until the invitations are ready, but don't bother trying to contact Peter tonight. It's just too busy in there and you've put in a long week at school and work. So, just rest up. Any plans for the weekend?"

"Actually, there's someone I am hoping to see on Saturday who might have some advice for me about Peter. I was going to spend time with Kathryn on Sunday, but she told me she has some personal business to deal with, so Riv and I might hang out. The heat is supposed to drop into the high sixties on Sunday, so we might go hiking."

"He mentioned that. Funny, people are freezing all over the country, and we're rejoicing that the temperature is dropping twenty degrees. That's desert life for you."

Larsen straightened the pile of nine-by-twelve envelopes on his desk. "I'm getting really excited about opening night, aren't you? If I have any brain power left tonight, I think I'll work on my monologue."

"I can't wait. Restoring this theater is wonderful, but I want to get into the real business of putting on shows and developing performers. I hope that the reopening of this theater will be something special for all of us, especially Peter and Kathryn."

Chapter 27

Larsen was grateful that the heat had subsided, but he felt ridiculous standing by the Mystekal Sands box office for twenty minutes all by himself.

"Someone stood you up, huh?" When the ticket clerk spoke to him through the loudspeaker system, he was so startled that he jumped.

Larsen turned to see a thirty-something-year-old woman with a cheerful smile and walked over to the window to speak to her. "Oh, no. I was just hoping a friend might join me, but I don't think she's coming."

"The afternoon shows bring in the crowds. It's only eleven o'clock. Not prime time for most moviegoers. What are you going to check out today?"

"I don't know. What's playing?"

"Well, there's a comedy and a love story that both start soon. The action movie doesn't play for another two hours. I'm thinking someone your age would prefer the comedy."

Larsen thought about it and dug his hand into his pants pocket. "Actually, I definitely want a ticket for the love story. Sorry, I only have a twenty."

The clerk smiled awkwardly as she slid his change and ticket under the glass partition. "Enjoy your show."

As Larsen walked through the lobby to Theater 3, he looked

to his left and right several times. Once inside, he saw only one couple in their seats and chose one that was farthest away from them.

Two hours later, as the film credits rolled, Larsen felt silly for having wasted his time, but not knowing what to do with himself, he sat back while the last song played.

"How did you like the movie, Larsen?"

"Martha Joy!"

"You remembered my name."

"Sure I do. I'll never forget your name. Or you."

"Nor will I forget you. This seems like an unusual choice for you. Did you need to get out of your house again like the first time we met?"

"No, um … actually, I moved out of my mother's house in late October. I'm living with this really nice lady named Kathryn Winterstrom."

"Oh, you moved. How did—"

"Martha Joy, can I be really honest with you? This is probably the weirdest thing I've ever said to anyone in my life … "

"Feel free to speak your mind. I've got plenty of time and an open mind."

"I actually came to see this movie because I was hoping you'd be here. And, no, it's not really what I would have chosen. But I liked it okay. I learn from watching different films, you know, about people and their behavior. And right now I'm just mumbling random stuff because I'm nervous, but I want you to know that I'm very cool with everything."

Martha Joy smiled warmly. "What exactly are you very cool with?"

"Um … something really bad happened to you about five years ago, didn't it?"

She paused to consider the question. "You mean when I saw

my husband kissing another woman in a Palm Desert restaurant?"

"Yeah. That. But, you know, the really bad thing that happened right afterward."

"Oh, you mean when he ran out to his truck trying to flee the scene and ended up killing me?"

Larsen felt lightheaded. "Yeah. That."

"You've done your homework. You've found me out. And I've tried so hard to make myself look just like you, meaning being a flesh-and-blood person. It takes an awful lot of strength, you know."

"I only found out about you because you told me about your husband. I knew you meant Reggie Lee White because your description of him matched my mother's new boyfriend."

"My, my. Such a small world. Such a small town."

"Yes. It is."

"Are you looking for advice on how to handle that man? I wish I could help you. If I had known how to do that, I wouldn't be caught between two worlds. I'd be in heaven, or I'd be alive."

"I'm so sorry … I actually didn't come to talk about Reggie or my mom."

"You didn't?"

"No. I saw you last weekend. You were standing outside with the crowds. I tried to reach you, but you disappeared."

Martha Joy chuckled. "That is one of the benefits of being a ghost."

"I think I'm dreaming."

"Please, Larsen, tell me how you think I can help you."

"Well, there's kind of another ghost in town, but he's not as easy to see or hear like you. In fact, it's an entirely different situation. Funny thing, though, you're both living at theaters. You're here at the movie theater, and he's living at the Desert Theater. I think he's been trapped in there for forty years."

"Do you know his name?"

"Yes. It's Peter Winterstrom. He's the son of the lady I live with. Just last week, she told some close friends the real story of his death. He was gay, like me, and his boyfriend's father hated his son and Peter so much that he tried to kill both of them. But only Peter died."

Martha Joy's warm smile turned to a worried frown, and Larsen could see the pain on her face.

"I'm so sorry. I've upset you."

"Well, I'm very unhappy to know there's another soul in such pain."

"Martha Joy, can you tell me why you're here? Can you tell me why he's here? How do I approach him? What should I say? What can I do? I'm sorry to ask, but—"

"I'm the only ghost that you know?"

Larsen felt the room begin to spin. "This is too bizarre. That's actually kind of funny. But, yes, that's what I'm trying to say."

"Well, dear, when we die, there's a very short time between our death and our transition to heaven. When I was killed, it happened instantly. There was a warm rush of luminous white light, and in it I saw my mother and my father. Their arms were outstretched, and they were beckoning me to come join them. A moment later, Snoodles, the beloved cocker spaniel I had as a child, appeared next to my mother, wagging his tail. Oh, Larsen, I so wanted to cross over. And in the distance, walking toward me, I saw my grandparents. For years, my heart ached because I missed every one of them. Joining them felt so wrong because my death had happened so quickly, and I didn't understand why. I wasn't ready to go.

"My mother kept asking me to come, and she tried to assure me that everything would be all right. But I simply couldn't leave. Even when the angels came for me, I still couldn't let go of this world despite my desire to live anew in the most breathtaking place I had ever seen with those that I loved and had longed to be with again. One day, when you travel this world, you'll find magnificent beauty awaiting you at every corner of the earth. But you'll never see anything as extraordinary as the glorious splendor that awaits you when it's your time. The pull toward the light was so great, Larsen, but I still felt tethered to the earth. And then, with great force, I was yanked back to this in-between world, where I have searched for answers, for joy, and for peace."

"It's been five years. Aren't you ready to leave yet?"

"You'd think so, but I'm not yet prepared to go." Martha Joy paused to reflect on the words she had shared.

Larsen waited patiently for her to continue. "Are you okay?"

Yes, thank you for asking. Now, let's talk about Peter. Yes, Larsen, you can help him."

"How? What can I say?"

"Like me, he stayed behind because the circumstances of his death were sudden and tragic. He wasn't prepared for the afterlife, nor could he begin to comprehend why he should be there. You must carefully reunite him with his mother and allow her to be the one to send him to the light. But before you do that, he must be able to trust you. Remember, his trust was shattered when he was alive. He carries enormous fear with him. When he is able to trust you, you will know. Truth brings forth the light. Truth is stronger than the darkness that we cloak ourselves in. Peter must have truth. He must know how much he is loved, but no doubt, his mother will remind him."

Feeling overwhelmed, Larsen lay back in his chair and stared up at the ceiling. Only seconds later, as he looked to address Martha Joy, she was gone.

Larsen got out of his seat, walked to the end of the row, then up the aisle toward the doors. As he walked through the lobby, he noticed something was different. There were three movie posters with a banner across the top corner reading NOW PLAYING. None of the posters were of the film he had just seen, nor were they of the other two.

Walking out of the theater, Larsen waited until the short line of people had purchased their tickets and gone inside. He went up to the window to see a sixty-something-year-old man with a well-trimmed, salt-and-pepper beard smiling at him. "How can I help you?"

"Oh, uh, I'd just like to talk to the woman who was working here earlier. You know, she's about thirty maybe, and she has shoulder-length brown hair. She was wearing a green blouse, like an emerald color."

The clerk looked confused. "I opened the window here today. I've been here since ten-thirty. Not only that, but we don't have any employees who match that description. Not even close. Sorry, son."

📖📖📖

Kathryn got out of her car and walked slowly toward the small gray stucco home with the round, teal-colored door. The cooler temperatures were a welcome relief, but what waited behind the door still made her sweat.

She checked her watch to make sure of the time. It was two o'clock in the afternoon. Steeling herself for the task, she knocked twice on the door. When there was no answer, she turned to go, then told herself that she needed to knock again—much louder.

As she heard movement on the other side of the door, she saw someone unlatch the peephole from the inside, and she knew her identity had been revealed. As the door creaked open, she felt her heart race, but not in a good way. She was terrified.

"Well, what the helllll do we have here?"

"Good afternoon, Mrs. Davis. I see you're in your robe. I

hope I didn't—"

"Did something happen to my boy? Are you here with bad news?"

"No, Larsen is just fine. He had a bad fever yesterday, but it broke late this morning. He'll be his old self in no time."

"He'll be his old self, huh? That's unfortunate."

"Mrs. Davis, that's a terrible—"

"A terrible thing to say? Well, it's the damn truth. Like I told him last Monday, he's dead to me."

Kathryn noticed that some of the neighbors were beginning to look in her direction, and Raylene's loud voice wasn't helping. "May I please come in?"

"You want to come inside my house? You want to interrupt my Sunday? My day to spend with the Lord?"

"Oh. I'm very sorry. I didn't realize … I would just really like to talk to you. Please."

"Better than having you stand at my door putting my business out there on the streets. Already bad enough everyone knows my boy don't live with me anymore."

Raylene stepped back and opened the door for Kathryn to walk through. "Gee, I'm sorry. If I'd known I was having such special comp'ny in the form of an old white lady who stole my son, I'd have tidied up."

Kathryn tried to ignore her words. She felt sick to see the empty liquor bottle on the coffee table with two overturned glasses and Raylene's clothes scattered around the living room. Next to the empty bottle, Raylene's double-D bra lay upturned on the coffee table, each cup partially filled with corn chips. She knew that Raylene was watching her as she made a quick study of the room and tried to avert her eyes to a landscape hanging on the wall.

"Sit down anywhere you like except my chair right here. And don't think I didn't see you looking at my bra. Mind your business.

Don't you go telling people nothin' you saw here."

"I won't say a word. You have my solemn promise. That's not why I'm here." As she tried to look away, Kathryn noticed a few framed pictures on some wall shelves had been turned downward. She knew they must be of Larsen.

"Well, this would be the perfect damn time to tell me why you are here, Mrs. ..."

"Kathryn Winterstrom."

"What's that? A high-society name?"

"Nothing of the kind."

"Just how long are we s'posed to sit here looking at one another? You gonna tell me why you came? State your business."

Kathryn folded her hands neatly on her lap. "Monday night, when you came to the Dalworths' home, you said something that I haven't been able to get out of my mind."

"Oh, really? Is that so? Well, I probably said a whole lot you people can't get out of your busybody minds. What in particular are you referring to?"

"It's something you said to me, not to Larsen."

"Well, unless you got an instant replay machine, you'd better tell me because I don't have all damn day to waste on this poppycock."

"You asked me if my husband left because he was gay."

Raylene fell silent, but her eyes penetrated Kathryn's gaze.

"Mrs. Davis, I am very sure that my husband wasn't gay. But it occurred to me a couple of days later that you asked me that because you were projecting your own situation onto mine. What I am trying to say is that it occurred to me that your anger toward Larsen is so great because he's not the only one you're angry with. Or maybe not the one you're really angry with. I couldn't help but wonder if Larsen's father was gay, too."

Raylene's jaw tightened, and her body stiffened. In an instant,

Kathryn knew she had stumbled onto the truth. She paused, hoping Raylene would speak, but she just continued to stare, her face filled with rage.

"I don't know your circumstances or your situation. But as a woman who briefly considered the same scenario and who had a gay son, I understand, if only a little. I beg you, please try to redirect your anger away from Larsen. He's such a wonderful young man. He's got so much talent, so much empathy, so much poise, so much intelligence, and, well, I just can't say enough about him. But despite all of the good things in his life, he's devastated believing that he's lost your love. You know, the Desert Theater is opening on the eleventh of January with a talent competition. I suppose you heard that on television Monday night. Larsen will be reciting his monologue, and I know it would mean everything to have you there. A piece of him is missing without you, Mrs. Davis. Won't you consider it?"

Raylene's angry face remained frozen. Her icy stare made Kathryn shiver. Very softly, she began to speak. "Now I'm only going to say this once, but you GET THE HELLLLLLLL out of my house!"

Kathryn jumped up and hurried to the door. "I'm so sorry. Please forgive the intrusion. But above all, Mrs. Davis, please forgive your son and accept him for who he is."

As the door slammed behind her, Kathryn stepped out into the bright sunshine, past the curious neighbors, and quickly got in her car, where she burst into uncontrollable sobs.

Chapter 28

River sat on a boulder and sketched the mountains in the distance, taking care to draw each cloud as he saw it.

"That's a beautiful sketch, Riv. I could go to sleep on those clouds."

Looking up to see Larsen standing there, River stuck his pencil behind his ear. "Thanks. Sit down, dude. Glad you could meet me."

"I didn't mind coming to school a little bit earlier. What's up?"

River closed his sketchpad. "I just wanted to make sure we got some time to talk privately. First, I'm bummed we didn't get to go hiking yesterday. I was really worried when I called Saturday night and Kathryn answered your phone. She told me you had a high fever and were out of it. I got your text on Sunday but was still worried. You okay?"

"Yeah, I'm fine now. Saturday was a really weird day, and then I ended up with a 104 fever. I was totally gone until late yesterday morning and figured I'd better take it easy."

"What happened?"

"Not really sure. Do you remember when we were at the Kafe and I saw Martha Joy?"

"No, dude. I completely forgot about when you got up from lunch to chase the dead wife of your mom's boyfriend down the street. Remind me."

"Okay, yeah, so that's not the kind of thing you forget that easily. Anyway, I had been thinking about Peter—you know, how to approach him and all—and I thought, who could give me better advice than—"

"Another ghost!"

"Right. Anyway, I went to the Mystekal Sands and looked for Martha Joy outside, where I had last seen her. She wasn't there, so I went to see this romance movie because I thought I might find her watching the film. But I didn't have any luck. Then, during the credits at the end, she shows up in the seat next to me. We had a talk. I gave her the news that I'd moved into Kathryn's house in October, and I told her about Peter and said that I needed her help. She gave me some advice, explained a little about why people become ghosts, and then, when I looked away for a second, she was gone. So I left. But when I walked through the lobby to leave, I saw that the movie posters had all changed and that completely different films were playing. The woman who I bought my ticket from wasn't there, and the guy at the window said no one fitting that description even worked there."

"Whoa. I'd be checking my temperature, too. I'd want to make sure I even had one. What happened next?"

"No clue, Riv. The next thing I remember was Kathryn sitting on the edge of my bed putting a cold washcloth on my forehead. I have no idea when that was. I could have come home and then gotten sick."

"Do you think you dreamed all of that?"

"I feel like it really happened. You saw Martha Joy in the theater, Riv, so you know she exists. That was the same day I first met her. You saw her again the Saturday before last."

River thought. "Hey, are you wearing the same pants you had on Saturday?"

"Yeah. But they just came out of the wash Friday night. Who are you? The laundry police?"

"Ha ha. Dude. I'm not checking to see how often you wash your clothes. I was just remembering if you knew how you paid for the movie or if you might have shoved a ticket stub in your pocket."

"Oh! I couldn't imagine why you were asking. I hate to admit it, but you really are pretty smart."

River laughed. "Let's not waste time dwelling on the obvious."

Larsen rolled his eyes. "Actually, I do remember. I paid with a twenty." He reached into his pocket and pulled out a twenty-dollar bill. "All my money is still here. I know I bought a ticket. She handed me change, a receipt, and a ticket."

"Do you remember giving the ticket to anyone?"

"No, I don't think I did."

"So nobody was there to take your ticket?"

"I can't remember."

"Okay, so if you saw a movie, tell me what it was about."

Larsen thought for a moment. "I have no idea. No memory of it whatsoever."

"You must have dreamed about Martha Joy, Lars."

"But it felt so real. And she told me things I didn't know about how people become ghosts. And I could just as easily have dreamed that someone took my ticket, you know?"

"Yeah, but in dreams we usually leave out the parts that don't matter."

"I don't know. Maybe I never will. But you're the only one I'm telling. I never did tell your mom about Martha Joy. I hope she wouldn't be angry about that."

"Nah. She'd probably be really interested, but since Martha Joy isn't a ghost at her theater, it's okay not to tell her."

"Good. Hey, I've never seen you sit outside school and sketch before. How come you're doing that today?"

"Because of a conversation I had with Avalon on Friday. It's no secret that she's been really down. It's been hard enough for her leaving Jersey City and having her mom do so much to mess up her life. Then she comes here to school and deals with the same lowlife bully crap as you do. She has a real passion and talent for painting like you have for the theater. She finally decided to start painting again. I was really glad to hear that. Anyway, it kind of hit home that I haven't been drawing as much since I started seeing Gina. I never want to get too far from my art, so I just thought I'd get back to drawing more, even if I'm just drawing scenery and not dead people. Of course, you never know when one will walk into my picture. So, how was the rest of your weekend?"

"Everything was way off, Riv. When I finally felt better, late Sunday afternoon, I could see that Kathryn was in a bad way. At first, I figured it was because she was worried about me, and then I thought maybe she was getting sick, too. But she just seemed upset and angry with herself about something she did. I could tell she didn't want to talk about it, so I didn't try to pry. She's done so much for me. I hated seeing her in such a state, and she wasn't really any better this morning. I wish I could repay some of her kindness by helping her out."

"She knows you care. Besides, you're going to help Peter, and I can't think of anything she'd want more in the whole world."

"Thanks, Riv. I appreciate that. Can I say one more thing?"

"Go for it."

"That pencil behind your ear makes you look like an accountant. Just sayin'."

River took the pencil away from his ear and stuck it in the coil of his notebook. "You're not right, dude. Ha ha."

📖📖📖

Larsen was heading to the trailer when Muggins appeared out of nowhere, jumping up and licking his face. "Hey, boy, where's your mom?"

"Here I am."

Coming into view was Arielle, carrying a stack of sample books in her arms. "Hey, Lars. Some of the guys are going to start prepping the old paint store so we can turn it into a school after Christmas is over."

Larsen reached out to take the heavy books from Arielle. "Please, let me carry these for you. They weigh more than you do."

"No, I've got them. Actually, I need you to do something else. I was downstairs in the theater measuring the kitchen when I got called away. I left my tape measure there. I need you to go grab it for me, then measure exactly how much space we have to install a new refrigerator. I'm going to be buying a full-size one for the theater and a small one for the school. We're also going to be buying two microwaves. Oh, and I was looking in the drawers, and all of the original silverware and utensils are still there. Can you take an inventory for me and let me know what condition everything is in? I left a notebook and pen down there, too."

"Sure, Mrs. D."

"Oh, and you and Kathryn are coming to Christmas breakfast on Wednesday morning, right?"

"For sure. I can't believe Christmas is only five days away. I'll see you inside the trailer in a bit, Mrs. D."

"Okay, Lars. And, hey, I think my canine son wants to come with you."

Larsen felt a bit nervous as he entered the basement area. He looked at the rehearsal space and wondered how many times it had been used. What plays had been performed? How many shows had Peter performed in?

Straight ahead, at the far end of the space, the flats, furniture, and large props that had been sitting idle for forty years overwhelmed Larsen. He noticed that he wasn't the only one.

"What is it, boy? Your nose is at full sniff right now. Darn, I wish you could talk. If I can talk to ghosts, it shouldn't be that difficult to talk to a dog."

Muggins seemed to understand and looked oddly at him, then went back to sniffing.

Larsen looked ahead to the left and saw Arielle's notebook and measuring tape on the kitchen counter. But those could wait. He felt compelled to wander over to the old sets, but the dog beat him to it.

There were several folded scenery flats against the wall. A few were open, as if the theater had been closed in a big hurry, and no one had time to put everything away. The flat depicted a New York alley with tall buildings in the background. Larsen felt certain it was from *West Side Story*, which was in rehearsal but never performed. He remembered what Kathryn had shared with him a few weeks ago after they left the Dalworths' home. After Willard Carrow killed Peter, he closed the theater for fear that any lingering clues to what really happened might be discovered.

Larsen brushed his fingers over the painted chain-link fence on the flat. He couldn't feel its barbed edges—only the sharp pain of knowing what had happened to Peter.

"Grrrr."

Feeling his heart race, Larsen walked on, very slowly, looking quickly at all of the scenery and props with forty years of dust on them. He passed by an old street lamp, an old-fashioned barber pole, and a bus stop sign.

"Grrr."

"Muggins ... what is it? Peter, are you here?"

Looking down at his arms, Larsen saw the goose bumps begin to appear and felt the chill that hugged him. "Peter, I think you must be here. I'm sorry it's been so long since the first time we spoke. I never thought I'd find you down here. I thought I had to wait until the workers in the theater were gone for the day. I really wanted to come back sooner."

Peter's presence was undeniable, but as Larsen looked around, he could only see the pieces of different sets in the empty spaces.

"Grrrrrrr."

Turning to speak to Muggins, Larsen put his hand quickly to his heart when he saw Peter vaguely forming in the open space, away from the sets. He didn't know if Martha Joy had spoken to him in a dream or in the Mystekal Sands, but he tried to remember her advice. It was about trust. He had to earn Peter's trust.

"Peter, do you remember what I told you? I live in your house, in your old bedroom. Your mom thinks about you every day. She has photos of you all over the house. She tells me that you had the most beautiful baritone voice on earth and that your life and your gifts were taken way too young. She remembers you just the way you look now."

Larsen couldn't hear his words, but he knew Peter was asking if Kathryn was happy. "She's as happy as she can be without you. She manages the high school cafeteria. When she was younger, she used to take in foster children. Nobody could ever replace you, Peter, but having children around helped ease her loneliness. You understand that, don't you?"

Peter's image, only slightly clearer, was listening intently to Larsen's words, and now, without hearing him speak, Larsen knew he was asking about his father.

"Nobody knows what happened to your father. A year or so after you died, he left and never came back. Your mom doesn't know what happened to him. I'm sorry."

Peter began to sob, only, unlike his words, his sobs were audible.

"Please let me help you."

Larsen saw Peter's mouth moving. His image was still faded, just like some of the old photographs of him in Kathryn's albums. Then, for the first time, Peter spoke aloud. "What happened to him? He didn't die with me. I've waited here for him."

Feeling a rush, Larsen knew Peter was asking about Ernest Carrow. He hadn't anticipated that as being a concern of Peter's. It seemed so obvious now, but he had overlooked it in his many musings about a situation that he could barely understand. "Ernie didn't die when you did, Peter. His father tried to kill you both, but only you died."

"Bring him here."

Larsen stammered. "I-I can't bring him here, Peter. Ernie … um, Ernest Carrow died two years ago. You might find this ironic … um, I know I do … but he was choked to death by a ghost."

Peter's image became sharper as the shock of Larsen's words registered on his face, begging Larsen to explain.

"Willard Carrow made Ernie's life a living hell. He forced him to pretend to be heterosexual and marry a woman. He even had a daughter, Eve. But by that time, after seeing you die in that theater and knowing that his father had killed you out of hate and tried to kill him as well, Ernie became every bit as mean as his father. I'm sorry, Peter. He grew up to be a really bad person. He was the principal at the high school. When Eve got pregnant as a teenager, he killed her boyfriend and set another guy up to take the fall. Almost eighteen years later, the ghost of the guy he murdered killed him."

Peter's sobs intensified as he realized he had waited forty

years for someone he could never see again. "I wanted to see him. Just once more. It happened so quickly. No good-byes."

"I know, Peter. I'm sorry. But your mother is still here, and she would love to see you. I'd really like to arrange that for you, if you'd let me. Remember I told you that the theater is opening in January? That's only a little more than two weeks away. We're going to have a talent competition on opening night. Did I tell you that? It will be harder for you to stay here after that. People will be around all the time. But you don't want to stay here anymore, do you? You can't possibly want that. This is no life—I mean, death—for you. You deserve eternal peace."

Larsen felt unsteady. He wasn't sure what he was saying. He felt like he was pulling dialogue from every ghost movie or TV show he'd ever seen. Did he sound completely ridiculous? He had no idea if his words made sense only to him, or if Peter was taking them to heart the way he had intended.

Peter stood stoically in one place. His head turned only slightly to look at Muggins, who had sat there staring at him the entire time. Larsen looked at the dog. "Hey, boy. You've been so quiet I forgot you were with me."

"I'll never see him again. I waited for him."

"I'm so sorry, Peter. I'm sorry about what happened to Ernie, and I'm sorry he did such terrible things to other people. But that's the truth."

"He was good. He made me happy. He had so much love in his heart."

Larsen frowned. "I believe you. But I'm afraid that Ernie's ability to love died when you did."

"I waited so long."

"I know, Peter, but do you …"

Muggins barked as the room became warm again. Larsen knew he'd have to try again another day. Peter was gone. He felt drained as he walked over to the kitchen area and grabbed the tape measure. "C'mon, boy, let's do some measuring for your mom."

"Woof!"

Wearily, Larsen looked at his four-legged friend. "Woof to you, too."

📖📖📖

"You know, Lars, when you didn't come back right away, something in my gut told me you were talking to Peter." Arielle typed some information into an online form as she spoke.

"Mrs. D, Peter has been waiting forty years for Ernie Carrow to come back. He can't understand that the boy he loved named Ernie became a horrible man named Ernest."

Arielle turned around to face Larsen at his desk. "Well said. Did you ask him about seeing his mother?"

Larsen began filing a stack of receipts on his desk as he spoke. "Yeah, I did, but he seemed to be in shock about Ernie. I couldn't get any further in the conversation after I gave him such bad news."

"You'll just have to try again. Today is Friday already. Time is flying by. Maybe you can talk to him on Monday. I don't want you to come in on Tuesday. It's Christmas Eve. If you can't find Peter on Monday, you'll just have to keep trying. I guess he has to process what happened to Ernie. If I waited forty years for someone and got that kind of news, I'd sure have to pause and reflect, you know? So, were you able to actually see him?"

"Yeah, I was over by the old sets, and he was sort of in the rehearsal space. Just standing there. He wasn't clear like you or … um, I mean, he wasn't clear, but I could see him. And I heard his voice today."

"You did? How amazing! That must mean he's beginning to trust you. You know, now that I think about it, when I saw him on the stage, he seemed faded, too. But he was too far away, and I think my brain just told me it was because of the plaster dust or something. I know; it's crazy. Nothing makes sense, and everything makes sense at the same time." Arielle paused. "By the way, it's been so busy that I haven't had time to talk to you about something very important. I want you to stay on as my assistant here after the theater opens, if you would. I'm not sure what your plans are after you graduate."

"First, of course I'll stay on. I'd love to! As for school, I'm not sure what I'm going to do. I'm applying to UCLA and some other theater schools, but unless I get a scholarship and some financial aid, I don't see how I can do it. If anything, I need to earn all I can."

"Fantastic. By the way, those vintage posters you ordered will be back from the framers after Christmas. I'm counting on you to help me decide where to hang them."

"Really? I'd love to help with that. You know, Mrs. D, I almost just asked you if you could fit one more seat at your Christmas breakfast table."

"For who, Lars?"

"Peter. It's really weird, but he's not like a ghost to me at all."

Chapter 29

River held Avalon's phone in his hands and looked down at it with great interest. "When you said you could paint, you didn't tell me you can really paint! This is beautiful. This house looks like it could tell many stories."

Standing outside by the main doors of the school, Avalon was keenly aware that Gina would be coming along soon and probably wouldn't be happy to see her talking to River. But she put it out of her mind as best she could. "Oh, it can tell stories. That's our home on Kensington Avenue in Jersey City."

"Was this drawn from a photo?"

"Sort of. But I turned summer into winter and added the two people outside. I think living in the desert has made me appreciate the cold weather more."

"Did your dad sell the house when you moved out here?"

"No, he rented it out for a year. He's hoping that if Erik finds a good job when he gets back, he can live there with Carrie Lynn and their baby. Plus, there's an apartment on the third floor that's always been rented out."

"That's nice to know that your family home isn't gone."

"Yeah, it is. And I don't like to sound selfish, but I hope Erik and Carrie Lynn do live there so I can move back after graduation. I feel like a fish out of water here, Riv."

"Well, this area isn't exactly known for its abundant water. Sorry, I didn't mean to make a joke out of the way you feel. Any more paintings?"

"There's one more."

River took his middle finger and swiped the screen from left to right. "Oh, wow!" He reverse pinched the screen to see the details in Avalon's painting. "You are a genius. You paint like someone who's been studying for a lifetime. What a kick-ass painting of New York City!"

"Yeah, we've got the best view in Jersey City. That's from Liberty State Park. You probably know that's the Hudson River."

River looked at Avalon and smiled.

"Oh, yeah. I forgot. You're real smart, and you know everything."

"Ha ha. That's what I want people to believe. But since my name is River, I've made it my business to know all of the main rivers of the world, numero uno River being myself. I'm the real Rio Grande."

Avalon giggled. "I totally know you're not kidding. And, yeah, of course you would know all the rivers. It's so you."

River was mesmerized by what he saw on the screen. "This is seriously good, Avalon. I want to ask you something, if that's okay."

Avalon pushed a green strand of hair away from her eyes. "You can ask me anything you want. You know I trust you."

River lowered his voice. "So, just wondering: since you've been painting again, have you painted any premonitions?"

"Nope. Nothing's come to me. I've just been painting from my photographs of back home and from my memories, too. Feels good to paint and helps with the homesickness and the breakup. But if I do feel compelled to paint something, I'm not going to fight it. I'll go with it, you know? I'm tired of dealing with bullshit and being afraid of things … and people." Avalon wiped a few beads of sweat from her brow. "I'm glad we only had a half day today. I'm sick of this school and this freakin' desert. Being here is just plain weird. It's tripping me out being hot as hell in December."

"Yeah. I can get why you painted the old Jersey homestead with snow. I have to take a look at that again." River swiped left on the phone. "This is great. So much character."

"Hi, Avalon. Is something special happening on your phone? Is there a party going on here?" Gina, who had just come outside, smiled and put an arm around River's waist.

"Just showing River my paintings. That's all. Erik is probably waiting by his car for me. Have a merry Christmas. See ya next year." Before River could respond, Avalon hurried away.

Gina could see the look of concern on River's face and worried that she had let her jealousy show. "Hey, Riv. How's my guy? My mom asked me to make sure that you're coming to our house for Christmas Eve dinner tomorrow."

Distracted, River's eyes followed Avalon into the distance as he watched her get into Erik's car. Realizing that Gina was asking him a question, he quickly averted his glance, but Gina knew exactly where he'd been looking and didn't like it.

"Sure, Gin. I'll be there. I told you I would be. I'm looking forward to it."

"I'm sorry for asking again, Riv. I just wanted to be sure. My mom's picking me up in about ten minutes, and we're going to finish the rest of our shopping. By the way, in case you were wondering, Taylor's not coming. She told my mom she wasn't kidding about never setting foot in this town again. My sister sure knows how to hurt my parents. I mean, it's not like they haven't gone to LA to visit her."

River gestured toward the closest boulder. "Let's sit down and talk before your mother gets here."

River opened his backpack and pulled out a water bottle. "You know, when Taylor used to bully Jess and the Jinxster, it's because being a bully made her feel better about herself. Secure people don't need to bully."

"Uh … right." Gina fiddled uncomfortably with the zipper on her backpack as River spoke.

"It doesn't sound like she's gotten any more confident being in LA for the past two years, or she wouldn't be so threatened by this town, especially since it's way more happening since she left it. Gin, I hope that you won't be that way. I mean, I hope you'll feel good about—"

Gina felt sick as panic settled in her stomach. She knew River saw right through her insecurities regarding Avalon. "I'm really sorry, Riv. I know what you're thinking."

River turned to look her in the eyes. "I can't tell you anymore that there's nothing romantic between Avalon and me. And I can't tell you enough times that she's never hit on me. She just wants a friend. You've got to deal with that, Gin."

Gina, aware that River had noticed her nervous fidgeting, looked uneasy. "Hey, can I have a sip of your water?"

"Sure, here."

She took a few sips of River's water, then handed the bottle back to him. "I know, it's just that she's got so much in common with you. You're both artists, and you're both different."

"Right. And that's why we're friends. Why can't you accept that it's not anything more?" River put a comforting hand on Gina's shoulder. "You're beautiful, baby, and you're the girl I want to be with. But I'm going to be really honest: it hurt me the way Avalon rushed off because you made it really clear you don't like seeing us talking. And you told me that you were Avalon's friend, too, but honestly, I'm not seeing that. You told me that you exchanged phone numbers, but I know you're never going to call her. And you know, that's okay. Just don't hate on her."

"I'm sorry. I just wish I had a talent to impress you the way she does."

River was frustrated. "You do impress me, baby. Have I done something to make you feel like I'm not feeling the love, or what?"

"No, Riv. I'm just being a jerk. Do you want me to call and apologize to her?"

"No. Just chill, Gina. Okay?"

Gina looked nervously at her phone. "You know, Riv. My mom just texted me that she's going to be a few minutes late and I've got to use the little girl's room. So I'll see you tomorrow night, okay?"

"Sure, Gin."

Gina gave River a quick kiss on the lips, stood up, then made a dash toward the school. She raced through the open front doors, bumping unapologetically into a few students who were on their way out.

📖📖📖

As Gina hurried into the girls' room, she found Bianca waiting for her by the sinks. "I got your text. What's up? Everything okay with you and Tonio?"

"Heck, yeah. Listen, I texted you to meet me here because I'm worried about you. I was outside with Tonio and we kept our distance because it looked like something heavy was happening with you and Riv."

Gina peeked under the bathroom stalls to make sure they were the only two in the room. "Yeah, sort of. I found Avalon outside showing River her pictures of her paintings on her cell. I asked what was going on, and she took off really fast just to get River's attention and make him feel sorry for her and angry at me. Bitch be like, 'look at my pretty paintings, Riv. Pay attention to me, Riv.' Ugh!"

"So is that what you two were just talking about?"

"Yeah. Riv was telling me how I needed to be more confident about our relationship and that he and the Jersey girl were just friends."

"He's told you that a few times before, hasn't he?"

Gina took her comb out of her purse and began styling her hair. "Yeah. You know, it's weird because I love him for being so smart, and then sometimes I hate that he is. Other guys would be so clueless."

Bianca sucked in her cheeks as she reapplied her blush in the mirror. "Girl, you may not like Avalon, but take it from your bestie: you better start acting like you do, or you're gonna be the one to kill your relationship, not Avalon. You hear me?"

Gina nodded. "I guess I have to sharpen my acting skills. Who knows? Maybe I've got some talent after all."

📖📖📖

Muggins went crazy with joy when he saw River enter the trailer.

"Hey, boy. Surprised to see me here, aren't you? But you don't have to give my face a bath or anything."

Muggins kept licking his human brother, while Arielle got out of her chair to give River a hug. "Aw, Riv. You just made my day coming to visit. And I owe this great honor of your presence to ...? And where's Lars?"

"I walked over here with him because I wanted to talk to you. And Lars is going downstairs in the theater to see if he can talk to Peter again."

"Oh, good. I hope he succeeds. I can't stop thinking about that poor boy, waiting forty years for someone who ceased to exist a very long time ago. Just not in the way Peter ceased to exist. It's really tragic. Sit down, Riv. Since when do you need a formal invitation?"

River sat in Larsen's chair as Muggins went back under Arielle's desk. "Since I became royalty."

"You've been a royal pain in the ass since you were born. I'll give you that."

"Ha ha. Good one, Mom."

"Is everything all right?"

River picked a pen up from Larsen's desk and began absentmindedly dismantling it. Arielle recognized his nerves right away.

"Riv, that pen didn't die. It doesn't need an autopsy."

Realizing what he was doing, River laughed and put the pen back together. "You're really funny today, Mom."

Arielle leaned forward and touched his knee. "Are you having problems with Gina? Did you come here for a heart-to-heart?"

"Yeah, but don't get all mushy on me, Mom. The thing is, Gina's really jealous of my friendship with Avalon. And even though I don't like that, I can pretty much deal with it. But I really hate the way it upsets Avalon. Every time she talks to me she's worried about Gina coming along. Gina's jealousy just creates so much tension. And for what?"

"Have you told Gina how you feel?"

"Yeah, I have. Several times. I've told her that she's the one I'm interested in and that it's just friendship with Avalon and me. But nothing I say makes any difference."

"And you were hoping I could help you."

"No, Mom. I'm here because I was hoping you had a rocket to the moon, and I could escape into outer space to avoid this drama."

"Okay. I deserved that. Riv, having spent a good part of my life being insecure, I can tell you, it's not an easy thing to overcome.

If I had been secure, I wouldn't have made most of my stupid mistakes. I would never have left my family, and I certainly wouldn't have shacked up in LA with a creep like Phil Hodges and spent years trying to please a narcissistic, misogynistic, movie-producing piece of scum. What I'm trying to say is, it took me years to get it together and really believe that I was worth a whole lot more."

"So, what are you saying? I have to wait years for Gina to realize she's a worthwhile person?"

"No. But you need to be aware that it's not easy for some people to really understand their own value. You just have to be patient and understand that she can't change that part of herself overnight. But she does need to be better at not being so blatant about it, though. Especially where Avalon is concerned. Do you love Gina?"

River picked up the pen again, but realizing what he was doing, he put it back down on the desk and looked uncomfortably at his lap. "I think so. I really care about her a lot. I feel good when I'm with her. Most of the time."

"Honey, all I can tell you is that you need to do all you can to make Gina feel good, but at the same time, you've got to know that there's a limit to your powers."

River pretended to be insulted. "No way, Mom!"

Arielle laughed. "You give Gina what you can and hope that it's enough. If you two are meant to be, it will work out. Just be true to yourself, son. You know, let your brain make your decisions, not your ... uh ..."

"Ha ha. You're like ten shades of red, Mom."

"Oh, yeah. Well, take a look in the mirror, Riv. Because you're twenty shades to my ten."

Larsen was sure he could hear his heart beating. As he descended the stairs without the benefit of his canine ghost detector, he felt a strong chill and realized he didn't need one.

"Peter. Are you here?"

Larsen saw Peter standing near the flats at the far end of the room. He was slightly more opaque than he had been the last time. Hoping that a sharper image meant that he was gaining Peter's trust, Larsen walked slowly toward the lost boy, then stopped. It was clear that Peter did not wish him to come any closer.

"I'm so glad to see you, Peter. I am sorry that I had to give you such bad news."

Peter's spoken response was adamant. "Bring him here to me. I want to see him."

"I told you, Peter. Ernie is dead. He's not coming."

"My father."

"I can't bring him here, either. I told you; I don't know where he is. Even your mother doesn't know if he's dead or alive. She stopped looking for him. I think she's afraid to find out. They got divorced a couple of years after you died."

"Why? They loved each other so much. The way Ernie and I loved each other."

"Who really knows, Peter? From what your mom has told me, he felt guilty. He said he knew how dangerous Willard Carrow was and should have moved away after all of the threats and bribes. But he didn't want to break your heart and tear your mom away from her home and friends. But then, when you were killed, he blamed himself for not being stronger and protecting his family. He couldn't handle the guilt, and I guess it wrecked the marriage. So, he went away, and your parents got divorced. Maybe he's in heaven, waiting for you."

"But not Ernie?"

"I don't know. It's not for me to say where he went. People in this town have their opinions."

"He was good. He was my soul mate. How can I go to heaven if he's not there?"

Larsen brightened. "Maybe the Ernie you know is there. Maybe the Ernest that other people knew went somewhere else. I don't know how the afterlife works. I'm not always too sure about this one. Maybe a soul can split. After all, the Ernie you knew really did die when you did. Only his body lived on to become someone else."

"I hope so. Look in the desk."

Larsen looked around. "What desk?"

"Over there."

Larsen looked over toward the props and saw an old rolltop desk pushed sideways against the wall. "This one?"

"Yes. Look in the bottom drawer. Show me what you see. Please."

Hurrying toward the desk, Larsen looked at Peter to make sure he did not disappear. He bent down and pulled the handle on the bottom drawer. It stuck just a bit but then opened easily. Larsen put his hand inside and found that he was holding a stack of photographs. He walked back over to where he had been standing and addressed Peter. "This is what you wanted me to see."

"Look at them."

As Larsen leafed through the photos, he found one beautiful large photo after another of Peter in rehearsal for *West Side Story*. Then he came to a photo of Peter with another boy. He knew love when he saw it, and the love he saw in the photograph was something he hoped one day to have for himself. "Is this you with Ernie?" Larsen held the photo for Peter to see.

"Yes. Look at him. He was a good person."

Peter was right. As Larsen stared at the photo, he saw warmth and light in Ernie Carrow's eyes that were far from the evil man he had heard about. It was no wonder Peter had trouble believing what he had told him. "These are beautiful photos, Peter. I can see you and Ernie were very much in love. Can I bring these photos to your mother? Or do you want me to leave them here?"

"Let my mother have them."

"Would you like me to bring your mother here?"

"No. She will want me to go to the light. I can't go if he's not there. I have to wait for him. I have to wait!"

"I understand, Peter. But in a couple of weeks, there will be people at this theater all the time. You know, there will be lots of people making new memories. I'm afraid there won't be as much room for yours. I was just hoping you would want to see your mother before the theater opens."

"I've waited for forty years. I'll wait forever."

Larsen opened his mouth to respond, but Peter was gone. Looking down at the photos in his hands, he couldn't help but think of the bittersweet moment when he would present them to Kathryn. If only he could tell her that it was possible to see Peter again.

📖📖📖

"Wow, look at this photo of Principal Carrow as a teenager! He looks like a completely different person."

"No kidding, Riv. It's amazing. He looks like he was a really nice kid. And then he turned into the devil." Arielle looked up at Larsen. "So Peter wants his mother to have these photos?"

Larsen stood against the wall of the trailer. "Yeah, he does. But he won't agree to let me help reunite them. It just kills me."

River stood up. "Here, dude. This is your desk. You sit down; I'll hold the wall up."

Larsen began to protest, but River was already out of the chair, so Larsen took his place at his desk. "He thinks she'll make him go to the light, and he doesn't want to go without Ernie. I told him Ernie won't be showing up and that it's going to be really hard to be here once the theater opens in two weeks."

River played with Muggins, who had come out to greet him. "Maybe he'll change his mind. He's been focused on one thing for forty years and hasn't had anybody to talk to about it. He needs a little time."

Arielle, lost in thought, kept going through the stack of photos, her face clearly indicating she had an idea.

"Hey, Mom, you've got your brain turned on. What are you thinking?"

"I always have my brain turned on, Riv. I just haven't always used it. But I do have a brilliant idea. What if we put a plaque in the lobby and dedicate this theater to Peter?"

"That rhymes, Mom."

"You think?"

"Ha ha."

"We can have some of these photos professionally restored and framed, then we'll place them around the plaque."

"That's fantastic, Mrs. D. Kathryn will be thrilled."

"Great idea, Mom!"

"I'm not done. Right now, our new school will have only three classrooms, a lounge, and an office. But if we do well and expand, I hope it will become something much bigger. I think it deserves a better name than the Desert Theater School of the Performing Arts. What if we call it The Peter Winterstrom School of the Performing Arts? Of course, Jinxsy and Eve will have to approve it, but I can't imagine they'd have any problem with it at all."

"Heck, no, Mom. Besides, I've got the Jinxster wrapped around my little finger."

"I dare you to tell Jinxsy that."

"Ha ha."

"Getting back to business; now, listen, boys, here's what I'd like to do. After I get approval, I want to publicize the fact that the theater is going to be dedicated to Peter. But when I emcee the talent show, after I make the official announcement, I want to surprise Kathryn and everyone else by revealing what the new name of the school will be."

"That's brilliant. We can keep a secret, Mom."

"That will be the best gift to Kathryn ever! It's a really cool gift to me, too."

Arielle laid the stack of photos on her desk. "I hope you're right, Lars. I feel really good about this. I want this school to embody young gifted students like Peter and you. I love the idea of having a name that really means something and that honors someone so special. And maybe in some way this will give Peter the closure he needs to move on. Maybe just by knowing that he has a legacy here on earth he will find peace."

Chapter 30

"Come on in, Larsen. River and I are just having breakfast."

Larsen opened the screen door to the Dalworths' home and walked into the kitchen, where Mick and River were eating. "Hey, Mr. D. Hey, Riv."

Mick pointed to an empty chair. "Sit down. Hungry?"

Larsen took a seat at the table. "Well, I sort of had breakfast at home."

River burst out laughing. "How do you 'sort of' have breakfast?"

"Well, I had a small bowl of cereal because I was too nervous to eat much. I can't believe this is the big day. Tonight the theater is going to open, and I'm going to be performing in the talent competition. Kathryn's going to find out that the school is being named after Peter, and Lisa and Josh will be filming it all for the TV show. And that's just for starters!"

Finishing his bowl of cereal, Mick wiped his mouth with a napkin and turned to Larsen. "I've never been prouder of Arielle than I am today. I'm proud of you, too. From what I've been told, you have one hell of a work ethic. I don't think Ari could have found anyone better to work as her assistant. I know it's going to be crazy getting everything ready for tonight, so why don't you sort of have some more breakfast?"

River laughed. "Good one, Dad."

Larsen chuckled. "I think that's sort of a good idea, Mr. D. I'm feeling weak already. Are you coming to the theater with us now?"

"Oh, no. I have to put in a half day at work. I normally go in later on Saturdays, but I wanted to get an early start so I can get to the theater to help in any way I can. I'm going to go kiss my beautiful wife good-bye, and I'll see you two later."

"Mom's in the shower, Dad."

Mick smiled crookedly. "And your point, River?"

Embarrassed, River shoved a spoonful of cereal into his mouth as Mick walked away laughing.

"You're a piece of work, Riv. No wonder your parents say you're from Mars. But thanks for getting up early to help us. You're okay."

"Speaking of being okay, dude, how are you? I know you were hoping to hear from your mom at Christmas."

"I never said that."

"C'mon, I know you. When we were sitting here on Christmas morning, I saw your mind taking a side trip from the conversation. I know you were thinking about her and your dad."

Larsen shrugged. "My dad is dead, and I'm dead to my mom. It's not like I can change any of that. But your family and Kathryn are like real family to me. I'm really grateful to know you all."

"How's Kathryn doing? Is she excited about tonight, seeing you perform and having the theater dedicated to Peter? Wait till she finds out about the school being named after him."

Larsen took half of a toasted bagel from the basket on the kitchen table and began buttering it. "She was overjoyed about the dedication. I haven't seen her ever smile like that. It just didn't last long enough. Remember that Sunday after I got sick when I told you she was acting different? You know, angry with herself?"

"Sure. I remember."

"Well, whatever she thinks she did wrong, she's not talking about it, and she sure isn't forgiving herself. She's trying to pretend everything is fine, but it's not. When you live with someone, you get to know that person really well. And when something's off, you can just tell. Of course, I don't need to live in the same house with you to know—"

"Ha ha. Better watch it!"

Larsen smiled and took a bite of bagel. "Where's Jessie?"

"Sleeping in. She'll probably come over with my dad or the Jinxster."

"How about Gina?"

"She's coming tonight with her parents. Gabe's kids are all coming tonight, too."

Larsen poured himself a glass of orange juice. "Gabe is really brilliant at what he does. He's a quiet guy to work with, and sometimes kind of intense, but he's a master craftsman, you know. It'll be really cool for his kids to see his work."

"Yeah, I hope so. Hey, one more thing I wanted to ask you before my mom is ready to go: have you talked to Peter since that day when he showed you the photos?"

Larsen looked unhappy. "Not really. I tried twice after Christmas, but no luck. Then, one day after New Year's, I went looking for him, and he appeared very faintly. He just kind of stared at me. He didn't speak out loud to me and we weren't talking telepathically, either. I could just read his mind, weird as that sounds. He was just telling me that nothing has changed and that he's not going to see his mother or stop waiting for Ernie. Then I went in there yesterday to remind him that we were opening tonight and that everything would change."

"What did he say?"

"Nothing. I never even saw him. I felt a chill, and I knew he was there. He heard me, but he wasn't up for any conversation. And that's basically it, except that I thought I heard him crying when I left."

"See you this afternoon, guys!" Mick smiled and hurried out the kitchen door.

"Looks like we should get ready to go, Lars. Let's head into the living room and wait for my mom."

Just as River and Larsen were entering the living room, Arielle came in from the other direction carrying an oversized dress bag and a small suitcase.

"Hey, Mom. Where are you going?"

Arielle plunked her luggage on the couch. "Same place you're going. To the theater."

River laughed. "Yeah, only we're not moving in. Ha ha."

"I hope you come back in the next life as a female, Riv. Then you'll know what it's like to have to doll yourself up for an occasion like this, among other things. Now, would you be kind enough to carry my stuff to the car?"

"Where's Muggins?"

"He's in the backhouse snuggling with your sister. I think he's going to stay home today. It's too chaotic. Besides, he doesn't have a ticket. Now, let's go to the theater and get this show on the road. I'm a nervous wreck. I've never worked harder for anything in my life. Please, let this day go like clockwork."

"Sure it will, Mrs. D. What could possibly go wrong?"

📖📖📖

Bianca made herself comfortable on Gina's bed as she lay back and put Gina's pink and purple pillows behind her head. "Okay, girl, so why did I need to haul ass over here at twelve-thirty in the afternoon?"

Gina smirked. "You only live down the street. You have to

travel at least five blocks to be legally allowed to call it 'hauling ass.' Besides, you're so tiny, there isn't much to haul."

"Okay, so why did you summon my petite butt to your bedroom? Your text sounded kind of urgent."

"Totally."

"What's the nine one one?"

"Are you serious? I told you yesterday that I have no clue what to wear tonight. This is the first chance ever for River to see me glammed up. I want to look like a movie star. First, you need to help me figure out which dress to wear and then what to do with my hair and makeup. I don't want to look tramped-out like my sister. I want to look like the classy girl that I am."

Bianca locked her fingers together and stretched her arms lazily over her head. "Okay, girl. I've got you covered. Hey, you've got a call."

Gina made a face. "I wonder who it is. That's my WTFRU ringtone."

"What?"

"My 'who-the-fuck-are-you' ringtone. It's the default one I set for people who aren't in my contact list." Gina looked at the number. "I don't know anyone with a 201 area code. Hello?"

"Gina, this is Avalon."

Gina's eyes opened wide. She put her hand over the speaker and mouthed Avalon's name to Bianca.

"Oh, okay. I didn't recognize the area code."

"Yeah, my family kept our Jersey numbers. Listen, Gina, this is really important. I need your help."

Gina rolled her eyes. "You need my help for what?"

"I know this is going to sound really bizarre to you, but you'll have to trust that I'm for realsies. I have a super urgent message for River. I don't have his cell number, and I called his house phone but only got voicemail. I didn't leave a message because I figured it would be too late by the time anyone checked."

Gina sat down on the bed next to Bianca, put the call on speakerphone, and laid the phone on top of a pillow. "Too late for what?"

"Too late for him to get my message in time to do anything!"

"So, what can I do for you, Avalon?"

"I need River's cell number."

Gina held up her middle finger to the phone while Bianca suppressed a laugh. "I don't ever give out anyone's number. That's totally uncool."

Avalon's frustration was mounting, and Gina was enjoying every sigh on the other end of the phone.

"You know Riv and I are just friends. It's not like I'm gonna be calling him all the time, Gina. I just need to tell him something super life-and-death important. I know my dad's at the theater with everyone, but no way do I want to go through him. He left for work stressed to the max. So can you puh-leeze give me Riv's number?"

Gina crossed her eyes and stuck out her tongue. "Sorry; like I said, that's uncool. I totally respect my guy's privacy. You know?"

Avalon's voice grew louder. "He won't be upset. He'd want you to give it to me. I'm positive. I just never had any reason to ask him for it. I should have. I just didn't do it because I was so afraid you'd take it the wrong way."

Gina made a mock innocent face. "Me take it the wrong way? Why would I be upset if a girl who glommed onto my boyfriend from day one, and who is diggin' him more than she's willing to admit, wants his number?"

Bianca put up her palm to advise Gina to slow down, but Gina waved her off.

"I don't like River that way. You don't even know me. Okay, well, if you hate me so much that you won't help me, I'll have to get Erik to drive me to the theater so I can give him the message in person."

Gina looked panicked but quickly recovered. "Hey, Avalon, I'm really sorry. You're a really sweet girl, and, honestly, I know you and Riv are just friends. Please excuse me for being a total twat."

"Okay, Gina. But you shouldn't call yourself a—"

Bianca looked at Gina curiously as she continued to pour on the bull.

"No, Avalon. Seriously, I deserved it. You know, my sister, Taylor, was the biggest bully in school and totally insecure. She still is. When you've got a big sister like that, sometimes you just pick up the worst habits, you know? Gosh, I'm so sorry."

Avalon's voice was calmer. "Yeah. I've got a younger sister named Isabella, and I know she watches me closely. I'm not perfect, but I really want to be a good example for her. I see her copy me a lot."

Gina pretended to stick two fingers down her throat and gag. "Does she have green-and-blue hair?"

"No. Listen, Gina, I really need to talk to River."

Gina grabbed Bianca's phone out of her hand and texted one letter to herself. "Oh, hold on, Avalon. My baby is texting me. Oh, how sweet is this? He misses me and wants me to call him right away! And he put a little kissy face in the text. OMG, is he the most romantic boyfriend, or what? So listen, Avalon, he's waiting for my call. You just give me the message, and I promise I'll tell him right before we have phone sex."

Bianca twisted her face in protest but Gina ignored her.

"Just kidding about that last part. Well, I mean, we're not gonna do that *now*. He's so busy helping his mom. So, what's your message?"

Avalon sighed loudly. "I really wanted to tell him myself."

"This is the best I can do, Avalon. If it's that important, then giving me the message is the right thing to do."

Avalon paused. "I guess. But it'll sound real weird."

"I grew up in a weird family. I'm cool with whatever you tell me."

"Okay, well, just tell River that this morning I painted a lady trapped in a castle with a dragon."

Gina and Bianca shared a look. Trying not to laugh, Gina turned away from Bianca. "Oh, no, you painted a lady trapped in a castle with a dragon. Was he a big mean, green dragon?"

"I don't think he's really mean. The thing is, after I kept painting, I realized that the lady I was painting was Mrs. Dalworth. I recognized her in my painting because I saw her on TV that time. Anyway, in my painting, she looked really frightened, and River needs to know."

Gina made a face. "That's kind of lame, Avalon. You painted the picture, right? So you could have made her look any way you wanted her to look. And how convenient that she looks like River's mom."

"I know how it sounds, but, no, I didn't paint anything on purpose. Would you please just give River the message?"

Still unable to make eye contact with Bianca, Gina went on. "Okay, so you just need me to tell Riv that you painted his mom trapped in a castle with a dragon, and she looked really frightened but not necessarily because of the dragon. Like, maybe the dragon was her friend."

"Except for the last part, yeah. Could you tell him that exactly as I said it, Gina? Please?"

"Sure thing. I better go, Avalon, you know, before River wonders why I'm not calling him. I'll give him your message first thing."

"Thanks, Gina."

Gina ended the phone call and burst out laughing. "Can you freakin' believe that girl? I've heard of lame-ass, desperate attempts to get to a guy, but telling his girlfriend that you painted his mom in a castle with a dragon? What kind of nut job besides Avalon Martelli comes up with that nonsense? Does she think I'm stupid?"

Bianca wasn't laughing. "Actually, I'm not sure what she's up to. But if I were you, I'd deliver that message no matter what. You need to worry about covering your ass with more than a pretty dress."

Gina blew air through her lips. "No way! Now, help me decide what to wear."

"Hey, Mom, where's your control panel? I need to turn down your electrical input a bit. You're so wired, your hair is gonna stand on end in a minute."

Arielle continued to look through a list of names on a computer screen. "Riv, I'll rewire your control panel and disable some of your favorite body parts, starting with your mouth. And don't even think about messing with my hair, even verbally."

Larsen laughed. "I love when you guys go at it. I wish my mother was only kidding when she said things like that to me."

"Oh, honey, I wish your mom only said nice things to you, too. But what makes you think I'm kidding?" Arielle winked.

River leaned against the trailer wall as Larsen continued to collate programs. "What did you need me to do next?"

Arielle, frantically trying to finish what she was doing, didn't turn to face River. "I need you to go into the lobby and make sure that the dedication plaque for Peter and all of his photos are nicely draped. When Jess comes in, she's going to take the before photos. We'll have a private unveiling before the public is allowed in. Lars, Kathryn knows to come early for that, right?"

"Oh, yeah. She'll be right on time. And Ms. Carrow, her

mom, and Jinxsy will be here early, too. Along with the press and the other VIP guests."

"Good. Riv, after that, I want you to go upstairs. The contestants will be using the two large dressing rooms. Just make sure that they're appropriately marked for guys and girls and that each room is stocked with everything on the list I gave you. If you have any questions, ask Raphael's wife, Natalie. She'll show you where everything is kept."

Larsen raised a finger. "Oh, Mrs. D, I hate to ask you this, but what you just told River reminded me. It's okay if I sit next to Kathryn in the audience, isn't it? I don't want her to be alone. I'm sure you know she bought a ticket for me. I'll leave in plenty of time to be on stage when I'm called."

Arielle continued to stare at her computer screen. "That's totally fine, Lars. I did know that. Don't forget to double check with Gabe to make sure you know who's handling the video feed. We've got TVs in both dressing rooms so that all of the contestants can watch the performances. If there's any issues, ask Josh when he and Lisa get here. He's a technical wizard."

"Sure, Mrs. D."

River looked at his mother. "Mom, seriously, you need to take a breath and drink some water."

Arielle sighed and turned around. "You're right. I do. I'm just trying to familiarize myself with this list of contestants so I don't mess up any names or information. I've never really been an emcee before. I'm used to playing characters, not myself. It may sound silly, but it's much easier to be someone else. Oh hell, where's my hard copy of this list?"

Larsen pointed to the stapled pages in front of Arielle's computer. "Right where I put it an hour ago."

River reached over for his mother's water bottle and handed it to her. "Seriously, Mom, drink. You've been burning your eyeballs staring at the computer screen for nothing."

Arielle took a long drink. "I'm a crazed woman. What can I say? Okay now, let's see. It's two-fifteen. We've got four hours and forty-five minutes until the unveiling in the lobby at seven. At seven-fifteen, the front doors open. After five-thirty, Natalie will be greeting the contestants at the back door and sending them upstairs. She has two people who are going to make sure everyone gets on stage at the right time. My head is spinning. I hope we get everything done.

"I'm going to finish going over this list, and then I'm going to go back stage and make sure everything is set up for the musicians. We've got twelve people coming."

"It'll all be cool, Mrs. D. They brought the piano in this morning."

"What would I do without you, Larsen? You're my sanity."

"And what am I, Mom?"

Arielle grimaced, a hint of a smile on her face. "You're my insanity. If you want a compliment, wait until this is all over and everything has gone according to plan."

River laughed. "It'll be cool, Mom. I'm going to take off and do everything that you asked me. What do you want me to do when I finish those things?"

"Meet me back here in the trailer, Riv, and I'll reassess my to-do list. I just need to see backstage with my own eyes and make sure it all looks good. Oh, and, Lars, make sure my podium is on the right-hand corner of the stage and the mic is working."

River walked over and gave Arielle a kiss on the top of her head. "You'll be awesome. I'm proud of you, Mom."

After Larsen and River took off to do their respective chores,

Arielle took another calming breath and straightened her desk as best she could. Then, jumping up, she hurried out of the trailer, across the lot, and opened the back door of the theater.

She could hear the confident voices of her team directing the setup on stage and smiled confidently. It finally felt as if everything were coming together. As she stopped for only a minute to pause before going backstage, she felt a large hand make a firm seal over her mouth and nose. Before she could physically react, the unknown assailant then pulled her toward the downstairs door. With every bit of strength, she tried to scream, but the hand was clasped so tightly over her mouth that nothing but a mere squeak was emitted. And she could barely breathe.

The downstairs door opened, and the assailant went through it first, pulling her with him, then shutting the door. After dragging her down the stairs and finding himself somewhat out of breath, he took his hand away from Arielle's face and turned her around so she could see him.

"Hi, honey. I'm home. Miss me, doll face?"

Arielle stared in disbelief. "Phil! You degenerate piece of walking sediment. How dare you slime this theater with your presence? How dare you smother me like that and drag me down here?"

Phil grabbed her firmly around the waist and pulled him against her. "That doesn't sound very friendly, Arielle. It doesn't sound very respectful, either."

"What the hell do you want?"

Phil smiled wickedly. "I'm only here for one purpose."

Arielle tried to wrest free, but he grabbed her arms. "What the fuck do you want?"

"Oh, not too much. I'm just here to make sure that I ruin your career before it ever gets off the ground. Hmm. I wonder who will emcee amateur hour when you're not there to play the hostess with the mostess. I wonder who will run this place after I bash your skull in."

"Let me go!"

"You even try to scream. I'll gag you. You play nice. We can talk. Reminisce about old times. Talk about how you ruined my career and maybe brainstorm about the many ways you're going to make it up to me."

"I can't do anything with my head bashed in, can I?"

"Maybe not. But I'll have to think about it." Phil licked his lips like a savage beast about to feast on a dead carcass. "Come on. I've found a great hiding place for us down here. It'll be like old times, baby."

"Let me go! I've barely got enough time to get everything done as it is. Just get the hell out of here, and I'll forget you ever came back to this town."

Digging his thick fingers into her upper arms, Phil held her at arm's length and took a good look at her. "What the hell happened to my breast implants? I paid thousands for those."

"I didn't need them any more than I needed you."

"Oh, what the hell; it'll be like doing you when we first met."

"You repulsive scum. Don't you dare touch me!"

Phil pushed Arielle toward the far end of the room where the scenery and flats were stored, then turned her face forward as he pushed her between pieces of old sets until they were both well hidden behind a large castle wall with a giant dragon head lying on top. Arielle looked down to see a brand-new spool of rope, a package of duct tape, a folded blue tarp, and some dirty rags on another piece of the castle wall.

Phil belly laughed as he saw a look of fear come over her face. "Oh, yeah, I brought some supplies with me. Snuck 'em down here no more than fifteen minutes ago. So, if you even think about trying to scream or get away, I'll shove those filthy gasoline rags in your mouth and tie your pretty wrists until they bleed. And all the while I'll be enjoying the rest of you in a way I never did before. Or maybe I'll make a snuff film with my cell phone."

Arielle's heart was racing as Phil pushed her down to the floor and sat next to her. "Look, Phil, I'm sure you really don't want to do this. I know your career isn't what it used to be, but what do you think it will be if you're arrested for kidnapping, torture, and rape? Isn't your Hollywood condo more appealing than a prison cell?"

Phil put his thumb and forefinger around her neck. "That lousy 700-square-foot condo *is* a fucking prison cell. You think I like all of that Hollywood Boulevard traffic outside my window? I had it made in Bel Air, and you lost everything for me."

"No, Phil. The truth is that you would have lost your connection with Ross years before if it weren't for me. He kept hiring you to produce his movies because of my friendship with Lisa. And with him, too. You lost everything because of who you are. And maybe you could have salvaged some of your movie career had you not driven your Jaguar down here two years ago to try to kidnap me. It's not my fault you got your head beaten in with a baseball bat."

Phil's bloodshot eyes stared with contempt, and his nostrils flared as he ever so slightly tightened his hold around Arielle's neck. "If you had stayed put like you were supposed to, none of that would have ever happened. You ruined my career and my face. Look at all of these goddamn scars I've got! And guess what, babycakes? After I have my fun with you, it's going to be payback time. You can say good-bye to your pretty face."

As Arielle began choking, Phil took his hands away from her neck, but he remained menacingly close to her. Remembering that Peter spent time in the very area where she was hiding, Arielle began to look for him, hoping that in some way, he might be able to save her by knocking Phil out or choking him to death. But she couldn't feel any presence whatsoever. Peter had very likely gone upstairs to the stage to watch everything that was going on.

"Who the hell are you looking around for? There's nobody here but us."

Arielle snickered. "Oh, I don't know—maybe that screaming woman you inserted into my promo trailer."

Phil pulled a large jackknife from his pocket and opened it. Seeing Arielle's fear, he gently ran it across her neck, watching with glee as her eyes watered. Arielle could only whisper. "Please stop."

"Stop? Babycakes, I'm having way too much fun for that. And by the way, I'll take your cell phone."

Chapter 31

River's face was dripping with sweat when he finally located Larsen backstage. "Hey, Lars …"

"Riv, you look like you've been out roaming the desert. What's wrong?"

"My mom told me to meet her back in the trailer at around two-forty-five. Dude, it's three-thirty, and I can't find her anywhere. Her cell just goes to voicemail. I've asked every single person here, and nobody has seen her. Where the hell could she be?"

Larsen was alarmed. "I don't know. I haven't seen her either. He thought for a moment. "Wait, she's using the big dressing room down the hall. Maybe she went in there to freshen up and decided to rest a little. Makes sense. Have you looked there?"

"I didn't even know it existed."

"Come on, let's go together. It's a little tricky to find." River followed Larsen down a hallway and around a corner to a dressing room with Arielle's name written on a piece of paper taped to the door. He knocked loudly, but there was no answer. "Mom! Are you in there?" River tried to open the door, but it was locked.

"I have the key, Riv." Larsen opened the door, and River rushed in.

"There's nothing here but her stuff, all of that luggage I was kidding her about this morning. The bathroom door is open. She's not in there." River ran into the bathroom and looked behind the shower curtain just to make sure. "Wait' I know where she might be!"

"Where?"

"This morning before you came to the house, she was saying that she wished Peter had agreed to see his mom tonight. Maybe she went downstairs where you've been seeing Peter to see if she could convince him. My mom is one determined person. Maybe she thought she could do the motherly thing and change his mind. And if she found him, she would definitely stay forty-five minutes if that's what it took."

"You're so right, Riv. Let's go!"

Arielle winced and squirmed as Phil kissed her neck. He could see the revulsion on her face, and it only aroused him. He rolled his tongue around in her ear but stopped abruptly when he heard the basement door being opened. Grabbing the folded tarp, he opened it and threw it over the two of them as he pushed Arielle's head to the floor, whispering in her ear, "You say one fucking word or utter one sound, I will slit your throat. And if whoever that is happens to be someone you care about, I'll make you watch as I slit their throat first."

Larsen looked distraught as he looked around the large room. Not only did he not see Arielle, but he knew instinctively that Peter wasn't around.

"Mom, are you here?"

"Mrs. D!"

Arielle whimpered at the sound of their voices.

"I'll kill your son if you make any more noise."

Shaking, Arielle stayed silent as River and Larsen continued to call her name.

"She's not here, Riv. Let's check upstairs. You know what?

She could have needed to do an errand. Maybe she just did it herself because everyone else is so busy. You know, that's just like your mom."

"Something doesn't feel right, Lars."

"We'll find her, Riv. She's got to be somewhere."

As soon as Phil heard the door shut, he sat up and threw the tarp off them. "Aw, isn't that sweet? Your kid actually sounds like he gives a shit about you. And you were such a rotten mother, too."

Arielle started to make a retort but stopped as Phil waved the gleaming knife in her face. "Now, where were we, babycakes? Oh, yeah—I was just going to have a slice of sweetie pie."

📖📖📖

"Larsen! Hi!"

"Oh, hi, Lisa. Hey, Josh."

Lisa stood in the breezeway of the theater with a big grin on her face as Josh said hello, laid some equipment down, then hurried outside to get the rest from his car. "This must be River. I've seen so many photos of you over the years and heard about your wonderful sense of humor. Hi, honey. I'm Lisa Finlay, you know, your mom's best friend. Speaking of whom, why isn't she answering her phone? I've been trying to call her for a good hour now."

Larsen and River exchanged worried glances, and Lisa knew something was wrong. "Whatever it is, tell me now."

Just as River was about to speak, Raphael came running over. "Larsen, where's Arielle? Everyone's looking for her."

"We don't know! The last time River and I saw her was at two-fifteen in the trailer."

Lisa looked at her phone. "Holy shit, it's four o'clock now. Where would Ari have disappeared to for almost two hours? This is so completely and utterly unlike her."

"Arielle has disappeared? How could she? Her car is still outside."

"Dad!"

Mick, dressed in his work clothes and carrying a garment bag, looked panicked. "I tried calling her three times to let her know I was on the way. She didn't pick up or answer my texts. Where could she possibly be? I checked the trailer before I came here."

"I don't know, Dad. Lars and I just checked her dressing room and the downstairs rehearsal space. Everyone else has been looking for her, too!"

"Where haven't you looked?"

"We haven't checked upstairs yet."

"What's up there?"

River looked at Larsen to explain. "That's where the group dressing rooms are and a few smaller ones. Oh, and the wardrobe room is …"

Before Larsen could finish, Mick rushed up the stairs as River ran behind him.

Lisa turned to Josh. "Let's look outside. Maybe she's wandering around taking photos or something."

Josh looked confused. "Why would she do that?"

"How the hell do I know? She's missing, and right now I can't think of anything that makes any sense at all." Lisa turned to all of the people who had gathered in the excitement. "I need every inch of this place searched until someone finds Arielle. This is making me sicker by the moment. And don't forget the light booth."

📖📖📖

Phil caressed Arielle's face. "It's so nice spending time with you again, Ari. He purred grotesquely. "You have such soft skin. I always liked that about you. Tell me everything you liked about me.

Come on."

"Nothing. I was a fool to be with you. Nothing! Let me go, Phil. You've had your fun. You've taken your revenge. Now, let me go."

Phil looked at his watch. "It's almost six o'clock. We've only been together a few hours. You know that's not enough time for me. I'm just waiting for the show to start at eight. I do have the starting time right, don't I? That's when our real fun will begin. Gee, I'm happy to say that three groups of people have been down here looking for you, and I do believe we have thoroughly convinced everyone that you're not here."

Arielle was covered in sweat as the tears rolled down her face. "Let me go, Phil. They're not going to stop looking for me."

📖📖📖

"Dad, please. Sit down."

Exhausted, Mick reluctantly sat on a chair reserved for the musicians on the stage. "Riv. Larsen. We've turned this place in and out. Nobody has seen her or heard from her. She didn't drive anywhere because her car hasn't moved. Where the hell can she be? I don't even know where to look anymore. Where did Lisa and Josh go?"

River sat in a chair next to Mick. "They went driving around the building and the neighborhood. They've come and gone about three times."

"River!"

River looked up to see Gabe rushing toward him with a cell phone in his hand as Lisa and Josh returned, coming from the opposite direction.

"What's up, Gabe?"

"My daughter, Avvie. I just called her to see if Arielle had called the house phone. I didn't even realize that I left my business cell in the truck. Soon as I told Avvie your mom has gone missing for the last three hours, she's been desperate to talk to you. She thinks she can help."

River stood and took the phone from Gabe. The phone was so sweaty he could barely hold it. "Hello?"

"Riv! My dad said your mother is missing."

"Yeah, Avalon. I have no idea where she is. We've searched every inch of this building."

"Didn't Gina give you my message?"

"What message? No! I haven't spoken to Gina. I've been way too busy here."

"You didn't text her around lunchtime?"

"No way. What are you talking about?"

"I called her around twelve-thirty and begged her to give me your cell number. I told her it was a life-and-death emergency. She said she wouldn't give it to me because that was uncool, and I pleaded with her so hard. I told her it was really urgent. She said you had just texted her. She said she was going to call you and deliver my message first thing. She totally promised."

"Well, my phone's been on all day, and nobody called or texted me. Believe me, I've been checking every five minutes. What did you want to tell me?"

"The premonitions came back. At least, I think so. Riv, I painted this picture of a lady looking very scared. I didn't realize until I had finished that she looked really familiar. Then I remembered she looked exactly like your mom. I saw your mom on TV on that promo thing with Larsen and the screaming lady. Anyway, I told Gina that I painted her in a castle with a green dragon. She probably thought that was bullshit, so she didn't tell you."

"You saw my mom in a castle with a green dragon?"

Larsen grabbed River's arm. "I think I know where she is!"

Mick stood up. "Where's that?"

"Avalon, I think you may have just found her for us. I have no idea what you're talking about, but Larsen seems to know. Just stay by the phone in case I need to call you back, okay? Thank you so much."

Larsen began to speak as River handed the phone back to Gabe. "There's an old castle set downstairs at the end of the rehearsal hall. I'm sure. I've looked through all of those sets. And there's a green dragon head lying around. The body is upstairs in wardrobe, but the head is downstairs."

Mick was wired. "I'm on my way!"

Lisa gasped. "No! Stop! Don't anybody rush down there! I think I've just figured it all out, and we have to be very careful."

Mick looked desperately at Lisa. "If my wife is downstairs, I'm going to get her."

"No, Mick! Hear me out first, or Ari will be in worse danger."

Mick could barely keep himself from taking off, but he knew he should at least listen to what Lisa had to say.

"When Josh and I were out driving around, we passed a silver Jaguar a couple of blocks away. Josh made a joke about how people with expensive cars hate parking lots. I didn't think anything of it, but there's one person I know who drives a Jaguar, and he's already tried once to mess with Arielle and this theater. And he wasn't avoiding the parking lot; he was avoiding his car from being seen!"

Mick reddened with rage. "Phil Hodges?"

"Yeah, I think he's got Arielle down there. Once he messed with our promo trailer, I knew for sure he hadn't moved on with his life. But when his stupid trick backfired and brought us nationwide press coverage, that must have really tweaked him. I saw him earlier this week because he works in my building. He didn't say anything; he just snarled at me. But he was mean in a way I've never seen him before. Mean even for Phil, and he's one son of a bitch. I think he's been obsessed with Ari, and his rage has been growing. It is highly likely he has a weapon, because if he didn't, somehow I believe Ari would have broken free by now or screamed for help when people came downstairs looking for her. We need to call the police."

Rattled, Gabe fought to stay composed. "Just called, Lisa. They're on the way. No sirens. We don't want to give that bastard any warning."

"I'm sorry, I forgot that your ex-wife lives with him."

"I don't give a flying fuck about that. Now, like I told the officers, there's a trapdoor backstage that goes to the basement. I'm going to show them where it is. If they can get in that way, hope to God they can nab the SOB before he hurts Arielle."

Mick balled his fist as if Phil was standing before him. "He better not have. I don't want to imagine—"

"Then don't, Dad! The cops are only two blocks away. They'll be here in a second."

Larsen looked around for the police and stopped cold when he saw Peter standing off in the distance, crying. Peter was saying he should have been downstairs to help, but Larsen was letting him know, telepathically, that it wasn't his fault.

River looked over and saw Peter, but he was too worried about his mother to do or say anything. Only moments later, four officers came rushing in from the back door.

"This way to the trapdoor! Larsen here will take you to the regular door."

Two officers followed Gabe as Larsen motioned for the other two to follow him.

The fourteen minutes that passed from the time the officers

took off felt like an eternity. Everyone had moved to the breezeway to be near the basement door. When Mick heard Arielle calling his name and running upstairs to him, he was overcome with relief as she came flying into his arms. "Oh, baby! Thank God. I was so worried. We were all so worried."

River, Larsen, Lisa, and Josh were all euphoric when they heard Phil loudly protest as he was escorted upstairs by two officers, his hands cuffed behind his back. "I didn't do anything. She wanted me. That skank bitch can't get over me. She won't stop calling me." Phil looked at the angry sea of faces. "She begged me to come down and do her before the show. You're all fools if you believe a word she says."

The officer who was now standing behind Phil held up a plastic bag filled with Phil's supplies. "Yeah, right. That's why you brought these little goodies along."

"She's kinky. She asked for them."

Gabe and River lurched for him, but an officer held them back.

"Remember what I said downstairs: anything you say can and will be held against you. Good going there, asshole."

As soon as the two officers had taken Phil out the back door, everyone took turns hugging Arielle. Wrecked, she looked over at the remaining two officers who had just come up the stairs. "I know you need much more from me than I told you downstairs. But really, I did cover most of it. Can I come by tomorrow and give you the despicable play-by-play? I just can't do it now. I've got to get ready for a show."

"Sure, Mrs. Dalworth. That will be fine. Come by after one when we'll both be there."

"I will. And thank you for saving my life. Thank you so much!"

The officers nodded and headed out as everyone added their

thank-yous.

"Wow, Mom. You're still going to go on?"

"Of course I am, Riv. There's no way that scumbag will take this night from me or anyone else." Arielle looked at Natalie, who was standing at the door, holding off the contestants who had been arriving. "Oh, Natalie, we need to get out of the way and let you do your job. I'm sure people will ask you about the man in handcuffs being taken away. Just assure them that everything is okay."

Natalie smiled. "Sure thing, Arielle. Don't worry. I've got this."

Arielle walked down the breezeway toward the stage as everyone followed.

River grabbed a folding chair leaning against the wall and opened it. "Sit down, Mom."

"But, Riv—"

River gently put his hands on Arielle's shoulders as she reluctantly sat down. "It's for your own good, Mom."

Arielle gave him a dirty look, but River saw the love in her eyes and smiled.

"Look, I know you all want to know what happened. But there's really precious little time for me to take a shower and get dressed and ready. I'll just say this much: Phil grabbed me earlier when I came through the back stage door. He put his hand over my mouth and dragged me downstairs and over to that castle set, where he'd left rope, duct tape, and old rags. Thank God he didn't use them on me. But he would've. He had a knife at my throat, and he would have killed me." Arielle paused to take a deep breath as she contemplated what had nearly happened. "Is there any water here?"

"Yeah, Mom. Raphael went to get you some. Here he is now." River took the bottle from Raphael and handed it to Arielle, who drank half the water before she began speaking again.

I'm so grateful that Phil was talking a bunch of garbage when the officers came up on us. His blabbering muffled any tiny noises they may have made. It was like a miracle. One moment Phil was threatening me, and the next he's got a gun at his back and another officer is pulling me to safety. It was the most horrid and surreal ordeal of my life." Arielle finished drinking her water before continuing. "Now, everyone here has a job to do. You know what they say: the show must go on."

Chapter 32

"Larsen! You almost gave me a heart attack. There's only six minutes until show time, and I wasn't sure you were going to take your seat."

"Sorry, Kathryn." Larsen sat in the seat next to her. "No way I wasn't going to make it. It was just crazy outside. We're completely sold out, but we were able to admit some people for SRO, you know, standing room only. This one lady was in tears because she'd just found out her granddaughter was performing and was devastated to hear there were no seats left. There was a man behind her who looked like he was crying, too. Must have been her husband. I wish I could have gotten seats for them, but they seemed happy to just be able to see the show any way they could. I hope it's as great as the anticipation, you know? Did you see all the press and media that are here? Even more showed up after the dedication ceremony."

"I still can't get over this theater being dedicated to Peter. What a beautiful thing to do for my son—and for me. I've never had such a stunning surprise. I'm so very grateful to all of you. And yes, I did see the media people."

Kathryn opened her program and began to read it. "The caliber of talented people competing tonight is something special. I was surprised to see that you're performing last, Larsen. Talk about anticipation! My nerves will be shot by then. But you'll be the last act the judges see, so they'll remember you the best."

Larsen looked uneasy. "I think I should tell you something, Kathryn. You'll find out soon enough anyway."

Kathryn touched the palm of her hand to her chest. "What is it? Should I be worried?"

"Oh, no. It's just that there's no way I can win this competition."

"Of course you can. You're a brilliant actor!"

"Mrs. D is the only other person who knows this because I had to tell her. I didn't even tell Riv. I took myself out of the competition."

"My goodness. Why?"

"Well, at first I was all for it, and it didn't seem to matter because the six judges from LA and Palm Springs aren't affiliated with the theater in any way. But I was afraid that if I did win, it could backfire in a big way. Even if I won legitimately, you know there would be people who would say it was rigged because I work here. I wouldn't want Mrs. D to have to defend that. It could get really ugly, and it would sort of be like pouring a bucket of slime over everything she's worked for. That we've all worked for. So, before I perform my monologue, she's going to make an announcement that I'm not under consideration and say that I've re ... um ..."

"Recused yourself."

"Yeah, right. That's the word."

"That makes sense, Larsen, but you won't have a chance to win the grand prize. You could use that money. And the winner will have a starring role in a future production. But I do agree, the appearance of impropriety can be just as bad as impropriety itself. Do you know that word? It means something dishonest or unethical."

"I do now! And what you just said is exactly how I feel. Don't worry about me; I can get a starring role without winning the competition. I really feel good about my decision, Kathryn."

Kathryn reached over and kissed Larsen on the cheek. "You have so much integrity, Larsen Davis. Have I told you lately how much I admire you?"

Embarrassed, Larsen was relieved when the lights began to dim. "Mrs. D is coming on stage. Wow, look at her! She looks so beautiful." Larsen stopped himself from inadvertently mentioning Arielle's ordeal. He was glad everyone had agreed to keep it from Kathryn until another time.

Arielle, dressed in a shimmery plum-colored dress, walked out on stage. In the audience, Mick and River had to fight back tears.

"Riv, your mother is the most beautiful woman on this earth. She looks radiant. Who would ever believe what she's been through today?"

"Mom's a champ. Look at Jess. She's taking about a million photos."

"Jess is going to give that camera quite a workout tonight. Your sister looks pretty darn beautiful, too."

"How about my beauty, Dad?"

Mick looked at River and just laughed.

On stage, Arielle smiled as the audience vigorously applauded. Walking over to the podium, she laid her papers down, adjusted the microphone, and began to speak. "Ladies and gentlemen, hello, I'm Arielle Dalworth. I want to thank you all for being here on this very special night. I'm glad my friend Josh McBride is filming it. I've been worried that I might wake up tomorrow and find that it's all been a dream."

The audience laughed.

"I want to thank Eve Carrow and Jinxsy Patterson for entrusting me with this beautiful theater. Being project manager has been a challenging and rewarding task, and no doubt, being director of our new school will be every bit as wonderful.

"I do have a special announcement, but first, I want to thank

Gabe Martelli, our brilliant vintage restoration specialist, and his team, Raphael Mendosa, Alejandro Jimenez, and George Sanchez, who have worked tirelessly for months. I also want to thank our many volunteers who have been working with us tonight. I want to thank Larsen Davis, my amazing assistant, who has saved my life in more ways than you'd ever believe. And now, if I may direct your attention to the stage, please say hello to our distinguished panel of judges and our very talented musicians who will be working their magic for us soon. Everyone's name and bio are in the program; I really wish I could mention you all now, but we might not have time left for a competition."

The audience laughed again, and Arielle took a sip of water before continuing her speech.

"We will have twenty-five contestants performing tonight. You can read all about our judging process, but I'll just tell you that each contestant has two and a half minutes to perform. We will have a fifteen-minute intermission after the fifteenth contestant performs.

"Before we begin, I have an announcement to make that is so very dear to my heart. As many of you already know and have seen in the program, earlier tonight, before our doors opened to the public, we unveiled a plaque in the lobby dedicating this theater to a talented young man named Peter Winterstrom, the son of Mystekal's Kathryn Winterstrom. Peter was a budding actor and singer when he died suddenly forty years ago. He was a performer with a passion for learning, honing, and practicing his craft. Peter was the embodiment of what every performing artist should strive to be. That is why, not only are we dedicating this theater to him, but our new school will be named The Peter Winterstrom School for the Performing Arts."

Kathryn let out a loud gasp that was heard by everyone. She turned to Larsen. "You knew this? Oh my goodness! Did Arielle just say what I thought she said? The school is going to be named for Peter? Oh my! This is the most wonderful surprise. Dedicating the theater was such a joy in itself, now this. My Peter will live on. I am so overjoyed. This must be what he meant about being a desert star. He just didn't know it."

Larsen's watched as Kathryn's face radiated with joy. "I think Mrs. D and the audience want you to stand up."

Kathryn seemed surprised to notice that all eyes were upon her. As Larsen helped her up, he saw Peter standing off to the side, behind two stagehands. He could see the anguish and joy on Peter's face on seeing his mother again. He quickly disappeared from sight, but Larsen knew he was still there.

The audience stood up and turned to honor Kathryn, who was so overcome that she could barely stand without Larsen's help. Choking out a thank you, she sat down again, and all eyes returned to Arielle.

Arielle wiped a tear from her eye. "I promised myself I wouldn't let my mascara run."

The audience laughed while Arielle took another sip of water before continuing.

"And now, I'd like to introduce our first contestant. She's a sophomore at Mystekal High, a soprano who will be singing 'Love, Look Away' from *Flower Drum Song*. Please join me in welcoming Miss Heather York."

"I'm spending every moment of intermission right here by Peter's plaque." Kathryn ran her fingers over her son's name as Jinxsy, Eve, Madeleine, Larsen, Mick, River, and Jessie looked on.

Jessie looked around at the crowd mingling in the lobby. "Mom must be so happy! She's been waiting for this day forever. I was hoping that the night would live up to her expectations, but I think it's exceeding them. The contestants are all so talented, and the audience is loving every minute."

Mick nodded enthusiastically. "Jess, it's my dream come true to see your mother so happy. And I don't think I've had a chance to tell you, but you look exquisitely beautiful. All of you ladies do."

River playfully nudged Mick in the ribs with his elbow. "How about me, Dad?"

Everyone cracked up.

"Hey, River."

River turned and was thrilled to see Avalon, dressed in a full-length vintage burgundy dress with lace, standing there. He gave her a big hug and walked her away from the group so that Kathryn wouldn't hear him talking about what had happened.

"Hey, you. First I've got to say that you look so amazingly beautiful. Do you know that you saved my mom's life today? I'm sure your dad told you that my mother's degenerate ex was holding her hostage downstairs. He found a hiding place inside the walls of an old castle set. And the head from a dragon costume was sitting on the ledge of one of the walls. Wow, you were right on, Avalon. You saved my mom, my family, this theater, and this night. You've got a friend in me for life."

Avalon blushed. "You're too nice, River. If I'm gonna have this crazy gift, I'm sure glad that something good came from it." Nervously, she began to finger the long strands of vintage beads she was wearing.

"Those are pretty necklaces. But you really are a standout beauty."

Embarrassed, Avalon put the focus on her necklaces. "These are Austrian crystal. They belonged to my grandma. She's still alive and all, but she wanted me to have them because I'm a bit nutso for this stuff."

River smiled and looked at her. "Like I said, beautiful."

Gina, who had been patiently waiting to reveal herself to

River, was seething as she watched him pay such rapt attention to Avalon. Wearing a tight black-and-green dress that hugged every inch of her body, her hair in a sexy side-swept style, and her makeup applied to rival a movie star, she walked over to them.

Seeing her, Avalon gulped, said a quick hello, and hurried away before River could stop her. Pleased, Gina looked at River, waiting for him to hug her, followed by an explosion of compliments about her glamorous appearance.

Gina was astonished to see River's face remain blank, and he only stared at her. "Oh jeez, Riv! At first I thought you looked angry or something, but I guess you're kind of blown away seeing me like this."

River said nothing as Gina stepped closer to him and whispered in his ear. "I have some very exciting news. I've been waiting to tell you that I'm ready. Baby, I am so ready!" Seeing that River's expression still hadn't changed, Gina pressed on. "You know, handsome hands, I'm ready for us to be together. In every way. I'm waiting to feel you throbbing inside me. I'm ready to do everything we've talked about. I wish we could go somewhere and do it right now. I just can't wait—"

"Why didn't you give Avalon my phone number?"

Gina looked across the lobby at Avalon, who was now standing with Erik and her sister, Isabella. "I can't believe she came over here to tell you that. What a brat! Can't she just get attention by being normal?"

River's jaw tightened with rage. "My mom was kidnapped today by a delusional degenerate from her past. You know where he took her? He hid her downstairs where a lot of sets are stored. As I just told Avalon, he found a hiding place in the middle of an old castle set. You know, with a green dragon head and all that. My mother was missing for over three hours. Luckily, Gina's dad, Gabe, left his business cell in his truck. But he thought he'd left it at home, so he called to see if my mom had tried to reach him. I mean, we were all fucking frantic, you know? So, when Gabe called home, that's when Avalon realized that her message hadn't been delivered. She's so sweet and trusting, she just took the word of someone who promised to deliver it. Gabe handed me his private cell phone because Avalon was desperate to talk to me. After I spoke to her and she described her painting, Larsen knew immediately where my mom was. Four cops came out and got the guy before he could rape or kill her. He had a knife, rope, duct tape, rags, and who knows what else. Are you getting the picture? Avalon saved my mom's life today. But my mom could've died because one particular person was too jealous to deliver a message to me or give out my phone number."

Gina felt the blood drain from her face as the impact of River's words hit her. "Oh, Riv, I'm so sorry. I just thought—"

"What? What did you think?"

"You know, that Avalon was making another desperate attempt for your attention."

River stepped back from Gina, still eyeing her with rage. "I'm not quite understanding what you mean by 'another desperate attempt.' I don't ever recall any desperate attempts. Are you talking about the time she wanted to tell me that she and Erik had seen Kenny Milano post Reinhardt's notes on her locker, and she was worried her brother, a freakin' mixed martial arts expert, might beat the shit out of him?"

"Uh, no, Riv. I mean … um …"

"What, the first day of school when kids were making nasty comments as they walked by her in the hall? That day, when I was the one who noticed what was happening and went over to introduce myself? Is that the desperate attempt you're talking about?"

"No, Riv. But it just seems like she's so needy, and you're always right there for her. Even now, you're taking her side."

River's mouth fell open. "Her side? Are you serious? My mother could have died today because of you, and this is what you're worried about?"

"Riv—"

"You know, you've always been so worried that you were like your sister, and I always told you that you were nothing like her. You know what? I still mean that. Because you're way worse, Gina. And we are so over!"

Gina put her hand to her mouth and rushed out the front doors as the lights began to flicker, indicating that intermission was ending.

Seeing what had happened, Mick walked over to Riv and put a comforting arm around him. "I'm sorry, son. I didn't have to hear a word of that to know what just went down. I know how much it hurts."

River could barely speak. "Thanks, Dad."

Mick, his arm still around River, squeezed him tight. "Would it make you feel any better if I told you that you're as beautiful as your mother and sister?"

River made a sound that was somewhere between laughing and moaning. "You're too much, Dad."

Mick smiled. "I learned my impeccable timing from my son. Hey, let's go watch the rest of the competition."

As she watched River and his father go through the lobby doors, Avalon couldn't help but feel sad. She only wished that Gina had believed her from the very beginning.

Eve stood in the lobby saying hello to people she knew as they made their way to their seats. Just as she was about to head back to her own seat, she saw Jax Reinhardt slip into the men's room. She hadn't seen him since he was officially expelled, and she felt an anxious knot forming in her stomach.

📖📖📖

Arielle stood at the podium and applauded as the next-to-last act took a bow.

"Thank you, Jeffrey Evers. Ladies and gentlemen, as you'll see on your program, we have one final act. My assistant, Larsen Davis, will be reciting a monologue from *Othello*. However, the competition is officially over, as Larsen has chosen only to perform, not compete."

Arielle waited for the crowd to quiet. "Even though I have nothing to do with the judging of this competition, Larsen felt that, as a member of my team, it would be wrong for him to compete tonight. That said, he wasn't about to pass up an opportunity to perform for such a fantastic audience. So, please, give it up for Larsen."

Larsen walked out on stage, nervous but excited.

In her seat, Kathryn was clasping her hands together, whispering softly to herself, "Break a leg, Larsen. You can do it."

As Larsen took a deep breath and prepared to speak, Jax came running down the right aisle of the theater. "We don't want to hear a monologue. Come on, Larsen. Sing!"

Some of the crowd, thinking that Jax was a friend, not an enemy, and that Larsen was actually a singer with a case of nerves, began to join Jax as they cheered for Larsen to sing.

Feeling his entire body stiffen, Larsen fought the overwhelming panic until he felt Peter's presence. He turned to his right and could see him standing in the wing. Peter looked entirely different than he had before. He seemed nearly normal like a flesh-and-blood human being, and he was no longer frightened. "Tell them to play 'Tonight' in D flat."

Startled, Larsen shook his head no, as some of the crowd, along with Jax, continued to call out, "Sing! Sing!"

Peter was determined to get through to Larsen in the same way Larsen had been determined to get through to him. "Sing the song. You can do it. It will be fine. And if you sing the song, I will talk to my mother when it's over. Go ahead. Tell them: D flat."

As if he were in a dream, Larsen turned to the musicians behind him. " 'Tonight' from *West Side Story*. In D flat, please."

A hush came over the audience as the music began. Larsen's friends all exchanged looks, then looked at him.

The musicians began to play. Larsen opened his mouth to sing, and to his utter amazement, out came the most beautiful baritone voice he had ever heard. The crowd gasped in unison, but nobody was anywhere near as stunned as Kathryn, who had just experienced a greater surprise than before. Putting her hands to her throat, she whispered to herself. "That's my Peter's voice. I'd know it anywhere. How can this possibly be? That's my Peter's voice!"

"Life is filled with miracles and surprises, Kathryn."

Turning toward what she thought was Larsen's empty seat, Kathryn could not trust what her eyes were seeing. "Martha Joy!"

"I know it feels like a dream, my dearest friend, but it is not. Peter has given Larsen his voice. Listen."

Kathryn turned to watch Larsen as he sung proudly with Peter's voice, turning every few seconds to confirm that her Martha Joy was still by her side. When she heard Larsen sing the line "And what was just a world is a star," she thought she would faint, but the electrified crowd and the sound of her son's voice took her back forty years to a time when her son's singing was her greatest joy. "You are my star, Peter! And now you've given your gift to Larsen. I have two desert stars now!"

As the song ended, the audience rose to their feet, and thunderous applause and cheers filled the room, like fireworks exploding in the sky.

Jax, who had been standing in the aisle in disbelief, turned to leave and practically knocked down a woman racing toward the stage.

"That's my boy! That's my Larsen! That's my son! I'm the proudest mom on the planet."

Larsen looked at Peter, who stood offstage, smiling, then at his mother, looking beautiful and well groomed, unlike the woman she had become over the past several years. His eyes welled up as she stood there cheering, telling anyone who would listen that Larsen was her son.

"Riv, why did Larsen tell us all he couldn't sing? Nobody with a voice like that could possibly think he had no vocal abilities. I don't get it."

"I think I do get it, Dad. But I'm just going to do what I always do and keep my mouth shut."

"I don't suppose if I told you to unzip it, you'd tell me."

River laughed. "Good one, Dad. But no. Just because I think I know what's going on doesn't mean I'm not flummoxed like everyone else."

"Flummoxed?"

"Yeah, it means—"

"I know what it means, Riv. But you are only seventeen. Never mind."

Up on stage, Arielle reentered and ran up to hug Larsen as she whispered in his ear, "What in the world, Lars? I thought you couldn't sing!"

"I couldn't. Peter gave me his voice."

"Are you serious?" Arielle followed Larsen's gaze and saw Peter, beaming proudly. "This has to be the most incredible day of my time on this earth."

Arielle walked over to the microphone. "Ladies and gentlemen, I know you were all as amazed by that performance as I was. We ask you all to remain seated while the judges deliberate. I'll have the results for you in just five minutes."

The audience was bustling with excitement, making it easier for Kathryn to speak out loud to Martha Joy. "How is it possible that you are here and Peter has given Larsen his voice? I've died and gone to heaven, haven't I?"

Kathryn raised her program to her face so nobody could see her talking. "What will people think if they hear your voice coming from an empty seat?"

"Only you can hear me. And, no, Kathryn. You're very much alive. Peter and I are the ones who have not yet gone to heaven. When I died five years ago in that terrible accident, I was unable to leave this earth. It was too sudden, and I was in such shock. I lived in the Mystekal Sands, even through its renovation, just to be in a place where I had happy memories. Before he moved in with you, Larsen came to see a movie, to get away from his home situation. We talked in the dark theater, and he had no idea I was a lonely ghost. But he figured it out. The next time we spoke, I came to him in a dream because I heard him calling me. He needed my advice. He told me there was a young man named Peter Winterstrom who had been living at another theater, this one, for forty years. Larsen wanted to help him. He wanted Peter to see you again and to be set free."

Kathryn dropped the program onto her lap and put her hands on either side of her head. "This is real? I'm not an old woman having delusions?"

"No, not at all."

"When you died, Martha, I was going to quit my job. Losing my best friend and neighbor was too much for me. If I hadn't stayed on at the high school, I never would have met Larsen, and none of this would ever be. Peter might have stayed trapped forever. I think I'm going to lose you both all over again, only this time, I'll get to say good-bye. You are going to leave this time, aren't you? You must go to heaven with that beautiful white flower in your hair."

Martha Joy smiled. "Reggie is here. He came with Larsen's mother. While she speaks to him, I will go make peace with my husband. When Larsen is done speaking with his mother, he will take you to Peter. You will see your son again just as you're seeing me."

"Oh!"

"This is truly our final good-bye, Kathryn. But we shall be reunited someday. But not for many years. I love you, my friend. You are the kindest woman I've ever known."

Kathryn put her hand on top of Martha Joy's. "I love you, my dearest friend."

Martha Joy smiled as she faded away.

📖📖📖

Larsen rushed down from the stage and into the arms of his mother. "Mom, I never thought in a million years you'd come. Not ever. How come you're here? And why do you look so different?"

Raylene put her arm through Larsen's and led him a few feet away. "Let's talk over here for a minute. I know that your boss lady is going to announce the winners in a few minutes, and no doubt your friends are all wondering what in hell your crazy mother is doing here, but just let me say a few words. We'll talk much longer at another time. That okay by you, son?"

As much as Larsen wanted to talk with his mother, he was frightened that Peter would leave. Looking up on the stage, he saw Peter smiling to let him know it was okay.

Feeling more secure, Larsen turned back to Raylene. "You really seem different, Mom."

"It's called sobriety, Larsen. I've been pretty much drinking my way through life since your daddy, Nathaniel, died, and it's no wonder you don't hardly recognize the sober me."

"I uh …"

"Hell, I don't blame you for not knowing what to say to me. But for once, I know what to say to you, starting with 'I'm sorry.' First, I'm here because that very brave lady you live with paid me a visit one Sunday. She figured out why I was so angry. Yup. She put the pieces together. Right to my face she told me she was pretty sure your daddy had been gay and that I was taking my anger out on you. Then she begged me to come here and see you. I kicked her out of my house, I'm sorry to say, but her words stayed with me. Tonight, I stood in the back the whole time. Left during the intermission. Didn't want you to see me and get nervous before your performance. My goodness, boy, where the hell did you learn how to sing like that? Maybe you could all along, and I just couldn't hear you. I couldn't hear much of anything, could I?"

"No, not really, Mom."

"Larsen, I knew your daddy was gay back when I fell in love with him sitting in a jazz club. But he wasn't like you. No, he wasn't able to come out. He kept trying to conform to society, and I thought I was just the woman to help him do that. Oh, yeah. I thought my love would turn him straight. And he did like women well enough, and we had some happy years. But he liked men more. I was still crazy in love with him when he died of AIDs; I was angry at myself for being such a fool and for living in denial all those years. And then, knowing that the son he gave me was gay, too, well, that drove Raylene Davis right to the bottle. And damned if that whiskey didn't turn me into one mean woman. I'm so sorry, Larsen. And just so you know, Reggie and I have both quit playin' with the devil in the bottle."

"Ladies and gentlemen, if I may have your attention, we have our winners."

Larsen looked at Arielle, then back at his mother. "That's great, Mom. I'm so happy. I'll see you one day really soon, and we'll talk about everything, okay?"

"You don't hate me, son?"

Larsen gave his mother a hug as Arielle watched from the stage. "Not even close. I've got to get back to my seat now. I really do."

📖📖📖

As soon as Arielle announced the winners, the joyous performers and their families posed for pictures, while people began leaving their seats.

"Larsen, if it's okay with you. I'd like to wait here a bit." Kathryn spoke softly. "I think we have some very important things to discuss. I still can't believe this is all real. My Peter has been lost in this theater for forty years, and you have found him. You have given him freedom, and he has given you his voice."

"It's really hard to believe. Wait, how did you know all that?"

"Martha Joy told me. She sat in your seat while you were singing."

"You know Martha Joy?"

"Sure I do. She's the best friend I lost, the one who lived next door. I've got a photo of her in the house. We're standing next to each other at the beach with our arms around one another."

Larsen recalled the photo in his head. "Oh, right. I just never put the two together. I can't even picture the faces in that photo."

Kathryn laughed. "No wonder. We were wearing these crazy sun hats her husband had bought for us."

"Where is Martha Joy?"

"She's off to find Reggie and make her peace with him so she can leave this world. I know exactly how he's going to feel when he sees her: pretty darn surprised."

"I guess I won't get to say good-bye, but that's all right. I think I already did. Kathryn, are you ready to see Peter?"

"What a question, Larsen. How do I even begin to answer that? But, yes, I'm so ready."

"You know, he stayed here all of those years because he was waiting for Ernie to come back. I had to tell him that Ernie turned into a very different person and wasn't coming back. He didn't want to hear it at first. He kept saying that he waited forty years and would wait forever."

"My poor child." Kathryn collected her thoughts before continuing. "I wish I had known he was here. I wish he had come to see me."

"I think he was trapped inside for all of the years that the theater was closed."

"Oh my. Where do we go to see him, Larsen?"

"I'm going to take you to the trailer. On the far side of it, without any doors, away from the theater, you'll be able to have privacy. Are you okay to stand up?"

"If I had legs of lead, they'd walk me to see my son." Kathryn stood up and smiled. "Take me to Peter."

📖📖📖

With Larsen by her side, Kathryn looked into the night sky.

Everything was so still. The bursting colors, the up-tempo medley of sounds and voices, and the stunning discoveries and revelations of the theater now seemed like a distant dream.

Kathryn didn't need to ask Larsen if Peter would be there. She knew that he already was. When Peter materialized in front of her, she felt exhilaration unmatched by even the sound of his voice singing. "Peter! My boy!"

Peter looked tearfully at his mother. He could see the passage of forty years on her face and her body. To her, he looked exactly the same, but her heart could feel the elapsed time that her eyes could not see.

"I never thought I would see you again, Peter. It pains my heart to know that for all these years you were suffering in an abandoned theater, waiting for Ernie to come back to you."

Peter frowned ever so slightly, but he did not speak.

"Larsen told you about Ernie. Everything he said is true. That boy died at the hands of his father the same day you did. He grew up to be a monster, just like his father. His father may not have destroyed his physical body, Peter, but he killed Ernie's soul. I was probably the only person in this town who didn't hate him because I knew what had happened."

Peter spoke out loud. "I'm very tired, Mom."

"Of course you are. That's why you have to go to your rest."

Peter smiled. "I told Larsen you'd say that."

Kathryn put her hand to her mouth and began to cry. "Oh my. You're just the same. It's like we've turned back the clock. You know me so well. Still. You may be leaving us, but you have left your love and your beautiful voice here on earth."

"Let him come here."

Kathryn looked saddened. "I've told you, Peter. It's impossible to bring Ernie here."

"No, Dad. Let him come forward."

Larsen swallowed a lump in his throat as he realized what Peter was saying. He remembered the woman who was crying because she wanted to see her granddaughter perform. He had just assumed that she was married to the man behind her, who was also crying. Only she wasn't. They were complete strangers. Turning, Larsen saw the same older man in the distance. He had long gray hair, a closely shaved beard, and wore baggy clothing. There was only one person he could be.

Following Larsen's gaze, Kathryn gasped, looking first at Larsen, then at Peter. "Is that Nicholas? Is that your father?"

Peter nodded.

"Is he going to the light with you?"

Peter smiled. "Not unless you kill him first. He's alive, Mom. Just like you."

Larsen laughed and looked at Peter. "As my friend River would say, 'Good one.'"

Kathryn stared at her long-lost husband as he slowly walked toward her. She wanted to run to him, but she was afraid Peter would disappear. She turned again to make sure Peter was still there.

"Go to him, Mom. Hurry. I won't leave yet."

As her magical night pushed on, Kathryn held out her arms and ran to Nicholas. Seeing her joy, he ran to her. Larsen and Peter watched as Kathryn and Nicholas became lost in their embrace and in their love that time had not diminished.

Finally, Kathryn pulled away and looked up at him. "My goodness, Nick. I never would have known you, but I recognize you now. How did you know to come here?"

Nicholas stroked her hair before speaking. "I read in the newspaper that the new Desert Theater was being dedicated to our Peter. I wanted to be here and to see you again."

"Where have you been all of these years?"

"Everywhere and nowhere. I never married again. I've been a

lonely nomad who never let anyone get too close. I couldn't bear any more loss. I never forgave myself for not protecting you and Peter."

"You have to forgive yourself, my darling. Willard Carrow was the monster, not you."

Nicholas looked sorrowfully at the woman he had never stopped loving. "You may forgive me, but wherever Peter is, he hasn't."

"Nicholas Peter Winterstrom, Would you like to bet on that?"

"I'll wager my last dollar, Kathryn Rose Marley Winterstrom. And just exactly how will we prove who is right or wrong?"

Kathryn looped her arm through his and walked ahead, watching her ex-husband's face as he recognized their son, still fifteen years old, standing ahead of them.

"I'm hallucinating, Kathryn."

"No, you're not. That's our Peter."

Nicholas stared incredulously at his son.

Larsen looked at Peter, then at Kathryn and Nicholas. "I'm going to join the Dalworths and everyone else in the lobby. I'm not needed here anymore. Peter, I just want you to know that I will take care of this precious gift that you've given me and live my life in a way that I hope will make you proud. And I'll never, ever stop looking out for your mom the way she's looked after me. And your dad, too. If he sticks around. I've never been in a situation like this, so I've got no idea how to say good-bye."

Peter motioned for Larsen to come forward. As Larsen stood there, Peter put his arms gently around him. "The same way you say good-bye to any friend. With a hug. Thank you for being my friend, Larsen."

Moved to tears, Larsen hurried away and left the family to exchange their final words.

In the lobby, Arielle stood with Mick holding her close. "That long-haired man is Kathryn's husband? You know, there was something about him that was just different. I just felt this kind of boiling-over emotion in him."

River laughed. "Yeah. Sure, Mom. Easy for you to say now."

Arielle made a face. "You are completely incorrigible."

Eve wiped away the tears from her eyes. "I will never forget watching Tommy go to the light."

Jinxsy put her arm around Eve's waist. "Neither will I. It was so beautiful and sad. But I hated it. I wanted to get to know him so much better."

Madeleine gently touched Larsen's arm. "Did you watch Peter go to the light, honey?"

"No, it wasn't my place. Peter needed me for a lot of things, but not to say his final good-byes to his parents. If Kathryn had been alone, I probably would have stayed. But not with Peter's dad there. It just wouldn't have felt right to watch them, you know what I mean?"

"Not really, dude. That would have been amazing. My eyeballs would have been bulging like this." River opened his eyes as wide as he could, making a failed attempt for his eyeballs to bulge.

"You're full of it, numbnuts. Even you would have had the class to walk away."

River suddenly became serious. "Yeah. You might say that's what happened tonight."

"Oh, Riv, sweetie. Your dad and I feel terrible about that."

"I really cared about Gina. A lot. But her jealousy was way worse than I thought. And that's not like a flu that goes away."

Arielle looked up at Mick. "Our son is wise beyond his years."

River looked downcast. "Yeah, well, sometimes you don't have as much fun being wise, but I guess you might not have as many regrets, either." River paused. "Hey, people, I think we should wait outside for the Winterstroms so they know where to find us."

Larsen nodded in agreement. "Yeah, as much as Kathryn would have liked a long good-bye, Peter had very little left in him. I'm sure he's gone by now."

Arielle smiled brightly. "Okay then, Gabe and the guys are still cleaning the place, and he's going to lock up everything, so let's step outside and wait."

Larsen hurried to the door and held it open for everyone as they stepped out onto the newly paved desert street. "This night air feels so good. Hey, I think I hear the Winterstroms."

Everyone turned to see Kathryn and Nicholas rounding the corner. His arm was around her, and she was sobbing, as she clung tightly to the man she thought was long gone. "He's gone. Our Peter has gone to his eternal rest. It was the most heartbreaking and exquisitely beautiful thing I've ever seen. And now that I've seen it, I will never fear death."

Eve and Jinxsy nodded sympathetically.

"Oh, dear, I forgot that you two had the same experience. Someday, when I am able to comprehend everything that happened here today, maybe we can compare notes."

River smiled. "You know, Kathryn, I'm thinking you probably could hold the Guinness Book of World Records for the person who had the most phenomenal surprises in one day and lived to tell about it."

"I think you're right, River."

As the group began walking, Larsen stopped in his tracks. "Kathryn, look! Peter knew all along. He must have. He did exactly what he told you he was going to do all those years ago."

Kathryn looked confused. "What's that, Larsen?"

Larsen pointed upward as everyone looked into the sky to see a sparkling star brighter than all the others, including the North Star.

Kathryn was jubilant. "Nicholas, look! Just like Peter said. Remember? One day he was going to be the brightest star in the sky so I could always find him. And there he is, taking center stage in the galaxy, my glorious desert star."

The End